Praise for the ~~New York Times~~ *New York Times* **bestselling authors**

HEATHER GRAHAM

"Graham wields a deftly sexy and convincing pen."
—*Publishers Weekly*

"An incredible storyteller."
Los Angeles Daily News

"Refreshing, unique...
Graham does it better than anyone."
—*Publishers Weekly* on *Hurricane Bay*

JO BEVERLEY

"Arguably today's most skillful writer of intelligent historical romance."
—*Publishers Weekly*

"One of the great names of the romance genre."
—*Romantic Times BOOKreviews*

"Wickedly, wonderfully sensual."
—*New York Times* bestselling author
Mary Balogh on *Something Wicked*

CANDACE CAMP

HEATHER GRAHAM

JO BEVERLEY

CANDACE CAMP

A Bride by Christmas

HQN™

ISBN 13: 978-0-373-77343-5
ISBN-10:   0-373-77343-9

A BRIDE BY CHRISTMAS

Copyright © 2008 by Harlequin Books S.A.

The publisher acknowledges the copyright holders of the individual works as follows:

HOME FOR CHRISTMAS
Copyright © 1989 by Heather Graham Pozzessere

THE WISE VIRGIN
Copyright © 1999 by Jo Beverley

TUMBLEWEED CHRISTMAS
Copyright © 1989 by Candace Camp

This edition published by arrangement with Harlequin Books S.A.

® and TM are trademarks of the publisher. Trademarks indicated with ® are registered in the United States Patent and Trademark Office, the Canadian Trade Marks Office and in other countries.

www.HQNBooks.com

Printed in U.S.A.

CONTENTS

HOME FOR CHRISTMAS
Heather Graham

PROLOGUE

Christmas Eve, 1864

A SOFT, LIGHT SNOW was falling as Captain Travis Aylwin stood by the parlor window. He could almost see the individual flakes drift and dance to the earth against the dove-gray sky. It was a beautiful picture, serene. No trumpets blared; no soldiers took up their battle cries; no horses screamed; and no blood marked the purity and whiteness of the winter's day.

It was Christmas Eve, and from this window, in the parlor that he had taken over as his office, there might well have been peace on earth. It was possible to forget that men had died on the very ground before the house, that lifeless limbs clad in gray had fallen over lifeless limbs clad in blue. The serenity of the darkening day was complete. A fire burned in the hearth, and the scent of pine was heavy in the air, for the house had been dressed for the season with holly and boughs from the forest, and bright red ribbons and silver bows. Hawkins had roasted chestnuts in the fireplace that morning, and their wintry scent still clung lightly to the room, like the mocking laughter of holidays long gone. He had not asked for this war! He hadn't been home for Christmas in four long years, and no scent of chestnuts or spray of mistletoe would heal the haunting pain that plagued him today.

She could heal the wound, he thought. She, who could spend the holiday in her own home, at her own hearthside. But she would not, he thought. And no words that he spoke would change her feelings, for it was almost Christmas, and no matter what had passed between them, no matter how gently he spoke, Isabelle took up the battle come Christmas, as if she fought for all the soldiers who rested in the field.

From somewhere he could hear singing. Corporal Haines was playing the piano, and Joe Simon, out of Baltimore, Maryland, was singing "O, Holy Night" in his wondrous tenor. There was a poignant quality to the song that rang so high and clear. Two people were singing, he realized. Isabelle Hinton had joined in, her voice rising like a nightingale's, the notes true and sweet.

She had forgiven the men, he thought. She had forgiven them for being Yankees; she had forgiven them the war. It was only him she could not forgive, not when it came to Christmas.

The sounds of the song faded away.

He closed his eyes suddenly, and it was the picture of the past he saw then, and not the present. Not the purity of the snow, the gentle gray of the day. He could not forget the past, he thought, and neither could she.

He tensed, the muscles of his arms and shoulders constricting, his breath coming too quickly. She was there. He knew she was there. Sergeant Hawkins had told him that Isabelle had requested an audience with him, and now he knew she was standing in the doorway. He could smell her jasmine soap; he could feel her presence. She would be standing in the doorway when he turned, waiting for him to bid her to enter. She would be proud and distant, as she had been the first day he met her. And just as it had that very first time, his heart would hammer within his chest as he watched her. She was an extraordinary woman. His hands clenched into fists at his sides. It was almost over. The war was almost over. He knew it; the lean, starving soldiers of the South knew it; she knew it—but she would never concede it.

He straightened his shoulders, careful to don a mask of command. He turned, and as he had known, she was there. And as he had suspected, she was dressed for travel. Her rich burgundy and lace gown was dated; her heavy black coat was worn, and beneath her patched petticoats, he knew, she would be wearing darned and mended hose, for she would take nothing from him except the "rent" for the house, and that she put away each month behind a brick in the fireplace. Once she had put it away for two brothers, but now one of them lay dead in the family plot that was hidden by snow, and so she put the money away for Lieutenant James L. Hinton, Confederate States Artillery, the Army of Northern Virginia, in hopes that he would one day come home. She took the money because the United States Army had taken over her house. Because she was determined not to lose her home, she had no choice but to let them use it. The Hinton plantation lay very close to Washington, D.C., and though the army had been forced to abandon the property upon occasion when Lee's forces had come close, they always returned.

Isabelle knew that. That he would always return.

Travis did not speak right away. He had no intention of making things easy for her, not that night, not when he felt such a despairing tempest in his soul. He crossed his arms over his chest and idly sat on the window seat, watching her politely, waiting. His heartbeat quickened, as it always did when she was near. It had been that way from the first time he saw her, and now that he had come to know her so well…

She was pale that night, and even more beautiful for her lack of color. She might have been some winter queen as she stood there, tall, slim, encompassed by her cloak, her fascinating gray-green eyes enormous against the oval perfection of her face. Her skin was like alabaster, and the darkness of her lashes swept beguilingly over the perfection of her flawless complexion. Her nose was aquiline, her lips the color of wine. Tendrils of golden hair curled from beneath the hood of her cape, barely hinting at the radiant profusion of long, silky hair beneath it. Watching her, he was tempted to stride across the room, to take her into his arms, to shake her until she cried for mercy, until she vowed that she would surrender.

But he would not, he knew. He had touched her in anger before, had shaken her to dispel the ice from her heart. He held the power, and sometimes he had used it, in despair, in desperation, and once in grim determination to save her life. But he would not touch her tonight. He loved her, and he would not force her to stay.

"Good evening, Isabelle," he told her. He had no intention of helping her. He would let her go, because he had to, but he would not help her abandon him to the barren emptiness of another Christmas without her.

"Captain," she acknowledged.

He didn't say a word. She lifted her chin, knowing they were both fully aware of why she had come, and that he would not make it easy for her.

With soft dignity she spoke again. "I would like an escort to the Holloway place, please."

"The weather is severe," he said noncommittally.

"That does not matter, sir. I will go with or without your escort."

"You know that you won't go two steps without my permission, Miss Hinton."

Her lip curled, and her rich lashes half covered her cheeks. "You would prevent me from leaving, Captain?"

Why didn't he do it? he wondered. He could turn his back on her, could deny her request. If she tried to leave him, if she tried to ride away into the snowbound wilderness, he need only ride after her, capture her, drag her back. It would be so easy.

But he had fallen in love with her, and he could never hold her by force. If she wanted to go, he would saddle the horse himself if need be.

"No, Miss Hinton," he said softly. "I will not prevent you from going, since that is your heart's desire."

He stood and walked to the desk, her brother's desk, his desk. It was a Yankee desk now, piled high with his paperwork, orders, letters, the Christmas wishes that had made it to him, the letters he had dictated to the parents and lovers and brothers and sweethearts of the men he had lost in their last skirmish, letters that had not yet been sent. He searched for his safe-conduct forms, drew out the chair, sat and began to fill in the blanks. Any Union patrol was to see to the safe passage of Miss Isabelle Hinton to Holloway Manor, just five miles southwest of their own location in northern Virginia. She would be accompanied by Sergeant Daniel Daily and Corporal Eugene Ripley, and she was not to be stopped, questioned or waylaid for any purpose.

He signed his name, then looked up. He thought he detected the glistening of tears behind the dazzle of her gray-green eyes. *Don't do this!* he longed to command her. Don't you see that in this very act you deny our love?

But she had never said that she loved him. Never, not while she was burning in the flames of desire, nor in the few stolen moments of tenderness that had come her way. And neither, God help him, had he ever whispered such words, for he could not. The war waged between them, and enemies did not love one another.

He stood, then approached her with the pass. Her gloved hands were neatly folded, but they began to tremble where they lay against her skirt.

"Isabelle…" He started to hand her the paper.

She reached for it, but her fingers didn't quite reach

it, and it drifted to the ground. He meant to stoop to pick it up, but he didn't. His dark eyes locked with hers, and the room seemed to fill with a palpable tension. Suddenly he discovered that it was the woman he was reaching for, not the paper. He drew her into his arms and knew that she was not made of ice, that warmth flickered and burned within her. A soft cry escaped her lips, and her head fell back. Her eyes met his with a dazzling defiance, yet they betrayed things she would not say, that she would deny until the very grave if he allowed her.

"Isabelle!" he repeated, staring into her eyes, devouring her perfect features, his callused fingers coming to rest on the gentle slope of her cheek and chin. Once more he whispered her name, and he felt the frantic pounding of her heart just before he kissed her. He touched his lips to hers, and the fire seemed to roar behind him as he delved deeply into her mouth, stroking the inner recesses with his tongue and evoking memories within them both. His lips caressed and consumed hers, and flames lapped against his chest, his thighs, his loins, until he thought he could bear no more. Her breasts thrust explicitly against his cavalry shirt as he filled himself with the sweet taste of her, a taste that would so soon be denied him.

If she had thought to fight his touch, he had quickly swept that thought from her mind. In the power of his arms she did not—could not—deny him. The kiss evoked memories. Memories of blinding, desperate passion and need, memories of tenderness, of whispers, of golden, precious moments out of time, when love had dared and defied the reality of war.

The kiss was hungry, and it was sweet, and in those stolen seconds it meant everything to him that Christmas should. It simmered with passion, yet reminded him deep inside his heart of the times when they had laughed together. Of the times when he had held her against the world. It had begun in tempest, and yet it whispered of peace and the commitment of the soul. It promised years together, evenings before an open fire with children on their laps and the sweet sounds of Christmas carols dancing in their ears. It was everything that a Christmas kiss should be....

"No!" she cried softly, breaking away from him. Her small gloved hands lay against his chest, and the tears that had glazed her eyes now dampened her cheeks. "Travis, no! I must go! Don't you understand? I have to be with my own kind for Christmas, not in the bosom of the enemy!"

"By God, Isabelle! Don't you see? You *are* home. *This* is your home—"

"Not with you in it, Travis!" she interrupted, backing away from him. "Travis, please!" The desperate sound of her tears was in her voice. "Please, let me go!"

He felt as if his body was composed of steel, taut and hard and rigid, but he forced himself to breathe, and, watching her, he slowly forced himself to bend for the paper. He handed it to her, and their fingers brushed as she reached for it.

"Don't go, Isabelle," he said simply.

"I have to!"

He shook his head. "The war is almost over—"

"I cannot be a traitor."

"Loving me would not be turning your back on your own people. The war will end. The nation must begin to heal itself, to bind up its wounds—"

"The war is not over."

"Isabelle! Lee's men are wearing rags and tatters. They're desperate for food, for boots. Don't you see? Yes, they've fought and they've died, and they've run the Union to the ground, but there are more and more of us, and we have repeating rifles when half the boys in gray are dealing with single-shot muskets! I didn't make this war, and neither did you! Isabelle—"

"Travis, don't! I don't want to hear this!"

"Stay, Isabelle."

"I can't."

"You must."

"Why?" she demanded desperately.

"Because I love you."

She froze as he spoke the simple words, her cheeks going even paler. But she shook her head in fierce denial. "We're enemies, Travis."

"We're lovers, Isabelle, and no lies, no heroics, no denials can change that!"

"You're a Yankee!" she gasped. "And no gentleman to say such things aloud!"

A pained smile touched his features. "I tried, but a gentleman could not have had you, and I had to have you. Don't leave. It's Christmas. You should be home for Christmas."

"No!" She shook her head fiercely and spun around and hurried toward the door. She went through, then slammed it in her wake.

"Isabelle!"

Travis charged after her. He heard her lean against the door, and he paused, fingers clenching and unclenching.

There was nothing left to say.

"You should be home for Christmas," he repeated softly.

He heard her sob softly, then push herself away from the door.

And then she was gone.

At length Travis wandered into the room and sat down before the fire. The flames leaped high, and he saw her face in the red-gold blaze. Come home! he thought. Come home, and be with me tonight.

He leaned back. It had been almost Christmas when they met, he thought.

From far away, he heard the piano again. The men's voices were raised in a rendition of "Silent Night." The fire continued to burn, and beyond the window the delicate flakes of snow continued to fall.

He could go after her, he thought. Maybe he should.

It had been almost Christmas, an evening like this one, when they had first met.

He closed his eyes, and he could see her again. See her as she had stood on the front steps, a woman all alone, ready to defy the entire Union Army.

CHAPTER ONE

December, 1862

THE SNOW HAD FINISHED FALLING, but the house sat like an ice palace, like something out of a fairy tale. Rain had glazed over the white, newly fallen snow, and when the sun came out, the house and grounds seemed dazzling, as if they were covered with a hundred-thousand diamond chips. The landscape seemed barren, a painting from a children's book. It was a place where the winter queen should live, perhaps—it certainly seemed to have no bearing on real life.

But real life was why they had come. Since the first shots had been fired at Fort Sumter, everyone had known that northern Virginia was going to be a hotbed—and that certain areas were going to have to be held by the Yanks if Washington, D.C., was to be protected.

Now, with the war raging onward, it was becoming more and more important to solidify the Union presence in Virginia. The Hinton house was just one of the places that had to be taken over. The little township was already filling with his men, and from studying his maps looking for strategic locations, Travis had known that the Hinton house would be the best place for his headquarters. His occupancy would keep the Rebs away, while he would still have easy access to the town nearby if it became necessary to pull back. In addition, he would be in a good position to join up with the main army should he be called.

The day seemed very cold and still. Travis could hear only the jangle of harness and the snorts of the horses as his small company of twenty approached the house. The breath of men mingled with the breath of the horses as they plowed through the snow, creating bursts of mist upon the air. He reined in suddenly, not knowing why, just staring at the house.

It was such an elegant structure, like a grand lady in the crystallized snow. Great Grecian columns rose high upon the broad porch, tall and imposing. The house was white, and the white, diamondlike snowflakes caught on the roof and the windows. Even the outbuildings were covered in crystal. Through one window he could see a flicker of red and gold, and he realized that a fire was burning, warm and comforting against the snow and cold.

"Captain? It's mighty cold out here," Sergeant Will Sikes reminded him.

"Yeah. Yeah, it's mighty cold," he said. He nudged Judgment, his big black thoroughbred, forward. His men, cold and quiet, survivors of Sharpsburg and more that year, followed in silence. Everyone had thought the war would be over by May. A few weeks. The Yanks had expected an easy victory, while the Rebs

had thought they could beat the pants off the Yanks—
which they had done upon occasion, Travis had to
admit—but they hadn't counted on the tenacity of Mr.
Lincoln. The president had no intention of letting the
nation fall apart. He was going to fight this war no
matter what. So the North had learned there was to be
no easy victory, and the South had learned that the war
could go on forever, and here it was, just a few days
before Christmas, and they were all preparing to bed
down in Virginia instead of returning home to their
loved ones.

Of course, for some, Christmas was destined to be
even gloomier. For some, the war had already taken
its toll. Fathers, lovers, husbands and sons, many had
returned home already, returned in packages of pine,
wrapped in their shrouds, and for Christmas they
would lie in their familial graveyards, home for the
holiday.

He was becoming morose, he reminded himself,
something he couldn't allow. He was in charge of this
group of twenty young men and the hundred he had left
behind in the town. He had no intention of letting
morale fall by the wayside, nor was he of a mind to
shoot any of his men for desertion.

"Seems a fair enough place, eh?" he called out,
lifting himself out of his saddle to turn and view the
troops. He was met with several nods, several half
smiles, and he turned once again to face the house.

That was when he saw her.

She had come out to stand on the porch. She had
probably heard the jingle of the horses' trappings, and

she had known that men were coming. She must have hoped it was a Confederate company, yet it seemed she had suspected Yanks, for she had come out with a shotgun, and Travis was certain it was loaded.

For the life of him, at that moment, he couldn't care.

She was clad in blue velvet, a rich, sumptuous gown with puff sleeves and a daring bodice that left her shoulders bare and gave a provocative hint of the ivory breasts that surged against the fabric. She wore no coat or cloak against the cold, but stood upon the top step of the porch, that heavy gun swept up and aimed hard at him even as a delicate tumble of sun-gold curls fell in a rich swirl against the sights. She tossed her hair back, and he knew that she was young, and though he couldn't see the color of her eyes, he knew they would be fascinating. He knew that he had never seen a more beautiful woman, more striking, more delicate and fine. For several seconds he lost sight of duty and honor, even of the fact that he was fighting a war.

"She looks like she intends to use that thing," Will muttered, casting Travis a quick glance. "What do you think, Captain?"

Travis shrugged, grinning. She couldn't be about to shoot them. One lone woman against a party of twenty men. He lifted a hand and twisted in the saddle to speak. "Hold up, men. I'll do the talking and see if we can't keep this polite."

He urged his mount forward, leaving the others by the snow-misted paddocks and gate. She aimed the shotgun straight at him, and he pulled up his horse, lifting a hand to her in a civil gesture.

"Stop right where you are, Yank!" she commanded. The voice matched the woman. It was velvet and silk. It was strong, but with shimmery undertones that made her all the more feminine.

"Miss Hinton, I'm Captain Travis Aylwin of the—"

"You're a Yank, and I want you off my property."

He dismounted and headed for the steps that led to the porch. His heavy wool cape flapped behind him, caught by the breeze. He tugged his plumed hat over his forehead in acknowledgement that he had come upon a lady, but before he could take the first step he discovered himself spinning in astonishment. She had fired the rifle and just skimmed the feather on his hat.

"Son of a bitch!" he roared.

Behind him, twenty rifles were cocked.

"Hold it! Hold it!" he shouted to his men. He jerked off his singed hat and sent it flying down on a snow-drift, then glared at this Southern angel, his dark eyes flashing with fury. "What the hell is the matter with you? If you had hit me—"

"If I had intended to hit you, Captain, you'd be dead," she promised softly, solemnly. "Now, get your men and move off my property."

He threw back his cape, set a booted foot on the first step, placed his hands on his hips and clenched his teeth. There was no easy way to take over a person's property, but this was war.

"So you didn't intend to hit me, huh?" he demanded.

"Don't you believe me, Captain?" An exquisite brow rose with the inquiry.

"Oh, yes, ma'am, I believe you. If I didn't, you'd be tied up and on the backside of a horse right now."

He watched her eyes narrow and a slow crimson flush rise to her cheeks. She started to aim the rifle again, and though he wanted to believe that she wasn't stupid or vicious enough to shoot a man—even a Yank—he didn't want to take any chances. He leaped up the remaining steps, sweeping an arm around her waist to wrest the rifle from her grip. A soft gasp escaped her, but her grip was strong, and his efforts to dislodge the weapon sent them both reeling off balance. Suddenly they were tumbling down the steps and careening into a snowdrift. Travis instinctively attempted to keep his body lodged beneath hers. He didn't know why—she wanted to shoot him. Maybe he just couldn't bear the idea of such a beautiful creature being hurt in any way.

When they landed, she was still seething and fighting. He wrenched her beneath him, securing her wrists, and spat out an oath. There was no nice way to do this, no nice way at all.

"Lady, in the name of the United States government—"

"The U.S. government be damned! This is the Confederacy! Don't threaten me with the U.S. government!"

"Lady," he said wearily, "this is war—"

"Get off my property!"

"In the name—"

"Get off me! I will not listen to a government that—"

He jerked her hands hard, dragging them high above her head, and leaned very close to her. "Don't listen to the government, then, listen to me. Listen to me because I'm twice your size, ten times your strength—and because I have twenty armed men behind me. Is that logical enough for you? Listen, now, and listen good. I'm taking this house. It's called confiscation, and it is something that happens during times of war. I'm sorry that your property happens to be so close to the border, but that's the way it is."

She blinked, and he noticed snowflakes clinging tightly to her eyelashes and dusting her cheeks. She was very white, and she was shivering beneath him. He didn't know whether it was the cold that made her shiver, or if she was trembling with rage. She moistened her lips to speak, and he found himself staring in fascination at her mouth, her pink tongue as it moved over her lips. They were wonderful lips, well defined, full, sensual, beautiful. He wanted to touch them. He wanted to feel the sizzling warmth he knew he would find within the recesses of her mouth.

He blinked, straightening against the cold of the day.

She spoke then, the breath rushing from her in a gust. "You're not going to burn the house?"

He almost smiled. She might hate having a pack of Yankees on her property, but she did want her property to survive.

He shook his head. "I'm taking the house for my

headquarters. These fellows will bunk here—I have another hundred men in town. We'll do our best to compensate you for what we use."

She was still staring at him, unblinking now. Her velvet gown was wet with snow, her golden hair lying like curious rays of golden sun against it, and her gray-green eyes were startlingly bright and deep against the pallor of her cheeks. He felt her tremble again and saw that the snow was touching her bare shoulders and her breasts where they rose above her bodice. Little flakes fell deep into the shadowed valley between them. Lucky snowflakes, Travis thought, then he realized that she was freezing and silent in her misery. He thought with a sudden, unreasoning fury that she was what the South was made of, that she would suffer any agony in silence, that her pride was worth everything to her. This war would go on until eternity because of all the damn Southerners just like her. They had something that all the Yankee weaponry and numbers could not best, that sense of pride, of honor.

"Get up!" he snapped suddenly.

"I can hardly do that, sir, when you're lying on top of me!" she returned, but he had already thrust himself upward and reached down to help her. She didn't want to take his hand, but he allowed her no nonsense, taking hers. He drew her to her feet and swept his cloak from his shoulders, then threw it over hers. "I don't need Yankee warmth!" she protested.

"Whether you need it or not, you'll take it!" he growled and prodded her toward the steps. "Who else is inside?"

"General Lee and the entire Army of Northern Virginia," she said sweetly.

"Sergeant! Draw a detail of five and shoot anyone inside that house who lives and breathes!"

"No!" she cried out in protest. She spun around, caught within his arms, but meeting his eyes again. "I'll tell you who's inside!" she snapped. "Peter, the butler, Mary Louise, my maid, Jeanette, Etta and Johnny Hopkins, all of them house servants. In the barn you'll find Jeremiah, the blacksmith, and five others, field hands. That's it. Just the servants—"

"Just the slaves?"

She lifted her chin, smiling with such a supreme sense of superiority that he wanted to slap her. "My parents are dead, and my brothers are fighting. The *servants* are all free men and women, Captain. My brothers saw to that before they left for the fighting. All free so that they could leave if trouble came—and not be shot by the likes of you!"

Her blacks were far more likely to be shot by renegade Confederates, but he wasn't going to argue the point with her. He turned around, trusting her suddenly, because she had no more reason to lie. "Sergeant, bring the men in. It's getting damn cold out here. Oh, excuse me, Miss Hinton." He bowed to her then bent to pick up his hat from the snowdrift. He started up the steps, then paused, for she was staring at him with pure hatred. "Lead the way, Miss Hinton."

"Why, Captain? I'm not inviting you in."

He walked down and caught her arm, a growling sound caught in his throat. He had assumed that the

Southern belle he had to wrest the house from might have the vapors, or faint at the sight of a Yankee detail. He hadn't expected her to come after him with a shotgun, nor had he expected this defiance.

"Fine. I can escort you elsewhere."

"What?" she said.

"I can see that you are sent elsewhere, if that is your wish. I can pack you south, Miss Hinton. Where would you like to go? Richmond, New Orleans, Savannah, Charleston?"

"You intend to throw me out of my own house?"

A tug-of-war was going on within her beautiful eyes. She didn't want to be near him—but neither did she want to desert her home. He smiled. "Lady, the choice is yours."

"Captain, you're not going to be here long enough to do anything to me."

"I won't be?"

She smiled serenely. "Stonewall Jackson rides these parts, sir. And Robert E. Lee. They'll come back, and they'll skewer you right through."

He smiled in return. "You hold on to that thought, Miss Hinton. But for now…well, you can talk to Peter about something for dinner, or I can send my mess corporal down to raid your cellars. My men are good hunters. They can keep you and yours eating well. Just don't interfere."

"Interfere—"

"God in heaven, woman, it's cold out here!" He grasped her arm hard and jerked her along, opening the door to the house and thrusting her in before him.

The servants she had spoken of stood along the elegant carved stairway that led from the marble-floored foyer to the second floor above. Doors lined a long, elegant hallway to the right and another to the left, but Travis was certain that she hadn't lied, that the servants were the sole occupants of the house. They were all staring at him now with eyes wide. That must be Peter, a tall, handsome man dressed in impeccable livery, and that would be Mary Louise at his side. The others were peeking out from behind them.

"Hello." He doffed his hat to them, smiling, aware that Sergeant Sikes was coming up behind him with half the men. Peter nodded gravely, then looked at Miss Hinton.

"Speak to them," Travis suggested.

She moistened her lips. "Peter, this is, er, Captain Travis Aylwin." He thought she was about to spit on the floor, but the manners she had learned long ago on her mammy's lap kept her from doing so. "Oh, hell! The damn Yanks have come to take over the house."

"They're not a-gonna burn us—" Peter began.

"No!" she said quickly, then shot Travis a furious stare. "At least, the captain has promised they're not."

"I don't remember promising anything," he said pleasantly. "But, Peter, it is not my intent to do so. Not unless your mistress is a spy. She isn't, is she?"

Peter's eyes went even wider. "No, sir. Why, you can see how it is here, winter and all. You can hardly go house to house in these parts, much less find an army to spy for!"

Travis laughed. He had to agree. They were just about snowbound for the moment, except that he was going to have to get word through to intelligence about his location and the situation here. "There are twenty of us here, Peter."

"And we're colder than a witch's teat and hungry as a pack of bears!" Sergeant Sikes said.

"Sergeant!" Travis barked.

But Sikes already appeared horrified at his own words. He was staring at their unwilling hostess as if he were too mortified for words. Travis found himself grinning. "I'm certain Miss Hinton has heard such words before, even used a few herself, perhaps, but an apology is in order."

She cast him a scathing glare, but her lips curled into a curious smile. "If I haven't used such language, Captain, I'm quite sure that I shall before I have seen the last of you."

"Supper, Miss Hinton?" Peter asked.

She lifted a hand. "Feed the rabble, since we must, Peter." She pulled away from Travis's side, letting his military cape fall to the floor. "Do excuse me, Captain, but I choose not to watch your ruffians eat me out of house and home."

She started up the stairway. He watched her warily as she went, but he did not stop her. She might very well be going up to find a bowie knife or a pistol, but for the moment, he would just let her go. It was time to settle in.

"Where is Miss Hinton's room, Peter?" he asked.

"Second floor, second door to the left, sir," Peter said uneasily.

Travis merely nodded and smiled. "Thank you,

Peter. Sikes, you find a room in the house, and find one for me, too. As for the men—"

"The barn has a full bunkhouse," Peter advised him. "Fireplace, wood-burning stove, all the amenities, sir. Sleeps thirty easily."

"But that leaves Sergeant Sikes and me alone in the house, doesn't it, Peter? You wouldn't be planning something, would you?"

Peter shook his head.

"But your mistress might be."

Peter lowered his head, but not before Travis saw acknowledgement in his eyes. She was dangerous, Miss Fairy-tale-princess Hinton. But he could handle the danger. "Fine, Peter, thank you. The men will take the bunkhouse. Sikes and I will find rooms here, and if you value your Miss Hinton's life, you'll take care to see that she behaves."

Peter nodded, but Travis had the feeling that he wasn't at all sure he was up to the task.

"I'll sure try, Captain. I'll sure try," Peter told him.

Travis started to walk along the hallway to find a room he could use as an office. He paused, turning back. "Why?" he asked Peter.

Peter grinned, his white teeth flashing as he smiled. "I don't want to see her shot up by you Yanks, Captain, and that's a fact."

Travis nodded, grinned and started down the hallway. He waved a hand. "See to the men, Sikes. And to yourself. Peter, when's dinner?"

"I can fix you up in an hour, Captain."

"An hour. Everyone in the house. It isn't quite

Christmas Eve, but we'll pretend that it is. Everyone at the dining table except for a guard of two."

"Only two, sir?" Sikes asked.

"Only two. The enemy lurks within the house tonight," he warned, then wandered down the hallway.

ISABELLE HINTON didn't appear for dinner. The men ate, warming their hands by the fire and gazing at the fine plates and silver and the crystal goblets as if they hadn't seen such luxury in years. It had been forever since they had sat down to this kind of meal. It seemed as if they had spent the entire year in battle. The worst of it had been at Sharpsburg, by Antietam Creek. Travis had never seen so many men die, never seen the bodies piled so high, never smelled so much blood. Great fields of corn had been mowed to the ground by gunfire. Yankees and Rebels had died alike, and that battle alone had taught them all that war was an evil thing.

While the men were in the parlor playing the piano and singing Christmas carols, Travis retired to the den he had found to use as his office. He sipped from a snifter of brandy and rested his booted feet on the desk, staring at the flames that burned in the hearth. He closed his eyes, and for a moment he felt the sun again as he had that day at Sharpsburg. He remembered how eerie it had felt to lead a cavalry charge, then watch as the men were mown down around him. He had taken grapeshot in the shoulder himself and wondered if it wouldn't be easier just to die than to wait for infection to set in. But he hadn't lost the arm, and he hadn't died—he'd lived to fight again.

The men were singing a rousing rendition of "Deck the Halls." The warmth of the fire enveloped Travis, and the pain of battle drifted slowly from his memory. He wondered what he would be doing if he was home. Well, he wouldn't be at his own house. Since his wife had succumbed to the smallpox, he had avoided his own house for the holidays, but never his family. He would have headed into town to his mother's house. There would be a huge turkey roasting, and the scent of honey-coated ham would fill the house. His sister, Liz, would be there with the kids, and Allen would be asking him all about West Point, while Eulalie would want a horsey ride on his knee. Jack, his brother-in-law, would talk about the law with his father, and all the voices would blend together, the chatter, the laughter, the love. They would go to church on Christmas Eve, and they would all remember, even in the depths of the deepest despair, that it was Christmas because a little child had been born to rid the world of death and suffering. And somehow, no matter how dark an hour they seemed to face, he would believe again in mankind. And even now, even here, far from home, he knew that Christmas would always convince him that there could be love again. He just wished that he were home.

The men were no longer singing; the house had grown quiet. Travis set his brandy snifter on the desk, rose and stretched. He had a pile of maps on the desk, but he would get to them tomorrow. Right now, he wanted to get to bed.

He found Peter in the hallway, returning the last of

the crystal glasses to a carved wooden rack on the wall. "Upstairs, Captain. We done give you the master suite, third door to the left."

"Thank you, Peter. Sikes?"

"He's gone up, sir. Third floor, first door to your left."

"It's a big house, Peter."

"Lordy, yes. Needed to be, before the war. There was parties galore then, cousins coming from all over the countryside to sleep for the whole weekend. Why, around now, at Christmas…"

Peter's voice trailed away. Travis clapped an arm on the man's shoulder. "Christmas is kind of hard all around right now, Peter. Good night."

Travis climbed the stairs and found the door to his room. The master suite. It was a huge room, with a four-poster bed against the far wall, two big armoires, a secretary facing a window and a cherrywood table with a handsomely upholstered French chair beside it by the fire.

He draped his sword and scabbard over a chair and unhooked the frogs of his jacket, then cast that, too, over the chair. His shirt followed. Then he sat to tug off his boots and socks before peeling away his breeches. He would have slept in his long underwear, but there was a big pitcher of water and a bowl on a small washstand by one of the armoires, so he stripped down to the flesh and found that the water was still a little bit warm. There was a bar of soap there, too, supplied by Peter, he was certain, and not his hostess. It didn't matter. He scrubbed himself the best he could, then dried himself, shivering, before the fire, before slipping into the bed. It wasn't quite home, but it was a good soft mattress and an even softer pillow, and it was, in fact, so comfortable that he wasn't sure he would be able to sleep.

He closed his eyes, and he was just starting to doze when he heard the sound. He opened his eyes, then closed them again swiftly, before allowing them to part slightly. Firelight danced on the walls, and for a moment he didn't know what he had heard. The door to the hallway had not opened.

But he wasn't alone. He knew it.

He waited. Then he sensed the soft rose fragrance of her perfume, and he knew that she had invaded his bedroom, though for what purpose he didn't know. He could see her through the curtain of his lashes. All that lush blond hair of hers was free, flowing like a golden cascade over her shoulders and down her back. She was dressed in something soft and floor-length and flannel, but the firelight ignored the chasteness of her apparel, playing through the material and outlining the alluring beauty of her form. Her breasts were high and firm, her waist slim and tempting, her hips and buttocks flaring provocatively beneath it. She carried something, he saw. A knife. And she was right beside the bed.

He snaked out an arm, capturing her wrist, pulling her down hard on top of him. She gasped in surprise, but she didn't scream. Her gray-green eyes met his with a fear she tried desperately to camouflage, but with no remorse. He tightened his grip on her wrist, and the knife clattered to the floor.

"What good would it have done to kill me?" he asked.

She tried to shift away from him. He gave her no quarter; indeed, some malicious demon within him enjoyed her flushed features and the uncomfortable way she squirmed against him. He hadn't dragged her into his bedroom; she had come of her own accord.

"I wasn't going to kill you!" she protested.

He skimmed both hands down the length of her arms, then laced his fingers through hers and drew her to his side, leaning tautly over her. She swallowed and strained against him, but still she did not scream, and she tried very hard not to look his way. "I see," he said gravely. "You came to offer a guest a shave, is that it?"

Her eyes fell to his bare chest. He could feel the rise of her breasts, the outline of her hips, the staggering heat coming from her skin. He knew that she was aware of the desire rising in him. She couldn't help but feel the strength of him hard against her.

"I—I just…" Her voice trailed off.

"You came here to murder me!" he snapped angrily.

"No, I…"

"Yes, damn it!"

Suddenly her eyes met his. They flashed with fury, with awareness, then fear. Then something more. "All right!" she whispered. "I—I thought that I would kill you before you violated my home! But then…"

"Then what?" he demanded.

She moistened her lips. Her lashes fell, and she was

so beautiful he could barely restrain himself. He wanted to live up to the reputation Yankee soldiers were given in the South; he wanted to wrap his arms around her, to have her, to make love to her at all costs. He would have traded every hope he had of heaven just to fill his hands with the weight of her breasts; he would have sold his very soul to the devil to feel himself within her.

"I realized that you were a man, flesh and blood.... I..." Her words trailed away, and her eyes met his. She had never seen the deaths at Sharpsburg; she hadn't watched them fall at Manassas. But tonight she had played with death, and she had discovered that it was not glorious, not honorable.

She had recognized him as a human being.

"I still wish you were dead!" she snapped, surging against him suddenly as if she was horrified that she had forgotten their fight. "You're still a damn Yank and—" She broke off, breathing raggedly. He smiled, because they were both all too aware that he was human, and very much a man.

"Please, Captain, if you would be so good as to let me up now...?"

He started to chuckle softly. She could still be such an elegant, dignified belle, so regal despite their position.

"Sorry," he said.

"Sorry!" she gasped, realizing that he had no intention of letting her go. "But—but..."

"I can't take the chance that you might decide you're

capable of killing me after all," he said, rolling over and dragging her with him. He had to forget modesty to bring her along with him so he could find a scarf. She tried to fight him, to look anywhere but at him, but he was ruthless as he pulled her along in his footsteps until he found a scarf, then brought her back to the bed, where he tied her wrists together, then laid her down with her back against him.

She swore and she kicked and she protested, and she wriggled and fought until his laughter warned her that her movements were pulling her gown precariously high on her hips.

Then she merely swore. Like a mule driver. Sergeant Sikes could have learned a thing or two.

"Go to sleep!" he warned her at last. "Aren't you afraid I'll remember that I'm a raiding, pillaging, murderous—raping—Yankee?"

He heard her exhale raggedly. She didn't know how close she had come to forcing him to discover that a desperate monster lived in every man.

But in time she slept, and so did he, and when he awoke, his arm was around her, his hand resting just below the fullness of her breast. His naked leg lay entwined with hers, while the golden silk of her hair teased his nose and chin. It felt so good to hold her. To want her, to long for her. Even to ache. Just seeing her, just touching her, evoked dreams. Dreams of a distant time, dreams of a peaceful future. In those first seconds of dawn, she seemed to be the most wondrous present he had ever received.

She twisted in his arms, instinctively seeking

warmth. She cuddled against his chest, her fingers moving lightly across his skin, her lips brushing his flesh. He pulled her against him. As the morning light fell into the room, her lips were slightly parted, slightly damp, as red as wine.

Carefully he untied her wrists, freeing her hands.

Then he kissed her. He touched his lips to hers, and he kissed her. A soft sound rumbled within her throat, but she didn't awaken right away. Her lips parted farther, and his tongue swiftly danced between them, and he tasted, fully and hungrily, everything that her mouth had to offer. Heat rose within him, swift and combustible, swamping him, hurting him, making him ache and yearn for more. His fingers curled over her breast, and he found it as full and fascinating as he had imagined. He touched her nipples beneath the flannel that still guarded them and he felt her stir beneath him as he drew his lips from hers.

Her eyes opened slowly, and he realized that she had been lost in her own dreams. Their gazes met, then a horrified whisper left her lips. She suddenly seemed to realize what the situation was, and she twisted violently away from him.

And he let her go. She leaped away from the bed, her fingers trembling as they touched her lips, her arms wrapped tightly around herself. She stared at him in fury. "You…you Yank! How could you, how dare you, how—"

"You tried to murder me, madam, remember?"

"But you tried to—" She broke off. He hadn't really

used any force against her. "You know what you did! You are no gentleman!"

"I never make any pretense of being a gentleman when I'm in the midst of trying to stay alive!" he told her angrily.

"A Virginian, sir, would have been a gentleman to the very end. A Virginian—"

She broke off as her gaze fell over him, over his nakedness, and she turned to run.

He caught her arm and pulled her hard against him. His eyes burned into hers. "I *am* a Virginian, Miss Hinton. And trust me, ma'am, nothing has hurt so bad as this war. I have cousins in blue, and cousins in gray, and do you know something, Miss Hinton? Every single one of them is a gentleman, a good, decent man. And sometimes I wake up so scared that I can't stand it because I just might find myself shooting one of my very decent cousins someday. My gentlemanly cousins. Most of the time I wake to my nightmares. This morning I woke to see you. It was like a glimpse of paradise."

The blood had drained from her face, and when her eyes met his they were filled with a tempest of emotion, but she did not try to pull away. For the longest time they just stood there, then he lightly touched her cheek. "Thank you. It was just like a Christmas present."

She didn't move even at that. Her hand rose, and she touched his cheek in turn. She felt the texture of his skin, rough from lack of shaving.

Then suddenly it was gone, that curious moment when they were not enemies. Her hand fell away, and she seemed to remember that she was flush against a naked Yankee. With a soft cry she whirled and headed across the room, and he discovered that there was a door in the wall, very craftily concealed by the paneling.

She disappeared through it without a word.

LATER THAT DAY she found him in her den, which he had taken over as his office. She wore a bonnet and cloak, and her hands were warmed by an elegant fur muff.

"You said that I could go where I chose, Captain."

His heart hammered and leaped as he looked up from his work. It would be best if she left. He would cease to dream and wonder; he would be able to concentrate more fully on the war.

He didn't want her to go. He would never know when she intended to pull a knife again, but he was willing to deal with the danger just to enjoy the battle.

"Yes," he told her.

"I wish to go to a neighbor's."

"Oh? You're not going to stay to protect your property?" he said, trying to provoke her. His eyes never left hers. Her lashes fell, and she reddened very prettily. She was remembering that morning, he thought, and he was glad of the flush that touched her cheeks, just as he was glad of the totally improper moments they had shared.

Her eyes met his again. "Don't worry, Captain. I'll be back. I just don't care to spend Christmas with the enemy."

He looked down quickly. She was going to come back. He opened his drawer, found a form and began writing on it. He looked up. "I don't know your given name."

"Isabelle," she told him.

He stared at her. "Isabelle," he murmured, a curious, wistful note in his voice. In annoyance, he scribbled hard. "Isabelle. Isabelle Hinton. Well, Miss Hinton, where is this neighbor?"

"Not a mile on the opposite side of town."

He nodded. "Sergeant Sikes and one other soldier will serve as an escort for you. How long do you plan to stay?"

She hesitated. "Until two days after Christmas."

"Sergeant Sikes will return for you."

"I hardly see why that will be necessary."

"I see it as very necessary. Good day, Miss Hinton."

She turned and left him.

CHRISTMAS DAWNED gray and cold. Restless, Travis went out into the snow with a shotgun. He brought down a huge buck and was glad, because it would mean meat for many nights to come.

At the house, Peter and the servants were almost friendly. There was a long and solemn prayer before they started eating the Christmas feast, and there was general good humor as the meal was downed. Travis tried to join in, but when he realized that his mood was solemn, he escaped the company of his soldiers and returned to the den. He did not know when Christmas had become so bleak. Yes, he did. It had become gray and empty when Isabelle Hinton left.

HE DIDN'T HEAR HER RETURN. He had spent the day poring over charts of the valleys and mountains, pinpointing the regions where Stonewall Jackson had been playing havoc with the Union Army. A messenger had arrived from Washington with orders and all kinds of information gleaned from spies, but Travis tended to doubt many of the things he heard.

By nightfall he was weary from men coming and going, as well as from the news of the war. Peter had brought him a bowl of venison stew and a cup of coffee, and that had been his nourishment for the day. Exhausted, he climbed the steps to his room, stripped off his cavalry frock coat and scrubbed his face. Then it seemed that he heard furtive movements in the next room.

His heart quickened, but then his eyes narrowed with wariness. He hadn't forgotten how she had come upon him that first night, even if she had stopped short of slitting his throat. Silently he moved across the room, wondering what she was up to. He found the catch of the secret door and slowly pressed it. The door opened, and he entered her domain.

A smile touched his features, and he leaned casually against the door, watching her, enjoying the view. Miss Isabelle Hinton was awash in bubbles, submerged to her elegant chin, one long and shapely leg raised above the wooden hip bath as she soaped it with abandon. Steam rose from the tub, whispering around her golden curls, leaving them clinging to her flesh. From his vantage point, he could just make out the rise of her breasts, just see the slender column of her throat and the artistic lines of her profile.

Then she turned, sensing him there.

Her leg splashed into the water, and she started to sit up straighter, but then she sank back, aware what she was displaying by rising. She lifted her chin, realizing that she was caught, and from his casual stance against the door, she knew he wasn't about to turn politely and leave.

"Welcome home," he told her.

She flushed furiously. "What are you doing in my room, Captain?"

"Seeking a bit of Southern hospitality?"

She threw the soap at him. He laughed, ducking.

"No gentleman would enter a lady's bedroom!" she snapped angrily.

"Ah, but no lady would venture into a man's bedroom, Isabelle, and it seems that you did just that to me. Admittedly, you came to do me in, but you barged in upon my, er, privacy nonetheless."

Ignoring him, she demanded, "Get out, or you shall be gravely sorry."

"Shall I?"

So challenged, he strode across the room toward the tub. Her eyes widened, and she wrapped her arms around her chest, sinking as low as she could into her wealth of bubbles. He smiled, crouching beside the tub. She stared at him in silence for a moment, then called him every despicable name he had ever heard. He laughed, and she doused him with a handful of water, but he didn't mind a bit, since her movement displayed quite a bit of her.

"I'll strangle you!" she promised. But he caught her wrists when her fingers would have closed around his throat, and then, even as she struggled, he kissed both her palms. Then he stood, releasing her and stepping back.

"Damn, I forgot to be a gentleman again," he apologized. "But I was just wondering whether you had a knife hidden under that water or not. Do you?"

She inhaled sharply. "No!"

"I could check, you know," he warned.

Her look of outrage made him laugh. He gave her his very best bow, then returned to the door that separated their rooms.

"I'm changing rooms!" she called to him.

He paused in the doorway, looking at her. "No, you're not. You chose it this way the night you planned my early demise. So now it will stay."

"I'll move if I choose."

"If you move, I'll drag you back. Depend on it. If you stay, I promise that we're even. I won't pass through the doorway unless I'm invited. A threat, and a promise, and I will carry out both, Miss Hinton."

Thick honeyed lashes fell over her eyes. She was so lovely that he ached from head to toe, watching her. "You will never be invited in, Captain," she said.

"Alas, you have a standing invitation to enter my room, Miss Hinton. Of course, I do ask that you leave your weapons behind."

Her eyes flew to his. He offered her a curiously tender smile, and she did not look away, but watched him. She was as still and perfect as an alabaster bust. Her throat was long and glistened from the water. Her golden curls clung tightly to her flesh, and if she were to move, he knew she would be fluid, graceful, a liquid swirl of passion and energy.

I'm falling in love, he thought.

"I missed you on Christmas, Isabelle," he told her. She did not answer, and he slipped through the door, closing it behind him.

CHAPTER TWO

ISABELLE HINTON had never wanted to like the Yankee commander who had come to take over her home. She spent hours reminding herself that the boys in blue were causing the war, that the South had just wanted to walk away in peace. She reminded herself of all the atrocities taking place; again and again she remembered that her brothers were out there, facing Yankee bullets daily, but nothing that she could tell herself seemed to help very much. He'd never claimed to be a gentleman, and indeed, his behavior had been absolutely outrageous at times. But still, as the days went by, he proved himself to be a true cavalier underneath it all.

She tried to ignore all of them at first. But one evening, when she knew that he was dining alone, her curiosity brought her to the table. Though she tried to bait him, he was calm and quiet during the meal, the flash in his dark eyes the only indication that she touched his temper at all. He was a good-looking man—she had admitted that from the start. His eyes were so dark a mahogany as to be almost coal-black; his hair, too, was dark, neatly clipped at the collar line.

He was the perfect picture of an officer when he set out to ride, his cape falling over his shoulders, his plumed hat pulled low over his forehead, shading those dancing eyes. Beneath the beard, his features were clean and sharp, his cheekbones high, his chin firm, his lips full and quick to curl with a sensuality that often left her breathless, despise the condition though she might. Even his tone of voice fascinated her; his words were clear and well enunciated, but there was something husky about them, too, just the trace of a slow Virginia drawl. And, of course, she was very much aware of the rest of him; even if she didn't see much daily, the picture lived on vividly in her memory.

She hadn't had a great deal of experience with men's bodies, but she did have two older brothers, and after a few battles she had gone to the makeshift hospitals to help with the wounded. She had gone from ladies' circles, where she and others had rolled bandages, to being thrust right into a surgeon's field tent, and she had learned firsthand a great deal of the horror of war. She had cleaned and soothed and bandaged many a male chest, but none of them had compared to the very handsome chest that belonged to Captain Travis Aylwin. His shoulders were broad and taut with muscle and sinew, and the same handsome ripple of power was evident in his torso and arms. His waist was trim, and dusky dark hair created a handsome pattern across his chest, then narrowed to a thin line before flaring again to…well, she wouldn't think about that. She had been raised quite properly, she reminded herself over and over again, but that didn't keep her from remembering him, all of him, time and time again. She couldn't cease her wondering about him, nor could she keep him from intruding upon her dreams.

She always awakened before anything could happen, though her cheeks would be dark with a bright red blush, and there was a burning behind her eyes as she longed to crawl beneath the floor in humiliation.

She tried hard to stay away from him. He respected the distance, as he had promised when he had left her room after Christmas, but she always knew he was there at night, just beyond her door. His men were perfectly courteous and polite, and they were good hunters; there was always plenty to eat. So much so, she knew, that when she mentioned that some of her neighbors were facing hard times, the Union officers were quick to leave a side of venison before a door, or a half dozen rabbits, or whatever bird had ventured too close to the hunters. It was Travis's leadership that led to their generosity and care, she knew. Travis did not relish war.

She began seeing him and his troops not as faceless enemies but as men, just like the friends who had come to her parties, just like the young Southerners who had come to her home to laugh and dream, to fall in love and plan a future. She had to tell herself that they were the enemy, and that she did not want her enemy to be flesh and blood.

It was late January when she came down to dinner with him again. He had been reading some papers, but once he masked his astonishment at her appearance, he quickly set them aside, rose and held out her chair. She sat, quickly picking up the glass of wine that had just been poured for him and swallowing deeply. He sat down again, a touch of amusement in his eyes. He must have been a true lady-killer back home, she thought. He was full of warmth and laughter, a quiet strength and a subtle but overwhelming masculinity. His eyes held so much, and his lips were so quick to curve into a smile. But he could be ruthless, too, she knew. She had learned that the first night, when he had held her beside him until dawn.

"To what do I owe this honor?" he asked her softly. He barely needed to lift his hand. Peter was there with a second setting almost immediately. More wine was poured for him. Peter glanced her way worriedly. She winked, trying to assure her servant that she was, as always, in charge.

"The honor, sir? Well, actually, I was hoping that the snow would be melting, that you might be marching out to do battle again soon."

He sat back, watching her. "Perhaps we will be. Will that really give you such great pleasure?"

She rose, not believing that he could make her feel ashamed for wanting the enemy to fall in battle. She walked around the room, pausing before the picture of her family taken by Mr. Brady just before the war. Her brothers stood on either side of her, and her parents sat before them. But already the boys were dressed in their uniforms, and every day she prayed that they would return. If they sat in some Northern house, would a girl there wish them into the field of battle, to bleed, to die?

"I just want you out of my house," she told him, turning back.

He had risen and was staring at the picture, too. He walked around to it. "Handsome family," he told her. "Your parents?"

"They died in 1859, a few days apart. They caught smallpox. My brothers and I were safe, I think, because we had very mild cases as children. Neither Mother nor Father caught it then, but one of the neighboring babies came down with it and then…" She left off, shrugging.

"I'm very sorry."

"It's a horrible death," she murmured.

"I know," he said, turning from her. He stood behind his chair. "Shall we have dinner?"

She sat. Peter served them smoke-cured ham from the cellars, apricot preserves and tiny pickled carrots and beets.

"Where is home, Captain?" she asked him.

"Alexandria."

Alexandria. The beautiful old city had been held since the beginning of the war because of its proximity to Washington, D.C., but many of its citizens were Unionists. It was a curious war. Already the counties in the west had broken away and a new state had been born, West Virginia.

"You're going to get your home back, you know, Miss Hinton," he told her.

"Am I?"

"Of course."

She set her fork down. "How do I know you won't decide to burn the house down when you leave?"

He set his fork down, too. "Do you really believe I intend to do that?" he asked her.

She watched him for several long moments. He buttered one of Peter's special biscuits, then offered it to her.

"General Lee lost Arlington House," she said. "And, I admit, I'm quite surprised that you Yanks haven't burned it to the ground."

He set the biscuit down and sipped his wine. "It's a beautiful house," he said softly. "And it overlooks the Capitol. General Lee knew the moment he chose to fight for the South that he would have to leave his home. His wife knew, his family knew, and still he made his decision. Some people were bitter. Some of the men who had fought with him or learned from him before the war wanted to burn the place down. It is Mrs. Lee I pity— she grew up there. And as George Washington's step-granddaughter, she has always had a great sense of history. She's a magnificent lady." He paused, as if he had said too much. Then he shrugged, setting down his wineglass. "They're not going to burn the house down. They've been burying Union soldiers there since the beginning of the war. The land will become a national cemetery."

"And Lee will forever lose his home."

"The South could still win the war," he told her.

Startled, she stared at him. She hadn't realized that she had displayed such a defeated attitude. "The South *will* win the war!" she assured him, but then she frowned. "You sound as if you're quite taken with the Lees."

He pushed back his chair. "The general is my god-father, Miss Hinton. We all lose in this war. He made his choices, and so did I. A man must do what he feels is right. And yet I tell you, Miss Hinton, that this fratricide must and will end, and when it does, if we are blessed to live, then he will be my friend and mentor again, and I will be his most willing servant."

She jumped up, wrapping her fingers around the back of her chair, staring at him in fury. It was almost blasphemy to speak so of General Robert E. Lee; he was adored by his troops, by the South as a whole. He was a magnificent general and a soft-spoken gentleman.

"How dare you!" she spat out, trembling.

He took a step toward her, grabbing her wrist, holding her tight when she would have fled his presence. "Would you make monsters of us all?"

"I've read about the things that have happened. I know what Yankees do."

"Yes, yes, and *we've* all read *Uncle Tom's Cabin*, but I've yet to see you whip or chain or harness your slaves. By God, yes, there is injustice, and some horror is always true, but must we create more of it ourselves?"

"I'm not creating anything." She jerked free of him and spun around, hurrying from the room, but he called her back.

"Isabelle!"

She turned. He stood tall and striking in his dress frock coat and high cavalry boots, his saber hanging from the scabbard strapped around his waist. His eyes touched her, heated and dark.

"I am not a monster," he told her.

"Does it matter what I think?" she demanded.

A rueful smile touched his lips. "Well, yes, to me it does. You see, I...care."

She gasped in dismay. "Well, don't, Yankee, don't! Don't you dare care about me!"

She fled and raced up the stairs.

THAT NIGHT and every night after that she lay awake and listened to his movements, but he never touched her door, and he never mentioned anything about his feelings again. He was always unerringly polite to her, and though she felt that she should keep her distance from him, she couldn't. She came down to a meal occasionally, usually when Sergeant Sikes or one of the other men was joining him.

Sometimes he disappeared for days at a time, and she suspected that he had ridden away to supply information about troop movements, or to receive it.

At the beginning of April Isabelle awoke to find that the house was filled with activity. The way the men were bustling around, coming and going from the office, she knew that something was going on.

She came down the stairs and presented herself in the den. Travis's dark head was bent over a map in serious study. He sensed her presence and looked up quickly.

"What's happening?" she asked without preamble.

He straightened and studied her as thoroughly as he had the map, a curious shadow hiding any emotion in his eyes. "We're pulling out. There's a company of Rebels headed this way."

"You're going into battle?" she asked him.

"That's what war is all about," he returned, and there was just the slightest trace of bitterness in his voice. He sat on the edge of his desk, still watching her. "You should be pleased. Maybe we'll all die."

"I don't want you to die," she said. "I just want you to go away."

He smiled and lifted a hand in the air, then let it fall back to his thigh. "Well, we're doing just that. Tell me, Isabelle, will you miss me at all?"

"No."

He stood and walked toward her. She stepped back until she was against the door. It closed, and she leaned against it, but he kept coming anyway, until he stood right before her. He didn't touch her, just laid his palm against the door by her head. "You're lying just a little, aren't you?" he whispered.

She shook her head, but suddenly she found that she could not speak, that her knees were liquid, that her palms were braced against the door so she could stand. He smelled of soap, of leather and rich pipe tobacco. His eyes were ebony coals, haunting her; his mouth was full and mobile.

"I could die a happy man if you would just whisper that you cared a little bit," he told her, the warmth of his breath creating a warm tempest against her skin while the tenor of his voice evoked a curious fire deep within her.

She kept her eyes steady and smiled sweetly. "I'm sure you say those words to every woman whose home you confiscate."

He smiled slowly. "Yours is the only home I have ever confiscated." He leaned closer. "And you've known for some time how I feel about you."

She wanted to shake her head again, but she discovered that she couldn't. His lips brushed hers, and then his mouth consumed hers as the roar within her soul came rushing up to drown out the rest of the world. She fell into his arms and felt the overwhelming masculine force of his lips parting and caressing her own; she felt the heady invasion of his tongue, so deep it seemed that he could possess all of her with the kiss alone. His hands, desperate, rough, massaged her skull, and his fingers threaded hungrily through her hair, holding her close. But she couldn't have left him. She had never known anything like that kiss, never known the world to spin in such delirious motion, never known the hunger to touch a man in return, to feel his hair, crisp and clean, beneath her fingers, to feel his body, his heat and his heartbeat throbbing ferociously against her breasts. The sweet, heady taste of his mouth left her thirsting for more and more, until sanity returned to her, some voice of reason screaming within her that he was the Yankee soldier who had taken over her home, a Yank who was leaving at last.

She pulled away from him, her fingers shaking as she brought them to her lips.

He watched her, his eyes dark and enigmatic, and sighed softly. His rueful smile touched his lips again. "Will you care if I come back, Isabelle?"

"You're a Yank. I hope you never come back," she told him. She wiped her mouth as if she could wipe away the memory of his kiss, then turned and hurriedly left the room.

But later, in her room, she lay on her bed and knew that she had fallen in love. Right or wrong, she was in love with him. In love with his eyes and his mouth and his voice…and with all the things he said. And he was riding away. Perhaps to die.

She rose when she heard the sergeant call out the orders, and she raced down the stairs two at a time. She forced herself to slow down and walk demurely out to the porch. There he was at the head of his troops, his magnificent plumed hat in place, sitting easily on his mount.

He saw her and rode closer, his horse prancing as he came near. He touched his hat in salute and waited.

"Well, I do hope that you don't ride away to get killed," she told him.

He smiled. "Not exactly a declaration of undying devotion, but I suppose it will have to do." He leaned closer to her. "I will not get killed, Isabelle. And I will be back."

She didn't answer him right away. She didn't remind him that she could hardly want him to come back, for if he did, it would mean that the Union was holding tight to large tracts of Virginia.

"As I said, I hope that you survive. And that is all."

His smile deepened as he dug his heels into his horse's flanks and rode hard for the front of his line.

Isabelle watched the troops until they were long gone.

NEWS CAME TO HER in abundance as spring turned to summer. There was a horrible battle fought at Chancellorsville. The Union had over sixteen thousand troops killed, wounded or captured; the South lost over twelve thousand, and though the South was accepted to be the victor, she had received a crippling blow. Stonewall Jackson was mistakenly shot by one of his own men, and he died on May tenth from his wounds.

Isabelle prayed for more news. She volunteered for hospital duty again. She worked endless hours, fearful that every Confederate soldier might be one of her brothers, anxious that any Union soldier who fell into their hands might be Travis.

She was working in the hospital in July when news came through that a horrible battle had been fought in a little town in Pennsylvania called Gettysburg. The losses in human life were staggering. And General Lee and his Army of Northern Virginia were in retreat. Men whispered that it was the turning point of the war. The South was being brought to her knees.

Isabelle hurried home, anxious to hear about her brothers, anxious to hear about Travis. In town she waited endlessly for the lists of the dead, wounded and captured to come through, and when she was able to procure a sheet she eagerly sought out her brothers' names. When she did not find them, she thanked God in a silent prayer, wincing as she heard the horrible tears of those who had lost sons, fathers, lovers and brothers.

She swallowed tightly, wondering about Travis, and prayed that he had made it. Shaking, she drove her carriage home. And that night she admitted in her prayers that she loved Travis Aylwin, and that even if he was a Yankee, she wanted God to watch over him always.

IN SEPTEMBER she was busy picking the last of the summer vegetables from her small garden when she heard Peter calling to her anxiously. She came running around the house, wiping her hands on her apron. Peter was on the porch, anxiously pointing eastward. Isabelle shaded her eyes from the afternoon sun. Riders were coming. She could see them. Her heart began to beat faster. There were about twenty or thirty men on horseback. In Union blue.

Her heart thudded. Travis was alive!

But what if it was not Travis? What if it was some other Yankee who lacked Travis Aylwin's sense of right and wrong, even in the midst of war?

She turned toward the porch and raced up the steps, shoving Peter out of her way. At the end of the hallway she tore open the gun case and reached for her rifle. With trembling fingers she attempted to load it. A hand fell on her shoulder, and she screamed, spinning around.

"You're going to shoot me again? Damn, I didn't survive Chancellorsville and Gettysburg just to be shot by you, Isabelle!"

He was thin, very thin and gaunt, and yet his dark eyes were alive with fire. She started to move, and the gun rose with her movement. His eyes widened, and he grabbed it from her, sending it flying across the floor. Then he swept her into his arms and kissed her hard, and she couldn't begin to fight him, not until he eased her from his hold. He clutched her tightly to him, his fingers clenched around her upper arms. "Tell me that you missed me, Isabelle. Tell me that you're glad I'm alive!"

She swallowed hard. She was a Southerner. A Virginian. Her heart was alive, and it seemed that her breath had deserted her, but she could not surrender while the South fought on. She pulled away from him. "I'm glad you're alive, Yank, but I wish heartily that you were not here!"

She ran upstairs, where she paced her room while the Yankees settled in. When darkness fell, she listened to his footsteps in the room beside hers. She heard them come close to her door; she heard them retreat. Again and again.

IT WASN'T TWO WEEKS LATER that the Yankee rider came racing to the house. He slammed his way into the house, then hurried into the den with Travis. Isabelle came hurrying down the stairs, wondering what was happening. Men were rushing into her house, knocking glass from the windows, then taking up positions with their rifles at the ready. Travis came out of the den in time to see her at the foot of the stairway. "Isabelle, you've got to get down to the cellar."

"Why? What's happening?"

"Rebels. Clancy's brigade."

"Clancy's brigade?" she said, her face paling.

"Yes, Clancy's brigade," he repeated. "They're on

their way here. They heard that Yanks were holding this house and the town, and they want a battle."

She was going to fall, she thought. She was too weak to stand.

"Isabelle, what is it?"

"Steven is with Clancy's brigade. My brother Steven."

She saw in his eyes that he felt her pain, but she saw, too, that at that moment he was in command of his men, that this was war, and that he had to fight to win. "You've got to get down to the cellar."

"No!"

Travis turned to the butler, who had just come on the scene. "Peter! Peter, I don't know who is going to win or lose here today, but I'll be damned if I'll let Isabelle become a casualty of this war! Get her downstairs."

Peter put his arm around her and rushed her toward the cellar stairs. Dazed, she let him force her down them.

When she heard the first cannon roar, she screamed and clapped her hands over her ears. Then the house shuddered, and she heard a burst of fire and shells, and the screams of horses and men. She never knew what goaded her, but she couldn't bear it, knowing that Steven was out there, bombarding his own house. She escaped Peter and hurried out, ducking as bullets whizzed through the open windows. She didn't know what she hoped to accomplish—of course she wanted the Confederates to win. But there was Private Darby with his freckles, crooked teeth and easy smile, and there was blood pouring out of his shoulder, and he looked as if he was in shock. Isabelle crawled swiftly to the window by his side, ripping at her petticoat, finding cloth to bind up his wound, to staunch the flow of his blood.

"Thank you, Miss Hinton, thank you," he told her over and over again. She stretched him out on the floor; then she heard Travis shouting her name in fury.

"Isabelle!" It was a roar. He came rushing over to her, spinning her away from the window, pressing her against the door. "You could be killed, you little fool!"

She didn't hear his words. She was looking out the window, and she wanted to scream. Steven, in his battered gold and gray, was coming nearer and nearer the house, sneaking toward the rear. He looked so close that she could almost reach out and touch him. Then he stiffened, and red blossomed all over the gray of his cavalry shirt, and he fell onto the grass.

"Steven!" She screamed her brother's name and jerked free of Travis to race toward one of the windows. She felt nothing as she slipped over the windowsill with its shattered glass. She knew no fear as she raced across the battle line to her brother's silent form. "Steven, oh, Steven!" she cried desperately.

"Get down!"

Travis was behind her, throwing himself on top of her, bringing her down to the ground. Bullets flew by them, lodging in the house, in the ground so very near them. "Fool! You'll get shot!"

"That's my brother, I will not go back into the house without him!"

"You have to!"

"He could die!"

"Get in the house! If you go, I'll bring him back. I swear it. By all that's holy, Isabelle, I have a chance! You have none!"

He rolled her away with a shove. Then, before she could protest, he was up himself, racing across the lawn to reach Steven. A Confederate soldier stood up, his sword raised for hand-to-hand combat. Travis was unprepared, and he fell with the man onto the verdant grass. Isabelle bit the back of her hand, repressing a sob. Then she saw Travis again, saw him reach Steven, saw him lift her brother and stagger toward the house.

When he neared it, several of his own men hurried out to meet him. Steven was carried in and set on the floor of the parlor. Isabelle fell beside him, ripping open his shirt, finding that the bullet had pierced his chest, frighteningly near his heart. She staunched the flow of blood, discovered that the bullet had passed cleanly through him and wrapped the wound, with her tears falling down her cheeks all the while. She realized suddenly that the sound of the battle had receded, that no more guns blazed, no more shouts or Rebel yells rose upon the air. She turned toward the doorway. Travis stood there, leaning in the door frame, watching her.

She moistened her lips. The Yanks had held their ground, but he had brought Steven to her. She owed him something. "Thank you," she told him stiffly.

He smiled his crooked smile, doffing his hat. "It was nothing, ma'am, nothing at all."

But then he suddenly staggered and keeled down

hard on the floor, and she heard herself screaming as she saw the blood pouring forth from his chest.

TRAVIS WAS GOING TO LIVE. The Yankee surgeon promised her that, although he had lost a good deal of blood, he was going to live. He was tough that way. Steven's injury was by far the worse of the two.

The Yank worked hard over her brother. And he seemed to be an enlightened man, using clean sponges for each man, washing his bloodied hands with regularity. She could not have asked for better care for her brother. The Yanks had morphine, and they kept him out of pain. They gave him their best.

But that night Steven died anyway. She held him in her arms as he breathed his last, and then she held him until dawn, sobbing. No one could draw her away from him.

She was only dimly aware, when morning dawned at last, that Travis was with her. In breeches and bare feet, his chest wrapped in bandages, and none too steady on his feet, he came to her. He curled his fingers over hers, and she slowly released her grip on the brother she had loved. He whispered to her, he soothed her, and she fell against his shoulder and allowed her tears to soak his bandage. Then she realized who was holding her, and she tried to pull away, slamming her fists against him. She didn't see him wince at the pain, and, indeed, it meant nothing to him. Though he had seen men die time and again in war, he'd had little opportunity to see what it did to the loved ones left behind.

And he loved Isabelle Hinton himself.

"Let go of me, Yankee!" she ordered him, but he didn't release her. And finally her sobs quieted. In time he lifted her into his arms, and carried her upstairs, where he laid her on her bed.

It was hours later when she awoke. And he was still with her. Bandaged and in his breeches, he stared out the window at the September fields where the war had come home. Where the blood of her brother still stained the grass.

"Travis?" she whispered, and tears welled in her eyes, because she wanted to believe that it had all been a dream, a nightmare. He came to her bedside, silent and grave. He stared into her eyes and found her hand, squeezing her fingers. "I'm sorry, so very sorry, Isabelle. I know you would have rather it had been me, but I swear that we tried—"

"Oh, God, Travis, don't say that, please! I—" She broke off, shaking her head. Her tears were very close to falling again; she felt that she had been destroyed in those moments when Steven had breathed his last. "Thank you," she said primly. "I know how hard you tried to save him. And you—you shouldn't be up. You're wounded yourself." Indeed, he seemed drawn and weary and haggard, and he had aged years in the months since he had been gone.

"I'm all right," he told her.

She nodded slowly. "So am I," she whispered.

"I'm always here if you need me."

"I *can't* need you!" she whispered.

He inhaled deeply, but he released her hand, turned and left her.

That afternoon they buried Steven. They stood by his grave, and the chaplain said that he had been a brave soldier, fighting for what he believed. Then Travis ordered that the musicians play "Dixie." Isabelle wasn't going to cry again, but she did. Then she ran away from the grave site and retired to her room. She spoke to no one for days. Peter brought her food on a tray, but she ate very little of it.

Steven had been dead for almost two weeks when a sharp tap on her door and then a thundering brought her from her lethargy. She swung the door open, furious that her privacy was being abused, but when she would have protested she fell silent instead. It was Dr. Allen Whaley, the surgeon who had tried so hard to save Steven. He looked grave and worried.

"The captain is dying, Miss Hinton. I thought you should know."

"What?" she gasped incredulously. "But he was fine! I saw him. He was fine, he was—"

"He shouldn't have been up. He lost more blood, and he courted infection. Now he's burning up with fever."

Isabelle raced to the door connecting her room to Travis's. She thrust it open and raced to his bedside.

He was burning up. The bandage around his chest had been curtailed to cover just the wound, and the flesh all around it was slick and hot. Sergeant Sikes had been sitting by him, ineffectually dabbing at his flesh with a wet cloth.

"Up, Sergeant!" Isabelle ordered quickly. She took over the task of soothing Travis's forehead and face with cool water. She touched his wrist and felt for his pulse. She flinched from the fire of his skin and glanced toward Doctor Whaley, who nodded his approval of anything she might try. She bathed Travis from his waist to his throat with the cool water. She began to talk to him, and she talked until she was hoarse.

Later Doctor Whaley came and they rebandaged the wound. The doctor lanced it, and they drained the infection, then wrapped it again. And still his fever burned on.

"Tonight will tell," Doctor Whaley told her. "If you would pray for a Yank, Miss Hinton, pray for this one tonight."

She tried to pray, and she kept moving. She soaked him again and again, trying to cool him. She wiped his forehead and his cheeks; she saw where the war had engraved lines around his eyes, and she thought of how dearly she loved his fascinating, handsome face. If he died, he would have died for her, she realized. She had wanted Steven. He had gone for Steven for her.

"Don't die, don't die, damn you! I—I need you!" she whispered fervently to him.

It couldn't have been her whisper. It really couldn't have been. But he inhaled suddenly, a great ragged breath, and then he went so still that she thought he had died. She laid her ear against his chest and heard his even breathing. She touched his flesh, and it was perceptibly cooler. She started to laugh as she sank into the chair by his bedside. "Oh, my God, he is better!" She breathed the words aloud.

And then Doctor Whaley was by her side, lifting her up. "Yes, he's better, Miss Hinton. And now you'd best get some rest before you fall apart on us!"

He led her away, and when she slept that night, she slept soundly, a smile curling her lips for the first time since Steven had died. There *was* a God in heaven; Travis had lived.

HE STAYED IN BED for a week before he summoned sufficient strength to stand. Isabelle kept her distance from him, not trusting herself with him anymore.

She heard him, though, the day he first rose. He shouted now and then when one of his men seemed to think he needed more help getting around than he did. His soldiers walked around that day with pleased grins, ignoring his tone. They were just glad to have him up.

Isabelle wanted to see him, but she couldn't bring herself to do so. She avoided the dining room; she avoided his office. She was afraid of getting too close to him.

November faded away. December came, and Isabelle made her plans to leave for Christmas. She was packing when she realized that someone was watching her from the open doorway.

That someone was Travis.

He was completely healed now. He was still gaunt, but his features were so striking that his thinness only accentuated the clean lines of his face. His eyes followed her every step, and wherever they fell, she was touched with warmth, with fire. He was striking in blue wool breeches, his high boots and regulation cavalry shirt, his officer's insignia upon his shoulder. "What are you doing?" he asked her.

"Packing."

"Why?"

"I'm leaving for Christmas."

"Why?"

"Because it is not a holiday to be spent with the enemy."

"I am not your enemy, Isabelle."

She shrugged and kept packing.

He slammed the door shut and strode across the room, catching her by the shoulders, wrenching her from her task. His eyes bored into her like ebony daggers.

"Let me go!" she cried.

"Why, Isabelle?"

"Because, because—"

"No!" he cried, and he tossed her leather portmanteau to the floor, bearing her down upon the bed. His fingers curled around hers, holding her hands high over her head.

"Travis, damn you!"

"I need you, Isabelle. I need you!"

She wanted to fight him. She wanted to deny everything that had happened, everything she felt, but then she thought that perhaps it had always been coming to this, from the very first, when they had fallen together to the snow. She opened her mouth to swear, to protest, but his whisper was already entering her mouth.

"I need you, Isabelle, my God, I need you!"

Then his lips were on hers, his kiss fervent, building

a fire within her. He whispered against her mouth, and his lips burned a fiery trail across her cheeks, to her throat, against her earlobe, then back to her mouth again. His tongue teased her lips, then delved between them.

She wrapped her arms around him, her fingers burrowing into his hair, and she came alive, rejoicing in the feel of his hair, in the ripple of the muscles in his shoulders and back. She wasn't sure when it happened, but it seemed that his shirt melted away, and she was torn between laughter and tears when her hands moved across his bare flesh, luxuriating in the warmth of him, in the feel of life. She touched the scars where war had torn his flesh, and she placed her lips against them as tenderly as possible. But after that few things were tender, as the tempest flared between them with a sudden swirling desperation. Her bodice had somehow come undone, and his face lay buried against the valley between her breasts. And then he was taking one into his mouth, his lips and teeth warm upon one pebbled, rosy peak, and the sensation was shattering, sending tremors of fire and yearning through her. She gasped, clinging to him, then she gasped again as she felt his hands upon her naked hips, then between her thighs. She moaned, closing her eyes, shuddering and breathing deeply against his neck as his touch became bold and intimate, stroking, delving, evoking need and searing heat and molten pleasure...

His breeches were shed; her gown was a pile of tangled froth around them; his features were both hard and tender as he rose above her. He gently pulled and tugged away the tangle of her clothing until she lay naked and shivering beneath him. And yet she trusted him, the enemy; he saw it in her eyes. He laid his head against her breasts, then he shuddered with a frightening force. "My God, I've needed you, Isabelle. I may be your enemy, but no enemy will ever love you so tenderly. No friend could swear with greater fervor to be so gentle…."

She cried out, finding his lips, drowning in his kiss. As they kissed, his hands traveled the length of her. He touched and stroked her endlessly, boldly, intimately….

And gently, tenderly.

Finally passion rose swiftly, wantonly, within her. Desire had bloomed so completely and surely in her that she knew nothing of distress or pain, and everything of the driving, blinding beauty of being taken by a man who gave her love. She knew the fury of his passion and the wealth of his rapture as he brought her to a peak of ecstasy so sweet that it was heaven on earth before he shuddered violently and fell beside her, the two of them covered in the fine sheen of their own sweat.

They were silent for the longest time. Then he reached out and touched a curl against the dampness of her cheek. "I'm sorry, Isabelle, I had no right…."

She caught his hand. "No! Shh. Please don't say such things, not now!"

He rolled over, stroked her cheek and stared unabashedly at the rise and fall of her breasts. "I love you, you know."

"No! Don't say that, either!"

She tugged away from him, trembling as she reached for her clothing.

"Isabelle," he said, rising, trying to stop her.

She didn't know why she was so upset. She wanted him—she had wanted him desperately! And she loved him, too.

But there was a war on.

"Travis, leave me alone. Please."

"Isabelle, I didn't—"

"No, Travis, you didn't force me. You didn't do anything wrong. You were—you were the perfect gentleman! But please, leave me alone now. I have to be alone."

He turned angrily and jerked on his shirt and breeches, then his boots. "I'll expect you at dinner tonight," he told her.

She watched him leave, then she washed and dressed and finished her packing. She walked down the stairs and into his office.

"I want to leave for Christmas, Captain," she told him.

He stood up, staring at her across the desk. "Don't leave, Isabelle."

"It's war, Captain."

"Not between us."

"I can't stay! Don't you understand? I can't spend Christmas with the enemy!"

"Even if you sleep with him?"

She slapped him. He didn't make a move, and she bit her lip, wishing she hadn't struck him. She didn't know what she was doing to either of them anyway. It was just that the sound of Christmas carols made her cry now. She wanted so badly to be home for Christmas, but she didn't know where home was anymore.

"I'll write you a pass immediately," he said curtly. "Sergeant Sikes will see to you."

"Thank you."

He scratched out the pass and handed it to her, then looked at the work piled on his desk.

Isabelle turned and headed for the door, then hesitated. She wanted to cry out to him; she wanted to run back.

But she couldn't. Something deep inside her told her that it just wasn't right. She might be in love with the enemy, but it was still wrong to spend Christmas with him.

CHAPTER THREE

ISABELLE SPENT CHRISTMAS and New Year's Day with Katie Holloway. Katie's place was an old farmstead, and Katie was as solid and rugged as the terrain that surrounded her. She had watched the British siege of Fort McHenry during the War of 1812, and she had lived long enough to say and do and think what she wanted.

"It's dying down now, mind you, Isabelle. This war, it's almost over."

"That's not true! Our generals run circles around theirs. Time and time again we've won the day with far less troops and—"

Rocking in her chair, Katie clicked her knitting needles and exhaled slowly. "When our men die, there's none left to replace them. Aye, we fight fine battles! None will ever forget the likes of Stonewall Jackson. But he and many of his kind are gone now, cut down like flowers in the spring, and we cannot go on without them. Not even Lee can fight this war alone. It's over. All over except for the dying."

Isabelle didn't feel like arguing with Katie; she just felt like crying. She didn't know how life would change when it was all over; she only knew that she had seen enough of it, and she was ready for it to end. She had buried one brother; she wanted the other to live.

She wanted Travis to live.

"I think I'm going to go home tomorrow," she told Katie. It was late January, the snow was piled high, and she wasn't supposed to go home alone. Sergeant Sikes or one of the men came by every couple of days to see if she was ready to leave. No one was due for a few days—she had been determined to say that she wasn't going back. Not until the snows melted. Not until the men went to war again.

But now, suddenly, she didn't want them to go to war. She didn't want *Travis* to go to war.

She hopped up and kissed Katie's weathered cheek, then she hurried into the bedroom to do her packing.

It was the end of January, and not even high noon brought much warmth. Despite Katie's protests that she shouldn't travel alone, Isabelle was going to ride home.

"You should wait for an escort! Captain Aylwin is not going to be pleased."

"Well, Katie, they haven't won the war yet. I can still do as I please," she assured her friend.

She mounted her bay mare and drew her cloak warmly around her. She determined not to go through town—there were too many Yankee soldiers she didn't know there. So she headed east, past small farms and decaying mansions. Everything was winter bleak, and her mare snorted against the cold, filling the air with the mist of her breath. Trees were bare, and the landscape was barren. It was always like this during winter, she told herself. But it wasn't. It was this barren because of the war.

She had ridden for an hour when she came upon the deserted Winslow farm. Thirsty and worried about her mare, she decided to stop to see if the trough had frozen over. She dismounted into the high drifts and led the mare toward the trough. She sighed with relief, because the water had only a thin layer of ice over it. She broke through with the heel of her boot, then patted the mare as she dipped her head to drink. Then she heard a noise behind her and turned around.

A soldier had come out to the porch. He was dressed in ragged gray and butternut, his beard was overgrown, and his eyes were hard and hostile and bleary. At first her heart had soared—one of her own. But as the man leered at her the sensation of elation turned to one of dread. She knew instantly that he was a deserter, and he was here hiding from the Confederates and the Yanks.

She pulled the reins around swiftly, ready to mount, but to no avail. The man threw himself against her, dragging her down into the snow. She pounded her fists against him desperately, and her screams tore the air, but neither had any effect on him. His breath was horrible and rancid, he was filthier than she had ever imagined a man could be, and the scent of him terrified her beyond measure. She knew what he intended, and she thought wildly that she really might rather die than let him touch her. But she was unarmed; she'd had no reason to travel with a weapon—Travis had always seen to her safety.

And now she was alone.

"Hey, ma'am, I'm just looking for some good old Southern hospitality!" he taunted.

She freed a hand and smashed at his face. A hard noise assured her that she had hurt him. She took the advantage and kneed him in the groin with all her strength. He screamed with the pain, but took hold of her hair and wrenched her to her feet, then dragged her toward the house. She started screaming again, but it didn't matter; he dragged her up the stairs and through the doorway. A fire was burning in the open hearth, and he tossed her down before it. She tried to scramble up, but he pounced on her. She twisted her face, frantic with fear, when he tried to kiss her.

Then, suddenly, the man was wrenched away from her and tossed hard across the room. Travis was there. Travis, in his winter cape, his dark eyes burning with an ebony fury. As Isabelle scrambled away, she saw the Rebel deserter draw his pistol. "Travis!" she shrieked in warning. She heard an explosion of fire, but Travis did not fall. A crimson stain spread across her attacker's shirt, and she realized that Travis, too, had pulled a pistol. He wasted little time on pity for the Reb but strode quickly to Isabelle, jerking her to her feet.

"What were you doing out alone?" he demanded.

"I was coming home."

His hands were on her. He was shaking; he was shaking her. "Fool!" he exploded, and he wrenched his hands away from her, turning his back on her. She wanted to thank him; she wanted to tell him that she was grateful he had come. She even wanted to cry out that she loved him, but she couldn't. He was the enemy.

"Thank God I decided to come for you myself this morning! Damn it, Isabelle, don't you know what could have happened? He could have raped you and slit your throat and left you in the snow, and we wouldn't even have known it!"

She moistened her lips. She couldn't tell him that she had been anxious to come home because she had been anxious to see him. He caught her arm and pulled her along with him until they got outside. Then he lifted her up on her mare before mounting his own horse, and they started off in silence. The silence held until they reached the house, where he dismounted and came over to her before she could get down herself. He lifted her down, his hands fevered and strong. Her hair tumbled in reckless curls around her face, golden beneath the sun. "What?" he asked suddenly, angry. "Are you upset that I killed the Reb? He was one of your own, right? A good old Southern boy!"

"Of course not!"

"Friend or enemy, is that it, Isabelle? And am I forever damned as the enemy?" His eyes were alive with fire, and his fingers were biting into her upper arms.

"What do you want from me?" she cried.

His grip relaxed slightly, and a slow, bitter smile just curved the corners of his lips. "Christmas," he told her quietly. "I want Christmas."

And suddenly Christmas was everything—everything he wanted and everything she could not give. She pulled herself from his arms and ran into the house.

TRAVIS DAMNED HIMSELF a thousand times for the way he had handled things. But finding her in the arms of that deserter had scared him to the bone, and he trembled to think that he would not have been there if he hadn't determined that morning to go to Mrs. Holloway's himself and bring her back.

And he had done that only because his orders had come. They were pulling out again. He was to lead his men to ride with Sheridan. Grant was in charge on the Eastern front now, determined to cage the wily Lee, whatever the cost. Grant knew that the other Union generals had been overmatched by Lee's abilities—and overawed by his reputation.

He had only a few days remaining to him here. Right or wrong, he was in love with her, and after the endless months of torture, he had found that she was not all ice and reserve, but that she could be fire and passion, as well. He wanted a taste of that fire upon his lips when he rode away again.

But it was lost now, he thought.

He sat in the dining room alone, waiting for Peter to serve him. But then he grew impatient with himself, with her. He slid from the table and strode up the stairs to his room, and, once there, he burst through the connecting doorway.

He paused sharply, for he had found her this way once before. She was cocooned in a froth of bubbles, one slender leg protruding from the water as she furiously soaped it. Her eyes met his as he entered the room, and a crimson flush rose to her cheeks. But she didn't deny his presence, and she even smiled softly.

"I was coming to dinner," she said quietly. She bit her lower lip. "It's just that I felt so...dirty after today."

Golden-blond ringlets were piled on top of her head, some escaping to dangle softly against her cheeks and the long column of her neck. He had no answer for her other than a hoarse cry and the long strides that brought him to her. He didn't reach for her lips, but paused at the base of the bath, smiling ruefully as he dropped to his knees, then caught the small foot that thrust from the bubbles, and kissed the arch, teasing the sweet, clean flesh with the touch of his tongue. His eyes met hers, which were shimmering with mist and beauty, and he heard the sharp intake of her breath. Her lashes half fell, sensual, inviting. Her lips parted, and still her gaze remained upon him. He stroked his fingers along her calf, soaking his shirt as he leaned into the water, but he didn't care. Brazenly he swept his hand along her thigh. Then he lifted her, dripping and soap-sleek, from the tub. He held her in front of the fire, kissing her, before he walked with her to the bed, cast aside his sodden shirt and breeches and leaned down over her.

No woman had ever smelled so sweet; no skin had ever felt so much like pure silk. She was the most beautiful thing he had ever imagined, with her high firm breasts, slender waist, undulating hips. He kissed her everywhere, ignoring her cries, drinking in the sight and taste and sound of her, needing more and more of her.

That night she dared to love him in return, stroking

her nails down his chest, dazzling him with her finger-tips. Dinner was forgotten. The night lingered forever. He didn't leave her, didn't even think to rise until the sun came in full upon them and he heard a knocking at his own door.

He kissed her sweetly parted lips and rose. Scrambling into his breeches and boots, he hurried to his own room and opened his door.

There was a messenger there from Sheridan, Sikes told him. He was needed downstairs right away.

He found a clean shirt and hurried down the stairs, where he closeted himself with the cavalry scout and received the latest news.

He had only until the fourteenth of February to meet up with other troops north of Richmond.

ISABELLE CAME DOWN LATER. She wore her reserve again, as another woman might wear a cloak. "You're leaving?" she asked coldly, sitting down across from him.

"Soon."

Her fingers curled around her chair, her lashes lowered. He rose and came to stand before her, then knelt down, taking her hands. "Marry me, Isabelle."

"Marry you!" Her eyes widened incredulously. Gray-green, brilliant against the soft beauty of her face, they were filled with disbelief.

"I love you. I would die for you. You know that."

She swallowed painfully, then shook her head. "It's not over yet. I can't marry you."

"Isabelle, you love me, too," he told her.

She shook her head again. "No. No, I don't." She paused for a second, and he sensed the tears behind her voice. "I *cannot* love a Yankee. Don't you understand?"

She leaped up and was gone. She didn't come down to dinner, and he wouldn't go to her. He ate alone, then drank a brandy, before he finally dashed the glass into the fire and took the stairs two at a time. He burst in upon her and found her clad in a soft white nightgown of silk and lace, a sheer gown, one that clung to the exquisite perfection of her form. She was pacing before the fire, but when she saw him, she paused. He strode over to her, wrenching her into his arms, shaking her slightly so that her hair fell in a cascade down her back, and her eyes rose challengingly to his. "If you can't marry me," he said bitterly, "and you can't love me, then come to bed with me and believe that I, at least love you!"

At first he thought she would lash out at him in fury. He bent over, tossing her over his shoulder, and the two of them fell together onto the bed. Her eyes were flashing, but she only brushed his cheek gently with her palm.

"I cannot love you, Yank!" she whispered. But her lips teased his, her breath sweet with mint, and her body was a fire beneath him. Her mouth moved against his. "But I *can* need you, and I need you very much tonight!"

IT REMAINED LIKE THAT between them for the days that remained. By day she kept her distance, the cool and dignified Miss Hinton, but by night she was his, creating dreams of paradise.

But neither paradise nor dreams could still the war, and in due course he rode out for his appointment with battle. She stood on the porch and watched him as he mounted his horse. And then, as he had before, he rode as close as he could to where she was standing on the porch.

"I love you," he reminded her gravely.

"Don't get yourself killed, Travis," she told him. He nodded and started away.

She called him back. "Travis!"

He turned. She hesitated, then whispered, "I'll pray for you."

He smiled and nodded again, then rode away. The war awaited him.

THEY SAID THAT THE SOUTH had been losing the war since Gettysburg, but you couldn't tell it by the way they were fighting, Travis thought later.

At the end of February, when Travis was joining up with Sheridan's forces, General Kilpatrick staged an ill-conceived raid on Richmond. Papers found on the body of Colonel Dahlgreen indicated an intention to burn the city and assassinate President Jefferson Davis and his cabinet. Meade, questioned by Lee under a flag of truce, denied such intentions vigorously, and Lee accepted that the papers were forgeries. Travis was glad to hear that both sides could question something so heinous, and that even in the midst of warfare, some things could be discussed.

In May, Travis and his troops were engaged in the Battle of the Wilderness, which would stand out in his memory forever. Rebels and Yanks alike were caught, confused and horrified, in the depths of the forest. Soon the trees were ablaze, and more men died from the smoke and fire than from bullets.

From there the survivors moved to the Battle of Spotsylvania. Next Travis followed Sheridan into the Battle of Yellow Tavern, where the cavalry, ten thousand strong, met up with Stuart's Southern troops on the outskirts of Richmond. Stuart brought over four thousand men, and the fighting was pitched and desperate, but Travis managed to survive. The great Confederate cavalryman Jeb Stuart was mortally wounded, however. He died in Richmond days later.

LATE IN JUNE Isabelle became aware of a man approaching the house on foot. She was upstairs in her room, and she watched from the window. She bit her lower lip, perplexed. He wore a gray uniform, but she couldn't trust Confederate soldiers anymore, not after what had occurred on her journey home from Katie's.

Travis had given her one of the new repeating rifles, and she hurried downstairs to the gun cabinet to get it. She loaded the gun and hurried to the window, but her worry fell away when she saw the man coming closer. With a glad cry she set the gun down and raced outside, flinging herself into the man's arms. It was her brother, James.

"Oh, my God, you're home!" She kissed him, and

he hugged her and swung her around, and she laughed, and then she cried. And then they were in the house, and Peter was there, and the other servants, too, all eager to welcome him home. He only had a few days' leave; he was a lieutenant in the artillery, and he had been lucky to receive even that much time.

Isabelle was determined to make his time at home perfect. She ordered him a steaming bath, dug out his clothes, supervised dinner, and when he was dressed and downstairs again, she was ready to sit with him for a meal of venison stew. He smiled at her, a very grave young man with her own curious colored eyes, slightly darker hair and, now, freshly shaven cheeks. He started to eat hungrily, as if he hadn't seen such a meal in years. Then he suddenly threw down his fork and stared at her, his eyes filled with naked fury.

"This is Yank stew!"

Isabelle bolted back in her chair, sitting very straight. She stared at her hands.

James stood, walking around the room behind her. "I just realized what this means. The house is standing, and there's food in it. What did you pay for those concessions, Isabelle?"

She gasped and leaped to her feet. "I didn't pay anything for concessions!" Guilt tore at her, but she had never paid for anything. She was protected, yes, but she had never paid for that protection. She had simply fallen in love. "They use the house as their headquarters—that's why it's still standing. And there's food in the larder because they bring it in, for their own use, and ours, too."

"And you stay here!" he accused, his hands on his hips.

"I stay here, you fool, for you and Steven! I stay so that they won't burn the house down around us. I've even taken the Yankee dollars Sergeant Sikes gives me as rent, and I've stowed them away to keep this place alive so that you and…and Steven would have a home to come back to!"

He strode from the dining room, down the hall and into the den. With a fury he pushed Travis's papers from their father's desk. Something fluttered to his feet, and he bent to pick it up. It was a record of her safe conduct form to the Holloway home for Christmas. He stared from the form to Isabelle. "What is this?"

"Safe conduct. I—I always leave for Christmas."

Suddenly he started to laugh, but she didn't like the sound of it. "Oh, this is rich! You play the whore all year, but then you leave for Christmas! Oh, Isabelle!"

She itched to slap his face, but he was too gaunt from all he'd been through, and besides, she felt the horrible truth of his words. She turned, a sob tearing from her, and raced up the stairs. She burst into her room, where she lay on her bed and sobbed. It was odd, she thought. It was Christmas she was suddenly crying for, and not the war, the death, the pain. It was the peace of the holiday that had been lost, the peace and the gentle dreams, and the belief that man could rise above his sins.

Her door opened. James came in and sat beside her on the bed, then scooped her into his arms. "I'm sorry,

Isabelle. I'm so sorry. The war has warped me. I know you, Isabelle. You're the sister who bathed all my cuts and bruises when I thought I was too big for my friends to see me cry. The one who stood by our parents. The one, Peter tells me, who ran out in the midst of a barrage of bullets to reach Steven. Isabelle, I love you. If some Yank has kept you safe, then I'm glad. Can you forgive me?"

She hugged him tight, because no words were necessary between them. Then they went down to their cold dinner, and when they had eaten, Isabelle took him out to Steven's grave, and she told him how odd it had been to hear Yankee musicians playing "Dixie."

He slipped his arm around her, then gave a silent salute to Steven before they walked to the house together.

Over the next few days he drew her out. He listened to the accounts of his brother's death, and he listened when she haltingly told him about the deserter who had attacked her. He also listened to her talk about Travis. He gave her no advice, only warned her, "Isabelle, you're in love with him."

She shook her head, watching the fire. "Even now he could be dead. He's fighting somewhere south of here." She swallowed. It was the front that James would soon return to.

James leaned toward her. "You *are* in love with him. And it sounds like he loves you."

"He is still the enemy."

"Will he marry you?"

"James, I cannot marry the enemy!"

"The war can't go on forever, even if it seems so. But it has taught me that life and love are sweet, and too easily stolen from us before we can touch them."

James left the next day. She forced herself to smile as she buttoned his coat and set his hat on his head. "You'll be home soon for good!" she told him.

He smiled. "Yes, I promise. I promise I'll come home for good." He kissed her cheek, and she walked him as far as the porch. He had to go a few miles on foot, since he was in Yankee territory. Somewhere to the south he would be picked up by a transport wagon. Horses were rare now, and he refused to take her mare. "They'll just kill her down there, Isabelle. Let her survive this thing. I may need her when I come back!"

She hugged him one last time, fiercely, and then he started out. She watched him from the porch, and he suddenly turned around. "Isabelle, don't marry him, if you feel you can't. But give him Christmas. He deserves Christmas."

Then he walked away, and she prayed that the war would soon be over. She assured God that she really didn't care in the least if the Yankees won, just so long as someone ended the damn thing.

THE BATTLES WERE FOUGHT fast and furiously on the Eastern front as summer progressed. Women were desperately needed to nurse the wounded, and Isabelle found transport south to the outskirts of Cedar Creek, where an old church was being used as a field hospital. A horrible battle had been fought on October nineteenth. The South had nearly taken the day, but in the end the Union had prevailed.

Rebels and Yankees both were being brought in, and Isabelle was grateful to see that no injured man was being left on the field. Still, each time she saw a blue coat with a cavalry-red stripe on it, her heart sank. Travis had ridden away to join Sheridan, and Sheridan's men had won this battle. Had Travis, too, ridden victoriously away?

At last she discovered that he had not, for she turned to a sheeted form one afternoon to discover it was Travis.

His face was as white as death, and he was barely breathing. She ripped open his uniform to discover that a saber had savagely slashed his side.

Isabelle turned to search out one of the surgeons. She wanted Dr. Hardy, a man with a keen belief in hygiene. If the wound didn't kill Travis, infection might.

"His pulse is good, his breathing is steady and, so far, no fever," Dr. Hardy told her a little while later. "Keep his wound clean, and he should make it."

She did as he'd said. She was careful to tend to all the men, but she reserved time daily to wash and re-bandage Travis's wound.

On the third day he opened his eyes. He stared at her incredulously; then his eyes fell shut again. The effort to hold them open was too much. "Water," he croaked.

She dampened his parched lips, warning him not to drink too quickly. He managed to open his eyes again, and she tried not to smile. Despite his long hair, he was still so handsome. His dark eyes filled with dismay when he realized that he was in a Confederate hospital.

"You might as well let me die," he told her.

"Don't talk like that."

"Andersonville *is* death," he reminded her sharply, and a cold dread filled her heart, because rumor said it was true, that Union soldiers died like flies in the Confederate prison camp.

"You're far too ill to be sent to Andersonville now," she told him, then moved away.

The next morning she was dismayed to find that Travis had stirred an interest among the Southern women helping out as nurses. She was unable to find him alone. If he was going to get that much care, she decided, she was going to keep her distance.

He healed more quickly than anyone had expected. Two weeks after his arrival, she was making the bed beside his when his fingers suddenly clamped around her wrist, and he pulled her to face him.

"What are you doing here?" he demanded sharply of her.

Her brows arched. "Helping!" she snapped.

He shook his head. "You should be home. Oh...I see. You want to find your brother."

"My brother is well, thank you very much. He was home on leave during the summer." She pulled away. "Perhaps I was looking for you, Captain," she told him quietly. Then she left him. It was becoming altogether too disturbing to cope with him.

She didn't have to cope with him much longer. Three days later, when she came in, he was gone. Trembling with raw panic, she asked Dr. Hardy what had happened to him.

"The Yank? Oh, he's gone."

"Andersonville?" she whispered in horror.

Hardy shook his head, watching her closely. "He escaped. Not that we have many men to watch the prisoners around here. He just slipped away in the night."

Three days later Dr. Hardy called her, and when she turned, he took her by her arm and led her outside. She held her breath, terrified that he was going to tell her that Travis had been shot during his attempt to escape.

But Hardy hadn't called her about Travis. He cleared his throat and squeezed her hand as they walked along the barren meadow. "Isabelle, Lieutenant James Hinton is on our list as a prisoner of war. He was taken at Petersburg."

"No!" She screamed the word, then sank to the ground, denying Hardy's news with everything in her. She wanted to scream, to keep screaming, to make the words go away.

Hardy knelt beside her. "Isabelle, listen—"

She didn't listen. She grabbed his arm. "Was he injured? Are they taking him west? Do you—"

"He wasn't injured, he was just forced by overwhelming odds to surrender. And he's being taken to Washington. Isabelle, he's alive! And well. He'll probably even be able to write to you. Isabelle, many men died at Petersburg! Be grateful that he's alive. He might be better off in that Yankee prison. He might have Christmas dinner."

She tried to smile, tried to believe Hardy.

Two weeks later, December was upon them and the place was just about cleared out. The injured men had been sent home to recuperate, or back to the battlefield, or they had died.

Hardy called Isabelle into his makeshift office and handed her a sealed document. She looked at him. "You're going home, Isabelle. Confederate soldiers will escort you to the Union line. That letter should give you safe conduct. You need to go home. The war is digging in for winter. I'm moving on to Petersburg."

He stood and kissed both her cheeks. "Merry Christmas, Isabelle."

She kissed him in return. "Merry Christmas."

He smiled and slipped something from his pocket, then handed it to her. "I was afraid you wouldn't think it was a very merry Christmas. I just received that letter two hours ago. It's for you. From your brother, James. He'd heard that the Yanks were in and out of the house, so he wrote through me."

She stared at him, then ripped open the letter, tears stinging her eyes. He was alive; he was eating; he was lucky, considering what could have happened to him. He ended his letter with a command: "Merry Christmas, sister! Have faith in the Father, and who knows, perhaps next Christmas will bring us all together again."

She kissed Dr. Hardy again, then she ran out, pressing the letter to her heart.

AS DR. HARDY HAD PROMISED, she was escorted to the Yankee line by two cavalry soldiers; then her papers

were handed over, and she was given an escort through
the lines to her doorstep. She had worried the whole
way about Travis. He must have been weak after his
ordeal; he hadn't been strong enough to return to battle.
She hoped fervently that he would be there when she
reached home.

He was.

Travis was waiting for her on the porch. The Yankee
sergeant with her papers saluted him sharply and re-
spectfully, and said that he had brought Miss Hinton
home at the Union's command, and that he needed
permission to return to his own unit. Travis quickly
granted him permission, saluting in return. He stood
tall and straight as he watched Isabelle dismount, then
ordered one of his men to take her horse. When she
walked up the steps, she saw that his eyes were alight
with a pleasure that belied his solemn features.

She walked past him and entered the parlor,
shedding her worn travel cloak and hat and tossing
them on a chair. Seconds later Travis was behind her,
pulling her against him, pressing his lips to her throat,
whispering things that were entirely incoherent.

She turned, ready to protest, ready to reproach him,
but no words would come. She didn't give a damn who
was in the house, who saw what, or what they might
think. Not at that moment. She wrapped her arms
around his neck, and he swept her into his arms, then
carried her into the huge master suite that he'd claimed
as his own. A fire was burning in the hearth, hot and
blazing. Darkness was falling, but the fire filled the
room with a spellbinding glow. Travis laid her down

on the bed, his fingers shaking as he removed her clothing. Then he shed his own and straddled her, and the loving began.

The fire cast its glow over them as the night passed. In that curious light he was sleek and coppery, and she couldn't keep her lips from his skin or her fingers from dancing over his rippling muscles. More scars were etched now across his flesh, and she touched them gently, kissed them with tenderness. She had wanted him so badly, and now he was hers. Right or wrong, she loved the enemy.

When morning came, Isabelle made no pretense of denial. She kissed him eagerly by the light of day, met his eyes openly, honestly, and smiled at his hoarse cry as she was swept into the ardent rhythm of his lovemaking.

She dined with him that evening. He told her about the battles, about Wilderness, about Cold Harbor, Chancellorsville. There was so much sadness in him. She kept a tight rein on her own emotions as she told him that James had been taken prisoner at Petersburg, but that she had heard he was in Washington, not Camp Douglas, in Chicago, which the Rebs feared so greatly.

TWO NIGHTS LATER the men started playing Christmas carols. They came in and used the piano, and they played their sad harmonicas. She felt for them, for their longing to go home.

She didn't run away when they sang, and when Sergeant Sikes prodded her, she even rose to sing herself. To the tune of "Greensleeves" she sang about the Christ child's birth, and when she was done, the room was silent and still, and the eyes of every man in the place were on her. At last Sikes cleared his throat, and Private Trent laughed and said that he had made a wreath, and he went out and brought it in. She told them that they could find the household decorations in the attic, and they raced up to bring them down. Soon the place looked and smelled and glowed of Christmas.

Travis, who had watched her from beside the fire, turned and left the room. She heard his footsteps on the stairs.

Rising, she determined to follow him.

He was in the room they shared, staring down at the half-packed portmanteau she had set in one corner. She stared at him in silence as his eyes challenged hers.

"You're leaving again?"

"Yes."

He walked across the room to her, pinning her against the door, his palms flat against the wood on either side of her head. He searched her eyes for a moment, then walked away to stand in front of the fire, his hands clasped behind his back.

"There's something for you on the table," he told her.

"What is it?"

"Go see for yourself."

She hesitated, then walked across the room to the round oak table by the window. There was an official-looking document there wrapped in vellum and red ribbon.

"Travis…?"

"Open it," he commanded.

She did so, her fingers shaking. There was a lot of official language that she read over quickly and in confusion, and then she saw her brother's name. Lieutenant James L. Hinton. She kept reading, trying to make sense of the legal terms and the fancy handwriting. Then she realized that James was to be exchanged for another prisoner, that he was going to be sent home.

She cried out and stared at Travis. She didn't know *how* he had arranged it, only that he had. She started to run toward him, then she stopped, her heart hammering.

"Oh, Travis! You did this!"

He nodded solemnly. "Merry Christmas. You never let me give you a gift. This year I thought you might."

"Oh, Travis!" she repeated; then she raced into his arms. He kissed her, and it was long and deep, and as hot and glowing as the fire. Breathless, she pressed her lips against his throat. "Travis, it's the most wonderful gift in the world, but I have nothing for you. I would give you anything—"

"Then marry me."

She was silent. She saw the fever in his dark eyes, the shattering intensity.

"I—I can't," she said.

Disappointment banked the ebony fires. His jaw hardened, and she could hear the grating of his teeth. "And tomorrow afternoon you will come down to the office as if we were perfect strangers, and you will ask my blessing to leave."

"Travis…"

"Damn you! Damn you a thousand times over, Isabelle!" He turned away from her.

"Travis!" she called again, and he turned to her.

He stared at her for several agonizing seconds, and then his long strides brought him to her, and he wrenched her hard into his arms. His kiss was laced with force and fury, and his hands were less than tender as he touched her. She didn't care. She met his fury.

"Isabelle!" Her name tore from him raggedly as his fingers threaded into her hair. In the end, the loving was sweet, agonizingly sweet, and accompanied by whispers that he loved her.

Lying with her back to him, she repeated the words in silence. *I love you.* But the war was still on; he was still the enemy. She couldn't stay, and she couldn't tell him how she felt.

Not even for Christmas.

TRAVIS LAY BY HER SIDE and watched the moonlight as it fell on the sleek perfection of her body. Her back was long and beautiful, and the ivory moon glow caressed it exquisitely. Her hair was free and tangled around him, and he thought with a staggering burst of pain about how much he loved her, how much he needed her. And perhaps God was good, because he *was* alive and able to hold her, and she was here with him. And, damn it, he knew that she loved him!

But he knew, too, that tomorrow would come, and that she would indeed enter the study and demand safe passage.

Suddenly he smiled ironically. He could remember

being young, could remember his parents asking him to choose the one thing he wanted most for Christmas. He would think carefully about it, and they always gave him the gift he chose.

If only someone would ask him now. He wouldn't need to think. There was only one thing he would ask for.

Isabelle.

He mouthed her name, then rose, dressed and stepped into the hall. The smell of roasting chestnuts was in the air, along with the scent of the pine boughs the men had brought in.

Tomorrow would be Christmas Eve. She would come down for her safe-passage form, and he would give it to her.

HE HAD BEEN RIGHT. At noon Sergeant Hawkins came to tell him that Isabelle had requested an audience with him.

And now he was alone.

CHAPTER FOUR

Christmas Eve, 1864

WITH HER SAFE-PASSAGE PERMIT in her hands, Isabelle closed the door to Travis's office behind her and leaned against it. Didn't he understand that it hurt to leave him, but that it was all that she had left? She was among the nearly beaten, the bested. She was a part of the South. Once she had thrilled to the sound of a Rebel yell; once she had believed with her whole heart that Virginia had had a right to secede; once she had followed that distant drum.

It was true, perhaps, that the end was near, but the South had yet to surrender, so how could she do so?

She hurried along the hallway. Sergeant Sikes was there, waiting for her with his light blue eyes clouded, his face sad and weary. "So, you're leaving, Miss Hinton. I had hoped that you might stay this year."

She adjusted her gloves, and smiled. "It's Christmas, Sergeant. We should be with our own kind, don't you think?"

"It ain't up to me to think, ma'am. I'm just the sergeant." He turned, opening the door for her. "Seems to me, though, that Christmas means we ought to be with the ones we love. Yes, ma'am, that's what it seems to me."

"Sergeant," Isabelle said sweetly, stepping onto the porch, "didn't you just tell me that you weren't supposed to do any thinking?"

"Um." He whistled, and their horses were brought up by one of the privates. She mounted without his assistance, and he sighed and mounted his horse. They started out, Sergeant Sikes riding behind her. Even so, he was determined to talk. "We celebrate a day when a little baby was born. Oxen and lambs flocked around him!"

"Right, Sergeant," she called back.

"There were angels floating around in heaven. Wise men made a journey following a star. Why, ma'am, God looked down from heaven, and he actually smiled. Miss Hinton, even God and the army know that Christmas is a time for peace!"

She turned around, smiling. "You love him a lot, don't you, Sergeant?"

"Captain Travis? You bet I do, ma'am. He's a great officer. I've known him for years. I've watched him put his personal safety behind that of his men every time. I've seen him rally a flagging defense with the power of his own energy, and I've seen him demand that the killing stop when the war turned to butchery. Damn right—'scuse me, ma'am—I do love him. And you do, too, don't you?"

She opened her mouth, not at all sure what she was going to say. In the end she didn't say anything at all. She only stared across the snow-covered fields and saw that another party was out that day, three Union soldiers heading south, trailing a hospital cart behind them. They were headed for the farmstead where she had been attacked the year before.

"Sergeant! There's a man on that cart."

"That's the way it looks, Miss Hinton."

"Come, then, let's see if we can be of help!"

She urged her horse on, then realized that she had forgotten the men were Yankees. Maybe it was Christmas magic that made her so concerned for the unknown soldier in the cart. She didn't know.

Her mare plowed through the dense white snow until she was nearly on top of the first soldier. "Sir! What's happened? I've been a nurse, perhaps I can be of some assistance."

The young officer paused, reining in, looking back as one of the other soldiers lifted a body from the cart and headed for the house. "I don't think so, ma'am. The old fellow isn't going to make it. We found him on the trail, barefoot and fever-ridden, and we've been trying to help him along, but, well, it doesn't look very promising."

Isabelle stared at him, then dismounted, tossing the reins over the porch railing. She caught up her skirts and hurried along the steps and inside.

One of the soldiers was working diligently to start a fire. The other was beside the old man, who he had laid on the sofa, and was holding a flask to his lips.

Isabelle stepped closer, and the Yankee soldier moved politely away. She gasped when she saw that the man on the couch was not a Yankee at all, but a Reb dressed in gray, with gold artillery trim. He was sixty, she thought, if he was a day, yet he had gone out to fight, and he had tried to walk home through the blistering cold with nothing but rags on his feet.

She knelt beside him, pulling the blanket more tightly around him. "I've done what I can," the Yank beside him said. He inclined his head politely. "Frederick Walker, ma'am, surgeon to the Ninth Wisconsin Infantry. I promise you, I have done all that is humanly possible."

She nodded quickly to him, but she didn't leave the old man's side. She took his hand.

"He wanted to get home. Home for Christmas. We were trying to see that he made it, but...well, sometimes home is a very long way away."

"Is he comfortable?" Isabelle asked.

"As comfortable as I can make him."

Suddenly the old man's eyes opened. They were a faded blue, rimmed with red, but when he looked at Isabelle, there was a sparkle in them. "God alive! I've gone to heaven, and the angels are blond and beautiful!"

Isabelle smiled. "No, sir, this isn't heaven. I saw the Yanks bring you in and came to see if I could do anything. I'm Isabelle Hinton, sir." She flashed a look at the doctor, wondering if she should be encouraging the old man to talk. The doctor's eyes told her that it was a kindness.

The old man wheezed, and his chest rattled, but he kept smiling. "What are you doing out on Christmas Eve, on a day like today? You should be warm and safe at home, young lady."

"And you shouldn't have been walking in your bare feet!"

"They weren't bare. They were in the best shoes the Confederacy has to offer these days!" he said indignantly. He sighed softly, then caught her eyes. "Oh, girl, don't look so sad! I knew my game was up. I was just trying to see if I could make it home. These nice young fellows tried to give me a lift." He motioned to her, indicating that she should draw near. "Yanks!" he told her, as if she hadn't noticed. Then he smiled broadly. "The doc here knows my boy Jeremy. Jeremy is a doc with a West Virginia division. They've worked together on the field. In Spotsylvania and Antietam Creek. Even at Gettysburg. Isn't that right, Doc?"

"Your son is in the Union?"

"One of them. Both my boys with Lee are still alive, and my daughters, they're back home. But you know, Miss Hinton, every year, whoever could get leave came home for Christmas. Not that we could get many leaves but…no matter what, we all wrote. My boys all wrote to me no matter what, no matter what color uniform they were wearing. And having those letters, why, it meant everything. It meant that I was home for Christmas." He broke off, coughing in a long spasm. Isabelle worriedly patted his chest. The young Yankee doctor offered him another drink. It soothed the coughing. Then he lay back, exhausted, but he looked at her worriedly. "Don't you fret so, girl. I'm going to a finer place. I'm going where the angels really sing. Can you imagine what a Christmas celebration is like in heaven? Where the war don't make no difference? Quit worrying about me. Go home. Go home for Christmas."

She shook her head, swallowing. "I—I don't want to leave you."

His eyes closed, but he smiled, his lips parched and dry. "Then stay with me. But when I'm gone, promise me that you'll go home."

"I don't know where home is," she whispered beneath her breath.

But he heard her. His eyes opened, soft and cloudy, but she knew that he was seeing her.

"Home is where there is love, child. Surely you know that. It don't matter if it's a shack or a palace or a blanket beside a fire, home is where love is."

His eyes closed again. Isabelle squeezed his hand, and he squeezed back. Then his lungs rattled again, and the pressure of his hand against hers faded.

Tears flooded her eyes and spilled over his blanket.

Someone was touching her shoulder. Sergeant Sikes. "You come on now, Miss Hinton. Let me get you to Katie Holloway's place."

She let him lead her to the door because she could hardly see. She couldn't bear the injustice of it, that the old man had to die so close to home.

She shook free of the Sergeant's touch and turned back. The old man seemed entirely at peace. The lines had eased from his face. He even seemed to be smiling.

She walked into the snow. Someone came to assist her into the saddle, and Sergeant Sikes remounted, too.

They could go on. She could go to Katie's for the holiday.

Or she could go home.

She cried out suddenly, pulling the reins with such force that the startled animal reared and pawed the air, spewing snowflakes everywhere.

"Miss Hinton—" the sergeant began.

"Oh, Sergeant Sikes! He hasn't died in vain, has he? He's in there smiling away, even in death. Because he's home. And I'm going home, too. It's Christmas, Sergeant!"

Let the Yanks think that she was crazy. It was true

that the war wasn't over yet. But for her it was. At least for Christmas.

She felt that she was flying over the snow. It was a day that promised peace to all mankind.

The snow was kicked up beneath the mare's hooves, and the wind whipped by them as she raced across the barren countryside. Sikes was far behind her, but he needn't have worried. She knew the way.

At last she saw the house. Through the window she could even see the fire that burned in the hearth in the office.

She leaped from her mare and raced, covered in snow, up the steps. She tore open the door, leaving it ajar, and flew on winged feet to the den. She didn't knock, just threw open that door, too. And then she stopped at last, completely breathless, unable to speak.

Travis was behind the desk. He stared at her in astonishment, then leaped to his feet, coming quickly around to her. She sagged into his arms.

"Isabelle! Are you hurt? What's happened? Isabelle—"

"I'm not hurt!"

"Then—"

"Nothing has happened."

"Then—"

"I'm just home, that's all. I've come home for the holidays. Oh, Travis, I love you so much!"

He carried her to the hearth and sat before the fire, holding her on his lap, his eyes searching hers. He whispered her name and buried his face against her throat, then repeated her name again.

"I do love you, Travis. So very much."

He shook his head, confused. "I think I've loved *you* forever. But you left...."

"I had to stop. Some Yanks were taking an old Rebel home, but he didn't make it. He died, Travis."

"Oh, Isabelle, I'm sorry."

"No, Travis, no. He was satisfied with his life. He'd known all kinds of love and...and he'd never cared about the color of it. It's so hard to explain. He just made me see... Travis, love is fragile. So hard to come by, so hard to earn. As fragile as a Christmas snowflake. Oh, Travis!"

She wound her arms around him, and kissed him slowly and deeply. Then her eyes found his again. "I— I'd like to give you something. What you did, getting James freed, was wonderful."

"Isabelle, you're my Christmas present. You're what I have wanted forever."

She flushed. "Well, I was hoping you would say that. Because I don't have anything to wrap for you. I've been so stubborn, so horrible."

"Isabelle—"

"Travis, do you really love me?"

"More than anything in the world, Isabelle."

"Then may I be your Christmas gift?"

"What do you mean?" He started to smile, but his eyes were suspicious.

"I mean, well, it would be a present for me, too, really. You—" She paused, took a deep breath and plunged onward. "You said you wanted to marry me. Our minister has gone south with the troops, but your Yankee chaplain is with you, and the church is just down the lane. Travis, I'm trying to say that I'll marry you. For Christmas. If you want to, that is."

He was silent for the longest time. Then he let out a shriek that rivaled the heartiest Rebel yell she had ever heard. He was on his feet, whirling around with her in his arms. He paused at last to kiss her; then he laughed and kissed her again.

When his eyes finally met hers again, they were brilliant with the fires of love, and his hands trembled where they touched her.

"Isabelle, there has never, never been a greater Christmas gift. Never. God knows, there is no gift so sweet or so fine as the gift of love."

She smiled, winding her arms more tightly around him. "And the gift of peace, Travis. You've given me both."

IT WASN'T HARD TO ARRANGE. The men tripped over themselves to decorate the church, and though little else could be done on such short notice, they did manage to bring old Katie Holloway in for the ceremony.

Isabelle stood at the back of the church, while Katie insisted she take her mother's pearl ring. "Something borrowed, love. You must wear the ring."

Isabelle smiled. Her dress was light blue silk, her undergarments were very old, and her love…her love was new. She was all set to become a bride.

"I wonder what's taking them so long!" she said, looking toward the back of the church. Travis was outside in the snow, along with half his men. He turned around suddenly, saw her and ran into the church. To her amazement, he dragged her out into the snow. "Isabelle! Do you believe in Christmas?"

"What are you talking about?" she demanded. "Travis, you're behaving like a madman."

He started to laugh, then he shoved her around in front of him. "Isabelle, all we were lacking was the proper person to give you away. Now, well, we have that, too."

For long moments she stared at the man in the gray uniform standing in front of her. Then she screamed with happiness and tore away from her prospective groom to catapult into the newcomer's arms. Travis, tolerant of her display of affection for another man, watched the dazzling happiness with which she greeted her brother.

"Isabelle!" James hugged her, then looked around at the blue uniforms surrounding them.

"Well, Yanks, is it a truce, then, for a wedding?"

Hats were ripped off and went flying into the air. A cheer went up.

Moments later they were all inside the church. James led her down the aisle and handed her over to Travis. The chaplain began the service, and she and Travis stated their vows. And when they were solemnly promised to one another, the chaplain stated, "On this date, Christmas of 1864, with the power invested in me by God and the state of Virginia, I declare Travis and Isabelle husband and wife. Captain, kiss your bride."

He kissed her and kissed her. And kissed her.

Sikes had found rice to throw at them, and James was quick to join in. Laughing, the newlyweds ran from the shower of rice to the supply buggy that had brought them, then headed to the house.

Peter had made the most sumptuous Christmas and wedding dinner imaginable, given the state of their larder, and though his feelings would change with the coming of the new year, James seemed willing enough to ignore the fact that the men in his house were Yankees, and the Yanks were more than willing to accept him as one of their own.

It was Christmas.

LATER, WHEN MOST of the soldiers had gone to their sleeping quarters, when Sikes and James were half asleep in front of the parlor fire, Isabelle realized that her new husband was nowhere around.

She found him out on the chilly porch, looking up at the sky. She hooked her arm through his, and he smiled at her.

"What are you doing out here?" she whispered.

"Following a star," he told her softly. He brushed her hair from her face. "I thought I was far away from home for Christmas, but now I know I'm not. I am home. Wherever you are, love, that's where I live. Forever, within your heart."

She said nothing, and he lifted her into his arms, preparing to carry her from the cold porch into the warmth of the house, and then to their room.

But he paused just before he stepped through the door, and he stared at the North Star, whispering a silent prayer.

Thank you, God! Thank you so much. For Isabelle… For Christmas.

THE WISE VIRGIN
Jo Beverley

PROLOGUE

"THEY'VE STOLEN THE Blessed Virgin Mary!"

The serfs of Woldingham gaped after the horsemen thundering away down the road into the winter woods, their captive's cries fading on the frosty night breeze. Then, like a flock of starlings in the field, they scattered. Most ran for their simple thatch-roof houses, hoping not to be connected with the disaster. The really cautious gathered their families and took to the woods themselves.

After all, who else but the de Graves would commit such a crime? And when the Lord of Woldingham clashed with his old enemy, no one was overcareful where the arrows and even the sword blades fell.

Soon only the village priest and headman were left on the moonlit road leading up to the castle, if one didn't count the abandoned donkey stolidly waiting, head down. Even Joseph had thrown off his borrowed cloak and scuttled away. The two men looked at each other in silent commiseration, then they set off at a run toward the castle that loomed nearby. Despite narrow hall windows blazing with festive light, and bonfires in the bailey, it was an ominous shadow against the starry sky.

Someone had to tell Henry de Montelan, Lord of Woldingham, that his daughter had been seized by his bitterest enemy.

At Christmastide, too.

The gates stood open, waiting for the traditional procession to bring the holy couple up to the castle seeking shelter on Christmas Eve. Unlike the wickedness shown in the Bible, the Lord of Woldingham would offer the shelter of his keep to Mary and Joseph, leading them into the luxury of his solar chamber. The play was a tradition dating back generations, to the last de Montelan to go on Crusade, a tradition closely linked to the blood feud between Woldingham and the nearby castle of Mountgrave.

The two guards stared at the hurrying men, then peered behind for sight of the procession. The priest, Father Hubert, and the headman, Cob Williamson, told of the disaster as they rushed through. The guards came to full alert.

Trouble.

And at Christmastide, too.

The two men threaded their way through the crowded bailey, calling their news but not stopping to answer alarmed questions. Tipsy cooks stopped basting the carcasses roasting on spits, and the sweating baker cursed, then called his assistants to clear tables of bread into baskets and out of the way.

There'd be armed men and horses through here soon.

And at Christmastide, too.

The noisy celebration in the great hall spilled golden

light out of the arrow slits and billowed jollity from the open, expectant door of the keep. The two men labored up the outer stairs then stopped to catch their breath. Within the hall, huge fires leaped to drive away the winter chill, spraying sparks as logs settled, blending smoke with the torches flaming on the walls. Around the room, the ladies and gentleman of Woldingham made merry along with guests, household knights and senior servants. A tumult of children—striplings to babes—romped under and around the tables, tangled with a pack of dogs.

Slowly they were noticed, and an expectant silence settled.

Lord Henry de Montelan rose, massive, gracious and rosy with good cheer. "Here at last, eh? Well, say your piece!"

The headman looked at Father Hubert and the priest accepted his role. He stepped forward. "Lord Henry, a terrible thing has happened."

The silence darkened. "What?" demanded Lord Henry, coming down off the dais toward them. His four stalwart sons rose, dazed but alert. A hound growled.

"What has happened? Where is the holy couple? Where is my daughter?"

The priest fell to his knees. "The de Graves have stolen her, my lord."

After a deadly moment a man howled. Sir Gamel, fiercest of Lord Henry's sons, leaped over the table in front of him in one bound, his teeth bared. "My sword! My sword! I'll gut them all. To horse! Revenge!" He stormed toward the door, brothers not far behind.

Lord Henry stopped him with a hand, perhaps the only man in England able to do it. Though Lord Henry's color stayed high, it was not a sign of good cheer anymore. "Aye, my son, we'll have revenge, and blood and guts aplenty, but we'll not run into a trap. Horses!" he bellowed, and the men in the hall burst into action. "Armor! Weapons! Gamel, Lambert, and Reyner—you hunt them down and bring Nicolette home safe. *Safe,* remember. Harry," he said to his eldest son, "you and I will stay here. In case."

Stalwart Harry agreed, but with a scowl of disappointment.

"At Christmastide?" young Reyner asked, sixteen but nearly as big as his brothers. "They'd steal the Virgin on Christmas Eve?"

"Nothing," growled his father, "is too wicked for the de Graves."

In moments the noise of the castle changed to martial tone, and the lord, his oldest son and his master-at-arms were huddled in military conference. Father Hubert and Cob silently congratulated themselves on coming out of it whole and slipped away down the steps. Since no one seemed to be in a mood for feasting, a hunk of roast pork and some loaves went with them. A bit of a feast for the poor villagers.

"A fine state of affairs," mumbled Cob around a piece of juicy meat.

"At Christmastide. At a holy pageant! Godless men. Godless!"

"It's to be hoped the poor Lady Nicolette comes to no harm, Father. For everyone's sakes."

"Indeed, indeed." Then the priest slid a look at his friend. "But do you know, Cob, I could have sworn I saw Lady Nicolette up in the gallery over the hall, peeping out."

The headman stopped. "What? Nay, Father, you must be mistaken. How could that be?"

"Well now, what if some other gentle lady played the part of the Virgin? I thought it a little strange that Lady Nicolette did not speak to me and kept herself so huddled in her cloak."

Cob swallowed the meat in one gulp. "But it's *tradition,* Father. A holy tradition. The youngest virgin of marriageable years in the lord's family plays the part of the Blessed Virgin. And by—"

"Being welcomed into the hall of Woldingham, instead of turned away to lie in a stable, brings God's blessings to everyone in the coming year. Yes, yes. It makes you think, doesn't it?"

"It makes you bloody afeard, it does! What's to become of us all with the tradition mucked about like that?"

"And what's to become of those involved when it all comes out?" the priest muttered.

He wasn't thinking about the peasants, or even the feuding men, but about the young women involved in this perilous deception.

And the possible reasons for it.

Father Hubert crossed himself and started to pray.

CHAPTER ONE

THE HUGE PADDED BELLY finally had a benefit, Joan of Hawes decided as she bounced across the horse, face down, in front of her captor. It cushioned the worst of this. She'd given up screaming and yelling. All that had achieved was a sore throat. Her captor was treating her as if she were a roll of fleeces, ignoring her—other than one strong hand in her belt that stopped her falling off, accidentally or on purpose.

Despite fury and fear, she was grateful for that firm grip. They were racing down a woodland track at a gallop, and she'd no mind to die over this. But who had snatched her off the donkey, and why? And why now, when it would cause such terrible trouble?

Suddenly the rider pulled the horse to a head-tossing, stamping stop, and hoisted her up just like a bundle. Before she could shriek, he turned her, and put her down sitting sideways in front of him on the horse. By the time her dizzy head had settled, they were off again and she'd only caught a glimpse of a dark-hooded form. Now, however, she could see other riders around. Strange riders, flowing dark, fast and fiendishly quiet through the winter-bare, frosty wood.

Earlier, they'd swooped down on the village in silence, like black hawks from the sky....

"Sweet Mary, save me," she whispered. Had she been seized by the forces of darkness?

She twisted to try to see if her captor had a human face, but saw only darkness. A shiver of unholy terror passed through her, but then common sense returned. He was hot like a man, and smelled like a man—sweat, wool and horse. Now she saw that his hood hung forward to shadow his face, and his skin was darkened in some way. A common raider of some sort.

Then she understood more. This galloping horse had no saddle, and the man she was squashed against wore no mail. The bridle and reins were rope. Not unearthly devils, then, but men without jingle of bell, harness or mail. All the horses were dark, too. No wonder they'd appeared as if out of nowhere.

It was—it had to be—the de Graves, her uncle's bitterest enemies, taking this opportunity to ruin the de Montelan's most sacred ceremony. All the same, she couldn't help admiring the planning and execution. She did so love a job well done.

But why, oh why, did they have to choose *this* year to make mischief, when it was going to cause such terrible trouble? Her cousin Nicolette had been supposed to play the Virgin, and no one must know that she and Joan had changed places.

Perhaps they'd let her go soon. They'd succeeded in disrupting the ceremony, and had no need to keep her. If so, could she get back to the castle before Nicolette was discovered there? Probably. If he put her down now.

"Sirrah," she said.

When he ignored her, she shouted it. "Sirrah!"

He paid no attention, intent on the dark road and speed. Speed taking them farther and farther from Woldingham. Joan eased her arm forward and jabbed back as hard as she could with her elbow.

The horse misstepped, and her captor grunted slightly, but he only said, "Stop that."

Then they were off again, and she knew—knowing men—that there'd be no stopping until he decided it was right to stop. May the devil rot his toes. She thought of throwing herself off the horse, but wasn't feeling suicidal. Just frightened and irritated.

What foolish mischief this was. But then, the whole bloodthirsty feud between the de Graves and the de Montelans was foolish. It had cost lives over the generations, and disrupted the whole countryside hereabouts, and all because of a piece of cloth carried to Jerusalem back in the First Crusade.

In the weeks since Joan had arrived at Woldingham to be companion to her cousin Nicolette, she'd learned all about the wicked, dishonorable de Graves family. They were supposedly guilty of everything from stealing that banner to putting the evil eye on the Woldingham sheep last August. The stories might be true, but she wasn't convinced, mainly because of the current head of the de Graves family.

Not that she'd met the famous Edmund de Graves, of course, but all England had heard of the Golden Lion—beautiful as Saint Michael, brave as Saint George, protector of the weak, defender of the right, dire vengeance on all who did evil…. Legends were told of him, and troubadours sung his praises.

The Golden Lion was son of the famous Silver Lion—Remi de Graves, mighty warrior and advisor to the king. Lord Edmund had been trained from boyhood by the best tutors and warriors, including the almost mythical Almar de Font, a renowned hero in his own right. At sixteen, the Golden Lion had carried the prize at a glittering tourney. At seventeen he had fought brilliantly in the war against France. At eighteen he had single-handedly cleared out a nest of outlaws, who were terrorizing the area around one of his estates.

It was possibly true that generations ago a de Graves had cheated a de Montelan out of the banner, but the Golden Lion could have nothing to do with wicked rivalry and revenge today.

Could he?

So, was she *not* in the hands of the de Graves?

The horse was pulled to a halt again, pressing her even harder against her captor. Whoever he was, he was a superb rider. This was a fiery destrier, heat and muscles seething beneath her, and her captor was controlling the beast with just legs and a piece of rope.

"Husha, husha, Thor," her captor murmured, leaning forward to pat and soothe the horse's arched neck. His massive chest almost crushed Joan and she squeaked a protest.

He straightened. "My apologies, Lady."

"Now, sirrah," she said, ready to argue for release, but he told her to wait and turned to the other dark riders gathering around, breath puffing white in the cold air.

To her irritation, Joan found herself waiting. She studied the half-dozen hooded men, seeking a clue as to where they came from. They wore no badge, and were almost silent shadows against the moon-silvered woodland, with horse-breathing and hoof-shuffling as the only sounds.

"All's well," her captor said, and without comment the others spun to ride off, scattering.

They really scattered, too, going in different directions, avoiding paths and melting into the woodland. This efficiency did hint at the hand of the great Lord Edmund, but she wouldn't believe he would stoop to something so petty.

It must be some of his men indulging in a prank. She'd heard that the men-at-arms and retainers of the two families were the ones most keen to make trouble. The main point here was to get free and get back to Woldingham.

"You are from the de Graves?" she whispered, as he turned his horse into the woods, in a different direction again to that taken by the others.

He leaned over her again, but this time to protect her from the prickly holly branch he pushed aside. "Of course. You are safe, Lady, never fear."

Safe. It seemed a strange thing to say, and he was wrong. Joan had never felt less safe in her life, and it had nothing to do with him. She and Nicolette had planned to switch back once the Holy Family was in the castle, but the more time that passed, the more likely it was that Nicolette would be found. Uncle Henry would think they had played a childish trick, and would be furious. If he found out *why,* though…. Joan couldn't even imagine the rage and violence that would result then.

She had to get back.

"Let me go," she said urgently. "You've achieved your purpose."

"Have I?"

"Of course—"

He put a large, callused hand over her mouth, and she heard what he'd heard—the distant howls of her uncle's hounds.

"Sounds carry on still winter air," he breathed into her ear. "Don't try to speak."

He removed his hand and they moved on, the pace slow now because of the unpredictable ground. *Don't speak?* How was she to hammer sense into his head if she couldn't speak? All the same, Joan sagged into silence. *What point in arguing?* How was she to get back to her uncle's castle undetected with hounds on their trail?

The thought of Nicolette, however, made her try again. Perhaps the hounds wouldn't be interested in her trail. "Put me down," she whispered, "then you can get away."

"We are getting away," he whispered back, with a hint of humor.

"You're alone. You can't fight them. And the hounds—"

"Have many tracks to follow. You find it hard to hold your tongue, don't you, Lady Nicolette?"

Before Joan could decide whether to tell him she

wasn't Nicolette, he said, "And here is the well-planned water, to hide our trail."

It was a shallow stream, gurgling noisily over rocks. The horse splashed into and along it, guided by its rider with only subtle shifts of his muscular body.

Clever yet again. "What do you want with me?" she whispered. "Why are you keeping me?"

"Can't you imagine?"

Imagine? Their plan was to disrupt the ceremony. What else?

Then a horrible thought occurred to her.

What if the plan went further than that? What if the plan was to stir the smoldering feud into a hellish fire? There were some at Woldingham who wanted all-out war, including her cousin Gamel. What if there were similar men at Mountgrave Castle? Men who wanted to pour oil in the fire.

Disrupting the pageant would be a mere splash of oil. Kidnapping only a cupful. But rape…rape of Lord Henry's only daughter would be a whole barrelful. It would start a conflagration quenched only by the blood of a whole family.

And if only Cousin Joan was available, well, a jug of oil would make a violent enough flame.

Joan sent an urgent, silent prayer to Mary, protector of all virgins, and tried desperately to think of a way to escape.

Fight him off? Ridiculous.

Jump off the horse and run? She'd be caught in a moment.

Push him off the horse and escape on it?

A trained warhorse wouldn't be taken, and she might as well try to push the hills alongside the stream as push this man off this horse!

Helplessness started an uncontrollable shivering, and a whirling panic in her mind.

"Cold?" he said. "We'll be in a shelter soon."

"Where? What? Where are you taking me?" Her voice turned shrill, and with a curse, he clasped his hand over her mouth again.

"To a cave," he said, sounding irritated. "It's prepared for a lady's comfort. Now, stay silent until we reach there, woman."

Since he kept his hand over her mouth, she didn't have a choice. However, Joan's fear shrank a little. Thrown back against him as the horse picked its way up what was probably a sheep track of some sort, she considered his irritated tone. Could a man intent on rape and murder really speak like that?

How could she know? With a bundle of brothers, she knew men quite well, but she knew nothing of how they behaved in war, or in a bloody feud. At the thought of her brothers and her family, tears smarted in her eyes.

In trouble again. That's what they'd say if she lived to face them. Her brothers would rush to kill her defiler, but that wouldn't do much good after the fact. They'd all think it was her own fault, and as usual, they'd be right.

WHEN JOAN HAD ARRIVED at Woldingham, wrapped in furs and hoping for new adventures, she'd found her cousin Nicolette a feeble, weepy sort of person. She'd been summoned, apparently, because of that—to be a companion and raise her spirits. Her aunt Ellen had informed her that Nicolette suffered from a case of a lovesickness—that she was even having to be guarded from running away with the man. She was not to be encouraged in her folly.

"Your parents report you to be a young woman of sense, Joan, and not given to foolish fancies."

Joan had not been feeling particularly sensible at that moment as she was temporarily staggered by the opulence of Woldingham—by the size, the number of retainers and the glittering treasures everywhere she looked. She'd mumbled meek agreement— she had promised her mother she'd behave—but ventured a question. "Whom does Cousin Nicolette love, Aunt?"

"It doesn't matter. He is completely impossible. Completely."

Joan couldn't imagine how Nicolette could be so silly as to imagine herself in love with a landless knight or a troubadour, and she was happy to help her recover. She herself was firmly of the belief that love could be guided toward sensible, suitable targets.

Nicolette had seemed to welcome companionship and distraction, and soon became a lively, charming friend—even if she did sometimes relapse into sighing, unhappy moments. Joan had enjoyed the wealth and comfort of Woldingham, and the rich selection of handsome, eligible young men paying suit to Nicolette.

She'd already decided an older, sensible man would suit her better as a husband, but she had no objection to flattering flirtation with toothsome gallants.

Even though Nicolette was clearly not tempted by any of her gallant swains, Joan had expected the excitement of Christmas to banish all sighs for a while. The closer it drew, however, the more distracted and melancholy Nicolette became. Her loving parents fretted, but never gave the slightest sign of bending.

The man must truly be impossible.

Then one day, Nicolette fainted. After she'd been carried into the luxurious bedchamber they shared and left to rest, Joan gave her a piece of her mind. "Nicolette, this is foolish beyond measure. No man is worth starving and fainting over!"

"Yes, he is," her cousin said mutinously, but then tears glistened in her eyes. "But it's not that exactly... I'm so afraid..."

"Afraid? Of what?"

"The...the play."

"The Holy Family one? On Christmas Eve?"

Nicolette nodded.

"What is there about that to make you ill? You've played the Virgin for three years, haven't you?"

"Since I started my courses, yes. The youngest virgin of marriageable age..."

"So?"

Nicolette's eyes searched the private room as if someone might be lurking, then she whispered, "I'm not."

"Not what?"

"A *virgin*."

Joan gaped. It was so outrageous she'd not believed it.

Except that it instantly explained so much.

"What's worse," Nicolette added, covering her face with trembling hands, "I'm with child! What am I going to do?" She looked up, wild-eyed. "Don't tell Father and Mother!"

"Of course not." Joan, however, felt ready to lose her breakfast herself. "Why? How…? I assume," she snapped in outrage and terror, "you weren't visited by the Archangel Gabriel! Were you raped?" It seemed the only explanation.

Nicolette sat up. "Of course not. I love him!"

Joan stared. Mooning over Sir Nobody, or a charming troubadour was one thing. Giving her body to him…? "When?"

"At the Martinmas Fair. I didn't plan it. I swear it. It just happened. We stole a few moments. We were so unhappy, and…oh, if only Father would relent! But I never thought until recently that I might have conceived."

Would Uncle Henry soften when he learned of the child? She knew the answer without asking. Nicolette's parents doted on her, but that meant that if they'd refused the match so firmly the man must have been truly unsuitable. A baby would change nothing.

Except that it changed everything.

She shuddered at the thought of the reaction when Nicolette had to confess. Would the baby save her from blows? From being thrown into the foulest dungeon? Would her parents' love survive the shock and shame?

Whatever the immediate reaction, Nicolette would end up in a convent until she bore her child, and it would be either strangled or given to serfs to raise. After that, she would either stay behind walls or be married off to whatever man would take money to overlook her flaw.

Joan gathered her weeping cousin into her arms, though she had no real comfort to offer. The growing child could not be hidden forever. It was all just a question of time.

When her cousin had collected herself a bit, Joan gave what little comfort she could. "Don't worry about the play. Nothing shows. No one will know."

Nicolette stared at her. "Joan, God will know! I can't represent the Blessed Virgin! It will bring a curse on us all."

"Your baby will bring a curse on all soon enough. What difference does a play make?"

"All the difference in the world!" Nicolette put her hands to her stomach. "I know I carry disaster, but that means I cannot add to it. Ever since the de Graves stole the Bethlehem Banner—" she hiccuped on new tears "—ever since then, Woldingham's well-being comes of the Holy Family play."

Joan hoped she was as good a Christian as any, but she had little belief in God paying attention to plays. The reenactment had a lot more to do with human rivalry than with piety.

The grand de Graves and de Montelan families had

many estates and moved between them, but they both celebrated Christmastide here in the area. The de Graves displayed the banner that had been carried into Bethlehem during the Crusade. In direct reaction, the de Montelans welcomed the Holy Family into their home, proving their superiority to the rest of mankind. Both families were thumbing their noses at one another rather than engaging in an act of piety.

"You're going to have to do it for me," Nicolette said, jerking Joan out of her thoughts.

"What?"

"Play the Virgin."

"I can't do that!"

"You have to. You *are* a virgin, aren't you?"

"Of course, I am!"

"Well then. I looked at the family records, and I think you are the youngest virgin of marriageable age anyway."

Joan considered what she knew. Her mother was Lord Henry's sister. Of three brothers, two were unmarried, and one had only sons. She had four older married sisters and five brothers. It did seem likely.

"But I can't pass as you."

"Yes, you can. To preserve the illusion of the Holy Family, you'll slip out of the castle secretly."

"With no guards?"

"The guards will just see you down to the village, then return. They won't notice anything. You'll be enveloped in a head-cloth and cloak, with a big cushion for the pregnancy. Besides, it's not their place to speak with you. And remember, when you appear in the hall no one here is supposed to recognize you, either, so you stay well swathed."

Joan had to admit that it seemed possible. "But what of you? You can't be seen. And won't anyone notice that I'm not at the celebrations?"

Nicolette leaned back, frowning over it. "Your courses!" she suddenly said. "You suffer so much from them."

"That's true," Joan agreed. She always had terrible pains and, for at least one day a month, had to take to her bed with soothing potions and warm stones to hug.

"You'll have your pains on Christmas Eve."

"My courses are not due until a week later."

"I don't suppose anyone will be counting. And I'll pretend to be you."

"That won't work. Your mother fussed over me the last time."

"You'll make it clear you don't want fussing, and then she'll be so involved with the Christmas Eve festivities that she'll not have time. I'll huddle down in the bed and moan if anyone comes."

"I can see a hundred ways for this to go wrong!"

"So can I, but we have to try. Please, Joan. I won't commit sacrilege."

In the end, Joan had sighed and agreed. "But the problem still remains, Nicolette. What are you going to do?"

For a moment she thought her cousin wouldn't answer, but then she whispered, "I've been in touch with *him*. I've told him about the child. He's going to find a way."

It was a solution, but a terrible one. "Run away? Leave your family?"

"I have no choice."

"Oh, Nicolette!" Joan leaned forward to embrace her cousin, tears stinging her eyes. It was tempting to berate her again for the string of follies that had led to this suffering, but she knew her cousin must recognize every single one. Now, in this dire situation, what choice was there? It would be hard enough to evade the guard around Nicolette and steal her away. Then Nicolette would be cut off from her family forever, and everyone at Woldingham would be cast into misery. And for what? For that phantasm called love, that wildness called lust.

The best Joan could pray for was that in this dreadful situation, Lord Henry would bend and decide that accepting an unworthy husband was better than losing his daughter forever. After a month at Woldingham, she had doubts. Though just, Lord Henry was relentlessly stern. The innocent were not punished, but the guilty were not spared. He seemed to regard any flexibility or hesitation as if it were a deadly plague.

And, she thought, clasped in the enemy's arms, here she was. Guilty of deception, and possibly sacrilege. What's more, Nicolette was stuck in the castle, presumably still huddling and groaning; the play and feast were both ruined; and the de Montelans were out in furious pursuit of the de Graves, murder on their minds.

CHAPTER TWO

THE HORSE HALTED, and she glared up at the man. "You," she said, "have made a stupid mess of everything."

"This mess is none of my making," he said shortly, sliding off the horse. He reached up and lifted her down as if she weighed nothing, which certainly wasn't true. She was instantly reminded that she was the prisoner of a very strong and ruthless man who might have evil intentions.

"Come into the warm," he said, leading her toward an ominous opening in the hillside. "Perhaps it will improve your mood."

A curtain had been hung at the cave opening, probably to hide the light, for inside, the space was lit by three dish-shaped oil lamps. There must have been an opening above, for the smoke wasn't choking them. It was a little warmer, but not much.

Hay and water stood ready for the horse, and he cared for the beast first. Joan hadn't been aware of how much warmth she'd drawn from his body during the ride, but now she shivered. Perhaps also with fear. A fire was laid ready, so she lit it from one of the lamps and held her hands to it as she looked around. Two fine wooden chests, three jugs and thick furs spread over a ledge of rock.

To make a bed? She swallowed, trying to decide if she were better off trying to pretend to be Nicolette. Then she shook her head. Even neighbors who were deep and ancient enemies couldn't help but meet. This man doubtless knew Nicolette by sight, and no one who knew them would confuse them.

Nicolette was slender, with fine hair the pale gold of rich cream. Joan was well-curved with curly hair closer in color to honey. The huge bolster that faked her ripe pregnancy was proving useful in hiding the shape difference, but that couldn't outweigh the rest when he had a chance to really look at her.

With a final pat of the horse's neck, he came over to her.

"Please, Lady Nicolette, take a seat," he said, gesturing to the furs.

Joan stayed facing the fire, putting off the moment. "Who are you, and what do you want with me?"

"I'm sorry," he said, sounding sincere. "I thought you truly would have guessed, Nicolette. Beneath dark cloth and grime lies Lord Edmund de Graves, and you are now safe in my care."

Joan turned slowly, dizzy with shock.

Golden hair, and beneath the soot on his skin, a face handsome enough for the Archangel Michael. His skill with the horse. The very quality of that horse. His effortless air of command.

The Golden Lion.

And he'd rescued Nicolette. Why?

Because, of course, he was her lover!

She took the few steps backward to the ledge and sat with a thump. What man would be attractive enough to turn her cousin's wits, and yet the most unsuitable husband in the world for Nicolette of Woldingham?

Lord Edmund de Graves.

"Don't be afraid," he said, pulling off his leather jerkin, revealing a rich green tunic beneath. "We're safe here. In a little while, the first hunt will have died down and we can make our way to Mountgrave."

He dipped a cloth into a bucket of water and scrubbed his face clean. Joan just sat there, stunned and bitterly disappointed. She supposed he was going to be as bitterly disappointed any minute now. Dense of him not to have realized he had the wrong lady, but after a lifetime with her dense brothers she wasn't completely surprised.

At least she needn't fear rape. Instead of pure relief, however, she ached with regrets. Regrets for a tarnished hero. Edmund de Grave—the sort of man to ruin a maid in some corner of the Martinmas fair.

He turned to her. "Please, my lady. We are safe. Make yourself more comfortable."

There was no point putting it off. Joan unwound the enveloping head-cloth.

The smile disappeared. "So. Who are you?"

"Joan of Hawes, cousin to Lady Nicolette."

He sank cross-legged beside the fire, in a breathtakingly elegant movement that seemed unconscious. "Then we have a problem, my lady."

Fighting tears, Joan stood and loosened the low girdle that held her paunch in place. With a wriggle, she made it fall to the ground so she could kick it away.

Well-shaped lips twitched. "Such a casual way with offspring."

"I'm sure many women wish pregnancies could be ended so easily."

"True enough. Why were you playing the part, Lady Joan?"

"You know that, my lord," Joan snapped, sitting down again, and gathering her cloak around her.

"Ah," he said, eyes widening slightly, "the virginity of the Blessed Mary. Truly, I should have thought of that."

"Indeed you should!"

His brows rose a little at her tone. They were lovely brows—golden and smoothly curved. His hair was lovely, too, waving down to his shoulders.

What a deception.

What a waste.

What a temptation, even so.

This was doubtless a lesson planned by heaven to reinforce her belief that a woman who chose a husband by looks was a fool.

Suppressing a sigh at a bitter lesson learned, she rose. "Now will you return me to Woldingham before folly turns to tragedy?"

He didn't move. "If I had a magic wand, I doubtless would, Lady Joan. As it is, we still must evade the first fury of the hunt. We'll have to rest here for a while." He swiveled, reaching for a jug and two cups, then poured wine for them both. He held one out, and Joan took it, noting that the cup was heavy silver, richly worked. When she sipped, she found rich mead. Even as a fugitive in a cave, Edmund de Graves did not live simply.

That part of the myth was true. The splendor of Mountgrave was part of the myth.

And part of the bitterness between the families, since the de Montelans attributed the de Graves's extreme wealth to their possession of the banner.

Joan wanted to insist that they leave but knew he was right. This area would be full of Woldingham men by now, men who would kill first and think later. The Golden Lion was reputed to be a warrior of almost miraculous skill and strength, but even if that were true, he couldn't defeat ten or twenty—especially unarmed.

Then she saw his armor and sword in the corner near the horse, dull steel and glittering gold, glinting in the firelight. Even armored, however, he couldn't get her safely undetected back to Woldingham yet.

Which blew away any hope of returning before Nicolette was discovered and their actions were known to all.

With a sigh she leaned back on the luxurious make-shift bench.

"Where is Lady Nicolette?" he asked.

"In bed, pretending to be me and unwell."

"Can she remain there undetected for long?"

At least he was as clever as described. No need to lay it all out for him. "Perhaps for a while, my lord. If no one suspects."

"Lady Nicolette is deeply loved by her family. No one will visit her to make sure she is comfortable?"

"You forget. It's not Nicolette. It's me. I'm a mere cousin."

"But a guest. It seems neglectful."

She really didn't want to discuss her private matters with the Golden Lion, but she said, "I have very painful courses, my lord. I've had one bout since arriving at Woldingham. Lady Ellen knows there is nothing to do for me but leave me alone for a while. And she will be busy."

"Ah, and by great good fortune, your courses came now? You are bearing up bravely."

Heat rushed into her cheeks. "They are some days off yet, my lord. We could only hope that Lady Ellen is not paying close attention to such matters."

He shrugged and sipped his wine. "How could you have hoped to pull off the deception to the end?"

She told him of the concealment on the way to the village. "Then, if everything had gone as planned, Joseph and I would have been escorted to the solar, and the feast would have begun. We would have put aside our cloaks and slipped out to join in the celebration. Nicolette would have appeared, of course, not me. I'd have taken her place in the bed. The deception would not have had to last for long. In an hour or so, I was going to have a miraculous recovery and join the company." Rather wistfully, she added, "I was looking forward to it."

"Poor lady," he said, with a hint of a smile. "We had no choice, however. Other than tonight, Lord Henry has kept his daughter under close guard, and I want no more bloodshed between us."

She thought of the howling hounds and gave him a look.

"There's been no bloodshed yet, and will not be if I can help it," he said.

"That's another reason you won't try to get me back to Woldingham now."

"Exactly. If your family managed to kill me, it would not promote peace."

"This whole adventure will not promote peace!"

"I know it all too well. How long can Lady Nicolette maintain the deception?"

Joan abandoned any thought of making him see how stupid it had been to seduce Nicolette to begin with. "It's impossible to say, my lord. Will Lady Ellen be distracted by the seizure of her daughter, or will she think to come to me with the story? I hope the former. It is possible that I'll be ignored until tomorrow. Can you return me before then?"

"Perhaps. It was never part of the plan. What will happen to Lady Nicolette if she is discovered?"

Joan shrugged. "She can't reveal the real reason, so she'll have to claim it was a girlish trick. Lord Henry will punish her for sure."

"How severely? You have destroyed Lord Henry's holy play. Perhaps committed sacrilege, or even treason."

Joan didn't need the worst put into words. "Lord Henry loves his daughter deeply."

"But I don't suppose he loves you that deeply. Perhaps it would be better not to return you to Woldingham at all."

"I will not leave Nicolette to face him alone." The noble statement was interrupted by a noisy rumble—from an empty stomach.

Lord Edmund's brows rose, but he stood to pick up a wooden box and put it open on the ledge beside her. "Pork, bread and a cake of dried fruits. Not a feast, but something."

He took none, and returned to his seat by the fire. Joan would have liked to match him in nobly ignoring the food, but she was famished. "Woldingham fasts on Christmas Eve," she said. "I've only had dry bread and water all day."

"Whereas I have eaten fish and other foods. Please, my lady, eat. It is for you. While you eat, we can decide what to do."

Joan tried to control her hunger in front of him, and took only dainty nibbles of pork and bread. "You have to return me to Woldingham, my lord, in case there's a chance to preserve the deception."

"If the deception has been discovered, however, it will go hard with you."

"I don't suppose he'll kill me. Or Nicolette," she added, suddenly struck by his lack of concern over his beloved. "Of course, when he finds out about the child…"

"I am aware of that danger, Lady Joan. This was all an attempt to bring Lady Nicolette to safety."

She opened her mouth to berate him for getting Nicolette with child, but she managed to control herself. "How long before we can attempt the return?"

He looked at the box. "With your appetite, not long."

With heating cheeks, she realized that, morsel by morsel, she'd eaten most of it. "I'm hungry."

"It's as well I'm not." Did his lips twitch again? Was he *laughing* at her? Joan was taking a hearty dislike to the Golden Lion.

Deliberately she picked up the last of the fruit and took a big bite. "*When* can we return me to Woldingham, Lord Edmund?"

"At dawn, perhaps. The serious hunt should have petered out by then. Your safe return will still leave Lady Nicolette imprisoned, however. Can you think of a way to help her reach Mountgrave?"

Joan was about to declare that she wouldn't do that even if she could, when logic intervened. This was the father of Nicolette's child, the man her cousin loved, and at last he seemed to be putting her welfare first. Nicolette would want to be with him, and would be infinitely safer with him than with her family once her belly started to show.

"Why should I help you?" she asked, hoping to find out more about his intentions. Did he plan to marry her cousin? How could he, without the blessing of her family, with Lord Henry doubtless howling his outrage to the king?

He sipped from his cup. "Wouldn't she like to be reunited with her lover?"

"I'm not sure. It will cause such grief and trouble."

"The cursed feud has been causing grief and trouble for generations. Her belly will cause more. Will Lord Henry soften when he knows she's with child?"

He clearly knew the answer. Joan put down the fruit,

her appetite truly gone. "This is such folly. Why must the enmity between you and Lord Henry run so deep?"

"It runs dry on my side, I assure you, despite the deaths over the years."

Joan remembered hearing that Lord Edmund had asked for a truce. "But he will not bend?"

"He's not completely inflexible. I think, deep inside, Lord Henry tires of this madness as much as I do. But this matter has turned it all back into chaos."

"As it was bound to!" Patience snapping, Joan leaped to her feet. "'Fore God, Lord Edmund, how could you have been so foolish?"

Ignoring his sharp movement, she carried on. "Seeing you, I can begin to understand why Nicolette was swept beyond wisdom, but you have more years and experience. You are the Golden Lion! You should have had strength for both." She turned to pace the confines of the cave, and her thoughts continued to spill out. "Ah, you men are impossible! You think with your—"

He grabbed her skirt and jerked her toward him. Short of toppling onto the fire, she had no choice but to go. "Stop that!" At the last moment, she fell down on her behind rather than go any closer, but he seized her waist and drew her implacably onto his lap.

"Seeing me?" he said, a strange glint in his angry eyes. "Lust after me yourself, do you, Lady Joan?"

May the clever man get warts, and she deserved them herself for revealing her folly.

Joan turned her face away. "I merely accept your appeal, my lord. To a susceptible young woman."

"And you, of course, though young, are not susceptible."

"Not at all." Hastily she added, "And please don't feel you need to prove otherwise—"

He cinched her closer, tight against his broad chest, forcing her to face him, to face teeth bared in a furious smile. "How well you know foolish men, Lady Joan. We can't resist a challenge, can we? Are you sure you were fit to play the Blessed Virgin?"

A hand slid up to settle beneath her breast. Only beneath. A subtle threat, but he could probably feel the frantic pounding of her heart. Why, oh, why hadn't she followed her mother's advice and learned to hold her tongue with men?

"My lord," she said, trying the soothing tone she'd use with a snarling dog, "you don't really have any interest in me, and you dishonor Nicolette by this behavior."

"But we men are impossible." Confining her with one strong arm, he seized her long plaits in the other hand. "And we think with our rods. That was what you were about to say, wasn't it, my foolish virgin?" He began to wrap her hair around his fist, drawing her head inexorably back, then back farther. She squeaked a protest, but it did no good. She ended up stretched like a bow, waiting helplessly for the attacking kiss.

Only then, his eyes on hers, did his lips slowly lower.

At the last moment, they slid away, down to her extended, vulnerable neck. A choked sound escaped her as he ran his hot lips up and down her throat, teasing skin, nerves, tendons and the pounding blood vessels beneath.

It was nothing.

It was terrifying.

"Don't. Please…" Her plea escaped as a whisper.

He ignored it and pressed his teeth into the side of her neck—not hurting, but showing ruthlessly how vulnerable she was. How he, like a ferocious animal, could sever skin and flesh to kill.

That wasn't, however, why she was so panicked. What terrified her was the ridiculous excitement bursting into flame within her. She'd never been handled like this by a man before—never. And her astonishing reaction was a breathless dizziness that was equal parts bizarre, irrational pleasure and blind terror at feeling this way.

He raised his head to look at her with dark, angry eyes. "Still think you are a good judge of men, Lady Joan?"

She could only stare, knowing her eyes must be white around the edges, feeling her heart thunder close to bursting.

"You thought me safe, and I am not. You thought I would take your sharp tongue without retaliation, which I will not. And then you thought worse. You impugned my honor."

With a sharp tug on her trapped hair, he said, "This has not been my idea of a perfect Christmas Eve. This enterprise was embarrassing to think about, tedious to arrange, and dangerous to carry through. It springs from stupidity, weakness and rigid minds. And now, by the thorns, it was all for nothing. I have the wrong woman, and she's a sharp-tongued bitch who wants to lecture me about wisdom and strength. Don't believe the legend of the Golden Lion, Lady Joan. I'm just a man, with all the faults of men. Perhaps I raped Nicolette. She is after all, the precious daughter of my enemy."

Joan found the power to shake her head as far as she was able.

"No? As I said, don't believe the legend."

Consciously or not, he'd relaxed his grip a little. Swallowing, she said, "Nicolette said it wasn't rape. She wouldn't lie about it."

"Will she stick to that story when her family's fury falls on her head?"

"She won't lie."

"Even though she has been such a foolish virgin?"

His cynical disdain was stinging places that had no right to care. "She was clearly a very foolish virgin to give herself to you."

Anger flashed and his teeth showed like fangs, but then, like light shifting, it became a true grin, and his expression gentled. "Ah, Joan, but you're beautiful when you're angry."

Before Joan could react to that ridiculous statement, his lips descended on hers at last, his strong arm holding her close against him, too close for struggle or escape. She tried to writhe, but even that was scarcely possible, and her bound hair meant she could not free her lips from the overwhelming assault.

She must have stopped struggling, because his left hand was now stroking her side. He started to rock a little, and his lips freed hers to murmur, "My honey, my pretty one, my sweet, fiery Joan. Give me your lips, give me your soft sighs. Melt to me. I'll never hurt you."

He kissed her again, and she couldn't stop her lips softening a little, soothed by his gentle, foolish murmurs.

Foolish.

Scarce believable. But...

Edmund de Graves. And her...

He kissed her cheeks, her eyelids, then her lips again. "Open to me, sweetheart. Let me taste you fully."

She wanted to taste him, just this once. She let the Golden Lion meld their lips, let him taste her mouth. Tasted his heat, felt his hand on her breast, rubbing the astonishingly sensitive peak.

Her head swirled as with a fever, but she knew this was madness. She must stop him. This was what he'd done to Nicolette, and look at where that had led!

Just a little more, though? A little more before fighting him off...

He suddenly lay back, their lips still joined, so she sprawled on top. Both hands seized her thighs, spreading them over him. He set her lips free, but stayed close, breath warm against her cheek. "I hunger for you, Joan. Let me feel more of you, just a little more."

He was big and hot, as if power glowed out of him and into her. She hungered, too. Dazed by him, by her effect on him, she cradled his strong face in her hands, loving that intimate contact. "A little, then…"

She wouldn't go too far, but she could enjoy a little more.

He pulled her skirts free so she was naked against his tunic. Murmuring soothing nothings, he eased up his own clothes. She stiffened then. No, she mustn't.

But it was only his belly he exposed to her. Her skin lay against his hot, hard flesh, so she felt each of his deep breaths in her most intimate place. Poised for flight, she still thought, *Not yet. Not quite yet. This is too extraordinary, too wonderful.*

He slid his powerful, callused hands up her legs, beneath her skirts, to grip her hips, to hold her pressed to him. "So hot and wet against me." He shifted his torso, moving under her, against her. "Beautiful lady. Give yourself to me."

Joan swayed, fevered, feeling almost as if she breathed through her secret places, breathed him in— his heat, his power, his vibrant essence. His eyes trapped her wits, gazing at her, into her, dark with desire.

For her.

No.

It was *Nicolette* he loved. Nicolette!

"No." She clawed first at one confining hand, then the other, making no impression through the cloth of her garments. "We can't! Let me *go!*"

His hands swooped free to ruthlessly trap her wrists. Oh, what a foolish maiden she had been. And yet, even then, she wanted. Perhaps, even, she wanted him to force her, to override her sense and honor and force her into pleasure.

If not for Nicolette.

Poor Nicolette, betrayed…

Helpless, Joan went still, tears escaping. "Don't," she whispered.

Suddenly Lord Edmund let her go, flinging her hands away. Thrusting off, she toppled free and scrabbled away from him, away to the far side of the cave. When she looked, he was rearranging his clothes.

He met her eyes calmly. "Let that be a lesson, Lady Joan, not to be so disdainful of weak, susceptible women."

After a shocked, agonized moment, she picked up a rock and hurled it at him.

He ducked, and it cracked against the far wall. "Don't do that again." It wasn't a request.

"You're vile! How could you do that when you love Nicolette?"

"I don't give a hen's hoof for Nicolette of Woldingham."

"But—oh!" She wished she had the courage to throw another rock at the heartless brute. "She loves you!"

"No, she doesn't. She loves my brother Gerald. I look forward to introducing you two. He, at least, deserves the sharp edge of your tongue."

"Your—" She let out a shriek of pure frustration. "You should have told me!"

"You should not have impugned my honor with your vile assumptions."

Joan covered her trembling lips with her hands as

she finally accepted what a fool he'd made of her. Deliberately. Effortlessly. And she'd crumpled.

And even now, under shock and anguished embarrassment, under the certainty that she would hate Edmund de Graves till the day she died, a little glow warmed her at the thought that at least he wasn't Nicolette's lover.

Fool, she told herself. Fool. Even if free, he was not for Joan of Hawes, and she wouldn't have him if presented on a golden platter by a choir of six winged angels!

He'd found his cup and was filling it with more mead. "I hope you've learned your lesson, Saint Joan. Seduction's an easy enough matter, especially for a man with a pleasing form. You women," he added, glancing at her, "are all too possible."

Joan actually curled her fingers around another loose rock, a lovely fist-sized one, but she knew when a threat was real. This was a man who'd take instant retaliation. She miserably accepted that she was frightened of him as she'd previously been of no man—that she'd met a will and an edge equal to her own. She'd rather die, however, than let him know. She turned her back in frosty disapproval.

He chuckled and moved. Her skin prickled with wariness, but the next she knew, he was through the curtain and out of the cave.

First came relief, then fear. Would he abandon her here?

His horse was still here, however, placidly munching hay. Despite his lesson, she did know men quite well. She had five brothers. No man would leave such a horse for long, nor his armor.

Private for a moment, she hugged herself and even let a few tears escape. Some of them came from fear about this whole situation, but mostly they came from shame. She hated him, but she hated herself more for being such easy prey, for that foolish, newly found part of herself that had wanted to believe his trickster lies.

That she was beautiful when she was angry.

That she could stir instant passion in a man like Edmund de Graves.

More than anything, however, the tears were a sign of her frustrated fury. Oh, but she wanted the last little while back, and a chance to behave differently. To win. Now she could think of all kinds of clever ways she could have turned the tables and made him look the fool.

She rubbed tears away. She couldn't turn back time, and a wise woman learned lessons so generously offered. Aye, she thought, sitting up and straightening her garments, she'd even be grateful to him for it. No man in the future would cozen her like that, and it did indeed make her more sympathetic toward her cousin. No wonder Nicolette had succumbed—and she had also been in love.

But not with him, a silly gleeful part of her noted. With his brother!

There, it was a warning against love, too! Joan had already decided that love was a folly, and that young men—especially handsome ones—were more trouble than they were worth. She planned to marry an older man, a placid one who would be happy to have a managing wife and who wouldn't want too much attention in bed.

Recent memories flared, saying that bed attention might not be all bad, but she stamped them out. It had been a lesson. Nothing more than a lesson.

She rested her chin on her raised knees and contemplated the glowing fire, trying to settle her mind to serious matters. How could everyone get out of this with a whole skin?

By sweet Saint Margaret, mother of the Virgin, it would be hard. Despite the dangers, she had to get back into Woldingham, and quickly. If Nicolette had not been discovered, and if Joan could sneak back in undetected, they could pretend that Nicolette had been the victim all along and had escaped.

That wouldn't solve Nicolette's true problem, but it would get them through Christmastide.

Lord Edmund didn't want to try to return her to Woldingham now, and Joan could see his reasons, but she felt they must try, and soon. In fact, it would be easier and safer if she attempted it alone. The worst that could happen would be that she'd be "rescued" by the men of Woldingham.

Despite the excellent sense of it, she knew Lord Edmund would not agree. It would offend his manly honor to let her go off alone. Perhaps if she put it to him sweetly and gently…

She sighed. She wasn't sure she was able to be sweet and gentle, even under this dire need. For the first time it stung a little. She knew she was too fond of speaking her own mind and making her own decisions. Her parents had seized on the invitation to Woldingham with glee, and not just because it was an honor to visit their grand relations. They'd hoped that Lord Henry's firm rule and Lady Ellen's gracious elegance might teach her better ways, ways more likely to find her a husband.

They had also hoped she would benefit from the example of the sweet-natured, soft-spoken Nicolette.

Lord Edmund was right. Despite liking her cousin, she had looked down on her for her gentle ways, and for letting a man trick her into giving him her maidenhead, no matter how much she might love.

Love. A weakness, not an inevitable part of human existence.

Lust, she admitted, was a part of God's plan, designed for procreation, and she'd just been given a short, sharp lesson in the power of lust. She really should thank him. She'd be forewarned and forearmed another time.

Another time.

With Lord Edmund?

She suddenly blew out a breath. What kind of thoughts were these? They were certainly unsuited to the moment. If she didn't find a way out of this predicament, she'd likely end up in a convent as punishment, with lust a matter that need no longer trouble her.

What was needed here was a sound plan, and she had it. All she had to do was convince the ever-noble

Golden Lion to let her make her way through the winter woods alone.

She sat up straight. If he'd gone any distance, perhaps she could just slip away. Before she lost courage, she stood, gathered her cloak around her, and went to ease out through the curtain.

CHAPTER THREE

SHE ALMOST WALKED INTO HIM, a dark silhouette against a starry sky. He turned at a sound. No chance at all of slipping away. Why had she expected it?

So, she had to persuade him, but Joan paused, caught by the scene before her eyes.

From their hillside, the land lay before them like a black cloth embroidered with fire. To her right and in the distance glowed Mountgrave. To her left, and closer, lay Woldingham, with lights in the keep and bailey. Perhaps they were continuing some semblance of the feast. People had to eat.

Between the two castles, the dark was scattered with smaller lights from peasant cottages in tiny hamlets, and in the middle, a bonfire of some sort. Above, like a high arched roof, the sky flickered with silver stars, God's protective mantle, with the Christmas star the most brilliant of all.

The star of the Prince of Peace.

"A wonder of God's work, is it not?" the man said quietly from beside her.

"God's beauty above, man's folly below. What of the lives of all the ordinary people down there, my lord, disrupted by a quarrel?"

She heard what might be a growl. "It is more than a quarrel, Lady Joan, and is no fault of the de Graves. We want only peace."

"Have you offered to return the Bethlehem Banner?"

"Return?" He turned to her, stiff with outrage, and they faced each other in the dim light like the warring castles. "The Bethlehem Banner never belonged to the de Montelans."

"They tell another story. They say a de Montelan carried it into Bethlehem. But does it matter?" She spread her hands, gesturing at the scene below. "Lord Edmund, someone is going to have to bend."

"Lady Joan, you are naive. To bend is to be defeated."

At that moment, the bell at the monastery of Colthorpe began to ring, counting the hour of terce. Midnight.

Joan sighed. "So Christ is born again to bring peace and brotherly love to the world. It is as well," she added pointedly, "that God's patience is infinite."

"It is not becoming of a lady to preach."

"It is not becoming of a Christian to refuse to turn the other cheek. Or to refuse to forgive your enemies."

He stabbed a furious finger toward Woldingham. "Go preach to your uncle, woman!"

"I tried!"

"And you still have your skin? You cannot have preached very hard."

Joan gave a wry smile, though Lord Edmund probably couldn't see it in the dark. "It was in the days before Christmas. Lord Henry takes the season seriously."

"But not seriously enough to end a pointless feud."

"How, when you will not bend? I'd hoped, from

your reputation, that you were a better man—" She caught herself, scolding like a shrew again.

She'd become used to thinking of herself as honest and forthright, someone who did not dress up her opinions in silk, and who would not be intimidated. Now, here, talking of Christian forbearance and humility, she began to think that perhaps her mother was right about more than tactics. Perhaps it simply wasn't very Christian to be so blunt.

"I'm sorry," she said carefully. "The feud is no concern of mine, except that it explains why the de Montelans will never allow Nicolette to marry your brother. For now, we had better discuss what to do next."

"Apart from beat you?" But then he shook his head. "Lady Joan, you are an unnatural, undisciplined woman, but I'll leave you to your uncle. He deserves such a cross to bear. As for our actions, I have decided that at dawn I will take you to safety in Mountgrave."

"Mountgrave!" She paused and moderated her tone. "My lord, for Nicolette's sake, you must return me to Woldingham."

"The possibility of her remaining undetected, and my returning you undetected, is just too small. The area still crawls with your uncle's men." He gestured, and she saw tiny, moving lights here and there. Parties from Woldingham, still hunting.

"I see lights near Mountgrave, too. Will they be your men?"

"No. My men have instructions to stay safely within the walls. I am trying to accomplish this without bloodshed. Just before dawn, my forces will ride out to clear a way to Mountgrave, so we should be safe."

"But you're casting Nicolette to the wolves! If I went alone, now, to Woldingham, I might make it in time."

He turned to her. "You jest!"

"About such a serious matter? Lord Edmund, I know it offends—" She bit that off. "I know it would be hard for you to let me make my way there unescorted, but it is the way most likely to bring everyone off safe."

"Impossible. By stealing you away, Lady Joan, I have made myself responsible for your safety. I cannot allow you to take such risks."

"I don't see why you have any right to prevent me!"

"Because you are a woman, and I am a man."

"Very well! If you insist on being so noble, my lord, escort me to Woldingham at dawn instead of to Mountgrave."

"I cannot risk making myself another martyr, and stirring deeper enmity. Your uncle's men will be forced back from Mountgrave, but they will keep both watch and search near Woldingham. Also, my men can come to our aid on my land, but not on Lord Henry's."

Joan tucked her chilly hands up the sleeves of her gown. "But what of Nicolette?"

"And what of you, in the end?" he said. "You tried to help your cousin, Lady Joan, and do not deserve to suffer from it." He suddenly moved, turning toward the cave and putting a hand to her back to steer her in that direction. "Come into the warmth and let us see if we can find a miracle."

Joan went, hoping he hadn't noticed her start at his touch. This power he had over women was most unfair.

As they sat on the ground, safely separated by the low fire, she raised a question that had been scratching at the back of her mind. "Tell me something, Lord Edmund. Where is your brother? Should he not be here with Nicolette rather than you?"

"Indeed, he should." He put another piece of wood on the fire, and it crackled into flame. Concern in his eyes, he said, "I don't know where he is.

"He was supposed to be in this role," he continued, "but he disappeared yesterday. Out on some business that went against my orders. I chose to go through with my plan. I pray he's returned to Mountgrave by now, and is keeping his hothead."

She suddenly had a terrible suspicion. "Did you tell him what you were arranging?"

He jerked to look at her. "Are you a witch, woman?"

"Are you a fool? Why didn't you *tell* him?"

"I do not need to tell my younger brother everything I plan. And he deserved to sweat for his stupidity!" He suddenly leaned forward, almost too close to the flames. "How did you guess? What do you know?"

Her mouth dried, but not from fear. Because she had bad news for him. "Lord Edmund, I'm very much afraid that Lord Henry has your brother in his dungeon."

"What?" He surged to his feet, and for a moment, she almost feared for her neck, but then he controlled himself and sank down again across the fire from her, not relaxed at all. "Speak."

Joan took a breath. "This morning, in the midst of all the preparations for the feast, some guards brought a prisoner to Woldingham. I didn't get a clear look at him. Perhaps it isn't your brother. And yet, he didn't look like a peasant, despite simple clothes. My uncle had him put into the dungeon, saying that he'd have no unpleasantness at Christmastide, but he seemed extraordinarily pleased about something, and he doubled the guards. I didn't think much about it, being more concerned with my own problems, but now, I fear it is your brother, caught while attempting some rescue of Nicolette."

"May the imps of hell torment him," Lord Edmund said.

"Lord Henry?"

"My brother."

"You should have told him. Of course he thought you didn't care—"

"A stick will do, Lady Joan. There is no need for the flail." He rested his head for a moment on tense hands. "So, we have two to get out now."

"And me to return." She held chilled hands to the fire, wondering whether Lord Henry's resolve about the peace of Christmas would hold when he thought his daughter was in the hands of his prisoner's family. Gerald de Graves might be under torture even now.

She looked at Lord Edmund. Despite arrogance, he clearly loved his brother, and was also one to take the burdens of the world on his shoulders.

"If I could return secretly, my lord, perhaps I could free your brother. Then he could escape and maybe even take Nicolette, as well."

"I thought you said that Lord Henry had him under double guard?"

"But it is Christmastide."

"If even one of my guards could be tricked or overcome by a woman, Christmastide or not, I'd have his neck. And unless I underestimate Lord Henry, he will have put his best men to guard a de Graves. He finally has the key."

"Oh." She felt stupid for not seeing it. "He'll offer your brother's life for the Bethlehem Banner?"

"And if you did manage to steal that chance for victory, your life wouldn't be worth a pin."

"He couldn't know."

"Once considered, who else?"

After a moment, she said, "Nicolette. If I managed to return undetected, Lord Henry would think Nicolette had been the Virgin, not me. If she then disappeared with your brother, he'd think she'd returned to free him. If they got away, all would be well."

It sounded hopeful to her, but he shook his head. "First, no one woman—or even two—is going to free a de Graves from Lord Henry's dungeon, especially without being recognized. Are you willing to kill the guards? Second, from what I know of Lady Nicolette, even her doting father would not believe her capable of attempting it. No, I'm sure he'd have to realize that you are the key to the whole thing."

Joan couldn't help but feel rather flattered by that.

"If I keep you," he continued, "I have an equal piece to offer for my brother's life."

"I'm not Lord Henry's beloved daughter."

"You're a relative under his protection. He could hardly refuse."

He was right. "That saves your brother *and* your precious banner, but leaves Nicolette and me exposed! You have to let me try to get back into Woldingham. Now, in fact. I promise to try to get your brother and Nicolette out."

"It's impossible."

"Lord Edmund, you are the most inflexible man I have ever met!"

"You are hardly bending in the wind of reason, Lady Joan."

"Because I'm right."

He leaned forward. "I cannot risk the banner my family has protected for generations."

"I will not risk my cousin's skin, without at least trying!" She'd doubtless have thrust her chin right up to him if not for the fire. As it was, the heat was flaring at her jaw.

"You are my hostage, Lady Joan, my means to save my brother. You will remain with me. If the two of you had not engaged in a foolish deception, all would have been well."

"No, it wouldn't, because my uncle would still have your foolish brother. And if you'd told him—"

"Stop flaying me! I have a family disaster on my hands, which is now going to make a feud I have been trying to end even deeper. I asked for none of this."

"Nor did I ask to be tossed over a horse, dragged to a cave, and…and assaulted!"

His tense face suddenly relaxed. "Yes, you did."

"What?" she spluttered.

"Ask to be assaulted. At least you asked for more. Begged, in fact."

She reached for a rock but then restrained herself.

"Very wise."

He smirked. It was definitely a smirk.

She picked up the fist-sized rock and threw it. Since she was daring the devil, she did her best to hit him with it, and throwing things hard and accurately was one of her skills. If he hadn't flung up an arm to defend his head, she might have knocked him out. Then she could have escaped.

At contact, he hissed with pain, but he was already lunging for her.

The fire was between them, but it didn't stop him. Probably he was through it so fast it had no chance to catch him. She scuttled back but had no escape. And anyway, mad impulse past, she was fixed in terrified paralysis.

He seized her around the waist and swung her over his raised knee. Through three layers of sturdy cloth, his strong hand stung, but she thanked heaven for those three layers of cloth.

He stopped much sooner than she'd dared to hope, and straightened her to face him, kneeling.

"No screams?" he asked.

"Over that?" she asked, with a bit of bravado, for she'd felt the swats. "You're not howling and you'll have a bruise."

"Did you not consider," he asked, looking as if he'd like to spank her some more, "the wisdom of injuring the weapon arm of a man who might be your protector?"

"I was aiming for your head. You probably don't need that to—"

The flare of rage in his eyes silenced her. "I'm sorry," she said quickly, and meant it, though she did hope he didn't think his hand had cowed her. "But if you're going to beat me for my unruly tongue, Lord Edmund, your hand will wear out."

"I might consider it a noble sacrifice for mankind. And, Lady Joan, I punished you not for saucy words but for a dangerous physical attack."

"You shouldn't have taunted me!"

"You can't return word attack in kind?"

That halted her for a moment, but then she said, "Your original attack was physical."

He let her go and stood. "Ah yes, I suppose it was."

His look suggested that he understood how devastating his original physical attack had been, and how that had led to this. All she could do was meet his eyes as if he were a man who stirred not a single lustful thought in her.

As if he weren't as beautiful as a warrior angel.

As if his rare smiles didn't make her want to be foolish.

As if her innards didn't tremble every time he touched her.

Her eyes almost stung with the effort of staring blankly at him, but she did it.

After a moment he shook his head as if she were a mystery to him. Good. Very good. "Lady Joan, why are you at Woldingham?"

She was still kneeling as if at a shrine. She hastily scrambled to her feet, taking the opportunity to straighten her clothes, the excuse to look down. "To change my ways and find a husband," she admitted.

"The men being driven away by your daggerlike tongue?"

She couldn't help but smile at him. "Is it as lethal as that?"

He burst out laughing. "Lord save the world. I think your father should put you in a convent that has a vow of silence."

"I'd break out. I'm not just a tongue, you know."

"No, you have a brain behind it, which is why your tongue is lethal. Tell me, why do you attack when you must know you'll be punished?"

She'd never really considered that before. "I can't seem to resist it. People are so infuriatingly stupid sometimes."

He smiled, turning away as if trying to hide it. "Yes, they are, aren't they?" He looked back at her and a connection of some sort made her heart do a silly little somersault. Immediately she guarded herself. Oh no, my lord, that won't work twice.

"Very well," he said, sober again. "Truce. We're engaged in matters too serious for this. Don't throw any more rocks when I offend you, and I won't retaliate for the things you say to me."

"Are you sure that's wise?" she asked. "I'm not sure I've ever unleashed my tongue."

"I think I can bear it. The question is, what can you bear? You were right to point out that if I use you as hostage for my brother, Lord Henry will have to know about the deception. You will suffer for it."

"So will Nicolette."

"She deserves some punishment. Perhaps I should return you to your own home, though you'll doubtless face punishment there, too."

Did he perhaps care about her safety? That tempted Joan to smile. "My parents wearied of punishing me years ago."

"It would have been better if they had persisted."

She cast him a reproachful glance and his lips twitched. "Unprovoked attack. I do beg your pardon, my lady."

"They will be disappointed," she admitted. "They continue to hope, you see, as if time might turn me sweet and pliant, make my hair silky and my figure willowy."

This time it was a definite smile. Lord save her, he had dimples. "Lady Joan, there is nothing at all wrong with your figure."

"Lord Edmund," she said, her thumping heart betraying her words, "I am immune to that sort of attack now."

"It's simple truth, Lady. Men's tastes vary as much as women's, and I like a woman of substance, one I'm not afraid of breaking."

"Oh." She realized she was running her hands over her generously curved body, and his eyes were following her hands.

More acting?

She told herself so. Whichever, she stilled her hands

and clasped them modestly before her. "I think I must balance the scales by complimenting you back. You doubtless know it all too well, but you are a very handsome man."

"More curse than blessing. Women make fools of themselves over me, and if they are married women, they create enemies."

Make fools of themselves. Oh, if there were words to armor a maiden to a man's charms—even this feast of a man—those were they. Whether given deliberately or not, she silently thanked him.

"Now we are equal again," she said, turning to pace as she spoke, and glad to break the taut connection between them. "Can we return to plans? Returning me to Hawes would ensure my safety, but Nicolette and your brother would still be in peril. Nicolette has no safe explanation for the switch, and your brother will die unless you return the banner to Wol—"

"Not return," he interrupted sharply. "It was never theirs."

Joan flung up her hands. "How can an apparently reasonable man be so…so unreasoned! Sir Remi de Graves and Sir Henry de Montelan—I'm surprised you aren't called Remi, my lord—"

"My older brother, who died when twelve."

Joan rolled her eyes. Two families trapped in an ancient quarrel. "Sir Remi and Sir Henry went on crusade together, cousins and brothers in arms. They carried with them a banner they hoped to bear victoriously into Jerusalem and into the place of Christ's birth in Bethlehem."

"A banner made by my ancestor's mother and sisters!"

"But carried by both, yes?" When he didn't deny it, she went on, "Unless the de Montelans lie, Sir Remi was wounded in the taking of Jerusalem, and Sir Henry alone rode with it to Bethlehem to complete their vow."

"Remi was wounded in saving Sir Henry's life. His blood stains the banner to this day!"

"No one denies that. But why do not the de Montelans have a right to the banner half the year, as they claim?"

"Because, Lady Joan, they would not return it."

"Are you not judging them by yourselves?"

She watched his hands clench into fists then, with effort, relax. "Are you saying," he asked grimly, "that if I gave the banner to Lord Henry now, he'd return it in a six-month?"

"No. But he has many a six-month to make up for. Lord Edmund, someone has to bend!"

"It will not be me. I will not betray the generations that have gone before."

"I see. You're afraid of them, and of what people will say."

His fists clenched again. "Take back those words, Lady Joan. I fear only God."

Joan wished she hadn't said it, largely because she could see it hurt him in ways she'd not expected or intended. She was past the point of return now, however. "I cannot take them back, my lord, unless you prove them not to be true."

He whirled away, looking up. "What sins have I committed, Lord, that you punish me with this woman? Her tongue flays me, yet my honor says I cannot strike back! My body burns—"

Though trembling with physical fear, Joan caught those chopped-short words.

Oh.

My body burns. One thing was sure—that had come deep from within. It had been no trick.

Of course, she told herself, there was nothing deep and meaningful about it. But it was undeniably satisfying to think that at this moment, the Golden Lion burned for her.

He turned to look at her, almost sheepishly. "Lust," he said.

She nodded. "You're probably used to it. It's new to me."

"You've never lusted?"

"Not like this."

He ran a hand through his hair, looking away. "We should not even be aware of these things at such a time. When so many important matters hang in the balance."

"It's not easy to stop, though, is it?"

His eyes rested darkly on hers. Flickered over her. Back. "No, it's not easy to stop."

What would happen if she touched him? She'd probably end up like Nicolette. At the moment, it didn't seem to matter. "Does your lust make it hard for you to think straight?"

"I would have thought that was obvious!" He turned abruptly to seize the jug of mead and fill the two cups.

Some splashed on the floor. He passed one to her and unsteady hands brushed, sending sparks up her. Their eyes held as they drank.

Broke free.

She wanted to ask many questions, the main one being, did this happen to him all the time with woman after woman, or was there anything special about it? Just a little bit special? Something about her?

Another one was, if she tried really hard, tried to become more gentle and sweet natured, to guard her tongue, would there be any hope…?

Oh, indeed, she was a foolish virgin. He wasn't trying to trick her again, but she was doing it all by herself!

"The first idea was better," he said, sitting on the rocky shelf covered with furs, as far as possible from her and the heat of the fire. "You will be my hostage to bargain for Gerald."

Matching his cool tone, Joan said, "I think it would be better for me to attempt to return to Woldingham, now."

"The woods will still be crawling with men."

"I'm one small woman."

"And hounds."

She'd forgotten the hounds.

"If I use you as hostage, I can make it clear that the raid was simply to gain a prisoner to balance my brother. Yes, Lord Henry will be angry at you and Nicolette for switching places, but if he does not punish during Christmastide, perhaps his rage will fade. If not, we still have twelve days to think of some other solution."

The thought of Lord Henry's massive hounds on the

hunt had definitely sapped Joan's courage for a lonely trek, but she said, "Your plan means Nicolette will have to face them alone. She'll be so afraid."

"Unlike you?"

"I'm with you, and she's with Uncle Henry."

His brows rose. "As you've seen, I have no scruples about meting out punishment at Christmastide."

She almost said that she didn't fear him, but he'd probably take it the wrong way. She would mean that she didn't fear terrible punishment from him unless she did something truly terrible, in which case she'd deserve it.

What if he did something terrible?

"What are you thinking now, you wretched woman?" But the smile in his eyes took any offense from it.

She surrendered to honesty. "I was wondering whether you'd let me punish you if you did something stupid or wrong."

"No."

"Why not?"

"Why should I?"

"Strength," she complained with a huffed-out breath. "It's most unfair."

"Woman was put on the earth to be governed by men, and man was given the strength necessary for the task."

"So," she mused in deliberate wickedness, "if you were weakened by injury…"

"I'd stay well out of your reach! Very well, Lady Joan," he said, "I take your point and will make you another bargain. If ever, during our brief adventure, I give in to temptation and strike you again, I will let you pay me back in even measure." Before she could quibble, he added, "And you may compensate for strength and size by using a tool—stick, rock, what you will."

"Even your sword?" she asked, eyeing the magnificently scabbarded weapon lying near his mail.

"If you think that just."

She pulled a face at him. "I have to be just? That takes the fun out of it."

He laughed, a natural open laugh despite the perilous nature of their problems.

Something deeper stirred inside her. Here was the first man she'd found that she could talk to without watching every word, who seemed able—after a fashion—to accept her blunt speech, and even give as good as he got.

Sad that it would only be a "brief adventure."

Enough of that. She resolutely turned her mind back to plans. "If you exchange me for your brother, nothing will have changed."

"True. It will be worse, in fact. I'll still have to rescue Lady Nicolette or Gerald will rush into danger again. And all hope of peace will be over."

He sighed and leaned back against the wall. "The irony is that Lord Henry was moving a little. I've been negotiating with him for nearly a year, with only moderate success, but recently he became much more open to suggestions. Two things happened simultaneously, just weeks ago. Gerald confessed his folly and told me Lady Nicolette was carrying his child, and Lord Henry proposed peace, sealed by a marriage, the matter of the banner to be sorted out later. It was almost complete capitulation."

"Nicolette and Gerald? But then—"

"Of course not," he said, looking at her. "Nicolette and me."

"Oh." Joan could see what a disaster that had been, but she was struggling with the thought that even Lord Henry had tried to bend. He surely couldn't have known which de Graves Nicolette loved, so he'd assumed the most likely and tried to obtain him for his daughter.

"Without Gerald's news, I would have accepted. As it was, all I could do was propose a marriage to my brother, which Lord Henry quite rightly took as an insult. If I'd been given any time to plan at all," he added with irritation, "I would have married again myself and thus been unavailable."

"You've been married?" Ridiculous to be hurt.

He looked at her strangely. "I'm twenty-five years old and destined to be Lord of Mountgrave since I was ten. Of course I've been married. It was arranged when I was thirteen. An excellent alliance, but my wife died of a flux two years ago."

"I'm sorry."

He shrugged. "I've been busy with warfare and attendance on the king since I was sixteen, so I never saw her for more than a week in a six-month. I'd say 'poor Catherine,' except that she was perfectly content in the situation."

"I can understand that," Joan said, struck by the charms of such an arrangement. Her parents, and the neighboring families she knew well, did not spend much time apart. With grand families, however...

Then she looked at him, blushing. "I wasn't referring to you, my lord!" Then she wished she'd not even hinted at marriage between them.

"You think you could tolerate my presence for a little longer than that?"

"Of course! I mean…" She collected herself from the embarrassing mire. "I merely thought that I might seek out a similar husband. One much engaged with national affairs."

"A husband who will leave you in sovereignty over your world?"

"You have to see, Lord Edmund, how ill suited I am to day-by-day compliance."

He leaned back, studying her. "But—and remember you agreed not to throw rocks at me—you seemed to enjoy a man's physical attentions."

Her blush was an answer. "But I doubt many men could make them as pleasant to me as you did."

He smiled, and looked away for a moment almost bashfully. Truly, at times, Lord Edmund was a tantalizing mystery, and it was his faults and frailties that fascinated her more than his obvious charms.

If only…

Don't be foolish, Joan.

He patted the fur beside him. "Come sit over here. It doesn't suit me to talk across the cave like warring factions." When she hesitated, he added, "You have my word. I won't hurt you."

CHAPTER FOUR

"I KNOW," SHE SAID, walking over. "You seem to have forgotten that I might have reason not to want to sit."

"I didn't think I'd been so harsh."

"You weren't," she admitted as she sat. She looked at his arm, hidden by his sleeve. "What of you?"

He pushed up the sleeve and, with a wince, she saw a dark red bruise near his elbow.

"Nothing that will impede my fighting," he assured her, flexing the muscular arm. But then he held it out to her. "Perhaps you should kiss it better."

She looked him in the eye. "Oh no. Then you might think you should kiss *my* hurts better."

Dimples flickered. "If you wish, my lady."

She stared into his eyes. "Don't."

As if he understood, his expression turned wry and he lowered his arm, leaning back against the wall. "So, my wise virgin, what are we to do?"

She grasped the assumption that they were talking about the feud, Nicolette and his brother. "I do admire your desire for peace."

"Even if I cannot bring myself to do what is necessary to create it, and surrender the banner?" His brows rose. "Silence? I pray I haven't cowed you."

"I'm practicing tact and tongue control, since I fear this will all end with me imprisoned in a convent."

"A terrible waste."

"Perhaps in time I'll become an abbess, able to flay the male world with impunity."

"A waste."

"My cleverness and administrative abilities would be put to full use."

"A waste," he insisted.

"A waste of what, my lord?"

"Of a great deal of heat and fire." He held out a hand. "Come here."

Though her body longed to leap at him, Joan made herself eye that tempting hand. "I've learned my lessons well."

"I have more to teach."

Joan swallowed. "I don't deny you have an effect on me, Lord Edmund, but two Woldingham maids carrying de Graves babies will hardly improve matters."

"I won't get you with child."

"Many a man says that."

That anger sparked in his eyes again, anger because she was doubting his honor. She didn't. Truly. And yet, she didn't trust any man in matters like this.

"Swear it to me," she demanded.

Frostily, totally without dimples, he said, "I swear on my immortal soul, Joan of Hawes, that I will not get you with child this night."

"Good." But she sighed. By obtaining the oath, she'd destroyed any chance of needing it.

But then his hand stretched out again, and her pulse started a nervous beat. "This is hardly the time—"

"This might be the only time. The feud is now likely to be cast in iron. Would even your tolerant parents allow marriage between us, to the great offense of Lord Henry?"

"*Marriage?* You can't expect me to fall for a trick like—"

"Joan!"

She covered her unruly mouth with her hand. "Oh, I'm sorry. I truly didn't mean… But—" she hardly dared put it into words "—are you saying you might want to *marry me?* Why?"

He captured her hand and tugged her closer. "Poor Joan. Have you been so unvalued?"

"N-no. I've had men interested, but none who interested me. But you…"

Dimples flickered. "Awed by the great Edmund de Graves? I'd have thought you'd learned better by now."

"I've learned nothing but good of you."

She was against his broad, warm chest.

"You see my faults as virtues. What more can any man want?" A hand slid beneath her plaits, rough hot against her neck. "I like you, Joan, as I've liked no woman before. I like your courage and your calm head. Now I've grown accustomed, I even like your sharp tongue, for it is wielded by a clever brain." He tilted her head up toward him. "Can you imagine how wearying it is to be surrounded by people who reverence every word I say. I'd welcome a truth sayer." His other hand found her thigh and stroked upward, over cloth. "And my body likes your body—very well, indeed."

"My body likes yours very well, too. But is this wise? We have plans to make."

"The plans are made. I'll bring you through this unscathed if I can, so at dawn I will take you safely to Woldingham."

Complete reversal. "But—"

He slid her off the bench, to stand between his legs. "We have a night to pass before dawn, and I have plans for that, too."

"But your brother!"

"I'll find some other way." He pulled her close and his head came to rest between her breasts.

She held him off. "What of the danger to you?"

"It is nothing beside the danger to you."

"This is folly. Take me to Mountgrave and bargain me for your brother. At least Nicolette and I will not lose our lives."

"Trapped in a convent? Close to death for you, Joan. Let me prove it. Prove that it would be a waste." His hands merely flexed on her hips, but she swayed, and her body, her inner body, ached.

"All women feel this way, but many become nuns, and happily so."

"All women do not feel this way. Some, though excellent wives and mothers, are cool. My Catherine was. She was a dutiful bed partner, but if she could have started a child with a hug she would have preferred it."

Joan found that impossible to believe. Her hands

rested on his shoulders, close to his bare neck. With her thumbs, she tilted his chin up. "Are you sure of that?"

"Yes, for we spoke of it. Though not as sharp as you, Catherine didn't hesitate to speak her mind. She was some years older than I, and experienced. Twenty when we finally wed, and two years a widow. I was just fifteen. She knew her needs and how to demand them, and did not mind if I took other women for more vigorous sex play."

Joan frowned, and his brows rose as he continued, "Are you saying that when you wed your busy man, you will expect him to be virtuous when he's away?"

"I'd hoped he would not be much interested in sex at all."

"That would be a waste of another kind. Even if your matings are few, Joan, you should want them to be fiery." He pulled her closer. "Do you deny the fire in you?"

Hot almost to sweating, she could only shake her head.

"And I burn. Do you think I burn for every lovely young woman I meet?"

"Yes."

He laughed. "Very well. A little, yes. But not like this, Joan. On my honor."

He looked completely honest, but her stern common sense was not dead. "It's only the night, and the cave, and the fear."

"I'm not afraid."

"You're probably never afraid."

"Any man fears when there is reason to. He does not let it rule him. But I do not borrow fear, and nor should you. What tomorrow brings, we will deal with tomorrow. Now is now and, yes, it's the night and the cave. But it's also you." He rubbed his face against her, and his mouth brushed—once, twice—across her nipples. "I never thought I'd like a woman with a sharp tongue, still less one who hurled rocks at my head. But you are like pepper to my senses—burning but delicious."

Looking down, she could see her brazen nipples pushing at the cloth. She watched as he repeated, "Delicious," and put teeth gently to first one, then the other.

Conquered, she let her weak knees give way so she knelt, supported by her arms on his thighs. "You shouldn't encourage me. I'm sure my tongue can get worse and worse."

"Then I will teach it other tricks." He captured her head and kissed her, engaging her tongue in another kind of battle.

When it ended, she clung to him, dazed. "You could blunt a tongue entirely that way."

He smiled, stroking her hair. "That's what I thought. But there are other ways." Sitting straighter, he dragged his tunic and shirt over his head, presenting a stunning, firelit torso, a sculpture of muscle. "Explore me with your clever tongue, Joan."

She reached for him, but he captured her hands, holding them on his thighs. "Just your tongue."

Her tongue stirred hungrily in her mouth as she studied him, already savoring the warmth, texture and taste. Broad chest, small, flat nipples, a trace of hair low down the middle, around his navel and lower…

His navel, just above the drawstring of his braies.

Slowly she leaned forward to circle it with her tongue, closing her eyes the better to savor the heat, the taste of sweat and salt, the texture of smooth skin and ticklish hair. She dipped her tongue into it and felt his ridged belly muscles shudder.

Oh, she liked that.

Deep inside, her body pulsed insistently in response. She wavered for a moment, fearful of her own hunger. Of conquest and consequences. But then she remembered his oath, and she knew the Golden Lion would keep it.

Putting her mouth to his navel, she kissed it, feeling his hands tighten on hers, feeling her own hands clench on his thighs. She took her mouth away to blow on his wet skin, smiling at his shiver. Glancing up, she saw that he was leaning back, his eyes shut, lost in sensations she was creating.

Smile widening, she trailed her tongue lower, easing beneath the tied top of his braies. She felt him move and looked up a little nervously, wondering if she'd gone too far.

His eyes were open, meeting hers, heavy lidded. "If I wasn't feeling kind, I'd dare you to go further."

"I'm sure you know I can't resist a dare."

"I thought you were a very sensible virgin."

"You swore an oath, and I'm a very curious virgin. I've never seen…" To her annoyance, words escaped her then. "I can feel that you are… I mean…"

"Yes, I am." He released her hands and untied the cord that held his woolen garment up, then leaned back, leaving her to do as she wished.

With a bubble of excited anticipation and a wave of hot embarrassment, Joan lowered his braies.

Oh, my. She'd heard enough jokes and whispered stories to know what to expect, but she supposed most women saw this coming at them with intent. Presented to her like this, he was beautiful and she wanted to taste him.

"Tell me if I hurt you," she whispered, before touching her tongue to the tip of his rigid shaft.

She thought he laughed, though it might have been a groan. He was hard as rock, but like a rock warmed by the fireside then covered in silk. A musky smell teased at her, warm, comforting in some way....

Reason said other men were made much the same way, but she couldn't imagine feeling like this about another man.

He'd been right when he'd said her family would never permit such a marriage, even to the great Edmund de Graves. It would offend family loyalty too deeply.

What was to become of her?

Fighting away tears, she ran her tongue up and down him. When she brushed the ridge near the tip he jerked. She noted that and returned to tease.

"Does doing this disqualify me from the convent?" she wondered, contemplating the glistening, vulnerable tip.

"You don't have to tell them." He did sound breathless.

Arms resting on his tense thighs, she looked up. "What's going to happen if I keep doing this?"

"I'll spill my seed. You won't get pregnant unless I spill it in you."

"Do you like what I'm doing?"

His eyes crinkled. "No. But I liked what you were doing."

With a laugh, she said, "Tell me what you'd like even more. Give my sharp tongue power over you, Edmund de Graves."

"Don't say sharp to a man at a moment like this!" But he was teasing, and he suggested things. With a smile, she did them, aware with dazzled astonishment of him falling apart, exquisitely, trustingly vulnerable here at this moment with her.

When his breathing steadied and he opened his eyes, she said, "You're right. I'm not suited to a convent. This is too much power to give up."

He laughed and pulled her up for a ravishing kiss. Before she knew it, his hand was under her skirts, his mouth was at her cloth-covered breasts. When she arched and cried out, astonished by building sensations, he stilled his clever fingers and raised his skillful mouth. "The power goes both ways, Joan. Do you want me to stop now, before you turn to mindless wax in my hands?"

She shook her head. "Serve me. Give me what I want."

He laughed at her parry and obeyed, and who was to say who was the victor, who the vanquished at the end?

They lay together on the fur-covered ledge, and for Joan, at least, it was a time of strange adjustment. He'd taught her a lesson earlier about lust, but this had been a more potent one. The lesson she had learned here was that lust had a beauty of its own, and that she didn't want to live without it.

She wasn't prepared to say that she could only experience the beauty with this man, but she felt quite sure such harmony of desire was rare.

Yet to have him was almost impossible.

Their marriage was no more impossible than Nicolette and his brother, a part of her argued, and that would have to be, despite the enmity.

She couldn't give him up.

She couldn't!

She rose up on her elbow to trace his lips with her finger. "I want to marry you."

Those lips twitched. "I'm good, aren't I?"

She punched him on the shoulder for cocky arrogance. Justified, though.

He turned serious and caressed her face, brushing wild escaping curls off her cheeks. "I'd like to marry you, too, but I don't see how. Duty comes first. I'm determined to end this feud. At the very least, I cannot make matters worse and steal you away, too."

"If your brother and Nicolette are to be together—"

He laid fingers on her lips. "Gerald is not me. He is not the Lord of Mountgrave. He can move to one of my other estates and be out of sight. He won't have to constantly deal with Lord Henry over local and national matters."

"Lord Henry will never forget or forgive the loss of his beloved daughter, even if they move to Spain!"

He closed his eyes. "I know it. But our marriage would be daily salt in the wounds."

Joan straightened, frowning. "Then there's only one way. We have to end the feud."

"Willingly. Point the way."

"There's always a way."

"I wish I had your faith." He captured her and drew her down to him. "As it is, all we have is now."

She didn't give up—there generally was a way if a person was determined enough—but certainly going around and around it now would be a waste of time.

Of precious time.

She slid out of his hands and off the ledge to remove his loose braies, taking deep pleasure in his long, muscular legs, only realizing then that she was down to her linen shift.

Yes, he was good.

When he was naked, she said, "Turn over. I want to explore your back."

He merely lay there. "Make me."

The resulting fight was a different kind of education to Joan, and equally enjoyable. She was like a child next to his strength, but he managed his power with control and was surprisingly vulnerable to tickles, so she ended up straddling his back, massaging his muscles, each flex of her spread thighs against him stirring her aching hunger.

Oh yes, she was hungry for him.

Famished.

Thank heavens, his oath could be trusted.

And curse it.

She thought he'd fallen asleep, but when she carefully eased off him, he turned and snared her, to stroke
and suckle her into wild pleasure again. In fairness,
she could only do the same for him, when they lay
together talking, but carefully—not of anything connected to their troubles—till at last, they slept.

When she awoke, a glimmer of light around the
curtain warning of dawn, she felt more starved than
sated.

If he'd planned to teach her that she was a lusty
woman, he had undoubtedly succeeded. She leaned up
to feast upon him with tear-stinging eyes. Two of the
lamps had spluttered out during the night, but by the
dying flame of the third she could see bristles on his
square chin. She ran her fingers tenderly over the roughness.

His eyes flicked open, smiling, but she thought she
detected the same sadness behind them as ached in
her. "We must return you to Woldingham, Joan."

"What of your brother?"

"Lord Henry won't murder him. I'll negotiate
something."

"You'll exchange the banner for him?" With sudden
hope, she realized that would end the feud.

He rolled on his back, arm over eyes. "How can
I?"

"It's a piece of cloth. He's your *brother!*"

The concealing arm fell away. "It's my family's
honor through four generations. Blood has been lost
over it many times."

"And clearly more will be." She was determined

not to scream at him, especially about things he must know perfectly well.

"I swore an oath," he said. "All the men of our family do at the time they become knights. An oath never to give up the banner to the de Montelans."

She shook her head. "And *they* swear an oath never to cease the fight to regain it. What madness it all is. All the same, when I'm back in Woldingham, I'll set your brother free. Somehow."

He gripped her shoulder. "I forbid it."

"If Uncle Henry won't kill your brother, he won't kill me."

His hand tightened. "He might not stop much short. Joan, for my sake, take no risks. The thought of you suffering weakens me."

She pulled free of his hand and stood. "The thought of you suffering weakens me, but I don't suppose it will stop you from fighting."

He sat straight up. "You are an unnatural woman!"

"So? I thought you liked that about me."

A wry smile chased away his frown. "My training is to control and protect you, Joan. It is the way of the world for men to fight and women to stay safe."

"Then why are you worried about what Uncle Henry will do to me?"

"It is also the way of the world for men to punish. You will not," he said, "try to rescue my brother."

"I'll not take unnecessary risks."

He gripped her arm. "You will take *no* risks!"

"And if your brother escapes," she continued, despite a scurrying heart, "he'd better take Nicolette with him."

"Joan!"

Though quivering, she met his angry eyes. "You can't control me, Edmund. I will do what I think best."

"You will put your foolish head in a noose."

"*Why* do you assume you are cleverer and more sensible than I am?" She tore free again and put distance between them. "I assure you, I no more want to be caught by Uncle Henry than you want that. I'll take no foolish risks. But if I see a chance to get them away safely, I will take it."

He pressed his hands to his face, then lowered them. "Promise me one thing."

"What?" she asked warily.

"If you get Gerald and Nicolette out of Woldingham, go with them. Do not stay to face your uncle's wrath. I'll see you safe back to your family."

"I'll try."

"Promise!"

"I promise to try!"

He glared at her. "If it's you or her, you'll stay to face the punishment."

"Isn't that what you would do?"

"That has nothing to do with it." Edmund stood to pull on his braies and knot the cord. He turned his back to do it.

Joan began to dress, too, not nearly as miserable as she ought to be. She'd enjoyed that battle of wills as much as she'd enjoyed their wrestling earlier, and she loved his obvious concern.

He was right. She was an unnatural woman.

She'd kept her shift through the night, but her other clothes were strewn around. As she collected them and put them on, she watched him dress, savoring his beauty.

He was hers. Deep inside, she knew it, even though she knew their happiness might be impossible. Such little time for so strong a bond, and yet it was there, tugging at her, already like a painful scar.

She knew he felt the same. That's why he was going to try to return her to Woldingham. It would put him in danger, and, even successful, would leave him in a weak position. *He* might have faith that Uncle Henry wouldn't torture his brother to death, but she wasn't entirely sure.

Joan pulled her tunic down over her head. "I think you should take me back to Mountgrave and arrange the exchange."

He turned to look at her. "That wasn't your plan."

"I've changed my mind. Your brother risks death."

"If it comes to that, I'll doubtless give up the banner for him. For his safety, and his marriage to Nicolette."

Joan should have felt enormous relief at that tidy solution to everything, but his anguish over it was obvious.

"Break your oath?" she whispered.

He sat to pull on low boots. "If he starts sending me my brother in pieces, what choice do I have?"

Joan put her hand to her mouth, sickeningly certain her uncle was capable of it. "But then—"

"Don't argue," he said curtly. "You'll waste time and tongue." He suddenly strode over and seized her, kissed her, putting her tongue to alternate use.

When he released her, she staggered, watching him go toward his armor, go toward becoming the Golden Lion, who was not for her. To the man who would risk his word and honor to give her the greatest chance of safety.

"This doesn't make sense!" she exclaimed.

He whirled. "Joan, you are the only innocent in all of this!"

"Innocent?"

"Gerald and Nicolette have committed sins both of stupidity and immorality. I pushed through this plan without truly thinking things through, and without involving my brother fully in it. This disaster is my fault."

Joan opened her mouth to argue, but he swept on. "You tried to help your cousin, and your plan was sound. If I'd not interfered, you'd be in no danger. Therefore you, at least, should come off safe. My honor demands it."

And there, she saw she was up against a wall as high and strong as those around both castles.

She went to help him into his armor, another thing she'd done for her brothers now and then. "My honor demands that I try to help you and my cousin."

He ignored her, and did without her help as much as possible.

As he put on iron embellished with gold, the change was completed. Her midnight friend and lover transformed into the Golden Lion, a creature of myth and glory—of another sphere.

Marriage? Had that really been whispered in the night? It just proved how foolish nighttime whispers were. Even if there was no enmity between their families, such a great lord was not for her. He might as well be the Archangel Michael as far as she was concerned.

It had, after all, just been the night and the cave, but she wouldn't have missed it for her chance of heaven.

And she still thought they ought to go to Mountgrave and exchange her for his brother.

CHAPTER FIVE

As MISTY GRAY HERALDED DAWN, they made their way down the steep hill toward flatter, more fertile ground. She was perched up behind Edmund on his big horse this time, hand in his belt. He only had padded cloth between himself and the horse, and the rope bridle, so they still moved quietly, except for the subdued rattle of armor. His sword was in its scabbard, but he carried his big shield on his arm, since he couldn't sling it on his back and had no saddle to hook it to. She couldn't help worrying that the weight must tire even him over time. She worried, too, that his right arm might have stiffened by now from her wound.

She smiled at her own ridiculous tendency to fuss over him like a mother with a delicate child. This was the Golden Lion, undefeated in tourney for many years.

For a while they moved through a misty world still silent as night, but then pink touched the sky and the first bird began to call. As the pearly light spread in the sky, Joan kept her ears alert for sounds of danger, as she was sure he was doing, but it was as if the hunt had ceased.

Here, at least.

She didn't know this countryside well, but she assumed that the deer paths he chose led to Wolding-ham, and if there were enemies about, that's where they'd be found.

Foolish man.

As when she'd been first captured, she thought of slipping off the horse to escape. It would be easier now since she rode behind him, but just as pointless. He'd capture her in seconds. Instead, she wrapped her arms around his mailed chest, hating the harshness between her and his flesh.

In the end, danger came abruptly, catching them in the worst possible place. Thor had just scrambled up the steep bank of a stream when four horsemen galloped along a nearby path.

Edmund immediately stilled the horse, and the men almost missed them. Then one glanced to the side and hauled his horse up, crying the alert.

To run was hopeless. To stand was surely to die!

"Get off and head for Woldingham. To our left and as the crow flies." Edmund dropped the reins and drew his sword.

"No—"

"Obey me, Joan."

The Golden Lion had spoken, and after a heart-breaking moment, Joan slid off the horse. He couldn't fight with her on his back—but she wasn't running away.

She ducked into the cover of some evergreen growth and wove as quickly and silently as possible to some-where else. Anywhere else. Yells and the clash of metal made her jump, and she peeped out from behind a big tree, to see a mess of men, horses and swords.

They'd kill him!

She only just stopped herself from running out in a futile effort to help.

Then Thor kicked backward and a horse went down, squealing, the rider tossed off and, at least, dazed. Immediately, he reared, startling another horse into shying away. Praise heaven, none of the attackers was on a warhorse. A mighty swipe of Edmund's sword unseated another rider.

Joan expected blood to gush, and when it didn't she realized the Golden Lion was trying not to kill. "Noble fool," she muttered, but she understood. Any new death would widen the rift between the families.

The two remaining horsemen were hovering, not quite so keen to get close. The one who'd been thrown was staggering up, however, sword in hand. Edmund could probably ride away, but he was trying to guard her flight. Should she go?

Then one of the horsemen turned to where she'd run into the bushes and called, "Lady Nicolette! Come out! It's safe."

A strange definition of safe, but she was thrilled that they still thought Nicolette was the stolen Virgin. If she sneaked back into Woldingham...

Then it occurred to her that these men could have been out all night. If Nicolette had been discovered, they would not know.

She hovered, uncertain, her mind momentarily wiped of all ability to make decisions, and before her, the men seemed motionless, too, no one knowing quite what to do.

Then, the man on the ground charged, his sword pointed. "He's murdered her! He's murdered the Lady Nicolette!"

As if goaded, the other two charged, and Edmund whirled in the middle, miraculously countering three blades, but blood suddenly gushed from his right arm. He still swung the sword, but for how long? She could not possibly run away and abandon him.

Urgent breath burning her throat, she ran back to the stream, heedless now of noise or secrecy, and gathered half a dozen fist-sized stones in her folded-up tunic. Then, with them bouncing bruisingly against her thighs, she ran back as close to the fight as she dared.

Just two on one now, and only one mounted, but Edmund was weakening, and the man on foot was creeping up on him. She fished out a rock, prayed, and hurled it as hard as she could at his helmeted head. The clang must have been enough to deafen him, and he wavered, then turned instinctively to face the new enemy.

Joan was behind another tree by then, watching Edmund ignore a perfect opportunity to run the man through. The moment let him wound the other man in the sword arm, however, disarming him. Then Edmund kicked him out of his saddle to the ground.

She hurled another rock at the man looking for her. She missed his head but by luck caught him on the sword hand. He howled and dropped the weapon. *Concentrate. Concentrate.* Her next rock found its exact mark in the middle of his forehead, and down he went.

The unseated man had remounted, but held his horse back, seeming not to like the odds anymore, but the first thrown one was staggering back to his feet. Joan hurled a rock at his legs. By luck, it took him on the knee, and with a howl, he collapsed down, hugging it.

When she looked back, the other man was unseated again, and when Thor reared up over him, he took to his heels. Edmund seized the nearest available horse. "Come on, my disorderly lady."

He was right. She was here in the open, hurling stones at her rescuers. She'd ruined all chance of a sneaky return. She scrambled up onto the big, nervous horse, and as soon as she was in the saddle, they raced off, one other loose horse driven before them. Edmund called, "Grip the mane!" and kept hold of her reins.

She obeyed, but screamed, "I can ride!"

He slowed for a moment, looking at her, then tossed her the reins. Side by side, they hurtled down a cart track, the free horse charging ahead. She dearly hoped they went in the right direction.

She *could* ride, but she'd never done that much flat-out galloping and the stirrups were far too long for her feet. She gripped as best she could with her legs, giving thanks that the saddle was high front and back, and took a firm hold of the pommel, as well.

She said a silent prayer of thanks, however, when Edmund slowed their pace, for she needed to catch her breath. Not for long, though, for their attackers might have regrouped, or the fleeing one might have found reinforcements.

When the warhorse came to a dead halt, she glanced

a query at Edmund and saw him sway and almost fall. Bright blood poured from his leg. Thor must have stopped on his own, sensing his rider's weakness.

How much blood had he lost? How long could he keep conscious?

"Edmund!" she said sharply. "Look at me!"

His head turned, but she wasn't sure his eyes were focused.

Joan crossed herself. "Blessed Mary, help us." Careful ears caught no hint of pursuit, but she couldn't trust to a smooth journey. She wasn't even sure they were going in the right direction.

"Edmund, is this the right way?"

He shook his head slightly and looked around. "Yes. Not far now to Mountgrave." A spark of anger lit his eyes. "You should have done as you were told, and gone to Woldingham. You heard what that man said. Called you Nicolette."

She tersely made her point about them being out of touch. "And anyway, it's an issue no longer. They saw me. You might as well use me as a hostage. If you can stay on long enough to get home. Can you get on this horse? The saddle will help."

He eyed it, and shook his head. "Better to stay on Thor. You get up behind to help."

Joan much preferred a saddle, and she wasn't quite sure how to get up on the big horse without Edmund lifting her there, but she slid off her mount. With relief, she saw a hump of ground ahead and led Thor there. Blood still flowed down Edmund's leg, so she used her head-cloth to make a hasty bandage. More seemed to be coming from higher, though, from under his mail. No time to find that wound, or to treat his right arm.

From the hillock, and with some wincing help from Edmund's left arm, she managed to scramble up astride and behind. She heard him murmuring to the big horse, and having seen Thor in battle, she could only be grateful.

She could feel the horse's tension, however, a kind of seething need to act, probably because of the smell of blood. She looked down and saw too much of it on the earth and grass below.

They had to get to safety.

She kicked the horse's sides—far higher than it was accustomed to, she was sure, for her short legs were spread over the top of his mighty back. Nothing happened.

She glanced frantically behind. "Edmund, get him to move!"

Edmund jerked as if he'd been slipping into unconsciousness, but he said something and shifted his body slightly, and Thor began to walk. She wanted to scream for speed, but that would toss them off.

She twisted to stare down the road behind. All was quiet. As they made their way slowly, she strained for sounds. Then she heard it. Pounding hooves. Out of sight as yet.

"They're coming. We have to go faster!"

He was clutching the mane, half-collapsed forward now. He couldn't stay on at any speed. If he didn't, she couldn't. She virtually perched on top of the huge beast and wasn't used to riding bareback, even at the best of times.

"I'll get off," she said, but he said, "No!"

He collapsed down, arms around Thor's neck. "Mount me, and take the reins."

Spurred by a raucous cry that meant their pursuers had caught sight of them, she scrambled forward so she was astride his waist. He choked a cry, and she almost retreated, but she looked back and saw the enemy. Five men with death on their minds.

She leaned forward to grab the reins, and screamed, "Go, Thor! Go!"

By a miracle, the mighty horse lunged into action, iron-shod hooves chipping frosty ground beneath, each pounding beat rattling her bones and threatening to shake both riders free. But it was almost as if the horse worked to keep his riders on, and she had only to grip with her legs and try to keep everything balanced.

Then she felt Edmund begin to slide. His left leg must have been painful or even numb, and his right arm hung useless. She shifted, trying to counter his slide. Thor stumbled, out of balance. An arrow whistled past, making her yelp in fear. A few inches left and it would have been in her back!

Perhaps that was why it was the only one.

Then Thor squealed and bucked. The whistle seemed to come later, so Joan only realized the horse had been hit by an arrow as she and Edmund began to slide off. She grabbed for the mane and fought it, and the brave horse stilled, shuddering, trying to help.

The hunting cries were almost at their back now.

They were taken.

Then, ahead, a true hunting horn.

Precariously balanced, she looked up and saw Mountgrave on its hill and an army pouring out. Too far. Too late.

But when she risked a twisting glance, she saw the five men behind had halted, staring at the rescuing force in frustration. One had a bow, and he nocked another arrow, aiming right for her. Another man pushed the arrow to one side, but he looked into Joan's eyes and promised retribution.

The men whirled and raced away down the path, back to safety, back to Woldingham with a tale of treachery.

Joan eased off Edmund's unconscious body and burst into tears.

The next little while passed in a daze, as release from immediate terror turned her almost faint. She was lifted onto another horse and carried back to the castle at a walk, faintly aware of somber concern all around, and not for her.

A reverent, whispering concern for Edmund de Graves. Dear Blessed Mary, was he *dying?* What terrible wound had caused all that blood? What harm had she done by sitting on top of him?

When they clattered into the castle, they were swarmed by another small army, this time of servants, some quick to help, others there to stare at their lord with distraught eyes. Joan, still carried in her rider's arms, saw Edmund being carefully eased off Thor's back.

He was silent and immediately submerged in a sea of caring bodies. He could be nobly suppressing pain. Or still unconscious. Or dead.

No, not dead. They'd be wailing if he were dead.

"Lord Edmund," she said to the man holding her. Older, with intelligent, experienced eyes. "I must go to him."

Did those eyes see too much? "No need, Lady. He will be well cared for."

"But…" Joan forced herself into silence. Her feeling that she should be by his side was nonsense.

"I am Almar de Font, Lady. And you, I think, are *not* Lady Nicolette de Montelan."

"Joan of Hawes. Lady Nicolette's cousin." Then she added helplessly, "*The* Almar de Font?"

His lips twitched. "If there were another, my lady, I'd be forced to fight him for possession of the name." He turned and called something to the people around, and in moments she was carefully handed down and assisted, with fussing care, to stand.

He swung off and stood beside her. "All a man truly owns, my lady, is his honorable name."

Joan looked around at the massive, mighty walls and keep, at hordes of prosperous servants, dozens of fine horses, a small army of well-trained men. Edmund owned a great deal more than his name, but she wondered how much pleasure he gained from it.

She let herself be guided into the keep, feeling as if she'd arrived in a mythical land. Almar de Font was perhaps more famous than the Golden Lion.

He had enjoyed many heroic adventures of his own, but fifteen years ago, he had settled to being the mentor and trainer of his friend and lord's two remaining sons. The name Almar de Font *meant* honor, honor to the death, and she was bitterly sure that he would never let his lord and student bend his honor enough to give the banner to the de Montelans.

Not even to save Sir Gerald's life.

"Lady Joan!" She suddenly found herself enveloped in silk and perfumes, all part of a babbling woman. In a moment it began to make sense.

"So brave! So saintly! Come. Come."

Joan was given no choice, but carried on silk and perfume to a small but exquisite chamber hung with tapestries and warmed by two extravagant braziers. By then she had sorted out that her captor was Lady Letitia, Edmund's sister, and that the army was a bevy of maidservants, each one dressed more finely than Joan.

Joan was still wearing the costume of the Blessed Virgin, the simple clothes of a carpenter's wife. But even if she'd been wearing her festive best, Joan knew she would not have matched Lady Letitia's ladies, never mind the lady herself.

It didn't matter, since they immediately stripped her down to her skin and placed her tenderly in a huge perfumed, linen-lined bathtub. Despite feeble protests, soon every part of her body was being lovingly attended to by someone. She lay back and stared up at Lady Letitia, who was orchestrating this.

Edmund's sister lacked his spectacular beauty. Medium height, medium hair somewhere on the brown side of blond, medium figure. It was confidence and a fortune in silks and jewels that made her seem like a goddess.

"What's happening?" Joan asked.

Lady Letitia smiled, a full and joyous smile. "My brother will recover," she said, as if that answered the question.

"God be praised. But I meant, why am I being treated like—" she couldn't think what she was being treated like, except that it had never happened before "—an honored guest," she ended limply.

"But you are!" Letitia exclaimed, and sank to her knees to take the comb from a servant and work it gently through Joan's tangled hair. "You saved Edmund."

Joan hadn't even realized that her hair had come free from her plaits and must be a tangled mess. She suspected that despite Joan's status as heroic maiden, Lady Letitia would not be pleased to learn that her brother had created most of the destruction. She was tempted to laugh, or cry, or both.

If marriage between them wasn't impossible because of their families, she saw now that it was impossible in every other way. She'd felt like a poor relation at Woldingham. Here, she felt like an intrusive pig-girl.

She surrendered and let them wash her, dry her, lay her on a bed and massage her with perfumed oils. As she drifted off to sleep, she thought idly that it was not the treatment given an honored guest. It was more like the special care given a lamb destined for the Easter feast.

A sacrifice. Which is exactly what she was to be.

The next step was to hand her over to Uncle Henry in exchange for Gerald de Graves, and then the slaughter would begin.

CHAPTER SIX

JOAN WAS AWOKEN by a gentle hand shaking her, and for a moment a strange softness and perfume confused her. Where was she? Then, reality rushed back, and she sat up straight, ready to face her fate.

She winced. She was sore and stiff in many places, some of which she would never admit to. Despite a hovering maidservant, she closed her eyes and tried to recapture a moment of the cave, a trace of her and Edmund, but it was like a dream, evading her conscious thoughts.

She opened her eyes and looked at the middle-aged woman. "Is it time?" Time to be handed over.

"Aye, Lady, it is. Come rise and let us dress you."

Joan saw two other servants, one older, one younger, and a spread of fine clothes. "Oh, that's not necessary." Perhaps if she was returned as the bedraggled Virgin, it would temper her uncle's fury. "What I came in will serve."

The woman pulled a face. "I'm sorry, Lady, but that's all been tossed in the rag pile. Nothing special to begin with, and soiled with mud and blood."

Joan looked at the glowing fabrics again. She didn't

even know what some of the garments were, but it was all silk, much of it wondrously embroidered. "Then perhaps something simpler?"

All three were staring at her. "For the feast?" the woman asked.

"Feast?" For an insane moment, Joan imagined herself the chief dish, dressed for slaughter.

The woman laid a hand on her hair, comfortingly. Perhaps her fear had shown. "'Tis Christmas Day, Lady Joan, and none here wishes you harm. Woldingham has agreed to return Lord Gerald safe tomorrow in exchange for you, so today we can celebrate. Soon all will be gathered in the hall."

Tomorrow.

What difference did a day make? And yet it did. She had a day before the ax fell, and why shouldn't she enjoy it? And if she was to feast with the de Graves, she welcomed the chance not to appear a pauper.

She rose from her bed and let them slip over her head a shift of linen so fine it felt like silk. The full-length gown that followed *was* silk, a winter warmth of silk that puddled ungirdled at her feet like richest cream, for it was that color. By contrast, the tunic that they dropped on top was light as a feather and almost transparent, so finely woven it was, except where it was embroidered in jewel-colored flowers. Joan looked down and smoothed her hands over the shining pattern it made against the cream—like summer flowers against snow—and could have wept at the beauty of it.

For a moment she wanted to reject it as too fine, too fine for Joan of Hawes, but instead she gripped both layers of silk. Tomorrow would come. For today, she would dress in silk and feast in grandeur, and even let herself dream a little that this could be for her.

Next came fine woolen stockings and pretty cream leather shoes that fit. Then the plump maid, Mabelle, opened a chest and took out a glittering snake. The girdle of gold and pearls was clasped around her hips, yet still hung extravagantly down to her toes at the front. A fine veil was draped over her unbound hair and secured with a circlet as fine as the girdle. She wished she could see herself like this.

Had she, like ordinary Lady Letitia, been transformed into a grand lady for a while? Or, as she feared, did Joan of Hawes squat like a toad among flowers, unchanged and out of place?

She stiffened her spine. This was her chance to experience grandeur for a few brief hours. She would take it.

When she was ready, the maidservants escorted her out past a reredos into a staggeringly noisy and brilliant great hall. Banners hung from the high-beamed ceiling, among coils of smoke from flambeaux, braziers and one great fire. The aromas of perfumes, spices and rich foods roiled in the air. Richly dressed people crammed tables all around, and servants lined the walls.

Waiting.

Waiting for her?

Embarrassed, she searched for her place, and Mabelle pushed her gently toward the grand high table to her right, raised on a dais.

Lady Letitia was there, and an older, even grander woman. A middle-aged man. Sir Almar.

Then she saw Edmund. Healthy?

No. Not Edmund, but the Golden Lion, sitting in the great central chair, dressed in crimson, with jeweled bracelets and a gold circlet on his hair—shimmering like a figure of gilt and jewels, scarcely human at all.

He was staring at her, too. Darkly.

He saw the toad.

Before she could panic and run, he pushed himself to his feet with his left hand—she could tell the movement hurt. Sir Almar, close by, and two attendants behind him, put out hands as if to help. When standing, Edmund bowed.

"Lady Joan. Welcome to my hall. Come, sit at my right hand."

To her breath-stealing panic, with rustles and scrapes everyone in the hall rose, even those at the high table. The knights bowed and the ladies curtsied, and the servants all went to one knee.

Joan stood there frozen.

Sir Almar came quickly down from the dais to her side and escorted her, dazed, up the steps and to the plain seat—but still a chair not a bench—at Lord Edmund's right hand.

She sat, and Edmund eased back into his seat. She noted that he accepted Sir Almar's discreet hand beneath his elbow to do it and that sweat glistened on his brow. He should be in bed. The hall sprang back into motion, but too many eyes lingered on her.

"I wish you hadn't done that," she whispered, head bowed, for she didn't know where to look.

His hand raised her chin and turned it to his pale face. She caught the flash of a number of large jeweled rings. "We do you honor, Lady Joan, that is all."

Once she met his eyes, he took his hand away, and, looking past him at the cool-faced older woman, she could only be glad. That must be his mother, the famous Lady Blanche de Graves, a grand lady in her own right, before marriage to his father. She was held to be at least partly responsible for the family's rise in fame and fortune.

The sort of woman he would marry next.

"I did not do so very much, my lord," Joan said.

"You saved my life, Lady."

"Thor would have brought you home safe, and you wouldn't have been in danger without me."

"You wouldn't have been in danger without me, Lady Joan, or *still* be in danger because of me."

"Ah," she said, breaking the disturbing connection with his eyes to look out at the hall. "Honoring the sacrificial victim. I see, my lord."

Liveried pages presented food, and Edmund silently selected choice items for her silver plate. She drank from a jeweled cup and began to eat, for she was very hungry. She wasn't entirely sure it would stay down, however.

Minstrels were concealed somewhere, playing peaceful, beautiful music, which would doubtless have delighted her in other situations.

She felt him lean back in his huge, magnificent seat.

"I have no choice now, Lady Joan, but to exchange you for my brother."

"I understand."

"It was your preferred course, if you remember." She could hear gritted teeth.

"But it's a shame I was forced to show my split allegiance so clearly."

"I didn't force you into anything. I ordered you to escape to Woldingham."

And it was clear he wished she'd done that. Perhaps it would have been better. They both would have been captured, but Lord Henry wouldn't have killed Edmund. To ransom the Golden Lion and his brother, Mountgrave would have had to give up the banner and all this would have been over.

But that wasn't true. If the de Graves lost the banner, they'd start a war to get it back. Their oaths demanded it.

"Lady Joan." She was startled into looking at his guarded face. "Tell your uncle that you helped me in order to prevent my murder by his men, because you knew he would not wish it, and does not approve of bloodshed at Christmastide."

After a moment she admitted, "That's clever."

"I am, sometimes."

Eyes say things that lips cannot.

His mother broke the silent connection, leaning forward to speak around him. "You have my deepest gratitude, Lady Joan, for assisting my son." Her heavy-lidded eyes missed nothing, and her thin-lipped smile did not warm them at all.

"I would not wish anyone to die over a piece of cloth, my lady."

The woman's fine nostrils flared. "It is not merely a piece of cloth, girl."

"No," said Joan, meeting her eyes. "It has been forged into a shackle for the men of two families. Doubtless in time, Lord Edmund will require a binding oath of his son that he never bend, never negotiate on the matter."

Edmund's right arm must have been heavily bandaged, but even so, he managed to grip her wrist. "Joan, be silent."

Joan saw his mother's features pinch, and it wasn't at her words. It was at Edmund's plain use of her name, and the tone in which he'd spoken. It had been a firm warning, but the tone had been almost intimate.

She saw him realize it. He removed his hand and pointed with his left hand, pointed to the right of the high table, where a length of dull cloth—faded reds and browns with some sort of stitchery on it—hung on a huge carved and gilded stand. "There it is."

The Bethlehem Banner. It hung like a figure of Christ on a golden crucifix.

War banners were rarely glorious after use, but this one was particularly faded and torn. Which, in a way, gave it additional power to move. She could believe that it had been carried into Jerusalem generations ago, had been stained with blood, then laid on the ground where Jesus had been born.

Or perhaps it was the suffering and blood through the subsequent years that gave it power.

Then she noticed how all the servants bowed to it as they passed.

She turned back to him. "Does it live there all the time?"

He was frowning at her tone. Perhaps everyone was, but she was intent on him. "Of course not. We have a special and secure chapel in the keep where it is kept, except at Christmas."

"It is locked away?"

"Six monks live close by to pray before it night and day, Lady Joan."

To pray for forgiveness, or to pray for yet greater glory for the de Graves, she wanted to ask. Seeing the grandeur in which he lived, sensing the reverence in which he was regarded, she understood better why the de Montelans believed the banner carried mystical power. Why they wanted it for themselves.

But it was all wrong. She felt as if that banner was trapped on that cross, as much a prisoner of coldhearted men as she would be tomorrow.

He touched her again with his right hand, gently. "Joan, what is it? No need to curb your tongue, you know that."

A hint of a smile in his eyes invited her to another place and time, but that was past. Done. His mother's watchful eyes told her that. She owed him some honesty, however. "If we can speak together before I leave, my lord—speak alone—I will tell you my thoughts on this."

After a moment, he nodded. "So be it. For now though, as a kindness to me, enjoy the feast."

Since there was nothing else to do, Joan obeyed, taking particular comfort in Sir Almar's presence to her right. Though a quiet man, he spoke easily on a number of simple subjects, and encouraged her enjoyment of tumblers, magicians and riddlers. From time to time, Lord Edmund claimed her attention, too, with some polite comment or question, or to ply her with yet more delicacies, but that was all. She knew why he gave her this limited attention. He was the center of his world, and always watched, so he must not seem too fond with her. However, it would raise suspicions if they were to ignore each other entirely.

He had no choice. She knew that. Even if he truly wished to, he couldn't marry her, and without the exchange, his brother would languish in prison, or perhaps face torture and death. She knew without assurance that Edmund would try to bargain for her safety, to mitigate any penalty, but he had to give her over to her uncle, and once Christmastide was over, Uncle Henry would not be merciful.

And Nicolette, of course, was likely confined on bread and water even now.

She wondered if any kind of feast was taking place at Woldingham.

She wondered if Nicolette had been forced to confess the true and greater sin.

All appetite fled, and Joan began to feel sick.

A warm hand covered hers again, concealed by the rich table coverings, but he said nothing. She glanced at him, and his eyes met hers briefly, full of the same knowledge that lay bitter within her. They were both powerless within a pattern of events created by others but made more tangled by themselves.

Then the music picked up pace and entertainers ran laughing from the center space to leave room for dancing.

"I wish I could lead you into a dance, Lady Joan." It was a polite nothing, but she hoped she read a touch of honest sadness in his expression. She needed to believe that his feelings had some truth to them, some lasting quality. That it had not just been the cave and the night.

"I am in no mood to dance, my lord."

Lady Blanche leaned forward again. "There are many men here who would be honored to be your partner, Lady Joan."

Joan smiled at her. "I would rather not, my lady."

Lady Blanche smiled back, but her eyes flashed a clear message. *Harbor no foolish thoughts, girl.*

Joan watched the dance start, then said, "I assume your wounds are not too serious, Lord Edmund."

"Just painful and awkward, Lady Joan. They might have been worse without your skill with a stone."

She couldn't help a fleeting grin at him, though she controlled it quickly. "It was a game my brothers and I played, my lord."

She allowed him to draw her into talking about her home, her brothers and sisters, and the rough-and-tumble years of growing up with parents too harried by ten children—all of whom miraculously survived—to be keeping close watch on any of them.

"Of course, the boys left to be trained in other households, but they were replaced by other men's sons. Not many, my lord," she added deliberately, "for Hawes is not a grand holding."

Mountgrave bubbled over with pages and squires who had won the privilege of serving the Golden Lion.

"And none of these hopeful young men courted you, Lady Joan?"

"A few did. They were not to my taste, however. Too young."

"Ah yes, I remember now that you favor a sober, older man."

With that, carelessly or deliberately, he summoned the memory of their night together, and as she had said that night, she whispered, "Don't."

His left hand lay on the rich cloth covering the table, and she saw it clench briefly. She also saw, made herself see, the three precious rings he wore, the worked gold bracelet around his wrist, and the heavy silk of his robe, embroidered red on red. He did not need to trumpet his wealth with gaudiness.

And then, she wondered suddenly how hard it was to be Edmund de Graves, the Golden Lion, at only twenty-five. She remembered him speaking of how wearying it was to be reverenced all the time.

Impulsively, irresistibly, she squeezed gently on the hand that still rested on her. He turned sharply to look at her, then carefully away. But beneath the cloths, his thumb gently, almost sadly, whispered against the back of her fingers.

After a moment, he eased his hand free and turned to his mother. "My lady, I fear I am too weary to preside over this feast any longer. May I beg you and Sir Almar to take my place?"

Lady Blanche put her hand to his face and kissed

him. "Of course, dearest. You know I wished you to keep to your bed."

"I could not disappoint everyone." He turned to Joan. "Be free, my lady, to stay or retire. You share my sister's room for the night."

Joan colored. She'd not even thought of where she would sleep. "I don't like—"

"It is no imposition, is it, Letty?"

Lady Letitia, on the far side of Sir Almar, cheerfully agreed.

Lord Edmund raised her hand with his left, and gently kissed it. "I wish you good rest, my lady. Be assured that I will do my best to assure your safety as you did mine."

Both kiss and words were suitable for a hundred pairs of eyes and ears, and yet Joan bit her lip to force back tears. She watched as he was assisted to his feet by two strong servants and helped to limp away, obviously in serious pain. Under the floor-length gown, there was no way to know how badly he was wounded, but she didn't think he put much weight on his left leg at all. Even so, before the banner, he paused to bow.

For a little while, last night, that body had been hers.

Hers to play with. Hers to care for.

She caught Lady Blanche's thoughtful eyes on her.

"How seriously is he wounded, my lady?" Joan asked directly. No point in trying to pretend she didn't care.

"As Lord Edmund said, Lady Joan, painfully, but not seriously."

"I bandaged his calf, but there seemed to be blood from higher. There was no time to deal with that."

"A blade slid up beneath the mail," said Sir Almar, and Joan turned to him. "Not a trick anyone could pull off, one on one. He was lucky it didn't penetrate all the way or he could have spilled his guts instead of a barrelful of blood."

Joan remembered the man on foot who'd charged with his sword. So close to death.

"But he will suffer no permanent harm?"

"If God is kind, Lady."

Infection. The ever-hovering danger. "He should not have left his bed. Surely he will keep to it now."

"He insists on delivering you to your uncle, Lady, and seeing his brother safe. But do not feel it is your fault. It must be done in person, on the neutral territory between the two lands. And no one wishes to delay matters."

"Neutral territory? I thought the lands met."

"They do, but at the start of this mess someone had sense to set apart four acres where the opposing parties can meet, honor-sworn not to spill blood. It's hardly ever used for that purpose, so the local folk use it as a common. They call it the Bethlehem Field."

She remembered a dark landscape and a flaring bonfire. "Do they light a fire there on Christmas Eve, Sir Almar?"

"They do, my lady. Peasants from both sides."

She looked at the banner and wished someone would throw it into the neutral fire.

"No, my lady," the man said as if he could read her thoughts.

She rose. "If you will excuse me, my lady," she said to Edmund's mother, "I would prefer to retire."

"Of course, Lady Joan. I will send some maids to care for you."

"There is no need."

"We would not want to fail in any courtesy."

Joan found herself accompanied by three younger maids, who she was sure resented being taken from the festivities, but who all insisted on remaining and settling to sleep on straw mattresses on the floor.

Alone in the bed she'd share with Lady Letitia, Joan smothered a grim laugh. Lady Blanche was clearly making certain that Joan engaged in no tryst with her son. It was flattering to be thought worthy of such measures, but a dismal confirmation that she was, after all, merely a toad.

CHAPTER SEVEN

JOAN WAS AWAKENED the next morning by early sun slanting through shuttered windows. It was warm under the heavy covers beside the sleeping Letitia, but the air nipped at her nose.

Though she didn't look forward to the day, she'd get up if she thought she had any clothes. She could hardly wear the feasting finery when she was taken to her fate.

Very soon a servant popped in to wake the three maids, and as they quietly began to dress and put away their mattresses, folding blankets into a large chest, she asked one to find her something to wear.

As she waited, Joan slipped out of bed and wrapped herself in one of the blankets. Then she opened the shutters a little and looked out over the castle complex and across the countryside that lay between here and Woldingham. Her breath puffed white, but she welcomed the sense of space, for even in this luxurious room, she felt imprisoned.

Perhaps an awareness of future imprisonment.

What would her uncle do?

She'd not just switched places with Nicolette for the

Christmas play. She'd attacked, perhaps seriously injured, some of his men to defend a de Graves, and very actively helped Lord Edmund to escape. What was worse, if she'd not allowed herself to be brought here, there would be no hostage to exchange for Gerald de Graves, except the banner.

She'd try Edmund's clever suggestion, but her faith in it was weak.

She hugged herself against a chill deeper than the frosty morning. Poor, poor Nicolette, whose situation grew worse with every twist of this tangled event.

The door opened and she turned. It was one of the maids with an armful of cloth. Clearly no silk, this time, and not too bright of color.

"Thank you," Joan whispered, and waved the woman away. She began to dress herself in a sensible brown wool gown and a heavy tunic of russet color. Practical. Warm.

Letitia stirred and opened her eyes, obviously taking a moment to remember who Joan was. "Oh." Then, in a different tone, she said, "Oh, I'm sure we can find something better than that for you, Lady Joan." She began to scramble out of bed, but Joan waved her back.

"These are fine. I'll be going out, so something warm is welcome."

Letitia huddled back under the blankets and furs. "If you're going out, you need more. I'll lend you my fur cloak. I insist."

Joan thought of arguing but didn't. It was a loan only. And she rather suspected Lady Blanche would prevent it.

She was tying the woven girdle when Letitia asked, "What happened between you and my brother?"

The question no one else had asked. "You know what happened."

Letitia shook her head. "He's in a strange mood over you."

Joan didn't want to create trouble here. "He considers me under his protection. He doesn't want to hand me back to my uncle."

Letitia pulled a face. "I'd hoped he might have fallen in love with you."

Joan gave a convincing laugh. "Hardly."

"Love has no logic. He looked at you once or twice last night, as if…well, as if."

Joan didn't want this conversation, but it seemed rude to leave. Instead, she posed her own question. "Are you not married, Lady Letitia?"

"I was betrothed, but he died of a festering wound."

Joan's heart missed a beat. It could happen to anyone, great or small. "I'm sorry," she said, but she longed to run to see if Lord Edmund was still healthy.

"So am I. He was a lovely man. I've not met the like."

Caught by her sadness, Joan sat on the bed. "How long ago?"

Letitia rolled onto her back. "Two years. Mother parades rich and handsome men in front of me like prize bulls, but Edmund won't let her push me."

"She wants you happy again."

"She also wants me well married. She takes pride in having well-married offspring. She's not going to like her younger son being entangled with Nicolette de Montelan."

"There's no choice now."

"Is Lady Nicolette strong?"

Joan knew what she was being asked. "Not in that way, but Ed—Lord Edmund said they'd live away from here, at one of his lesser properties."

"And never return. That will be hard for her. And Gerald."

"They made their own fates," said Joan grimly.

Letitia considered her. "Does that mean there's no chance you'll have a similar fate?"

Joan felt her face heat and stood. "Absolutely none."

"Oh." Letitia sat up, huddling coverings around her. "Are you saying that the Golden Lion doesn't attract you in the slightest? That makes you a very unnatural woman."

"That's what he said." Joan considered Lady Letitia's astonishment and laughed. "You're right. There are forces of nature that no one can withstand. Of course, I'm in love with your brother. But I harbor foolish hopes."

With that, she did make her escape.

The castle was strange to her, but she could hardly get lost. In the great hall she helped herself to some of the bread and cheese set out as a breakfast, and sourly regarded the Bethlehem Banner. Two armed guards stood beside it, and in front on his knees, a monk prayed. The passing servants still bowed.

She turned away, trying not to be bitter, but unable to forget that the piece of cloth was the price of everything, and despite his fabulous wealth, it was the one price Edmund de Graves would not, could not, pay.

A young man appeared before her and bowed. A squire, she guessed, but close to knighthood, and with the gilded confidence of wealth and power. "My lady, Lord Edmund would speak with you, if you will."

Her foolish heart couldn't help a little flutter. "Where?"

"In his chamber, Lady."

She almost asked if it were proper, but the squire was not the person to ask, and anyway, Lord Edmund's chamber would not be a private place. She let him lead her back behind the reredos to the private quarters and to a richly carved door. With some wryness, she thought it looked like the door to a shrine except that an armed guard stood outside.

Who, exactly, did they think might attack their lord within his own castle?

The door swung open and she took one step through before halting in amazement. She couldn't help it. She had never seen a room as magnificent as this.

What walls were not hung with brilliant tapestries were painted with flowers and animals. All the structural woodwork was carved and painted, as was every piece of furniture. Two windows lit the room, glazed in plain and colored glass and, between them, a roaring fire was set in the wall. Uncle Henry had a fireplace set into the wall of his chamber, but it easily belched smoke. This one had a hood that stuck out into the room—a hood of plaster, she thought, for stone could not be so finely detailed—sweeping up to the ceiling.

It seemed to ensure that all the smoke went up the chimney and outside so that the room was pleasantly warm without smoke at all.

And on the floor at her feet, halting her, lay a thick woven cloth in a rich design of red, blue and cream.

There were many people in the room in addition to Edmund, who was on his dais bed, and they were all looking at her. They were all also standing on the precious cloth. Swallowing, she walked onto it, too, and curtsied. "You wished to speak to me, my lord."

His bed was like the resting place of a precious relic, carved and decorated like everything else here and hung with heavy cloth woven in rich colors. Thick furs lay folded near the end, for show, no doubt. No one would ever need furs in a room this warm.

"If it please you, Lady Joan, sit." He indicated a chair by the side of his bed and the squire stepped forward to assist her to it.

As she brought her bedazzlement under control, she noted who was in the room. The squire, two menservants, a rosy-cheeked page, a monk at a desk writing on a long sheet of parchment and a black-robed figure who might be a doctor.

A chair, she thought, as she settled into it. And padded, too. Before coming here she had never sat on anything but a bench or stool. Was it as great an honor as it seemed, or just part of the astonishing luxury of Mountgrave?

Uncomfortably aware of an audience, she said, "I hope you are well, my lord."

"Healing wounds hurt, Lady Joan, but it appears I am healing, so I have no complaint."

"It might injure you to ride today."

"Dr. Hildebrand has sewn me up quite firmly and thinks I will not split again."

She could imagine the pain, past, present and future, but supposed that even great wealth had not spared him from it in his life. And despite the pain awaiting her, she did want this over. This place was too rich, too grand, for her, and Edmund was too great a temptation. Even now, she wanted to lean toward him, to touch his hair, to soothe his hurts, to be touched, to be soothed....

She sat straight, hands in lap. "You had something you wished to say to me, my lord?"

"Last night, you said you had something you wished to say to me, Lady Joan."

Her heart sank. In the sillier parts of her mind she'd been thinking he had summoned her because he needed to, because, despite hopelessness, he wanted to see her one more time. Instead, he was just courteously granting her request for audience.

She glanced around. These were doubtless his trusted people, and he must carry on his private business in front of them all the time, but she said, "I request privacy, my lord."

A mere gesture of his hand, and everyone bowed out of the room. Joan watched the door close, then looked back at him. "It must get very wearying."

He laughed shortly. "And yet it is all I know."

He was reclining against full pillows and wearing a

red robe under the covers. His thick golden hair waved down to his broad shoulders, and seeing him leisurely for the first time in daylight, Joan discovered that his eyes were not the clear blue she'd imagined, but a blue muted by gray and perhaps even by green. Softer, subtler, and somehow comforting.

"What are you thinking?" he asked.

"I think I heard an unspoken 'you wretched woman' after that, my lord." As his lips twitched, she said, "I was thinking that the Golden Lion should have piercing blue eyes. I like your eyes better."

She sat to his left, so when he extended a hand to her it was without pain. Knowing it was unwise, she put her hand into his, and at first contact, at the gentle curl of his fingers around hers, something inside cracked and melted.

That wasn't good. It melted into threatened tears.

"Don't," she said, and pulled her hand free. "Don't."

"Not even a touch?"

"If I'm any judge, your lady mother will be here as soon as she learns that we're alone. I would not like to distress her."

After a frowning moment, he leaned back. "As you wish, my wise and foolish virgin. What did you want to say to me? Something about the banner, I assume."

She saw him brace to refuse, to refuse to bend, to break his oath, and she almost held back her words. He would never understand.

"Tell me, Joan. At the very least, give me your honest tongue."

That made her color flare embarrassingly, but she

met his eyes. "I know this will seem a madness to you, but when I looked at the banner hanging in the hall, it seemed to me like Christ hanging on the Cross."

He frowned. "The frame is supposed to suggest the Cross. It contains fragments of the true Cross."

She shook her head. "That's not what I mean. It seemed…it seemed trapped there. Hung there. Tortured." She stopped, hearing her words sound crazier by the moment.

"Joan, a banner is designed to be hung. It must be the strain of this—"

"And then you said that you lock it away," she continued, determined to spit it out and be done with it. "Like a prisoner in a dungeon."

"It's a *chapel*. It's more splendid than this room! It's a small monastery, with chambers beside for the monks who care for it and pray before it."

"And if you were locked away in here, my lord, would it be luxury or dungeon?"

He moved both hands, then winced and ran only one through his hair. "As you said yourself, Joan, it's a piece of cloth. What do you want me to do with it? Don't tell me. Burn it."

She sat resolutely silent.

"It has to be guarded. You must see that." After a moment he said, almost yelled, *"What do you want me to do?"*

The door opened and his mother glided in, trailing expensive sleeves, hems and veil. "Edmund? Is something the matter?"

Joan rose and curtsied, prepared to be thrown out.

"No, Mother, though I was speaking to Lady Joan privately." It was clearly a reproof, and the lady stiffened.

"I heard you shouting, my dear."

"Then I was shouting at Lady Joan privately." His lips had softened, however, and mother and son shared a loving acceptance of his ridiculous statement.

She walked to the right side of his bed and leaned to brush his forehead. Secretly checking for fever, Joan was sure, as she'd wished to do. He caught his mother's hand in his left and kissed it. "I am well, Mother." Then he added, "I would ask you to do something for me, however."

"Anything, my dear."

"Go to the hall and stand before the banner. Look at it for me."

She straightened, frowning. "I do not need to look at the banner. I have seen it through Christmastide for thirty years."

"Yet that is what I wish you to do for me, Mother. Stand, or kneel if you choose, and look at it for me. For as long as it would take to say twenty Paternosters."

Clearly both puzzled and concerned, Lady Blanche looked at Joan with no kindness at all. "And Lady Joan?"

"Will stay with me."

"It is not proper, Edmund."

"I am in no condition to ravish her, and she is far too sensible to assist me to her ruin."

"Are you, indeed?" Lady Blanche asked Joan.

"I fear so, Lady Blanche."

After a startled moment, a touch of humor twitched at Lady Blanche's thin lips, and perhaps a prickle of womanly connection passed between them. But then she said, "I will do as you wish, Edmund, though it is folly," and swept out.

Joan and Edmund looked at each other, and for lack of alternative, she sat down again. She couldn't bear much more of his company, however. It was like starving at a feast.

"If times were right, would you be my wife?" he asked abruptly.

"We have not known each other long enough."

He didn't misunderstand. "Yet we have."

She gestured at his room. "I could not cope with this."

"You could cope with anything."

"You overestimate me, my lord."

"I don't think so. But if you wish, I would have it peeled back to wood and stone and whitewashed like a nun's cell."

She looked down at her clasped hands. "That would be a shame. Don't do this."

In silence she heard the fire crackle and the distant life of his bustling castle, and tried to estimate the length of time needed to say twenty Paternosters.

She looked up. "What do you expect your mother to say when she returns?"

"If I'd known, I would not have sent her."

"If you'll be able to ride shortly, you could have gone to the banner yourself."

"But I know what I want to see."

"I don't understand—"

They were interrupted by an autocratic child's voice beyond the door. "We wish to enter!"

The rumble was doubtless the guard. The response to whatever he said was, "But it's Christmastide!" and a wail that seemed to be a second voice.

Edmund pulled a face, but there was a smile in it. "If you please, Lady Joan, go and admit them."

Puzzled, she went to open the door to see the guard confronted by two blond children—a firm-chinned girl of about seven, and a much younger child in a trailing gown, thumb in mouth. They both instantly ran past the guard toward the bed, crying, "Father!"

Joan whirled. "Don't leap on him!"

Children. Why had she never thought that he must have children from his first marriage?

The girl turned with haughty anger, but then flushed. "We weren't going to," she said, but it was clearly a lie.

"You can sit on the bed if you're careful," Edmund said. "It's my right arm and my left leg that are wounded. And no bouncing on top of me for a while."

The girl lifted the younger child up onto her father's left side, and the toddler snuggled against him, thumb in mouth. Secure. The girl sat more sedately on his right-hand side, but Joan sensed she wanted to cuddle, too.

Motherless children, but at least they had one parent they loved and trusted, and who loved them.

"I will go," she said, but he shook his head.

"Wait until my mother returns. Come and meet my

children. Anna, give Lady Joan your best curtsy, for she saved my life. Remi, you may stay where you are, but say thank-you to her."

The little boy extracted his thumb and said, "Thank you, my lady," then shoved it back in again.

Anna, who strongly reminded Joan of Lady Blanche, made a perfect curtsy. "We truly are most grateful to you, Lady Joan, and also that you will be the means to save Uncle Gerald from the wicked de Montelans."

Joan flicked one glance at Edmund, but then smiled at the girl. "I am happy to be able to prevent bloodshed, Lady Anna."

The girl returned to her seated study of her father, and, lacking an alternative, Joan went back to her chair. The boy's head turned, watching her curiously.

"The de Montelans are not wicked, Anna," Edmund said, though it sounded like a struggle.

Anna's straight spine straightened farther. "Father, of course, they are!"

"But Lady Joan's mother is a de Montelan. And your Uncle Gerald is hoping to marry the Lady Nicolette de Montelan."

She frowned over that. "Then it is just the men of the de Montelan family who are wicked."

"Adults make a great mess of things sometimes, Anna. It is good to be faithful to your family's interests, but rarely is one group of people better or worse than another."

It was perhaps as well that Lady Blanche returned then, brow furrowed. She smiled at the sight of her grandchildren, however, and Anna went to hug her.

The wicked de Graves. A happy, loving family.

The wicked de Montelans. Even if Lord Henry was older and sterner, still it was a happy, loving family in its own way. She could even believe that he'd tried to bend to secure Nicolette's happiness.

How sad this all was.

"Well, Mother?" Edmund asked.

She sat in another chair, one closer to the fire than the bed, and Anna leaned against her. "What do you want me to say?"

"Whatever you wish. That is why I sent you with no guidance."

She sighed, staring into nowhere. "It is strange. I have never looked long and closely at the banner since I came here as a bride, and I do not recall what I thought then. But now…" She looked at her son. "At first I was impatient, thinking it a waste of time. Slowly, however, I began to really see it. It is a sorry piece of cloth by now, but that is not the point. It seems out of place on that huge, ornate holder. Perhaps we need to build it something smaller, more delicate…."

She looked at him, clearly searching for a hint whether she was saying the right things or not. Joan knew he was deliberately not giving any response. But what was the purpose of this? Even if his mother's reaction was the same as hers, what could he do other than give the banner a prettier frame and perhaps not lock it away from sight for most of the year.

"What's going on, Father?" Anna asked, standing straight, a slight edge of panic in her voice.

"It's all right," Edmund said. "Nothing terrible is

happening. We are all just thinking about things long ignored. Mother, was there anything else?"

Lady Blanche frowned almost in exasperation. "It sounds foolish to say, Edmund, but the banner did not feel *happy*. I found myself wondering whether Christ Himself would like a holy relic that had touched the place of His birth being the cause of so much enmity. It wouldn't be the first time, however," she added. "The Crusades themselves have been fought over Christ's holy places."

"True, but this is our relic, and our responsibility."

"You cannot give it up," Lady Blanche stated.

"Father!" Anna exclaimed, but he raised his hand.

"Anna, this is not for you to debate. I must think on it."

"But *Father!*"

"No, Anna. You must take Remi now. I will spend more time with you later, after I have returned Lady Joan to her family."

Lady Blanche rose and shepherded the reluctant children away. She glanced once at Joan but did not herd her out, too.

Joan stood on her own. "I will leave you to think. I know there's nothing you can do, so I do regret putting this extra burden on you, my lord. I felt that I had to speak."

He nodded. "I understand." He held out his left hand again, and she put hers into it, letting him pull her closer so he could kiss it. "Joan of Hawes, whatever happens today and in the future, know that I am honored to have met you. Never let the world cow you into silence."

Surrendering to folly, she leaned forward and lightly kissed his lips. "I'll do my best. God guide and keep you, Edmund."

Then she fled the room.

She found the castle strangely unaffected by the turmoil she was experiencing, though she gathered some traditional outdoor games had been postponed because of the planned meeting with the de Montelans at Bethlehem Field. In the bailey horses were being groomed and prepared to make a magnificent show. A number of men were already in armor surcoated in the livery of the Golden Lion. They were eating and drinking festive food in high spirits, though one or two glanced at her with casual compassion.

They knew her fate.

She supposed it was like this when men had prepared to take the sacrificial virgin out to the dragon. In this case, Saint George was not going to ride to the rescue.

She was surprised when Lady Blanche found her and insisted she return to the hall and eat, but the woman didn't say anything of importance, either about her son or the banner. She didn't protest, however, when Lady Letitia insisted that Joan wear her fur cloak.

As Joan left the hall she turned to look one last time at the banner, surprised to find that pity for it had driven out anger. Both emotions were foolish, she told herself as she went down the stairs into the bailey. It was an inanimate object.

It was men who had made it what it was, and men—and women—who suffered.

CHAPTER EIGHT

A FINE DUN PALFREY had been prepared for her to ride, and Joan appreciated the quality of the horse, though she was surprised to be given one almost as big as Thor. The destrier waited beside, caparisoned magnificently and summoning a smile by the way he preened, knowing himself to be the center of attention.

Astride her tall mount, she watched Edmund emerge from the hall. When he let two men carry him down the stairs, she knew he was not recovered enough for the venture. He hobbled between the servants to Thor and she couldn't help but say, "You shouldn't be doing this."

"It has to be done, and I'll be better once I'm on the horse."

Getting him there, however, even with a mounting block was neither easy nor painless, and by the time he was in the saddle, he looked pallid.

"Edmund—"

"I do not need another woman to nag me about this!"

Joan literally bit her tongue to suppress words. At least this journey could be accomplished at a walk, and his saddle was a jousting saddle, high in the front and back and shaped to cradle his thighs. Even if he fainted, he'd probably stay on.

He wore no armor, but a magnificent crimson gown embroidered with gold thread. This, clearly, was not an occasion for subtlety. She realized she was the only person not glittering in the red and gold of the de Graves.

They moved out in procession, banner-carrying foot soldiers at the front, then herself and Edmund, side by side, with about two dozen armed squires and knights behind. She watched him anxiously. Perhaps he'd been right; his color slowly returned, and she sensed his pain lessened. He held Thor's reins in his left hand, however, and she suspected he'd rather his right was in a sling rather than resting on his thigh.

Needing to break the silence, she said, "Your children are delightful. Are there just the two?"

"My rare visits. Though Catherine was with child when she died."

"How sad."

He shrugged, and indeed, what was there to say about the hazards of life?

"Will your brother and Nicolette be able to marry?"

"It ought to be so, but first I must see Lord Henry and try to judge his mood. He and I have only met once since my father died." He glanced sideways at her. "You do not look comfortable."

"I could have wished for something smaller to ride."

"I didn't think you'd be happy bobbing along at my knee."

"No," she said. "No, I wouldn't. Thank you."

"No matter what happens today, Joan, I want you to know that I'm going to have the banner treated differently. And I will continue to work for peace between the families. Surely in time we can break the shackles we have put on each other."

"I will pray for it."

"And I promise you, Joan, that my sons will not have to swear an oath on the matter."

"I wish such an oath did not burden you."

"Oaths have their uses. Will you swear to me to try to make the richest use of your life, your courage and your wit?"

She quirked her brows at him. "I think my courage will be well used, and soon, but my wit is best kept in check."

He tightened his lips and looked away. Perhaps she shouldn't have said it, but there was no point hiding from unpleasant truths.

They rode the rest of the way in silence, except for jingling harness and falling hoof. The day was cold but lovely, with clear blue sky and sunshine gilding frosted furrows and bare trees. Crows cawed as they flew from their dark nests high in the trees, but no birds sang until a robin fluttered to a hawthorn branch and trilled at them.

The Bethlehem Field was outlined by a thick hedge all around with only two breaks, facing each other. When they arrived, the de Montelans were already on the other side, banners flying, ready to enter.

Edmund raised his left hand and made a gesture. His

squire rode up alongside. "Lady Joan and I go in alone."

The squire wheeled to pass the message back, and Joan went alone with him into the large, open space. They were sworn to peace here, so she hoped all would be all right, though clearly in the past the whole parties had entered.

She saw some consternation among her uncle's people, but eventually, Uncle Henry rode in, every bit as magnificently dressed as Edmund, only in the de Montelan's blue and gold. He was leading another horse by the reins. Gerald de Graves's hands were tied in front of him and to the pommel of his saddle.

It had never occurred to Joan to try to escape. Would that be held against her, too?

They met in the center, and her uncle's glare made Joan shiver inside the thick fur. Noble sacrifice was all very well, but in the end it was real and frightening.

As the two lords greeted each other, she looked at Gerald de Graves. He was lighter built than his brother, but nearly as handsome, even dungeon-dirty and bruised. He met her eyes sympathetically but sadly. He gained his freedom here, but not what he truly wanted—Nicolette.

Lord Henry was holding out the horse's reins to Edmund, but Edmund said, "If you will, Lord Henry, I would speak with you."

The reins were pulled back out of reach. "You break your word?"

"Never. I wish to speak of more important things. The banner, for one."

A smile touched Lord Henry's lips. A hungry one. "The de Graves have come to their senses?"

"You know we swear an oath never to give the banner to the de Montelans."

"And we swear an oath never to rest while it remains in the hands of the de Graves."

Joan had to suppress a sigh.

The silence lingered so long that she thought it was all over, but then Edmund said, "Lord Henry, do you wish this feud to continue, generation after generation, poisoning this area with enmity, costing lives and happiness?"

"I do not. But I cannot accept the banner being in your unworthy hands."

Joan sensed Edmund taking a special breath. "What if it were in neither of our hands?"

"Edmund, no!" Sir Gerald exclaimed.

Lord Henry's horse stepped back, clearly stirred by some unwary movement. *"Destroy it?"*

"No. What I propose, Lord Henry, is that the de Graves and the de Montelans build a monastery here on Bethlehem Field, and house the banner in it. We would both swear to protect it, and to never try to move it from this place, and here it could be reverenced by any who wished to come."

Lord Henry looked around, frowning, and Joan bit her lip. It was a brilliant solution, but would her uncle agree? He'd never struck her as a quick-witted or flexible man, but he wasn't stupid, and she suspected he truly was as weary of the enmity as Edmund was. And he knew Nicolette loved Gerald de Graves.

The still moment was broken by pounding hooves, and everyone turned to see a horse galloping toward the field. The pale gold flying hair could only belong to Nicolette. The horse soared over the hedge and raced foaming right up to them. Joan had never suspected that her cousin was such a magnificent rider.

"Father!" she declared, "I must go with Gerald."

Joan saw a wince of exasperation on Edmund's face, but was herself tempted to wild laughter. Would nothing about this go according to plan?

"I left you locked up, daughter, where you belong!"

"I will not be kept from this, because it concerns me, Father. You know I love Gerald. If you will not permit our marriage, I must still go with him." She raised her chin, though she'd turned deathly pale. "I am carrying his child."

Lord Henry turned fiery red and swung on the bound man, fist rising.

"Stop!" Edmund's authority halted the older man. "I cannot interfere without starting a bloody battle here, Lord Henry, but I will not let you strike my brother. Save for the feud, he and Nicolette would be happily married, and if you consent to my plan, they can still be so. Proof of better days."

Lord Henry glared around, clearly teetering on the edge of bloodshed for bloodshed's sake. Nicolette extended her hand to him. "Father, I love you, but I love Gerald, too. And now, because of my sin, I *must* go to him. Pray heaven, I do not have to lose you."

Lord Henry's lips wobbled through his glower. "Sin indeed, daughter," he said. Though he doubtless intended to growl, it sounded simply unhappy. "But at least you didn't soil our tradition by playing the Virgin."

Joan stared at him. She had never expected such instant understanding and approval.

"And you, Joan," he said, turning to her. "You did well. But not," he added, voice recovering, "in helping de Graves to escape!"

Joan swallowed and produced Edmund's clever explanation. "I believed your men would kill him, Uncle, and I knew you would not want that."

Lord Henry looked nothing so much as baffled. "I see, I see."

Edmund spoke. "My death or serious injury would certainly have made peace more difficult, Lord Henry. If we do not settle this now, however, such a death might happen, sealing us all in turmoil for yet more generations."

Lord Henry looked between Gerald and his daughter for a moment, and Joan could almost hear him muttering that this man was not worthy of her, but then he dragged Gerald's horse over to Nicolette and put the reins in her hands. "Here, daughter, have him." But he leaned to grasp the startled Gerald's tunic in his hand. "Harm her, neglect her, be unfaithful to her, lad, and there'll be violence that'll make this feud look like May Day."

"I love her, sir," Gerald said.

"Keep it so."

Lord Henry turned his horse. "What now, Lord Edmund?"

"You agree to my plan?"

Lord Henry nodded.

"Then the sooner the building starts, the sooner the banner can be moved. Perhaps by May Day."

Joan couldn't keep silent. "There could be a wooden chapel while the monastery builds. It could be up before the end of Christmastide."

Neither man looked pleased. She suspected Lord Henry glowered just because she had interrupted, but Edmund's frown could be because he'd rather delay the final step. But then he nodded. "It can be so. Lord Henry, will you lend men to help build?"

"To get the banner out of your hands? By Jerusalem, I will! In fact, I and my sons will help in this holy task."

To forestall Edmund stupidly making the same offer, Joan said, "Lord Edmund is wounded. But Sir Gerald will doubtless help. Perhaps he and Nicolette can be married—"

"Joan," said Edmund.

"Joan!" bellowed her uncle.

Her uncle continued, "Hold your tongue! I don't know what imp has invaded you, niece, the way you speak out on men's matters!" He leaned forward and grabbed her reins by the bit, drawing her horse away from Thor. "Come. And you, too, Nicolette. Until you marry, you'll pretend to be a proper maid!"

Nicolette had untied Gerald, and they were both off their horses, kissing and exploring each other's tear-damp faces in a way that brought an aching lump to Joan's throat.

There was no true barrier now between her and

Edmund, but clearly he'd realized that she was unsuited to be the bride of the Golden Lion. He was quite right, too. She'd be miserable in such a situation.

As she was led away, however, he spoke one last time. "Lord Henry."

Her uncle looked back and Edmund continued, "Of your kindness, do not punish Lady Joan for her adventures."

Her uncle's look at her was sharp and questioning, but he said, "If she keeps her tongue mild and respectful, she'll have no hurt from me."

CHAPTER NINE

THE FIRST REACTION AT Woldingham was consternation, but soon happiness bubbled up, along with a subtle warmth and relaxation that showed how deeply the frost of enmity had cut. Though resentful at first, her male cousins took their father's point of view, and threw themselves enthusiastically into the building of the wooden chapel, seeing it as a victory over the de Graves.

Mountgrave would no longer have the banner!

She wondered how everyone was taking it there. She was sure some would see it as surrender, as weakness of some sort, but Edmund's status as the Golden Lion would likely carry him over that. As for herself, she worked hard at banishing folly. Despite an unexpected friendship, there was nothing lasting between her and Lord Edmund de Graves.

Lust, a part of her whispered. She had to accept that, yes, there was lust. That wasn't enough, however. She wasn't trained to be a great lady, and he was doubtless wise not to tempt her with the notion.

The last thing she wanted was for anyone to guess at the foolish part of her mind, the part that would marry Edmund de Graves if asked and hope that a clever tongue could make it all work.

Meanwhile she tried hard to behave well, did her best to enjoy Christmas, and threw herself into her cousin's ecstatic preparations for her wedding. Gerald even visited, riding into Woldingham one day, unescorted, testing the truce.

Though to begin with, the air boiled with tension, Nicolette's warm greeting and sensible Aunt Ellen's welcome brought it down to simmering point. Soon, though rather hesitantly, the castle moved again, accepting the enemy in their midst.

Joan, however, had the task of chaperoning the two during the meeting. She sat in a corner, sewing and trying to ignore their soft murmurs and occasional laughter. At a silence she glanced over and saw them lost in a kiss she doubtless should not permit. But what harm in it?

Except to her.

She and Edmund had not kissed like that, a leisurely kiss that promised aeons. There hadn't been any aeons to promise. She was dreading Twelfth Day, when the wedding would take place, and the banner would be brought at last to neutral territory. Could she survive it without making a fool of herself? After that, she would go home, for what was there to keep her here?

Eventually light faded and Gerald had to leave, though clearly he'd rather have stayed forever. He took Joan's hand and kissed it. "You are a most excellent chaperon, my lady."

"From a suitor's point of view," she said tartly.

Golden as his brother, he was a handsome man who could doubtless charm birds to his hand, but beside Lord Edmund he would pale.

He smiled. "Of course. But if Lady Ellen had wanted more decorum, she would have stayed herself. It's a clever woman who knows when the horse has left the stable."

Joan gave him a severe look. "I'll have you know, Sir Gerald, that I consider you a scoundrel for seducing Nicolette into what could have been disaster."

He glanced at his beloved. "Is it always the man at fault?"

Nicolette blushed, but Joan said, "It is always the woman who pays the price."

Gerald looked at her, head cocked. "Edmund said you were a very sensible virgin. I see what he meant."

And then he left.

Nicolette said, "Joan? What's the matter?"

Joan laughed it off, but she could have wept. A sensible virgin. It was likely to be her epitaph, and she'd like to die soon if that was the sum of Lord Edmund de Graves's assessment of her.

IT SNOWED A LITTLE on the way to the wedding, but cleared to crisp gray by the time the de Montelan party approached the Bethlehem Field with its new wooden chapel to one side. The center of the field was left open for the monastery that would rise there soon.

The red and gold of the de Graves was approaching on the other side, but around, the ordinary folk hovered, keen to see this great day, and to see the Bethlehem Banner, but ready to flee at the slightest sign of trouble.

Joan didn't blame them. All around her, beneath handsome surcoats and cloaks, armor and weapons jingled. Most jaws were tense, most eyes watchful. No one truly believed that today could pass as planned, without violence. She hardly did herself.

This time both parties passed through the openings and into the field. The armed men formed opposing ranks, and the principal families rode to meet in the middle. Joan noticed Lady Ellen and Lady Blanche bow to each other with just as much caution as the men.

She scrupulously did not look at Edmund. She couldn't risk it.

Then the de Graves forces split, and through the middle passed the six monks, singing the Te Deum, the two front ones bearing the banner on a simple holder. Just in front of Joan, Lord Henry heaved himself off his horse and down on one knee. In the next moment, all his men followed, and then the men of de Graves.

Joan couldn't help but look at Edmund, but by then he was off and kneeling, and she couldn't tell what it had cost him.

The monks passed into the chapel, and the men rose. The ladies were helped down, and the two families followed. The air crackled with danger, and Joan saw that her male cousins all had their hands on their swords. Edmund and Gerald did not.

A good job had been done on the building. It was simple but straight and sturdy, and the main posts and beams had been carved with crosses. The walls were painted white, and ample long windows let in light. They let in cold, too, but that could not be helped. They also allowed those outside to glimpse events inside, which was doubtless wise.

On the end wall behind the altar, a frame had been prepared in which the banner could hang, with shutterlike doors that could be closed over it in harsh weather. The monks carefully placed it there and knelt before it.

Someone had clearly put together some kind of ceremony, for now Lord Henry and Edmund walked forward and knelt behind the monks. Edmund still favored his leg, but didn't seem to be badly troubled by it.

One monk turned and held out a crucifix to them. Edmund first and then Lord Henry, they vowed to guard the banner here, to never try to remove it, and to cease the feud, putting all lingering hurts aside. They bound their families and their heirs to this cause.

When they stood, a silence settled, as if no one could quite believe that it had happened. But then tentative smiles broke, someone laughed and, outside, people began to cheer. Aunt Ellen and Lady Blanche shared a genuine smile.

Lord Henry's priest came forward then, and guided Gerald and Nicolette through their betrothal and wedding vows, blessing their union, though his brow twitched when he said the part about going forth to multiply. Nicolette blushed a fiery red.

When the couple ran out into the fresh air, however, hand in hand, clearly nothing clouded their happiness.

Despite everything, neither family had quite been willing to attend a wedding feast in the other's castle, so food was laid here on trestles, and barrels of ale stood ready. There was plenty for everyone.

Joan nibbled a piece of pork and looked around at playing children and chatting adults content, despite her own unhappiness, with her work. There was lingering wariness, but the seeds of peace had been sown. She had created some of the seed, and it would be a worthy harvest.

As the ladies and gentlemen prepared to return home, leaving the remains of the feast to the peasants, she stepped into the chapel to contemplate the banner one last time. A monk was already in the first vigil there, and a number of simple people knelt in prayer. She stayed back so as to not disturb them. The cloth was still as timeworn and stained, but she fancied it did look more content in this simple place, a cause of harmony not strife.

She turned at last to leave—and came face-to-face with Edmund.

"Oh."

Dimples showed. "Is that your most eloquent commentary on this all?"

Her throat ached with tears, but she must not show it. "You startled me. It went very well, didn't it?"

"Exceedingly. This is all your work, you know."

She wanted to escape, but he blocked the door. "You came up with this solution."

"But you lit the way." He captured her hand. "I was going to wait, but I sense that you are about to flee."

"You're blocking the door."

"I am clever, sometimes. But I mean I fear you plan to leave from this area."

She tugged her hand, but could not free it. "It is time. I came to be companion to Nicolette." She looked back at the people in prayer. "My lord, this is not the place…"

"It is exactly the place." He captured her other hand. She noted that his arm must be healing well. "Joan, I had to wait until this proved successful."

"Wait?" she queried, looking up at him.

"I want you to know that about me."

She felt as if her mind was hopelessly tangled. "Know what?"

"That I cannot always do what I most want to. That I have to put head before heart."

"Heart?" She heard herself sounding like a complete fool.

"When we left the castle to exchange you for Gerald I wanted to speak then. To tell you that I wanted a chance to win you as my wife. But I couldn't. If I couldn't make peace, we couldn't wed."

Joan just stared at him, trying not to breathe too hard and blow this all awry.

"I've fought over twelve days not to send you a message. I snarled at Gerald because he could risk visiting Woldingham and I could not. But now it seems as if this has worked. Incredibly, perhaps we have peace." He went to one knee.

"Oh, don't!" She'd seen him wince. She glanced behind and saw the peasants had turned to stare. A woman grinned at her.

"Joan," he said, drawing her attention back to him. "You are a wise virgin. I value the first, but very much wish to change the second."

A laugh escaped her. Someone behind chuckled, and he grinned unrepentantly. "Be my bride. My wife. My truth sayer."

She sank to her knees in front of him. "But not stone thrower?"

"Reserve the stones for our enemies." He let go of her hands and cradled her face, searching her eyes. "Do I have you?"

She covered his hands, part tenderness, part defense. "I don't know how to be Lady of Mountgrave."

"It needs your irreverent style, but my mother will teach you."

"Your mother doesn't like me!"

"My mother is waiting anxiously for me to tell her I haven't made a mess of this. She was only worried about yet more trouble with the de Montelans. Say yes, Joan. Please." He winced. "My leg feels tortured."

She leaped to her feet and helped him up, scolding. "How could you be so foolish! There was no need to kneel to me."

He captured her and kissed her. "Yes, there was. But if I'd not thought you'd run away, that was another reason to wait a week or two."

"What did you think I was going to do? Go straight to a convent and take vows?"

"I would put nothing past you. Or you might have seized the first lazy old man you saw and married him."

She snuggled against his chest, dazzled, dazed—

and slightly scratched by his gold embroidery. She pushed away.

He touched her face with a grimace. "As you see, I will not always be a comfortable husband. You haven't said yes. I cannot change much for you, Joan. I am the Golden Lion and the Lord of Mountgrave. Too many people depend on me."

"I don't want you to change." She reached up to touch his face. "I'm sure there'll be days when I wonder why I fell into this gilded trap, but you make me so happy, Edmund. And you seem happy with me. With *me*."

He turned his head and kissed her palm, then lowered to kiss her lips. "*You* are my most precious treasure, Joan of Hawes. You."

"You're going to make me cry," she said, rubbing her face against his chest—and scratching it again. She pulled free. "Take it off."

After a moment, he grinned, unfastened his belt and struggled out of the long, glittering gown to stand in a simple shirt and braies. "That, at least, I can do." He pulled her into a warm—and painless—embrace.

When they emerged from their kiss, cheers started, and Joan looked around to find every window crowded and a throng behind Edmund. She hid her burning face against his chest, and this time it didn't hurt.

Laughing, he swept up his rich garment and tossed it to his grinning squire, then led her out into the fresh air and smiling faces. His mother beamed, and brought his two children over to be the first to hear the news.

Before going to greet her new family, Joan turned at the last moment and curtsied to the silent banner. "Bless us all, Lord Jesus, de Montelan and de Graves, and all the simple people here. Bless us all forever."

TUMBLEWEED CHRISTMAS
Candace Camp

CHAPTER ONE

THE HOUSE ROSE up from the dry earth, as stark and bleak as the landscape around it. Melinda Ballard stopped the buggy and sat, simply staring at the house, for a long moment. There were no trees around it to soften its lines or shield it from the harsh Panhandle weather. Undoubtedly once white, the sun, dirt and wind had turned it a muted gray, much the color of the chill November sky behind it. Several shutters were missing, and others hung at a slant. Even the wide porch across the front managed to look unwelcoming.

Melinda's heart sank. She had set out this morning buoyed with hope, thinking that she had found a way to earn the money she and Lee needed so badly. She had been at her wit's end yesterday morning when she'd gone into town to buy flour and sugar and the heavy gloves she would need for this winter. The eggs she had taken in to sell, as she did every two days, had hardly put a dent in the bill she'd built up at the store, and Mr. Grissom had told her flatly that he could extend her no more credit. Melinda had turned away, fighting to keep back her tears.

It had been two years since her husband, Robert,

died, and ever since she had been struggling against financial ruin. She hadn't been able to farm their land by herself, even with Lee's help. After all, Lee had been only seven when his father died. She had managed to raise food for them to eat, but not a cash crop. She had had so many debts to pay—not only the costs of Robert's funeral, but also the loan at the bank for seed and expenses that they got every spring and paid off in the fall from their profits, as well as their account at the hardware and grocery stores. Gradually Melinda had had to sell their very small herd of cattle, and even the wagon, plow and mule team, in order to pay off their debts and keep them alive. Now it looked as if they would have to sell the milch cow and chickens, and then what would they have left to sell? Only the land, which Melinda had wanted so desperately to keep for Lee; it was his birthright.

But as she had walked away, blinking back her tears, Mr. Grissom's wife, a kind and sympathetic woman, had hurried after her and told her that "Ol' Daniel MacKenzie" was in need of a cook, if Melinda was interested in work.

Of course she had been interested. She had often tried to think of some way to earn more money than the pitiful amount she got from selling eggs, but there were few jobs for women, and those few, such as taking in laundry or sewing, would have meant buying or renting a house in town, which she couldn't afford to do.

Mrs. Grissom had warned her that she might not find the job to her liking. MacKenzie had a reputation for being difficult to deal with, and it was said that he didn't like women, usually hiring only men to cook for him and the cowhands at the ranch. But Melinda had paid no attention to that. What did it matter if the old man was grumpy and bad-tempered? Her own father had had a volatile temper, and she'd always been able to stand toe-to-toe with him and argue until they both gave up—laughing, as often as not. In fact, there had been times in her marriage to Robert when she had almost missed those fiery exchanges with her father. She and Robert had grown up friends long before they'd fallen in love and gotten married, and they had rarely fought.

Mrs. Grissom had given Melinda directions to the MacKenzie place, which lay several miles west of town, and had even lent her the Grissoms' buggy to drive out there. This morning Melinda had dressed in a plain, serviceable dark brown blouse and skirt and skinned her hair back into a tight braid, which she wound in a knot atop her head. When she'd looked in the mirror, she had been appalled. She knew the hairstyle wasn't attractive on her, but she hadn't realized how much her dark brown hair had lost its luster during the past year or so. Once it had gleamed, golden highlights glinting within it, but now it just looked plain and dull. And the bare hairstyle, lacking any softening effect, pointed out how thin and worn her face had become. They hadn't had enough to eat for some time, and she had lost weight, particularly in her face. As a result, her large, expressive gray eyes looked sad and too big, and her color was poor, no longer strawberries-

and-cream. There were lines of worry etched on her forehead and around her eyes and mouth. She was twenty-nine, but she appeared years older.

She had reminded herself that that was the way she wanted to look. A sober, practical appearance was best when applying for this sort of job. Prettiness or youth would be a detriment, making an employer think that she was inexperienced or incapable, or even that she would be available to his advances. She had to avoid that. Let him think she was older and unattractive. Still, she hadn't been able to suppress a pang at how much she had lost her looks. Once she had been considered pretty.

She had shaken off her mood and driven to the Mac-Kenzie ranch, hopeful that her money problems had been solved and that she and Lee would have a better life. But now, looking at the house, Melinda's heart sank. It looked so desolate, so cold. She suspected that its bleak exterior was a reflection of the owner's personality. She had never met the man, but over the years she had heard things about him, and now they all came flooding into her brain: he hated people, and women in particular; he was mean and angry and harsh; he had a tongue like vinegar and didn't hesitate to use it on whoever displeased him. He wasn't married and he had no children; Melinda had heard that it was because no woman could stand to live with him. She'd also heard that it was because he disliked people so much that he didn't even want a family.

It might be horrible to work for him, worse than anything she'd ever known. Melinda hesitated, her hands clenching and unclenching around the reins. Then she sighed and clucked to the horse, slapping the reins lightly across its back. Why was she worrying about whether she should go on? She had no choice. She was more desperate for the job than MacKenzie was for a cook. Without the money it would bring in, she would have to sell Lee's land, or they wouldn't survive the winter. And she was determined not to do that; the half-section of land was Lee's only inheritance.

She drove the small buggy up to the house and jumped down, tying the horse to the hitching rail in front of the porch. Up close, the house looked even less inviting. She walked up the three shallow steps to the porch and knocked on the door. There was no answer. She waited, then knocked again.

Melinda shivered. It had been cold in the buggy, but at least the vehicle had protected her from most of the wind. But now the freezing north wind whipped around the corner of the house and cut right through her. She had worn Robert's old coat over her dress, having cut up her own woolen cloak to make Lee warm pants and a shirt for the winter. The too-big coat hung halfway to her knees and down over her hands, and she had the collar turned up around her throat, but even its warmth wasn't enough to combat the chill.

She sighed and turned away, rubbing her arms in an effort to warm up. He wasn't home. She'd driven all this way, even borrowed a buggy and horse, and it had been for nothing. She glanced around. There was a small frame house to the side and back of the big house, as well as a barn, a corral and a few sheds. Farther away, past the barn, was a long, narrow building, which she presumed to be the bunkhouse for the cowboys, and across from it lay another house. That was probably the foreman's house, she thought. MacKenzie obviously had a big spread. But nowhere did she see a sign of people.

Melinda started down the steps toward the buggy, her spirits low. She glanced at the small rise behind the house. There was a windmill at the top of the little hill, positioned to catch the full force of the wind. But the blades of the windmill were not turning, and there was a man working high up on the platform. Melinda brightened. Perhaps it was Mac-Kenzie—or at least someone who could tell her where he was!

Quickly she crossed the yard and climbed the hill to the base of the windmill. She looked up at the man working on it. At that distance and with his face shadowed by his hat, she could see nothing of his features. "Hello?" she called, and the wind snatched away her voice. She cupped her hands around her mouth and tried again. "Hello!"

The man looked down, and though she could not see his face, impatience was evident in his posture, even in the way he turned his head. "Yeah?"

"I'm looking for a Mr. Daniel MacKenzie."

"You got him." His voice was rough and loud, whipped by the wind.

Melinda hesitated. Why didn't he come down so they could talk like normal people? It was difficult to discuss anything shouting back and forth like this. "Uh, I understand you're in need of a cook."

He cupped his ear in a pantomime of deafness. "Couldn't hear you!"

Irritation stirred in Melinda. "I said, I've come about the job of cook!"

"I don't hire women." Daniel MacKenzie stared at the woman below, his mouth pulled into a grimace. Silently he cursed the cook who had quit weeks ago. It was such a damn fool waste of his time to find a replacement. But he had to feed his men, and his foreman's silly wife was digging in her heels about cooking for all of them any longer. If he didn't get someone soon, he just might lose Will, and Will was the best foreman Daniel had ever had.

Melinda's chin came up. She would not back down, no matter how gruff and rude this man was. She had to have this job. She was determined to fight for it. "The way I hear it, you don't have much choice."

She had him there. MacKenzie frowned. Women housekeepers and cooks were trouble. He'd found that out years ago. They cried when you complained about the quality of their work and got a stubborn, muley look on their faces when you gave them orders. Worst of all, if they weren't too old, they got ideas about making the position of housekeeper into the permanent one of wife. Daniel wasn't about to give in to that, of course, but he hated the bother of avoiding their maneuvers and hints and traps. Almost as bad was the fact that if the woman was attractive, he had sometimes felt the stirrings of desire and been tempted to take her into his bed. But that sort of thing could prove to be just as entangling as marriage and wasn't the impersonal, clean relationship he wanted with his housekeeper. Sex was something to be had with the women of the night in Amarillo, a matter of money exchanged for services rendered, with no involvements or pain.

He considered the woman below him. At this distance it was difficult to see her clearly, but she looked neither young nor attractive. Her shape was bulky, her clothes plain and dark, and her face was pinched and colorless. As she'd gazed up at him, her bonnet had fallen off to hang down her back, and he could see her dark hair pinned up tightly in a fashion that aroused not the slightest interest in seeing it down or feeling it glide through his fingers. She seemed a plain and practical sort, not the kind to tempt a man or to try to inveigle him into marriage. She could be a hard worker who would stick to her own business and let him be.

"I'm considered a very good cook," Melinda went on. "You could give me a try, let me cook something and see how it tastes. I can also keep house."

He frowned. Frankly, he was desperate. He couldn't afford to be choosy. Besides, she was willing to clean the house, which his male cook had refused to do. "All right," he said reluctantly. "I'll hire you to cook and take care of the house—as a trial, to see how you do."

Melinda sagged with relief. For a moment she had been afraid that he would say no. And no matter how cold and lonely this house seemed, or how unpleasant he was, or how sure she was that she wouldn't enjoy working here, she had to have the money. "Thank you. You won't regret it."

He grunted, a sound expressive of doubt. "We'll see." He gestured with the wrench in his hand. "I want to make one thing clear—I'm a bachelor, and I like it that way. I've got no plans to marry, and if you're thinking about trying, you might as well forget it."

Melinda stared. The gall, the conceit, of this man! As though she would chase him, trying to get him to marry her! She set her fists on her hips and glared at him. "Well, I'm happy the way I am, too. And you can rest assured that if I were hunting for a husband, you wouldn't be in the race."

MacKenzie blinked, taken aback. A chuckle rose unbidden in his throat, and he forced it down. "You can take the little house in the back. You'll start work tomorrow. I'll send one of the hands to move your things. Where are they?"

"The Ballard farm, southeast of here. It's on the road to the McClure place."

MacKenzie nodded. "He'll be over first thing tomorrow morning."

He turned back to his work. Melinda stood for a moment, still staring up at him. Daniel MacKenzie had to be the rudest man she'd ever met. He hadn't even asked her name or a thing about her. She cupped her hands around her mouth again and yelled, "My name is Mrs. Ballard!"

MacKenzie glanced down at her as though surprised to find her still there. Then he swung around and went to work without a word. It was the first time—but not the last—that Melinda thought she would take great delight in kicking him in the shins.

MELINDA RETURNED to the small sod hut where she and her son lived. Lee was already home from school. She grabbed his hands and waltzed him around the one-room house, laughing. "I got the job! I got the job!"

She didn't tell him that her future employer was so high-handed and rude that she wondered if she'd be able to work for him. *Imagine just telling her that she would move the next morning, without a single by-your-leave or can-you-do-it!* Apparently Daniel Mac-Kenzie expected his employees to jump whenever he said so. It was no surprise to her that he had so much trouble keeping a cook.

But there was no point in spoiling Lee's happiness. Anyway, she had work and that was the important thing. She would be able to provide for herself and Lee and not have to sell Lee's land. And, perhaps best of all, they could move out of this tiny excuse for a house, built half below the ground and topped with sod. A sod hut might be warm and practical in this part of the country where there were almost no trees, but it smelled of dirt, and there was hardly enough room to turn around in. Sometimes, in the winters, when they were imprisoned in the hut by snow or cold weather, she had thought she would go crazy from the lack of space and privacy.

But now they would have a real house to live in. It might be small, but at least it was made out of wood.

She had peeped inside it before she left MacKenzie's place, and it had two little bedrooms as well as a living area. Not only that, but it would be fun to cook big, healthy meals without having to scrimp and make do and worry about the cost.

So what if Mr. MacKenzie was rude and gruff? She could handle him—and more than him, if it meant Lee would be warm and well-fed.

Lee shouted, "Yippee!" and twirled with her enthusiastically until they were both so dizzy they had to stop. Melinda flopped down onto a chair to catch her breath.

"Oh, Mama!" Lee exclaimed. "We'll live on a ranch! I've always wanted to live on a ranch. Will he let me help with the horses and the cattle? Did you tell him I helped Daddy with the cattle a lot?"

"No. We, uh, had a rather brief conversation. He just said he'd send a man over tomorrow to help us move."

"That soon? Then I won't have to go to school tomorrow?" Lee's face brightened even more. He had little interest in books.

"No, you won't." A frown creased Melinda's brow. She wasn't sure how often he'd go to school after that, either. He would be too far away to walk to school, and he didn't have a horse to ride.

"Where will we live? In ol' MacKenzie's house?"

"That's no way to speak about your elders."

"Yes, ma'am. Well, will we?"

"No. We'll have a house of our own."

"Really? What's it like?"

"Just a small frame house."

Lee grinned, an impish dimple beside his mouth. "Then at least it's above the ground."

Melinda chuckled. Lee knew her feelings on the subject of living half-below the earth. "Yes. And it has its own little porch and a bedroom for each of us."

"Really? Golly! What does MacKenzie's house look like? Is there a big barn? Did you see the horses?"

She shook her head. Horses had become one of Lee's favorite topics of conversation in the past year. One of the McClure boys rode to school on a pinto, and Lee had repeatedly described the horse to her, his voice wistful and admiring. She knew how much he wanted a pony of his own, and it hurt her that they didn't have the money for him to have one. What made it even more painful was that Lee, fully aware of their straitened circumstances, never asked her to buy him a horse. Childlike, he thought that because he didn't ask, she was unaware of how much he ached to own one.

"I didn't see any animals," she said. "But there's a big barn, and a corral. I'm sure you'll see the horses after we live there."

"Do you think he'd let me help take care of them?"

"I don't know. Perhaps, after a while, when he sees how good and careful you are."

Lee continued to talk and ask questions about their new home while Melinda settled down to work. She had to get everything ready to go by the next morning. Fortunately, there wasn't much to pack; they'd had to get rid of the bulk of their possessions four years ago, when they had moved to the Panhandle from their home in East Texas. She had only the bare minimum of pots, pans, dishes and utensils, and she already kept her blankets and linens stored in trunks.

Lee pitched in to help, taking care of most of the evening chores. They ate a quick supper. Melinda watched her son put away his food and smiled. She couldn't ask for a better son, hardworking and obedient—for the most part—yet all boy, too. He was big for his age and already beginning to take on a husky shape. He had done his best to be the man of the family for the past two years. Thank heavens, now he wouldn't have to feel as if he had the weight of the farm resting on his shoulders. He would be free to be a young, curious, active boy.

After supper, Melinda walked the mile to their nearest neighbors, the Hendersons, and asked them to look after her cow and chickens until she could sell them. Then she returned and finished packing. She had to stay up late to do it, working by the light of a wavering kerosene lamp, but at least the next morning, when two of MacKenzie's ranch hands arrived to move her things, she was ready to go. It made her feel as if she had somehow proved something to the nasty-tempered rancher himself.

The two men introduced themselves as Carl and Jimmy, and immediately set about loading her possessions into the large wagon they'd brought. Carl was a friendly sort and kept up a steady stream of conversation the whole time they were loading, telling Melinda how much the men were looking forward to having a lady cook on the premises again. Jimmy, on the other hand, only grinned at her shyly.

Lee ran in and out with the men, holding the door for them and carrying the smaller things. Melinda made coffee, and they drank it with thanks and more assurances on Carl's part that they were glad she was coming to the ranch. They finished the loading quickly, and the four of them climbed into the wagon, the two men and Lee perched on the high seat and Melinda sitting in her rocker, securely surrounded by her possessions, in the back.

The chair faced the rear, so that she was looking at the farm as they drove away. She had lived here for four years. She thought that leaving it ought to bring a tear or two to her eyes, but it didn't. She had never had any love for this farm; her life here had not been enjoyable. She had been raised in East Texas, with its creeks and trees and the wildflowers blanketing the earth in the spring, and she had found this treeless, dusty land ugly and barren. She had seen no beauty in the reddish dirt or the flat landscape broken by gullies like wounds slashing the earth, or the dusty grays and greens of sagebrush, mesquite bushes, cacti and yuccas. She had loved Robert ever since they were children, but he hadn't been enough to assuage her loneliness at being away from all her family and friends. For the first time she and Robert, always friends, had quarreled a lot, and the sweet love of their early marriage had begun to sour. Then she had lost him entirely.

No, she didn't mind leaving here. Her only thought was that she hoped the Hendersons' daughter would remember to look after the animals.

WHEN THEY ARRIVED at the MacKenzie ranch, Melinda climbed down from the wagon and, for the first time, entered her new house. She loved it immediately. There was a hardwood floor beneath her feet, there were normal walls around her, and the ceiling was high above her head. Everything was coated with dust, of course, but with a little cleaning it would be just perfect.

While the men unhitched the wagon and unloaded the furniture, Melinda quickly swept the dust from the floors. That would have to do for the moment, but later she would scrub the floors and wax them until they gleamed, as well as wash down the counters and cabinets in the kitchen. Last, she would attack the windows with ammonia and water. She smiled, looking forward to the work. It had been so long since she'd had a proper house to work on.

She glanced out the window and saw a man emerge from the barn and walk across the yard to the ranch house. His hat was pulled low over his face against the cold, and she could see no more of it than she had been able to yesterday. But she was sure it was Daniel Mac-Kenzie; she recognized his build and the heavy jacket he wore. He looked once toward her house. He must have seen his hired hands carrying in her belongings, but he didn't come over to greet her and welcome her to his ranch. Instead, he kept walking straight into his house.

Rude. Melinda's mouth twisted. It was obvious that he didn't intend to extend even normal courtesy toward her. She believed the stories she had heard about him hating women. He certainly seemed to have taken a dislike to her on sight. For some reason that idea made her even more determined to do an excellent job for him, to show him just how wrong he was.

When her furniture was squared away, Melinda left her house and walked across the side yard to the back door of the big house. She had plenty of work to do in her own house, and she was sure that Mr. MacKenzie wouldn't expect her to start cooking this afternoon, but she wanted to take a look at the kitchen she would be using. She would be in there bright and early tomorrow morning fixing breakfast, and she wanted to know where everything was.

Melinda knocked on the door and, receiving no answer, turned the knob and walked inside. She stopped, her mouth falling open. She stared around her in disbelief. It was a big kitchen, as befitted the house, with an enormous cast-iron stove. But it was in a state that no self-respecting cook would endure. There was dust everywhere, on counters, the table, even the stove. The stove was also slick with grease and there were stains and blackish lumps scattered over it. The cabinets were in almost as poor a condition. She opened the low cabinets and found pots and pans, most of them dusty and more than one looking as if it had not been cleaned properly. She opened the pantry. There was a flour sack, almost empty, and a sugar sack that was crawling with ants. She could find no cornmeal, no baking soda, no baking powder. There were no jars of home-canned vegetables. The Irish potatoes were so old they had twisted roots growing out of them, and the jar of molasses was sticky on the outside, with only an inch of molasses remaining in the bottom. The honey had gone to sugar.

She left the pantry and simply stood, hands on hips, stunned. She couldn't believe that this was the kitchen of a wealthy, important rancher. Poor white trash wouldn't have a larder like that. How could it have gotten into such a condition?

There were footsteps in the hall, and a man entered the room. Melinda got the second shock of the afternoon. The man was Daniel MacKenzie. She recognized the jacket. But this time his hat was off, and she could see the sharp lines of his face, handsome in a rough sort of way. She could see the blue eyes, startlingly pale and bright against the tanned skin. And she could see that "Ol' Daniel MacKenzie" wasn't old at all!

CHAPTER TWO

"WHY YOU'RE NOT OLD!" Melinda gasped without thinking, then clapped her hand to her mouth in embarrassment. Normally she would not have blurted out the first thought in her head, but his appearance had shaken her out of her usual politeness. From the way she had heard him talked about, she had assumed that Daniel MacKenzie was past his prime, but this man was definitely *in* his prime. His hair was thick and black, as was his beard, with only a sprinkling of gray in either one. Although his face was lined and weather-beaten, that was often true of men who spent their lives outdoors. It was obvious that Mr. MacKenzie was no older than forty, if that much. Melinda decided that she should have asked Mrs. Grissom, not just assumed his age. After all, she was a Texan and knew that "ol'" was a common appellation that didn't necessarily have anything to do with age.

MacKenzie's eyebrows shot up. "Indeed?" His voice was rough, almost rusty sounding, as if he didn't use it often. "Should I take that as a compliment or an insult?"

Melinda's cheeks flamed red. "I'm sorry. I just,

well…" There was nothing she could think of that wouldn't make the situation even worse. "I'm sorry."

"You're not exactly what I thought, either," he admitted. His eyes swept down her. It had been only the bulky coat and the angle at which he'd looked at her that had made her look squat, he realized. Up close, he could see that she was short, but with a trim, curving figure. Her clothes were plain brown, but the blouse and skirt couldn't hide the fullness of her breasts or the narrowness of her waist. Her hair was done up in a softer style, and she didn't seem as unattractive or as old as he had thought. His lips tightened with irritation at his misjudgment. "There are eight hands, and supper's at five thirty," he snapped, his voice sharp with his annoyance.

"What?"

"I said, supper's at five-thirty," he repeated, raising his voice. Was the woman hard of hearing or just inattentive?

"You mean—you want me to begin tonight? With supper?"

MacKenzie frowned. He wasn't an ugly man by any means, but the combination of that frown, the thick black beard and the sharp angle of his face gave him a fierce look that made her forget the general handsomeness of his features. "What the hell do you think I mean? That's what I hired you for, isn't it?"

Melinda stiffened, and her eyes flashed. "Mr. Mac-Kenzie, may I remind you that you're in the presence of a lady?"

"What?" He looked as dumbfounded as she had felt a moment before.

"Your language," Melinda explained.

"What language?" He continued to stare; then his face cleared, and he let out a short bark of laughter. "You mean 'hell'? Lady, if that's the worst you'll hear around here, you can count yourself lucky."

"I'm not accustomed to being sworn at."

"Then you'd better toughen up. I don't plan to let some prissy old maid censor what I say."

Prissy old maid! He managed to insult her practically every time he opened his mouth. Melinda started to retort, but clamped her lips together tightly. She couldn't afford to get this man angry. She needed the job. And she had known before she started that he would be difficult to deal with.

She drew in a breath and spoke calmly, if icily. "How you speak is, of course, your business. I am here only to cook. Presumably we shall have little need to speak to one another."

He looked a little disgruntled, as though he'd been left with nothing to say. He cleared his throat. "Yes. Right. Then, supper at five-thirty."

Melinda would have liked to give him her opinion of his high-handed ways. How could he expect her to move in and immediately begin cooking, especially in a kitchen in this condition! It was clear that he was a tyrant, the kind of employer who worked his people to death. No doubt that was why he didn't usually hire women, considering them too weak to work as hard as he required. Well, she'd been a farm girl all her life, and for the past two years she'd handled everything on her own. Daniel MacKenzie didn't know the stuff she was made of, but she intended to show him.

"Of course," she answered, her jaw clenched.

MacKenzie hesitated for a moment, feeling strangely as if he'd lost when it was crystal clear he'd won their argument. Melinda spun around and began searching through the cabinets. Behind her she heard him leave the room. When he was gone, she turned around and shot a seething look at the doorway. If she weren't a lady, she thought, she would have turned the air blue with cussing. As it was, she could only content herself with banging boxes and bottles around as she searched for the makings of supper.

She finally found an old box of baking powder. She could throw together some biscuits. And beans. There was a sack of lima beans in the pantry. Of course, to taste their best, they should be soaked all night before they were slowly simmered for a good, long time, but Melinda hadn't been cooking since she was ten without learning a few tricks. She'd let them boil full speed for a while, then simmer, and if she threw in a little salt pork and some spices, they'd be edible.

She pulled out a huge cast-iron pot and set it in the sink. There was a pump handle at the sink; indoor water was something she'd never had before. She pumped it cautiously and water trickled out. Melinda smiled and pumped harder. She scrubbed the pot thoroughly, then filled it with water and dumped in the beans. She found a rag that looked as if it had been washed in recent memory, dampened it and wiped off the stove. She would have to save a thorough cleaning for later. There wasn't time now. She stacked the wood—at least the wood box beside the stove was full—in the fire door of the stove, added some pieces of kindling, stuffed in crumpled newspaper and set it alight. Not for the first time she longed for the variety of wood they'd had back home. What she needed now were some splintered pine logs to make a quick fire. But here one didn't have a choice of oak for a long fire or pine for a quick fire. There was only mesquite wood or the little knobby logs of what was called shinnery, or, occasionally, the broken limbs that had fallen from the cottonwoods and larger oaks by the creek. She had learned to make do with what she had.

Once she had the pot of water and beans boiling, she went in search of meat. There was none in the kitchen, so she looked outside. One of the small sheds had a pipe sticking out of the roof; it must be a smokehouse. She went to the shed and opened it. Inside it smelled deliciously of meat juices and mesquite smoke, baked into the very wood of the structure. Long strings of beef jerky hung from the narrow rafters, as well as an assortment of hams, sausages, slabs of bacon and ribs. She carved off a slice of salt pork and cut down one of the large hams. Back in the kitchen, she tossed the chunk of pork into the beans and set about slicing away the thick, salted rind of the ham. Then she took out two large skillets, cleaned them and set them on the stove with a large blob of grease in each. When the grease was sizzling, she took the thick slices of ham and laid them in the skillets.

While the ham fried, she found a flat cookie sheet

and a large mixing bowl and, after washing them, she mixed the biscuits, rolled them out and cut them with a small glass, being unable to find a tin biscuit cutter. She laid the flat biscuits on the greased sheet and popped it into the oven. She couldn't locate a tablecloth to protect the long wooden table in the kitchen, so she set the dishes on the table itself. It had obviously been eaten on that way before, judging by the stains, scars and burned rings on the wood surface. She only wiped the dishes, not having the time to wash them thoroughly. Presumably the men had eaten on them in this condition before; once more wouldn't hurt.

She put the food in serving dishes and set it on the table, then turned her attention to brewing a pot of coffee. Last, she made a big bowl of red-eye gravy from the meat drippings left in the skillets. She was carrying it to the table, holding it with her skirts in lieu of cloth holders, when she heard the scrape of boots on the steps outside, and the cowhands began to stream in the door.

The first one in was Carl, and he grinned and sniffed the air appreciatively. "Oh, ma'am…" he breathed. "I knew I was going to like you the minute I set eyes on you."

One by one the men filed in after him. Like Carl, they were dressed in heavy flannel shirts, denim trousers and jackets and dirty, work-scarred boots. Two pairs of boots clanked with spurs. Mentally cringing, Melinda thought of what the spurs must be doing to the wooden floors. Now she understood why the floors were so pitted and gouged. All the men pulled off their hats, smiling at her, some shyly and others boldly. Melinda smiled at the shy ones and favored the bold ones with a cool stare that soon had them dropping their gaze. There were eight of them in various sizes and shapes, some with beards or mustaches and some without, hair and eyes in all shades, but all of them were hard, spare and browned by the sun into a kind of sameness.

They introduced themselves to her politely, but their eyes kept sliding over to the table. Melinda smiled. "Go ahead and sit down. Would anyone like some coffee?"

"Yes, ma'am." They were quick to follow her suggestion, scrambling for seats at the table.

Most of them wanted coffee, and she went around the table, pouring the coffee from the enameled pot, a small rag wrapped around the handle to keep it from burning her fingers. The men dug into the food without ceremony, heaping their plates. They began to eat, and all around the table came a chorus of, "This sure is good, ma'am," and, "Awful good cooking, ma'am."

The inner door opened, and Mr. MacKenzie stepped into the room. The hands barely paused in their eating to glance up and nod. MacKenzie looked at the table, and Melinda thought she saw a gleam of interest enter his eyes. He sat down and speared a piece of ham, then ladled red-eye gravy on top of it. Like the others, he cut open two biscuits and doused them with the gravy, then began to eat. Melinda waited expectantly for him to tell her it was good, as the others had. He didn't say a word.

Melinda walked over to him. He looked up questioningly, and she resisted the urge to dump the coffee in his lap. Instead she smiled stiffly and asked, "Coffee, Mr. MacKenzie?"

"Sure." He held out his cup. When she had filled it, he returned to his eating.

Melinda set the pot on the table and went to the sink. She set a large dishpan in it and pumped it half full of water, adding a few chips of soap, then began to wash the pots and pans she had used to cook in. Earlier, before the men had come in, she had prudently set aside two plates of food for herself and Lee. They would eat when the men had left. She had not been asked to join them, and she would never think of plopping herself down at a table full of men uninvited.

It didn't take the men long to finish. They went through the food like a swarm of locusts through a wheat field, and there were several hopeful inquiries as to whether there were any more biscuits. Obviously she would have to make more biscuits next time. The men sat back, chatting, enjoying their last sips of coffee.

"Sorry there wasn't any time to make dessert," Melinda apologized as she began to pick up their plates and carry them to the counter.

"Oh, ma'am, this was wonderful," Carl assured her, and there was a general chorus of assent. Melinda was watching Daniel out of the corner of her eye, and she noticed that he made no comment. He was probably blaming her for not being able to whip up a nice apple pie in the past hour, too.

One of the younger men jumped up to help her clear

the table, and she smiled and thanked him. Two of the others quickly rose to help. MacKenzie stood up.

Just at that moment, the back door burst open, and Lee tumbled in. "Mama? Can I eat yet? I'm about to starve."

Melinda held up an admonishing hand. "Quietly, Lee. And it's 'May I eat?' Just let me get the table cleared."

"You have a son?" MacKenzie's voice was quiet in a way that stopped all movement and chatter in the room.

Melinda turned, her stomach doing flip-flops, her fingers curling into her skirts. "Yes."

"You didn't say you had a boy." Her employer's face was hard and cold.

Melinda swallowed. She thought he would have looked the same way if he had accused her of being a thief. "You didn't ask me. I presumed it wasn't a matter of importance."

The cowhands began to stir, reaching for their hats and mumbling their thanks, shuffling out the door. Melinda wondered whether their departure meant they judged the threat of storm to be over—or just beginning. Lee came up beside Melinda, and she sensed protectiveness as well as fear in the rigid set of his body.

"I wouldn't have hired you if I'd known you had a child," MacKenzie said flatly.

Melinda bridled. "Lee's a good boy. He'll be no trouble to you or anyone else."

"I don't want children in this house."

Tears sprang into Melinda's eyes. She wasn't sure whether they were from anger or hurt. Maybe it was both. Her voice trembled despite her effort to keep it even. "Then I promise you that Lee won't set foot inside it again. My son and I will take our meals in my house."

She whirled and strode toward the door, pulling Lee along with her. She twisted the doorknob and pulled the door open, but MacKenzie was there in front of her, his hand flat on the door, pushing it shut.

"Don't be any more of an idiot than you have to be. I'm not exiling you to your house."

Melinda lifted her chin and stared straight at him. She refused to let this man intimidate her, especially when it came to her son. "No? Then what are you doing? Telling me I can no longer work here?"

Daniel looked at her. He would have liked to tell her exactly that. "No children" was a rule that was never broken in his house. Even Will's children kept scrupulously out of his way. This woman was already a burr under his saddle. He knew life would be easier without her. He felt tricked and deceived. She was younger and shapelier than he'd thought. She had a child. And her eyes were huge and a clear, soft gray, rimmed with thick lashes. They were lovely eyes, even if they were too big in her thin face.

His mouth twisted, and for a moment Melinda thought he would tell her to leave the ranch. But instead he sighed gustily and turned away, muttering, "Hellfire and damnation!" He stalked off toward the door, then swung back. "No, I'm not telling you you can't work here. My men would probably rise up in riot, after that meal tonight." He would never tell her so, but even he, who usually didn't care what he ate, found his mouth watering at the thought of her next meal. "You can stay. But I don't want him underfoot. Is that understood?"

"Perfectly." Melinda kept her expression as cool and regal as she could make it. MacKenzie looked at her for a moment, then jammed his hands into his pockets and walked out of the room, muttering again.

Lee turned his wide eyes up to his mother. "Mama, what's the matter with him?"

"I haven't the slightest idea," she replied crossly. "I think maybe he was just born mean. But I'll tell you one thing. We're going to save every penny I make, because you and I aren't going to stay here a day longer than we have to!"

MELINDA AROSE EARLY the next morning. The sky was still dark when she left her house and walked across the cold yard to the big house. Work began early out here, and the person who cooked breakfast had to be the first one up. She slipped softly into the house and laid the fire in the stove, then prepared the biscuits and coffee. While the stove heated, she went back to her house and shook Lee awake, instructing him to go to the barn and milk the cow while she gathered the eggs. He nodded, rubbing his eyes sleepily, and obediently climbed out of bed.

Melinda walked to the dilapidated chicken coop, swinging the basket she had brought from her kitchen.

Stooping, she opened the door and stepped inside. There was only a trace of the pungent odor of a henhouse. And there were no hens sitting in straw. In fact, there wasn't any straw. She glanced around. No chickens? No eggs?

She stepped out and surveyed the yard. There was no other building that could be the chicken coop. Shaking her head, she went to the smokehouse. Obviously there was going to be nothing but meat this morning, so she took a large slab of bacon as well as two rolls of sausage.

As she walked to the house with the food, Lee ran up to her. "Mama! Mama! You won't believe this, but I promise it's the truth. I looked all over that barn, and there's no milch cow."

"No cow?"

He shook his head. "I swear. I checked every last stall."

"Don't swear," she replied automatically. "I believe you, sweetheart. This place is a disgrace."

She whipped up a respectable breakfast of bacon, sausage and biscuits. Once again, the men gulped it all down and told her how good it was. "Eatin's never been this good on this place," one of them commented. Mr. MacKenzie didn't say a word.

After the men had left, Melinda opened the door from the kitchen to the rest of the house and walked inside. She felt vaguely guilty as she walked down the hall, as though she was sneaking in somewhere she didn't belong. The house was so still and quiet it was unnerving. She found herself walking on tiptoe.

With a grimace, she stopped herself and firmly set her heels on the floor. She had a right to be here; after all, Mr. MacKenzie had hired her to clean the house as well as cook.

Something felt gritty beneath her feet, and she glanced down. There was dried mud on the floor. There was also dust along the baseboards, and in the corner she spotted a cobweb. Automatically she looked up. Yes, cobwebs in the corners of the ceiling, too. She opened one of the closed doors lining the hallway, thinking that it wouldn't be so gloomy if only MacKenzie would open the place up a bit.

The room was dark, shrouded with heavy drapes. Melinda crossed the room and opened them. Dust fell on her, making her cough. The windows behind them were dirty, but at least they let in the light. She glanced around the room and shook her head in disbelief. No wonder MacKenzie kept the room closed up; the sight of it would horrify anyone. It was a formal dining room, obviously unused. Dust coated every piece of furniture, and she could see the tracks of her feet in the dust on the floor. Cobwebs decorated the baseboards, ceilings and legs of the furniture. A glass chandelier hung over the massive dining table, dulled by an accumulation of dust and tangled with cobwebs.

She plopped down on a chair, and a puff of dust rose up from it. Melinda hopped up and wiped at the dirt on her dress. Anger rose in her. The place was furnished beautifully. The table was mahogany under its coat of dust, and the drapes were velvet. The rug that covered the center of the room was Persian. It was a crime to let everything go to ruin like this!

She went through the rest of the downstairs, fueling her anger. It was all in as bad a state as the kitchen was. The leather couch in the sitting room had a rent in it, no doubt from a careless spur. The draperies were thick with dust—as was every other surface in the house. The floors didn't look as if they'd been waxed in years—or even cleaned, probably. She didn't have the heart to go upstairs.

How could even Mr. MacKenzie neglect a lovely house so? His solution to the mess seemed to be to close the doors.

The last straw was when she discovered mouse droppings in the parlor around a chair, then found that the mice had chewed through the cushion of the chair, no doubt to make a nest. It was a chair that was covered in what had once been beautiful, expensive damask.

Melinda made a noise of frustration deep in her throat and charged out the side door, grabbing her coat as she went. A glance at the hill showed her that MacKenzie wasn't working on the windmill today. She strode across the yard and into the barn.

"Mr. MacKenzie? Mr. MacKenzie!" He wasn't in there, either. She went out and looked around, shielding her eyes. She caught sight of him standing by the corral, one foot on a slat of the fence, watching the horses milling around. Two men stood beside him—one of the hands who'd eaten her breakfast and a man she'd never seen before.

Melinda marched toward them. "Mr. MacKenzie!"

All three men swiveled to look at her. Daniel MacKenzie's eyes widened, and he couldn't keep a grin from sneaking across his face. His new housekeeper was stomping toward him with the light of battle in her eyes, but the effect was spoiled by the coat hanging ludicrously big on her, its sleeves so long her hands disappeared, and by the fact that her face was smudged with dirt and her hair was tangled and coated with dust, half of it falling out of its careful roll.

Beside Daniel, Will Moore, the foreman, murmured, "That woman looks madder'n a wet hen."

"She's riled about something," Strack, the hand, agreed on the other side of him.

"I believe I have some work to do back at the house," Will decided. He'd seen that look in his own Lula's eyes, and he wasn't about to stick around to catch a lecture that didn't even belong to him.

"Uh, yeah." Strack sidled away. "Just remembered something I gotta do in the barn."

"Cowards," MacKenzie muttered as the two men melted away. The grin kept twitching onto his face, and he felt a certain sense of anticipation as he straightened, facing her.

Melinda saw the grin, and it stoked the fires of her irritation. What in the world did he find funny when she was so mad she could spit? She stopped two feet away from Daniel and planted her hands on her hips. "Mr. MacKenzie, your house is a disgrace!"

"I beg your pardon?"

"You have a beautiful house, and you've let it fall to rack and ruin. I've never seen such a pitiful sight."

"I'm sorry it doesn't meet with your approval," he commented dryly.

"It wouldn't meet with anyone's approval, unless they were blind! It's filthy! How you could allow a lovely place to get into such a state, I'll never know. There are mice—mice!—setting up house in your front parlor! And your kitchen is deplorable. You don't have the most basic staples. The flour is gone, the potatoes have sprouts as long as my hand, and the sugar is swarming with ants. There are no chickens in your henhouse, no milch cow in your barn, and not a single canned vegetable or even a jar of fruit preserves anywhere! How do you expect me to cook a meal? I couldn't even feed one person supper tonight, let alone a whole ranch full!"

"Why the devil do you think I hired you?" MacKenzie retorted. "Clean the damn place!"

"I don't have anything to clean *with!* There's not a single bottle of ammonia in the house. It's obvious that there hasn't been in quite a while. There's no wax, no—"

"Then get some! Get all the flour and whatever else you want. What are you crying to me for? You're the one who's in charge of all that. Make a list of what you need and give it to one of the men, or have one of them drive you into town."

Melinda opened her mouth to say something, then stopped. She was still sizzling, and she would have liked to continue to argue, but she realized that Daniel had pulled the rug out from under her. She had expected him to grumble and gripe about having to buy a whole batch of supplies, to defend the state of his house and larder. Instead, he'd simply told her to buy whatever she needed, somehow making it sound as if she were incompetent. It was completely irritating. "I still need some hens and a cow," she said finally, her expression mulish.

He grinned again. She looked just like a little girl who'd been caught grubbing in the dirt. "Then get them. I'm sure somebody around Barrett has a few chickens and a cow for sale."

She thought of her own livestock. "Well, actually, I have some back at my farm."

"Then send one of the hands for them. Now, are we finished? May I return to work?"

Melinda's eyes flickered toward the corral. She would hardly call standing around watching a bunch of horses "work." But she swallowed her words and said only, "Certainly," in a voice like ice. She swung around and walked away, lifting her skirts up a little from the ground.

MacKenzie stood watching her until she reached the house. He wished the jacket she wore weren't quite so concealing. Then, catching the direction of his thoughts, he turned to the corral, scowling.

CHAPTER THREE

MELINDA STORMED into the kitchen, closing the door after her with a resounding thud. She would have liked to shake it off its hinges. Daniel MacKenzie was an infuriating man.

She went around the kitchen, jerking open one drawer after another, searching for paper and a pencil to write the list of goods she needed from town. Typically, she could find nothing. Finally she stormed out and went across the yard to her own house, where she dug a sheet of paper and a small pencil stub out of the bottom drawer of the dresser in her room. She straightened up, glancing into the mirror above her dresser as she did so. What she saw there stopped her in her tracks.

A wild woman stared back at her, eyes wide with horror. Her hair was twisted and tangled, half undone and covered with dust. There were smudges of dirt on her forehead and cheeks. No wonder Mr. MacKenzie had kept smiling. It was a wonder he hadn't burst out laughing! She thought of how she had stood there, ranting at him about the untidiness of his house, and all the time she had looked like this!

She stared at herself, her anger wavering, and suddenly she began to laugh. She laughed until her sides hurt and she had to wrap her arms around herself and struggle to regain her breath. She sank down on the floor, giving herself up to her hilarity. Finally her laughter subsided, and she leaned against the dresser. The tension of the last two days had drained out of her, along with her anger.

Melinda sighed. Mr. MacKenzie was right. It was her job to get things in order; that was what he had hired her for. Naturally he would expect her to purchase whatever she needed. It would be fun, actually, to stock a kitchen from scratch without having to worry about pinching pennies.

She cleaned herself and redid her hair. Next she went to her own kitchen and got an apron, a few dish-cloths and her basket of cleaning materials. She wasn't about to wait for MacKenzie's hand to get back from town with the supplies before she started cleaning that house.

She returned to the big house and drew up a long list of urgently needed supplies. She gave the list to Carl and instructed him to go out to her farm afterward and bring back the chickens and the milch cow. With that done, it was time to attack the kitchen.

Soon the kitchen was filled with the acrid scent of ammonia. First she cleaned away years of accumulated grease, dirt and burned food from the huge iron stove. Next she scrubbed the cabinets, pantry shelves and counters. Finally she tackled the floor, getting down on her hands and knees with a tough-bristled brush and working carefully over the entire floor. By the time she finished, she ached all over and her head hurt from the ammonia fumes, but the kitchen was gleaming. Wearily she took her last panful of ammonia water outside and dumped it in the yard. As she did so, she saw a woman walking across the yard toward her. She was tall and raw-boned, with a cheerful, lively face.

The woman called and waved a hand, and Melinda waved back. "Come in and visit." She would be glad for the chance to rest and chat.

The woman climbed the three wooden steps to the small side porch. "I'm Lula Moore, the foreman's wife."

"Mrs. Moore. It's a pleasure to meet you. I'm Melinda Ballard."

"Call me Lula. We'll get to know each other well enough. We're the only women for miles around."

Melinda opened the door and ushered Lula inside. Lula stared around the kitchen in amazement, then let out an unladylike whistle. "Land o' Goshen, girl, you've managed a miracle!"

Melinda chuckled. Only another woman would appreciate what cleaning up this kitchen had involved. "Thank you." She put a pot of coffee onto the stove to brew, and she and Lula sat down at the table, smiling at each other. "It will be wonderful to have a woman close by."

"Isn't that the truth? Sometimes I get so tired of nothing but men and young 'uns and cows that I could scream." Lula grinned at her conspiratorially. "I didn't plan on coming over this morning. I was going to let you settle in first. But then Will told me about that fight you had with Mr. MacKenzie, and I just had to come up and meet you. I've never met a lady—or many men, for that matter—brave enough to take on Daniel Mac-Kenzie."

Color rose in Melinda's cheeks. "Oh, dear. You must think I'm awful, creating a scene like that. I should have waited to speak to him in private. My wretched temper got the better of me. It's not the first time."

Mrs. Moore chuckled. "Don't go apologizing for it! It's the best thing that's happened on this ranch since Jimmy killed a seven-foot rattler. It's the first time Daniel's ever met a woman who'll stand up to him. I remember when Will and I first came here, there were about three women housekeepers in a row, and when Daniel barked at them, they just cried or quit, or both. They say there was one who was tough enough to tell him off, but she got so disgusted that she up and left. She said she didn't plan to spoil her widowhood arguing with another man."

The two women giggled. "That's why it's been men up here ever since."

"I know," Melinda commented dryly. "I could tell from the condition of the house."

Lula shook her head. "Poor thing. I don't envy you cleaning it up. Tell you what, I'll send my oldest girl, Opal, up here to help you for a couple of days."

"That's very kind of you."

Lula made a dismissive gesture. "No trouble at all."

The coffee finished brewing, and Melinda got up to

pour them each a cup. For a moment they were quiet as they sipped their coffee, but Lula Moore wasn't one to let a silence last long. Soon they were talking about their children, the ranch, Lula's husband and whatever else came to their minds. Before long the conversation turned naturally to Daniel MacKenzie. Melinda related how harshly he had reacted to finding out that she had a child.

Lula shook her head, her face sad. "He's got no fondness for children, that's a fact. But it isn't that Daniel's mean, or that he's got anything against your boy. It's just—well, I don't mean to gossip, but I reckon you ought to know about Daniel, so you'll understand. Maybe you won't get so riled up about the things he does and says if you know what happened to him."

Melinda's eyes widened. "What happened?" Her voice lowered, and she leaned forward, as did Mrs. Moore.

"Well, this took place a long time before Will and I came here, so I only heard the story secondhand myself. Daniel was one of the first ones to settle in the Panhandle, way back in the late seventies. He was a young man, not even twenty. His father was a wealthy man back East, I understand, and he sent Daniel to stay with some cousins who had a ranch south of here. Daniel had always been kind of sickly, and—"

"Sickly?" Melinda echoed in astonishment, seeing MacKenzie's broad shoulders in her mind's eye.

"Hard to imagine, isn't it? He's tough as a cedar post now. Apparently fresh air and sunshine and plenty of hard work were what he needed. He loved it here and decided to stay. He bought some land and started ranching. He worked for years, building it up, buying more and more land, until the Lazy M is one of the biggest ranches around. Not like the XIT, of course, but big and prosperous. His father died when Daniel was about twenty-eight or so, and he went to the funeral and to settle the estate and all, and he stayed there a few months. Well, while he was back East, he fell in love."

"Mr. MacKenzie?" That was another thing Melinda had trouble believing. She couldn't picture him as anything but angry or remote.

Lula nodded, smiling, caught up in her romantic story. "They say she was beautiful, blond and dainty, like a porcelain doll, and she dressed in the most beautiful clothes. Daniel got engaged to her, and he came back to the ranch and built this house for her. Brought in lumber, fancy chandeliers, expensive furniture. He didn't spare any expense, and of course he could afford it. So he married her and brought her home. That must have been, oh, ten years ago, about 1885. There still weren't a lot of people living around Barrett."

"What happened to her?" Melinda asked, thinking of the beautiful, fragile young girl, dressed in elegant laces, satins and velvets. No doubt she had come from a wealthy, sheltered background in some cool, green flowering place back East. What must she have thought when she arrived in the Panhandle and found this flat, empty land? How had she felt when she heard the wind whining around the corners of the house, or saw the snow driving down endlessly in a blizzard? Melinda was washed with pity for the girl. No matter how much she had loved Daniel—another thing Melinda found difficult to envision—she must have been lonely and unhappy.

"Well, for two or three years, they were happy. They were young and in love. She had a baby, a little boy, and they say Daniel was mad about the child. He carried him with him everywhere and was always talking about teaching him to ride when he was older and showing him the ranch and all. But when the baby was only three years old, Daniel's wife went into town one day in winter. It started to snow real hard, and they should have stayed in town, but the girl insisted they leave for the ranch. She was sure they could make it before the snow got bad, and she didn't want to be separated from her baby. It was a servant she'd brought out from the East who was driving her, so he didn't know any better than she did. They set out, and the snow turned into a blizzard. They drove off the road, and when Daniel and the men found them, they'd both frozen to death."

"Oh, no!" Melinda felt tears starting in her eyes for the girl she hadn't known, but for whom she felt much sympathy. "The poor thing."

Lula nodded. "Yes, but that wasn't the worst. That very same winter, only a month or so afterward, the baby got pneumonia and died, too."

"That poor man." Melinda's heart stirred with pain and empathy for Daniel MacKenzie.

"It was a terrible tragedy. It scarred him. They say he's been sour on life ever since. That's why he never married again and why he can't bear to have children around."

"Oh, yes." Tears glimmered in Melinda's eyes. She was a woman of ready feeling, and if her temper was often right below the surface, so were warmth and sympathy. "I can understand." She had often thought that if Lee died, she would not be able to bear it. She had been delivered of a stillborn child once, and it had almost broken her heart.

Besides, he had lost both a child and a wife. Daniel MacKenzie was a man to be pitied, not disliked. Now that Melinda knew about his past, it was much easier to understand him—and not to blame him. No wonder he had closed off those beautiful rooms with the elegant furnishings he had bought for his beloved bride! No wonder he didn't want women and children around!

"Thank you for telling me," Melinda said to Lula. "It explains so much."

Lula nodded. "Yes. It's a sad story." She sighed. "So tragic. So beautiful and romantic."

Melinda wasn't sure how beautiful and romantic it was to have one's life wrecked by the deaths of a beloved wife and child, but it was certainly tragic. From now on, she vowed, she would have more patience with Mr. MacKenzie. She wouldn't let herself be wounded by his gruffness or lack of gratitude. She would keep a lid on her temper and not blurt out the first thing that came into her head, as she was wont to do. She would keep Lee out of his way, and she would try to steer clear of anything that would remind Mr. MacKenzie of his loss. It might not be easy at times, but she was sure that with patience and perseverance she could bring about a more comfortable relationship between herself and her employer.

WHEN CARL RETURNED in the middle of the afternoon with Melinda's supplies, she stored them away happily in the spotless kitchen. It gave her a feeling of pride, almost of ownership, to see the results of her labor, as if her work had somehow made the place her own. Then she set to work on supper, whipping up a huge meal of chicken-fried steak, mashed potatoes, gravy, biscuits and a mess of greens. There was even time to make a deep-dish apple cobbler for dessert. She had found a clean oilcloth during her cleaning, and she laid it on the table before she set it. It wasn't very attractive, but at least it would protect the table from further scarring.

When the men came in, the way they sniffed the air and closed their eyes in a pantomime of ecstasy was enough to make her fast, furious efforts worthwhile. Many of them noticed the change in the condition of the kitchen. Even Daniel glanced around the room in a bemused way, then dug into his food with a hearty appetite. He had a second helping of the cobbler, too, she noticed, though, typically, he didn't say a word of thanks or praise. The other men made up for that, however, lauding her cooking skills until she had to laugh and blush at their extravagances.

The next morning after breakfast Melinda made bread. After first mixing, then kneading, she finally stuffed the dough into bread pans and set it aside to rise, covered with dishcloths, while she prepared the noon meal. When the bread had risen, she adjusted the oven to exactly the right temperature through the judicious use of wood and the damper, then put the loaves in to bake to a golden brown. While they were cooking, she started on her second batch, this one of sourdough loaves and rolls, made from the starter that she had brought with her from her own house.

When the hands trooped in for the noon meal, they found a platter of succulent roast beef, a bowl of brown gravy made from its drippings, a platter of sourdough rolls and a sliced loaf of golden-brown bread, both fresh from the oven and smelling heavenly, as well as bowls of potatoes, carrots and green beans. To top it all off, there were two sweet-potato pies on the counter, cooling.

The men attacked the food as if it had been weeks since they'd eaten. Melinda went around the table filling up their coffee cups, then returned to the counter to slice the pies and dish them up onto dessert plates. She also put a second pot of coffee on to brew, having learned that the men used up one pot quickly and wanted another to drink with their dessert. She glanced at the table and saw that the bread was gone, so she took another loaf, sliced it and carried it over.

She picked up an empty serving bowl and was just turning away to carry it to the counter when MacKenzie's voice stopped her. "Why the devil do you keep jumping back and forth? Sit down and eat."

Melinda assumed that this was Daniel's ungracious way of issuing her an invitation to eat with them. She faced him and replied calmly, "I'll eat after you all have finished."

He grimaced. "Stop sulking and sit down and eat. I don't have the foggiest idea what you're mad about, so your show is wasted."

"Sulking!" Melinda's eyes flashed, and she set the serving dish on the table with a clatter. "I am not sulking. My job is to cook, not to eat with you!"

Daniel glared at her. "Well, you've finished cooking. Why the hell won't you eat like everybody else?"

"An employee doesn't just plop herself down to eat at the same table with her employer if she hasn't been asked."

"I'm asking you now!" he roared.

Melinda set her hands on her hips pugnaciously. Daniel's own hands were clenched tightly around his knife and fork. They leaned forward, each one's eyes boring into the other. All around the table, the men watched interestedly. It wasn't often that they had a delicious meal as well as a bang-up fight.

"And I refuse," Melinda replied. "I am free to eat whenever I please, and I'll wait to eat with Lee."

"Lee? Who's Lee? There's no one—"

"My son." Melinda clenched her jaw, waiting for him to fly off the handle again about her child. She didn't care if he did have a tragic history, if he said so much as one bad thing about Lee, she'd—

"The boy?" Daniel's eyebrows lifted in surprise. Then he scowled. "What the devil is he doing out of school in the middle of the day?"

"It's too far for him to walk!" Melinda snapped. She waited, her heart in her throat, for MacKenzie's suggestion that she board him in town during the week. It was what some people did who lived too far away from the school. But Melinda couldn't bear to have him gone that much.

"Well, for—" Daniel began in exasperation. "Why didn't you say anything about it?" He glanced down the length of the table. "Jimmy, find a horse for the boy to ride." He glanced up at Melinda. "Can he ride?"

"A little." His father had started to teach him, but after his death, they'd had to sell the horse.

MacKenzie turned back to Jimmy. "Give him a gentle one. And teach him to ride."

Melinda stood looking at him, dumbstruck by his generosity. Of course, lending one horse probably wasn't much to a man who owned as many as Daniel MacKenzie. But considering how he felt about Lee's being here, it was amazing. It would mean so much to Lee to have a horse to ride and someone to teach him. "Thank you," she said, her voice low and earnest. "That's very kind of you."

MacKenzie waved away her thanks, looking slightly embarrassed.

Later, when dinner was over and the other men had left, MacKenzie lingered behind. He held his hat in his hands, sliding it around and around through his fingers, and he kept looking down at it as though it held some wisdom. Melinda glanced at him questioningly. First generous, then embarrassed, now ill at ease. She would never have imagined Daniel MacKenzie being any of those things. What had come over him?

"Mrs. Ballard…"

"Yes?"

"I'm not a tyrant."

"I beg your pardon?"

"I wouldn't make a woman and a little boy wait to eat until the rest of us are finished. What I said the other day—well, I didn't mean he couldn't sit at the same table with me. I just—"

Knowing what had happened to him, Melinda's heart was touched with sympathy. "I understand."

"Do you?" His words sounded bitter.

"I think so. After Lee, I had a stillborn baby."

His eyes narrowed, and his face, which had looked almost human before, turned cold and closed. He made no comment on her words, just snapped, "I expect you and the boy to eat at the table with the rest of us. Is that understood?"

Melinda resisted an urge to salute. His reaction had squelched her sympathy. It was like offering friendship to a porcupine. "Yes. Perfectly. And 'the boy' is named Lee."

Daniel didn't reply, but simply walked out of the kitchen.

AFTER DINNER, Lula's daughter Opal arrived, as promised, and they started cleaning the house. It was a lengthy process and one that took several days to complete thoroughly. They swept, mopped and waxed the hardwood floors until they gleamed. They dusted and polished the furniture and the banister on the stairs. All the baseboards and windowsills were washed. The rugs, both elegant Persians and simple braided ones, were carried out and the dust beaten from them. The drapes were taken down and treated in the same fashion. They dusted the valances and all the cobweb-holding corners of the rooms. Every dish in the china cabinet and every knickknack on the tables and mantels was washed thoroughly, as were the windows. Melinda even had one of the hands take down the crystal chandelier in the dining room, and she washed each delicate prism until it sparkled.

One by one she opened the rooms as they finished cleaning them. She drew back the heavy draperies so that the sunlight could stream through the now-sparkling windows, giving the house light and warmth. She waited warily for some comment from MacKenzie about her opening the rooms he had closed off, but he said nothing about it.

They started on the second floor. The only bedroom that was actually used was Mr. MacKenzie's, so Melinda set about making it habitable first. It gave her an odd feeling to enter a man's bedroom, as though she were doing something slightly wicked and exciting, despite the fact that she had a perfectly legitimate reason to be there. It was even more peculiar to wash his clothes, to handle the shirts that had lain next to his skin or the sheets upon which he slept. His things still smelled faintly of his scent, a mixture of horse, tobacco, sweat and leather, and she found it disturbing—but not exactly in a bad way.

There was a kind of intimacy implied in the task, as there was in entering his room. He was a stranger to her, really, yet she knew how his bedroom was arranged and where his brush and comb lay on the bureau. She had ironed his shirts, and she had seen the indentation where his head had lain upon his pillow. It gave her a funny, shivery feeling.

After Mr. MacKenzie's bedroom, they cleaned the upstairs rooms one by one, leaving them in the same pristine condition as the lower floor. Melinda drew back the curtains and drapes and opened the doors into the hall, so that it was no longer a gloomy tunnel. The only exception was the second room down the hall from MacKenzie's. The day she opened its door, tears sprang into her eyes. It had obviously been a small child's room. There was a small bed, and in one corner sat a cradle. A rocking horse stood in the center of the room, carved out of oak and beautifully painted. A tarnished silver-backed baby brush and comb lay on a tray on the dresser, and there was a wooden spinning top on the chest of drawers. A painting of a child at his prayers hung on one wall.

Melinda swallowed hard and set about dusting and cleaning the room. After that, she always made sure the room was kept clean. But she left its door closed, as it had been for years.

CHAPTER FOUR

DANIEL MACKENZIE was aware of the house changing around him. At first it was only the food. Once they had eaten dry, tasteless stuff, sometimes burned, at other times almost raw, even now and then bizarrely both, but now, instead, their meals were delicious and savory. The vegetables were seasoned and not boiled to death; the rolls were light and flaky and not black on the bottom; the sourdough biscuits practically melted in his mouth and were accompanied by pale yellow butter in molds.

They continued the custom of slaughtering a steer every week for the large ranch population, but in the past the men had barbecued the animal and eaten the barbecue every night for a few days. But now they cut up the beef and stored it in the cool cellar dug into the side of the windmill hill, and Melinda cooked several different, interesting meals from it—barbecued ribs and briskets, stew, roast, pan-fried steaks, ground hash, pieces of round steak breaded and fried. There was always some kind of gravy from the meat drippings, too. Now and then, just for variety, she served up fried chicken or maybe a ham or fried pork chops. The crowning touch, always, was one of her sweet desserts, like apple dumplings or big pale sugar cookies or sweet-potato pone.

The men made pigs of themselves—including himself, Daniel was forced to admit. Meals were a delight to be looked forward to now, not simply a chore to get through in order to fill an empty belly. And it wasn't only the food. There was something about having a lady at the table. Suddenly the men were coming to the kitchen scrubbed and clean, and their language improved. They made an effort to keep the conversation interesting, instead of just discussing their work. It was pleasant to look down the table and see Melinda's pretty face and soft form, to hear her quiet laughter over some joke. It made Daniel feel a little confused and disturbed, yet he always looked forward to seeing her.

Then she started changing the house. He was so used to the place being dark and closed up, as his insides had been since the day Matthew died, that at first he didn't notice the difference, just walked through the house and out without glancing around. But gradually he began to notice that the place was somehow lighter. He began to look around, and he saw the scrubbed and shiny floors. He saw the rooms opening up, more every day, clean and filled with light. He glanced around him at the gleaming fine wood and the sparkling glass of the chandelier and oil lamps; he stared through the spotless windows at the unending stretch of land outside them.

The house was once again as clean and rich as it had

been when Millicent was alive and had her servants scurrying around—except that there was more light, for Millicent had hated the sight of the flat land outside and had kept the heavy curtains drawn. The sun hurt the furniture, she said, and perhaps it did, but there was such freedom in being able to look out and see clear to the horizon. Nor was the house as formal as when Millicent had been there, when Daniel had felt uneasy about setting a cigar down in one of the elegant china or glass dishes and had always seemed to be stumbling over some maid or other.

Daniel told himself that he didn't like the way Mrs. Ballard had changed the house. She was pushy, a bossy female who took too much on herself and didn't know when to keep her mouth shut. None of his other women housekeepers had dared to argue with him or to tell him he was in the wrong. Unfortunately, those women, like Millicent, had had a remarkable tendency to cry over the slightest complaint or terse order, or to tighten up and get that wounded-female look on their faces, as if he were a snake that they were forced to put up with. He had always felt guilty after he yelled at them and, perversely, that had made him even angrier.

But with Melinda, there was something enjoyable about exchanging hot words. Afterward he felt a pleasant sense of release, and he found himself thinking back on what she'd said and how her eyes had flashed, and he smiled. He wasn't left feeling as if he was a brute who had picked on a weaker creature. Melinda Ballard could stand toe-to-toe with the best of them, he thought, and as like as not come out on top.

It seemed crazy, and he didn't like to admit it, but he rather enjoyed arguing with her.

If he was honest, he had to admit that part of that enjoyment was in seeing her fire up. Her big gray eyes turned so clear and sparkling, in contrast to their usual softness, and her cheeks flushed with color. There was always an electricity about her when she got her back up, and he was reminded of those hot, velvet black nights in the summer when lightning crackled across the sky in the distance.

But then, she was a pleasure to look at anytime. She had changed almost as much as the house. Proper nutrition and an abundance of food had taken away the gauntness in her cheeks and put back the natural luster of her hair and the tone of her skin. In a matter of weeks she had gone from being a woman he thought old and plain enough to be his housekeeper to being a young woman who was too lovely for him to feel comfortable with her around all the time.

He found himself thinking about her far too often—in the day while he worked, in the evening when he read or caught up on his book work, at night as he lay in his bed, trying to go to sleep. In his mind, she was Melinda, not Mrs. Ballard, and he was afraid he would slip and speak to her too familiarly. He daydreamed about her big gray eyes and her rich brown hair, worn now in a softer, fuller style that made his hands itch to touch it. He thought about the womanly curves of her body, the full breasts and little waist, the swell of her hips hidden beneath her full skirts. At night his thoughts turned downright indecent, imagining what her legs looked like beneath her skirt or picturing her clad in only a lacy chemise that barely covered her breasts, veiling but not concealing the deep rose-brown circles of her nipples.

It was a mistake to start thinking about her like that, because then he couldn't stop. He couldn't work, couldn't think, and he would lie awake for hours. Invariably the next morning he was at his crabbiest, barking at everyone, but especially at Melinda.

It irritated him excessively that he should feel desire for her. It wasn't as if she displayed any interest in him. Indeed, unlike most of the younger housekeepers he had hired, she hadn't shot him a single coy look or given him a flirtatious smile. She hadn't even tried to maneuver him into a situation where they were alone. Besides, even if she had seemed to like him, he couldn't have let himself take advantage of a woman who was both under his protection and under his power— though, God knows, one would never know it by the way she acted!

So he could not have a brief, purely physical encounter with her, and he certainly wouldn't consider anything more than that with any woman, no matter how desirable she was. He had tried marriage once, and he was positive that the state was not for him. He had neither the patience nor the good temper to live with a woman, and he had found out with Millicent how quickly the sheer veil of love was ripped away by the struggle of daily living.

And, as if Melinda wasn't bothersome enough, there was her boy. Melinda had maintained her word and kept him out of Daniel's way, but he couldn't help but see Lee around the place, following one of the hands around or playing or riding a horse. He was also at the table every morning and night, where Daniel couldn't miss him. No matter how hard he tried, Daniel couldn't keep his eyes from drifting over to the lad. Lee wasn't of the coloring that Matthew had been, and he was far older, but every time he saw him, Daniel thought of Matthew. They would have been about the same age now, if Matthew had lived. And Matt would have been running around, learning all about the ranch, too, except that it would have been Daniel, not Jimmy, whom he would have tagged along behind. Just the thought of it reawakened the old pain, long ago put to rest, and though it wasn't as severe and slashing as it had been once, Daniel hated even the memory of his past loss.

It was, all in all, a damned nuisance having Melinda Ballard here. He ought to fire her, but he couldn't bring himself to do it. It would be unfair, considering how well she performed her work, and besides, he would probably have a mutiny on his hands if he took those delicious meals away from the men. He kept hoping that Melinda would quit, as the others had. But she showed no signs of that, even when he was in his surliest moods. She just ignored him when he was like that, which made him feel even more irritable, or she snapped right back at him and they wound up arguing, and then he was left with a bubbling, unfinished excitement inside.

Daniel would have been amazed to learn that he

was often on Melinda's mind, too, and in ways that surprised her. After she had learned the sad story of his family from Lula Moore, she had felt more kindly disposed toward him, even when he barked at her or fixed her with one of his black looks. One Saturday morning she was gazing out the kitchen window at her son, whom Jimmy was teaching to ride, when out of the corner of her eye she saw Daniel step onto the front porch. He started toward the yard, then stopped when he saw Lee and Jimmy. For a moment he stood there motionless, his eyes on the boy on the horse, and Melinda saw such bleak pain and longing in his eyes that it made her heart twist within her. Then he turned abruptly and stalked through the front door. He was in one of his foulest moods for the remainder of the day, but Melinda held her tongue.

That wasn't the case often, of course. When he snapped at her, she usually answered him back in kind. She had never been a timid woman, but sometimes her tart retorts surprised even herself. There were times when she thought for sure that he would release her from his employ. But he never did. It made her wonder if perhaps he secretly enjoyed their spats. Melinda knew that she often experienced a certain tingly excitement during their arguments; they could be oddly invigorating. There were even moments when, facing his bright blue eyes, his body taut with anger, she had felt, deep in the pit of her stomach, a stirring that was— well, frankly sexual.

She wouldn't have admitted that to anyone, of course, any more than she would have admitted that she

thought Daniel MacKenzie was handsome, or that she
enjoyed looking at him. Considering the way he felt
about her and how much they fought, she knew she
shouldn't like him in any way. Yet she found herself
stealing glances at him during meals, and more than
once she went to the kitchen window to watch him
cross the yard when she heard the closing of the front
door. She liked to see his long legs striding across the
ground, firm and tight inside his heavy denim trousers.
She liked the set of his shoulders and how he carried
his head. She even liked the way he tilted his hat down
in front over his forehead.

He had wonderful hands, large and strong, with
long, supple fingers. They were tanned and callused,
the nails short and blunt, the backs lightly sprinkled
with silky black hairs. Masculine hands. Melinda often
looked at them; she especially liked to see them curled
around one of the blue enameled coffee cups. She
would think of the roughness of his palms and finger-
tips and imagine how they would feel upon her skin.
Would his fingers be tender when they curled around
a woman's breast?

She rebuked herself for thinking such things. It
wasn't proper. And it wasn't possible, either. Daniel
MacKenzie would never dream of touching or kissing
her. He disliked her thoroughly. And, of course, she
wouldn't permit such a thing, even if he did want to.
Still, sometimes after she went to bed at night, she lay
looking out the window beside her bed at the big house
across the way, all silver and shadow in the moonlight,
and she would think about Daniel. Her breasts would

ache a little, her nipples tingling, and she could feel heat spreading through her. Her lips would feel alive and tender, and she would lightly rub her fingers across them, wondering what his lips would feel like. Would his beard scratch? If it did, she didn't think she'd mind. Embarrassingly, moisture would start between her legs, so that she pressed her legs together hard to stop it, but that didn't work.

Once she ran her hands slowly down her body, over her nightgown, touching her sensitive breasts and sliding down the plane of her stomach to her legs. Her eyes drifted closed as her body clamored for the touch that would ignite it. It had been two years since Robert died, two years since her body had known a man's hands. But she hadn't missed it until now, hadn't thought about it until she came to Daniel MacKenzie's house. She didn't know why he affected her this way. She didn't even like him. She wondered if she was turning into a loose woman. Could that be something that crept up on one unexpectedly? Could she change overnight from a lady into a slut? It seemed absurd. It couldn't be true. But why then was she suddenly man-crazy?

No, not man-crazy. It wasn't any man who stirred her. It was just one man. Daniel MacKenzie. Daniel MacKenzie, with his vivid blue gaze and his thick black hair, his hard, strong body. Daniel MacKenzie, who didn't even like her.

It puzzled her. It annoyed her. But she enjoyed it.

EARLY IN DECEMBER Melinda was awakened one night by the sound of hundreds of little taps against her window. Foggily, she came awake and lay listening to the tiny popping sounds. Sleet, she thought, and snuggled deeper into her covers. The sound meant bitter cold outside, and she shivered, thinking of it, and was glad for the warmth of her quilt and blankets.

The next morning her room was so cold when she made herself leave her bed that her teeth chattered. She wrapped the heavy robe around her and thrust her feet into her slippers, then hurried straight into the main room of the house to light the Franklin stove. She stirred the banked coals to life with the poker and shoved in kindling and heavier logs, as well as shavings to bring the red coals to life. The fire flamed up, and Melinda adjusted the damper. Sleepily, she huddled in front of the stove for a moment, seeking the warmth that would soon be pouring from the small metal furnace.

But she knew it would be some time before the stove became really hot, and she had no time to waste. Morning was her busiest time; that was why she rose so early, before dawn was even streaking the sky. Wrapping her arms tightly around herself, she dashed into her bedroom and pulled out her hairbrush and the clothes she would wear today. Then she ran back to the stove and laid the clothes over it to warm while she took down her hair, brushed it out and pinned it up. She had done it so many times she didn't need a mirror. She pulled on her woolen stockings, long-legged pantalets and petticoats without taking off her nightgown and robe; it was far too chilly, even by the now-roaring fire, to disrobe. Finally, however, there was no choice, and she had to let her robe and nightgown drop so that she could slip on her chemise, blouse and skirt. Last, she sat down on a footstool, pulled on her shoes and laced up the high tops.

Fully dressed, she returned to her bedroom. She broke the thin layer of ice in the wash pitcher and poured a bit of water into the bowl. She dipped her washrag into it and, grimacing, swiftly washed her face. She dried it with even more haste, then brushed her teeth with baking soda.

Her personal chores completed, she went into her son's small room and gently shook him awake. She sympathized with his groan and mumbled protest, but he had to get up. He had to leave for school early, and before that there was milking to be done. When she was sure that he was indeed awake and groping his way out of bed toward the stove, she left him. Her husband's heavy coat hung on a rack by the front door, and she pulled it on, buttoning it all the way down. She wrapped a long knitted scarf over her head and around her throat and opened the front door, pulling on her gloves as she started out. Then she stopped and stared at the scene before her. Even though she had lived in the Panhandle of Texas for over four years, she had never seen anything like this.

Icicles of various diameters and lengths hung from the roof of her porch and, across the way, from the roof, shutters, railings and gingerbread trim of the main house, as well as from the barn and all the outbuildings. All the walls of the buildings and the ground itself were covered with ice. Each twig of every branch of the mesquite bushes and twisted little shinnery trees was encased in ice, and from them dangled thousands of tiny icicles. Ice also covered the yucca plants, the scattered cacti and the blades of the low clumps of grass. Even the line of tumbleweeds that had blown up against the corral fence and lodged there was coated with ice and decorated with icicles.

The sun, rising palely in the east, touched the ice all across the yard, and it sparkled like prisms in the sun. Melinda stared. It looked like a fairyland, so delicate, crystal-clear and gleaming. She had never imagined that this bleak place could look lovely and enchanted. She smiled and went to the edge of the porch, gazing around her in delight.

A noise from the direction of the main house brought Melinda back to what she was supposed to be doing. Beautiful as the scene was, she still had breakfast to make. She wrapped one gloved hand around the narrow wooden porch column and ventured cautiously onto the ice-slick step. With the same slow movements, she stepped onto the ground. She was used to icy stairs; she had encountered them before. She was not used to ice so thick that it didn't crunch and break beneath her feet. She felt her feet slip with her first step, and she slid, her arms flailing for balance. Fortunately, she didn't fall, though she wound up several feet away in a direction she hadn't intended to go.

Determinedly, she turned toward the main house and began to make her way toward it. She walked with her arms outstretched, her eyes fixed on the ground, her steps small and tentative. Her feet slipped and skidded

so much that she appeared to be doing some outland-
ish dance, but she kept on.

Daniel MacKenzie, who had come out of the side
door of his house on his way to the barn, paused to
watch her. She was wearing that coat again; the sight
reminded him of how much the garment irritated him.
It was way too big for her, and the cut was mannish,
as well. She needed a woman's coat or a cloak, something warm and feminine, as befitted her. He wondered
what she had done with her own coat; obviously her
financial straits had been the cause of it, whatever it
was. Why hadn't her husband provided better for her?
It wasn't right that a lady like Melinda should be
reduced to having to become a housekeeper for some
churlish, ill-tempered man.

Frowning over his thoughts, MacKenzie went down
the steps and started across the icy ground. He, too,
stepped carefully, although his greater weight and the
heels of his boots kept him from sliding as much as
Melinda. He was walking past her, a few feet away,
when suddenly her feet went flying, and without
warning she slid across the ground and slammed into
him. Instinctively Daniel's arms went around her, and
he battled to steady them both. For a moment they
were flat against each other, his arms encircling her, her
hands clutching at the front of his coat.

Then his feet slipped, too, and suddenly he landed
flat on his back, with Melinda stretched on top of him.
They lay staring into each other's eyes. Though their
heavy winter clothing made it impossible for them to
actually feel each other's bodies, they were both in-

tensely aware of their position. With their faces only inches apart, Melinda could feel Daniel's breath on her skin. She had never been this close to any man except her husband. She couldn't keep from thinking about his arms, his legs, his chest pressed against her body. Beneath all the layers of clothing, her nipples started to tingle, and her thighs relaxed and grew warm. Her eyes widened at the sensations budding within her. Then she realized with horror how long she had been lying there on top of him, staring and making no effort to remove herself. A blush started in her cheeks, adding to the rosiness already put there by the cold.

She began to struggle to get up at the same time that he did, but all they accomplished was another fall. This time when they landed, it was MacKenzie who was stretched out atop her. It was, if possible, an even more suggestive position. His weight was heavy on her, pushing her into the chilling ground, but Melinda felt no pain, only a delicious heaviness in her abdomen and legs. Her skirt had become rucked up, and she could feel the coarse material of his trousers against her stockinged legs. She gazed up at him, her breath coming fast and hard in her throat. He could feel the quicker movement of her chest against his, see the heightened color of her cheeks. His eyes went to her mouth, pink and moist, lips slightly parted, and he could not look away. Melinda could see his eyes darken. Unconsciously she sucked in her lower lip. His eyes followed the movement, and he moved his legs apart and down on either side of hers, clamping hers in between them. His head lowered, and for a wild, brief instant Melinda thought that he would kiss her.

Then a child's laughter erupted from the porch of her house, and Daniel's head snapped up. He scowled over at Lee, who had come outside and had seen them go tumbling twice. When Daniel glared at him, Lee clapped both hands over his mouth, but even that couldn't stifle his laughter. Daniel looked back down at Melinda, and his frown grew even fiercer. He rolled away from her, and she tried to scramble to her feet. She managed to make it to her hands and knees before MacKenzie, also trying to rise, went sprawling on the ice and knocked her legs out from under her. Irritated, she rolled over to her back to try to get up that way, and as she turned, her elbow slammed into Daniel's side. He grunted, clutching his side, as he fell again.

"Damnation!" He glared at her. "Are you trying to kill me?"

"Kill you!" Melinda retorted heatedly. "Who just knocked *me* to the ground?" She tried to jump up indignantly, but her feet skidded out from under before she could get even halfway up, spoiling the pose.

"You came barreling right into me, not the other way around!"

They bickered as they thrashed around, unable to get a purchase on the slick ground. Melinda slipped, and her foot jolted the back of Daniel's knee, sending him tumbling; he rolled just as she reached out to steady herself with a hand on his shoulder, and she went sprawling. It seemed as if any progress either of them made was immediately ruined by the other one's flopping around.

Up on the porch, Lee abandoned any attempt to

hide his laughter. He doubled over, shrieking with merriment. Melinda, struggling vainly to rise on the slippery ice, wasn't sure whether she wanted to hit him or MacKenzie more. Daniel got up on his hands and knees, but he couldn't haul himself to his feet, because his hands and knees kept slipping with every movement he made. Melinda, looking at him, was reminded of a dog she'd once had that would run onto a freshly waxed floor, then scrabble frantically to stay on his feet. She began to giggle; then she was laughing. Suddenly her irritation and frustration exploded into hilarity.

MacKenzie shot Melinda a black look and started to explode into a tirade concerning her lack of respect and general want of sense, but just as he opened his mouth, his hands and legs began to slide slowly in different directions. He was powerless to stop them, and Melinda, watching him, wrapped her arms around her waist and laughed even harder. Suddenly, unexpectedly, Daniel grinned. Melinda had never seen him smile, *really* smile, and it almost took her breath away. The next thing she knew, he was lying flat on the ground and had given himself up completely to laughter. She thought she had never heard anything so wonderful.

CHAPTER FIVE

MELINDA PUSHED ASIDE the heavy curtains and looked out the parlor window. The ice had made it impossible for the children to go to school, and they were celebrating the unexpected holiday by sliding down Windmill Hill. She smiled, listening to their shrieks of laughter. They had better make the most of it today, for the sun was out and already at work melting the icy wonderland.

She watched one of the foreman's boys zooming down the hill on a sheet of tin. Lee was struggling to make his way up the hill, having already slid down. His feet seemed to slip back as much as they went forward, and he was making his way primarily by pulling himself from one skinny tree or bush to the next. His feet slipped out from under him, and Melinda winced. But he clambered to his feet, laughing.

She thought about Daniel and her struggling on the ice early this morning, and a chuckle rose in her throat at the memory. Her face softened as she thought of their hilarity. She didn't think she had ever heard Daniel laugh before. Oh, sometimes his mouth twisted into a sarcastic smile, or he let out an ironic chuckle, but never a deep belly laugh of pure fun.

Smiling, Melinda tied back the heavy draperies and began to dust. The cold and the shrieks of laughter from outside made her think about Christmas. It was already December, so the season was getting close. She needed to make the fruitcakes soon; they required several weeks to set. And she should ask Daniel—that is, Mr. MacKenzie—to bring out the Christmas decorations. Melinda's smile grew wider. It would be fun having a big house to decorate again, and enough kitchen and storage space that she could make a real Christmas meal. Christmas had been so cramped and awful those years in the sod dugout. This year, at last, she would have some money to buy Lee toys. She had gotten her first month's salary, and just this once she planned not to save a bit of it, but to splurge on Lee for Christmas. He'd been so good the last two years, never complaining, even though she hadn't been able to buy the set of tin soldiers he wanted.

Well, this year he would get them. She'd seen a lovely set of British soldiers in the hardware store, their coats a shiny red and their guns deep black. She could get him a chess set, too, and—oh, there were so many things. It would be fun to prowl through the stores, not the agony it had been last year.

Humming, she finished her household chores quickly. By midday she was through, and after the hands had eaten and she had cleaned up the dishes, she sat down with the makings of fruitcake and several large metal pans. She poured a pile of pecans onto her chopping block and started chopping. Sacks of pecans had been one of her first purchases after she arrived at the ranch, for she had known how many would be needed for the various Christmas and winter dishes. Practically every evening she and Lee had shelled pecans when their other work was done, picking out the meats and storing them in tin cans. There was still plenty of shelling left to do, but at least she had enough nuts for the fruitcakes.

When she had chopped up the pecans, she started on the citron, dates and candied orange peel. It was a long, tedious process, her least favorite in the fruitcake making, for the candied fruit was sticky and messy, clinging to the knife, the board and her hands, and clumping up in the bowl. As she worked, her thoughts strayed back to East Texas and the Christmas celebrations there, and she sighed wistfully. She remembered the sounds of the pecans plopping onto the roof in November. When she had awakened to those noises as a little girl, she had known that it wouldn't be long until Christmas season. Soon after, there had been the pecan gathering, when they had spread bedsheets and blankets out on the ground and shaken the trees, then picked up the pecans and poured them into gunnysacks.

She remembered the way the cold had crept up on them more gradually than it did here, and as it had gotten colder, her excitement had grown. Melinda's hands stilled, and she leaned back in the chair, thinking of the hot kitchen at home, the windows fogging over from the cold outside. Mama and Gran had bustled around, making the oyster stuffing from the recipe that had been handed down through the family clear back to Gran's grandmother, who had grown up in coastal

Georgia. A couple of weeks before Christmas, Daddy, who had already scouted out the best pine or cedar tree in the long woods between their farm and Uncle Clinton's place, would come in one day carrying the tree. After that, the children's excitement had been almost more than they could contain.

She and her older sisters had fashioned swags of evergreen and decorated the mantels and doors. They had made strings of popcorn and cranberries, and paper chains, to hang on the tree with the ornaments, and on top there had always been an angel with hair like spun sugar and gossamer wings. Daddy had brought home a box of oranges and a big clump of bananas, as well as a sprig of mistletoe shipped in from Central Texas. He would always tiptoe in the kitchen door, hiding the mistletoe behind his back, and sneak up behind Mama and hold it over his head while he stole a kiss from her. It made the children squeal with laughter, and Mama would shake her finger at him and pretend that she was angry, but everyone knew that her face was flushed more from pleasure than from the heat of the stove.

Melinda remembered their stockings hanging from the mantel and the excitement of sneaking downstairs at dawn the next morning to look with wonder at all the gifts. Then, when the presents had been opened, they had trooped into the kitchen for crisp golden waffles and bacon, and Daddy had read the Christmas story from the Bible before they ate. There had been mountains of food the whole day through, and in the afternoon, the house had swarmed with relatives and friends who'd dropped in to visit. By evening all the aunts and uncles and cousins were there, and when it got dark they'd set off the fireworks. Gran was a staunch Rebel still, who often reminded them that Gramps had fought under Stonewall Jackson, so their family hadn't gone in much for fireworks on the Fourth of July. It was Christmas when they set them off. She remembered running across the lawn in the dark, a sparkler fizzing in her hand and firecrackers popping in the background, the cold stinging her cheeks. It had seemed as though nothing in the world could be more wonderful.

Tears gathered in her eyes. Suddenly Melinda realized that she was sitting with her hands idle, crying over Christmases past. She shook her head and straightened, blinking the tears from her eyes, and went back to work.

She was surprised a few minutes later when there was a knock on the door and Mrs. Moore bustled in, wrapped up in heavy coverings from head to toe. Lula giggled as she began to unwind the woolen scarf from her head. "Do I look like a woolly bear? It's still cold as floogens out there, even if the sun is shining. So I figured I better wrap up, 'cause I knew it might take me a while to get here." She stepped out of the man-size boots she wore over her shoes and untied her cloak. It took some time before she was free of her outer garments.

"Whew!" she exclaimed, plopping down across the kitchen table from Melinda and automatically taking up a knife to help work. "What an undertaking. But I had to get out of the house. Will doesn't have anything to do outside. It's too slippery to even ride out to check the stock. He's been prowling the house all day long, until I was ready to go out of my head. I had to get out of there."

Melinda smiled. "I'm glad of the company."

"Making fruitcake?" Lula asked, nodding toward the citron, dates and candied peel.

"Yes. I figured I'd need to make a lot, considering that crowd of men."

"They sure can eat," Lula agreed. "I'll have to start on my fruitcakes tomorrow, I guess. I've been working the past couple of days on Opal's and my dresses to the Cowboys' Christmas Ball. What are you wearing this year?"

Melinda paused in her work and looked at the other woman. "You know, I hadn't even thought about it. I haven't gone the past couple of years, since Mr. Ballard died." The Cowboys' Christmas Ball was a huge party and dance held every year by Austin Carter, the owner of the Barrett Hotel, on the Saturday before Christmas. It was the major social event of the year, and people came from miles around. Despite its name, everyone was invited, not just the ranchers and their people, but the townspeople and homesteaders, as well. Melinda, Robert and Lee had attended the first two years they had lived here.

"But you'll go this year, won't you? Daniel never goes, but all the hands do, and so do Will and I and the children. You can ride with us."

Melinda thought about it. It would be fun to go to a party again, to dance and talk and laugh. It would be a rare occasion to dress up, as well as a chance to get together with other women and chat. Living out here, where there were often miles and miles between neighbors, could get very lonely. "I'd like to…." She hesitated.

The problem was a dress. She had only one nice dress, a blue wool, Sunday-go-to-meeting kind of dress. Not only had she worn it on every special occasion for the past few years, but it also wasn't really a dance dress, for it was high-necked and rather plain. The first two years when she had gone to the ball, she had worn a green velvet party dress that she'd brought with her from East Texas, but it was old and its nap had become worn. She'd had it for ages, and it wasn't new and stylish, and she—well, face it, she wanted to look pretty and special.

"Then it's settled," Lula went on assuredly. "You'll have a grand time. I always do. Will won't dance, but there's plenty of other men that do." She grinned meaningfully at Melinda. "A lot of unattached men, too."

"I'm not in the market for a husband."

"Pooh." Lula waved away that objection. "What single woman isn't?"

They continued to talk as they prepared the fruitcakes. Melinda discovered that Mrs. Moore's fingers moved as fast as her mouth, and by the time Lula left that afternoon, eight fruitcakes had been mixed and put into deep, narrow cake pans. After Lula's departure, Melinda cleared a space on the pantry shelves for several wide, shallow biscuit tins, into which she poured steaming hot water. She covered the fruitcake pans with clean linen napkins and set them into the biscuit tins for the slow steaming they required.

As she worked she thought about the upcoming Christmas dance and what she could wear to it. The more she thought, the more she wanted to go. However, while she had enough money to buy Christmas things for Lee with her first month's salary, she couldn't afford the yards of expensive material she would need for a ball gown, too. And Lee came first.

When dinner was over, she went to her house and looked through her clothes, as though something would pop out that she had forgotten. Unfortunately, they were all the same: serviceable dull black, brown and blue skirts and blouses. She sighed. She didn't have time to make anything, anyway, even if she had the money. She would be busy with her normal work, which was exhausting, as well as the extra Christmas tasks. She would just have to wear her blue Sunday dress. That was more befitting to a widow who had a child and wasn't young anymore.

As she turned away, she caught sight of a big brown box on the top shelf of the wardrobe. She stopped. She had forgotten about that. When they had moved here, she had been unable to throw away her wedding gown and had brought it with her. No doubt it had turned yellow and was falling to pieces by now. Melinda hesitated, then stretched up on tiptoe and pulled down the box. She untied the string that kept it tightly shut and opened it. Lace and satin cascaded out. She pulled out the gown and spread it on the bed. The style was too old-fashioned, of course, and the color was all wrong.

But it was beautiful, expensive material, suited for a ball gown, and if she dyed it another color and did extensive alterations...

Melinda smiled. She could make something of it. It was probably unfeeling of her to use her wedding dress for a mere party dress, but she couldn't help it. The idea of having something pretty and new to wear was too tempting.

Smiling to herself, she found a piece of paper and began to sketch what she would do.

TWO NIGHTS LATER Melinda sat in her parlor beside the Franklin stove, her head close to the kerosene lamp to catch every bit of its light, cutting and stitching on what would become her ball gown. It was after ten o'clock, and she should have been in bed, for her mornings always started early. She had undressed and put on her nightgown and bed robe, and her hair hung loose around her shoulders. She had been on her way to bed, in fact, but she hadn't felt very sleepy, and she had been unable to resist doing a little more work on her dress.

The wind whined around the corner of the house; it was a lonesome, chilling sound, and Melinda shivered, even though she was warm enough beside the metal stove. The sun had shone brightly for the past two days, melting the ice except for the patches protected by shade, but the temperature continued to be cold, especially at night.

There was a sound outside, and she paused with her hand over her dress. She sat motionless, listening. It had sounded like a shout. There it was again, only closer. She stood up, leaving the dress on her rocker, and went over to the window to pull aside the curtain and peer out. It was a dark night; there was no moon. For a moment she could see nothing. Then she detected a flash of movement on the porch of the big house, and suddenly the bell that hung there rang out. Melinda jumped, startled, and one hand flew to her heart.

The bell ringing at night could only mean that there was some sort of emergency. Was someone sick? No, there would have been no need to awaken everyone on the ranch for that. It must be something that required help. The bell continued to clang. Lights sprang to life down in the bunkhouse and the foreman's house. She saw the front door of the ranch house open, and Daniel emerged holding a kerosene lamp. His hair was rumpled, as though he had been asleep, and his shirt-tails hung down outside his trousers. She watched as the cowhand left the bell and ran to Daniel. He gestured in an agitated manner and pointed toward the barn. Daniel whipped into the house, then came out again without the lamp, and the two men ran toward the barn.

Melinda could see nothing unusual. She hurried to the front door and opened it. There were men running toward the barn from all over now. Behind her she heard Lee's sleepy voice, "What is it, Mama?"

"I'm not sure." Then she saw a peculiar glow at the far end of the building, and she gasped. "Oh, my Lord in Heaven! It's a fire! Quick! They'll need everybody's help."

Melinda ran into her bedroom and exchanged her

soft at-home slippers for her work shoes. She didn't take the time to change into a dress. Every minute counted with a fire. Instead, she just threw her coat on over her robe and gown and grabbed a pail from the kitchen. She ran out the door and across the yard toward the barn, the bucket bouncing against her leg. Lee was right beside her.

Some of the men, including Daniel, were wearing bandannas over their faces to protect them from the smoke and were bringing the fear-maddened horses out of the barn and turning them loose. Will Moore ran to the corral gate, where the horses were already shifting around nervously and whinnying. He flung it open and let the animals out. Other men hurried back and forth from the small round metal stock tank inside the corral to the barn, carrying buckets of water to throw on the flames. It was obvious to Melinda that the water in the tank would not be nearly enough, so she went to the pump handle and began to pump vigorously. Lee took the bucket, scooped up a pailful of water and ran to join the men in the barn.

Melinda pumped and pumped until she thought her arms would fall off. When she could do it no longer, Lee switched places with her, and she carried the bucket, heavy with water, to the fire. Before long it was clear that the barn could not be saved, and Daniel shouted at the men to leave it. They concentrated on wetting down the corral fences and the ground around the barn. After that, the side of the bunkhouse and the outbuildings were soaked with water. The worst was not losing the barn; that could be rebuilt rather easily, considering the number of hands who worked for Daniel. The real danger was that the fire might spread from the flaming barn to the surrounding buildings and destroy them or, worse yet, spread to the grass and blaze across the prairie.

She traded places with Lee again and continued to pump. Now and then she paused to straighten her back and rest her hands and arms. Even accustomed as she was to hard work, her muscles were crying out in protest, and she could feel blisters forming on the palms of her hands. She wished she had thought to grab her gloves when she ran out the door. Whenever she stopped, her eyes roamed over the men until she found Daniel. He wasn't hard to find, for he was always in the thick of things, shouting orders and throwing himself into whatever needed to be done. His face was lit eerily by the glow of the fire in the dark night. Sweat shone on his skin, and despite the cold, dark patches of wetness had formed on his shirt. He looked hard and strong and competent.

As she watched him, Melinda's heart squeezed within her chest, and she felt as if she were suddenly spinning crazily. She bit her lip and returned to her pumping with renewed vigor, her irritation with herself pouring into work. It wasn't love, she told herself sternly. She couldn't possibly have any feeling for a man like Daniel MacKenzie. Desiring him was one thing; he was, after all, a handsome, powerful man, whatever his faults. But his faults were plainly there, and surely she wasn't foolish enough to ignore them. He was rough, rude and hard; he disliked women, and he didn't want her son around.

But then she thought of the piercing blue of his eyes and of his thick black hair. She thought of the warmth that always started in her stomach whenever he looked at her. She remembered the tragedies that had marred his life and thought that perhaps they had soured him, that he hadn't always been like this. She remembered his laughter the other morning and his unexpected, flashing grin, and she thought that perhaps he was changing. Might not that hard shell crack and fall away under the warmth of a woman's love?

Her hand slowed on the pump handle. She realized what she was doing and shook her thoughts away. Sternly she returned to pumping. She looked up when she felt a hand on her arm. Lula Moore stood beside her. "They've just about got everything watered down," she told Melinda. "They're starting to dig a fire trench around it now. There's nothing you can do here. But you could make some sandwiches and coffee. I have a feeling that when this is over, they're going to be mighty hungry."

Melinda nodded, grateful to give up the job. She walked up to the ranch house while Lula returned to her own home. Inside the kitchen, Melinda peeled off her coat. The fire and hard work had made her hot, and she was grateful to get out of the heavy garment. She would have stripped it off outside, she had grown so warm, but it had seemed too bold, considering that she had on only her robe and nightgown underneath. She started a fire in the stove, then washed the dirt and soot from her hands. She prepared two pots of coffee and put them onto the stove to boil while she began to make thick sandwiches for the men.

When she had a tray piled with sandwiches, she called Lee and gave it to him to pass around. She put her coat back on and carried out a tray of cups and the coffee. The men grabbed the sandwiches and ate hungrily, then gulped down the coffee. They were almost finished with their task, and they returned to it with renewed energy now, with food and hot coffee in their stomachs. Melinda went back to the house to replenish both pots of coffee. At the porch, she turned and looked back. The barn was burning fiercely against the black sky, casting a red, flickering light over the toiling men. It reminded her of a scene from an illustrated book of Dante's *Inferno* that she had seen in her parents' house.

But she could see that the fire wasn't spreading, no matter how awful it looked. The men were winning the fight. She pulled herself away from the scene and went inside to wash out the pots and make more coffee.

She was standing by the stove, her coat off, waiting for the coffee to finish, when the side door opened and Daniel walked in. His clothes were stained with sweat, dirt and soot, and his shirt hung open down the front, the tails outside his pants. His sleeves were rolled up, and he had obviously washed his face and arms under the pump outside, for they were clean and still damp. His face was weary and marked by sleeplessness, but he was smiling.

"You did it!" Melinda guessed.

He stopped, as though surprised to see her there. He stared at her, and Melinda was suddenly very aware of her state of dishabille. Heavy and unrevealing as her gown and robe were, they were still nighttime clothing, not the kind of thing to be wearing in front of a man. And her hair was unbound. No man except her husband had seen her with her hair unbound since she was fourteen. Nervously she pushed it back from her shoulders. If only he wouldn't stare so!

"Yeah." Daniel's voice sounded a little rusty. Frankly, he was surprised he'd even been able to say anything. He hadn't expected to see Melinda in his kitchen; he had thought she had finally gone back to bed. But here she was, in his house, standing there in her nightclothes. They covered up more of her skin than lots of evening dresses, but somehow the knowledge that this was what she wore to sleep in, that only one layer of cloth lay between that robe and her bare skin, made his own skin feel as if he were standing in front of that fire again.

Her hair hung loosely around her face and down to her waist, thick and soft and dark. He had never seen her hair down before; it was a husband's privilege. His fingers itched to reach out and touch it. Almost involuntarily he moved toward her. "Yeah, we stopped it," he told her, hardly aware of what he was saying.

He stopped only a foot away from her. Melinda was startled by how close he had come, but she didn't step back. A frisson of excitement ran along her skin, sparking a warmth deep in her abdomen. She could smell the smoke on him; she could see the drop of water, like crystal, that nestled in the hollow of his throat. She thought that she would like to lick that drop of water from his skin with her tongue, and she pressed her lips together tightly. What if he read her thoughts on her face?

But Daniel had no interest in trying to interpret her expression. He was too lost in her big gray eyes, too busy grappling with the violent emotions churning inside him. When he'd come in he had been tired but elated, charged with their successful escape from danger. Somehow, when he saw Melinda, the elation had exploded into something clse—an eager, electric, intensely sensual excitement. He wanted her, right here, right now, as badly as he had ever wanted any woman. Maybe worse.

He reached out a hand to her hair, and his fingers skimmed lightly over it. The silky strands caught and clung to the calluses on his fingertips, and it was like fire licking through his abdomen. God, her hair was lovely, so thick and soft. He wanted to sink his hands into it; he wanted to bury his face in it. He could see his fingers trembling slightly, and he didn't know if it was from the physical strain of what he'd done tonight or from sheer desire.

"I saw you earlier, pitching in to fight the fire. You're a brave woman."

Melinda gazed up into his face. His touch, the expression in his eyes, the heat of his body so close to her, made her feel weak and liquid. Her thoughts were scattered and confused; she struggled to pull together a coherent sentence.

His hand slid down her hair and onto her arm, then to her hand. His fingers grazed one of the raw places on her palm, and she winced involuntarily. He frowned and lifted her hand to look at it. "You hurt yourself!"

"Just some blisters." She offered a small, self-dep-recating smile. "I forgot to put on my gloves."

"I'm sorry."

"It's not your fault."

"You hurt yourself trying to save something that was mine." He didn't tell her that the thought made him feel both angry with himself and yet fiercely proud and possessive.

Daniel led her to the sink and gently washed her hands, cleaning the raw places with infinite care and blotting them dry. He took an unguent from the medicine box in one of the cabinets and spread it over the reddened and blistered skin. Then he wrapped gauze carefully around each palm and tied it.

They stood there for a moment, her hands resting in his. Slowly, never taking his eyes from her face, Daniel raised Melinda's hands to his lips and gently kissed each one. She stared at him, her eyes huge, her chest rising and falling with her rapid breathing. She was filled with yearning and anticipation, hardly daring to breathe or move, lest it break the enchantment lying over them and make Daniel leave.

Instead, he came closer, his head lowering to hers, and Melinda went up on tiptoe to meet him. His hands slid down her arms and sides, brushing her breasts in passing, and stopped at her waist. He pulled her up and close to him, and her arms went around his neck. Their lips met and clung as his arms slid around her, squeez-ing her to him, and he deepened the kiss. His mouth was hot and urgent. Melinda's lips opened beneath his insistent pressure, and his tongue moved inside her mouth, wet and velvety. He explored her mouth, arousing wild, tingling sensations that shot all through her as his harsh, rasping breath sounded in her ears.

Melinda shivered and clung to him. She felt dizzy and breathless, as though sparklers were shooting through her. Her tongue touched his, and she felt Daniel shudder. His skin grew hotter, and he pressed her more tightly against him. His response was like a match to the dry tinder of Melinda's desire. She was suddenly aflame, conscious of nothing but heat and urgency. Her tongue stroked and tangled with his, and he groaned. Feverishly his hands ran down over her buttocks and back up, bunching up her robe.

There was the sound of feet on the wooden steps outside, and Lee's voice called, "Mama? Are you in here?"

They sprang apart, and Melinda whirled away. Her hands flew to her burning cheeks, and she wondered if it was clear from her face what had been going on. She heard Daniel's boots crossing the floor, and then the sound of the outside door opening.

"Mama?" Lee came into the room, babbling excitedly. "Did you see it? We stopped it. I watched that ol' barn burn, and oh, boy, was it somethin'!"

Melinda drew a deep, calming breath and turned around. Lee was chattering and reaching for one of the leftover sandwiches, hardly even glancing at her. Except for him, the room was empty. Daniel was gone.

CHAPTER SIX

MELINDA AND LEE returned to their house, but after she lay down, she tossed and turned, too keyed up to sleep. She couldn't stop thinking of what had happened between her and Daniel. She blushed at the thought of how boldly she had behaved, and she wondered what he must think of her. But then she remembered the force of his own passion, and she giggled, smothering the sound with her pillow. Surely, with the way *he* had kissed *her,* he wouldn't think her forward. She was amazed when she remembered how hungrily he had kissed her, how his hands had moved over her back and hips. She had thought he didn't even like her!

Just tonight she had realized that she was beginning to feel too much for the man who employed her, and then he had taken her in his arms and kissed her like that. It must mean that he cared for her. And yet…the idea was absurd. How could he care for her? He'd hardly spoken two civil words to her the whole time she'd been here. But then, she reminded herself, it seemed just as unlikely for her to feel anything for him. Yet, crazily enough, she knew she did. She thought about him almost all the time; her hands lingered longer than was necessary over his clothes when she folded them; she cleaned the two rooms that were most particularly his, his bedroom and the study, more often than any other rooms in the house, except the kitchen.

When he had taken her into his arms, it had felt so right, so wonderful and exciting. She couldn't remember ever feeling that kind of wild, leaping desire, even with her husband. Certainly she had never kissed Robert with such fervor. The intensity of the sensations she had felt stunned her. Could this be love? It wasn't at all what it had been with Robert. She and Robert had been friends all their lives, long before they grew to love each other. Their love had had a solid basis of friendship, respect and shared memories. Their courtship had been sweet and innocent, and on their wedding night he had been gentle and slow with her. They had argued, of course. What married couple didn't? But their arguments had been quiet differences of opinion that were usually resolved with a kiss and a hug. And if at times they had grown a trifle bored with each other, well, that was the way life was. That was the way love was. Wasn't it?

Was it possible that the wild and stormy feelings that Daniel MacKenzie engendered in her were also love? All the bright, burning anger, the desire bursting in her like fireworks when he kissed her, the excitement that rippled through her whenever he was around—were those surging, conflicting emotions love?

Melinda didn't know what to think. She didn't know what to expect from Daniel. She didn't even know what she wanted. But she knew she could hardly wait until the next day to see him again.

MELINDA AWOKE FAR LATER than usual the next morning. She ran anxiously to the big house to prepare breakfast and was relieved to see that the ranch hands weren't sitting there waiting hungrily for their food. After the hard, late night they'd all had, everyone must be sleeping late. She scurried around, getting breakfast, her ears cocked all the time for the sound of the inner door opening and Daniel entering the room. But it didn't happen.

Some time later, when the food was prepared and she had rung the bell calling them to eat, the ranch hands began to file in. Daniel was among them. He must have been out working already. Melinda turned toward him, her heart rising in her throat, waiting for a smile or a special look. But he didn't so much as glance at her. She sat down at her place, feeling sick inside, and pushed her food around. It was all she could do to hold back the tears.

Later, when the hands had left, Daniel lingered, standing behind his chair, his hands clenched on the wood so hard that his knuckles turned white. Hope began to rise in Melinda again. Perhaps he had been embarrassed to show anything for her in front of the men. That made sense. She went to the table on the pretext of carrying some dishes to the sink. In fact, what she wanted was to be close to Daniel, to give him an opportunity to speak to her. Her heart was pounding like mad with anticipation. She lowered her head, suddenly too shy to look into his face.

Daniel cleared his throat. "Uh, Melinda…that is, Mrs. Ballard. I…I apologize for last night." His voice was as stiff and cool as if she were a complete stranger instead of the woman he had fervently kissed only a few hours ago. "It was inexcusable of me. It was late, and we had all been working hard. I fear that my jubilation carried me away."

So! It wasn't any feeling for her, or even desire, that had made him kiss her. It was simply that his excitement about their victory over the fire had bubbled over, and she had happened to be the only person around to kiss. Melinda kept her head down. She couldn't bear to let him see the tears forming in her eyes. She refused to let him know how he had hurt her.

"Of course," she replied, pleased that she could keep her voice so steady and cool. "I understand. No doubt it was the same for me."

She turned and walked to the sink. She scraped off several dishes and set them into the soapy washing pan, all the while keeping her back to Daniel. He stood for a moment without saying anything. Then she heard the sound of his boots on the floor and the inner door swinging shut. He was gone. Melinda went to the table and carried another load of dishes over. She worked quickly and efficiently, as she always did. But now, as she scraped and washed and rinsed, tears poured silently down her cheeks.

MELINDA TOLD HERSELF that she was no worse off than before. She had never believed that Daniel wanted her until that kiss. Now she knew for sure that he didn't.

Or if he *had* wanted her, even a little, he must have been disgusted by the forward way she had flung her arms around him and kissed him back. But her life was not changed. She still worked here, still had her son, still had—well, whatever she had had before. At the moment she was experiencing some difficulties in counting her blessings, but they were there, she knew. Things were the same. *She* was the same.

The only problem was, that was a lie. She wasn't the same. She was hurt, confused and angry. And she couldn't forget the taste of Daniel's mouth on hers or the strength of his arms around her—or the wild feelings that had risen up in her in response.

For the next few days Melinda avoided Daniel as assiduously as he avoided her. They were together only at mealtimes, and then neither one of them looked at or spoke to the other one. If a dish of food was sitting in front of Daniel, Melinda would have starved rather than ask him to pass it to her. She talked to the other men as she always did, laughing at their jokes and listening to their stories, doing her best to pretend that she was not hurt.

Unfortunately, she knew she could not avoid Daniel much longer. She had to ask him about the Christmas tree and decorations. She refused to let her feelings of shame and hurt keep her from putting on a proper Christmas for Lee. She would have to brace herself to talk to Daniel, and soon. There were only two weeks left before Christmas.

She realized that it would be easier to speak to him with other people around. At least it wouldn't appear as if she wanted to steal a moment alone with him.

So, as dinner was ending one day, she summoned up her courage and looked down to the other end of the table. "Mr. MacKenzie."

Daniel's fork clattered onto his plate, and his head snapped up. He was grateful for his beard, because he was afraid he was blushing. Hearing her speak his name, which hadn't happened in three days, had startled him, but even more upsetting was the response that shot through him. He was hungry, shamefully hungry, for any word or look from her. If she had shown him even a smidgeon of encouragement, he thought he would have gone down on his knees to her, begging her for her love.

Oh, damn! There he went again. His lips tightened, and the familiar self-anger surfaced. He hated himself for kissing her. He hated himself for feeling this way. Why was he such a fool where women were concerned?

It had been contemptible of him to kiss her the other night—and he knew how much further he would have gone, blind to anything but his lust, if her boy hadn't barged in on them. Melinda Ballard was not a woman of light virtue. He couldn't just take her to his bed and enjoy her, then cast her aside, as he could the women in the red-light district in Amarillo. He couldn't ease his hot, surging desires with her soft, womanly flesh. She was a lady, a woman to be loved and cherished and married, as well as to take pleasure from. He had been close, dangerously close, to doing all those things.

But he knew that falling in love with Melinda would be foolish in the extreme. He had sworn after Millicent died that he would never love another woman, never marry again. His own bitter experience had taught him what a mistake love was. He had fallen head over heels in love with Millicent, carried away by her feminine sweetness and beauty. He had married her and brought her proudly to this home that he had built for her. But their love had died, crushed under the sledgehammer of reality.

He wasn't meant to be married. He loved this land; women hated it. Millicent had cried for hours when he brought her to the ranch, and she'd never adjusted to it. She had wanted desperately to leave, and after a few months he had been willing for her to go home to Maryland. Standing in the wreckage of his hopes and dreams of love, he had agreed to a separation, but then she had found out that she was pregnant. After his son was born, he couldn't bear to lose Matthew, so he had refused to let her go unless she was willing to leave Matthew with him. They had continued to live together in a loveless, miserable state. Then she had died. The land she had hated so much had killed her. He had killed her by refusing to set her free.

Daniel had tried to tell himself that it was just Millicent who had hated it here, but he knew it wasn't true. This was a harsh, hard country, unsuitable to a woman's soft nature. He had heard many other women complain about the Panhandle—the loneliness, the hardships, the weather, the bleak, flat landscape. One afternoon a week or so after Melinda came to the ranch, he had overheard her in the kitchen talking to Lula Moore, extolling the virtues and beauty of East Texas.

She had told Lula that her dream was to save enough money to move back there. She hated it here, just like any other woman. Just like Millicent.

But it wasn't only the land that had killed his love for Millicent. She had, quite frankly, irritated him with her weakness, her vapors and her ceaseless complaining. She had had no interest in him or the ranch, only in dresses and hairstyles and gossip. It seemed as though she knew how to do nothing useful. Of course, that was the way women were supposed to be. He remembered finding her idle chatter charmingly girlish before they were married, and he had smiled indulgently when she'd pouted prettily and begged him not to talk of business and "such man things." At that time he had been eager to talk instead of the glory of her blond curls and the glow of her skin and the velvet beauty of her eyes. He had been happy to shelter her from the silly little things that frightened her.

But the charm had quickly turned to irritation when she had cowered under the bed covers during a thunderstorm or squeaked with horror at the idea of riding around the ranch with him or refused to take her meals with the "rough, wild men" who worked for him. Her sweet, maidenly shyness had turned out to be coldness and repulsion in the marriage bed. At first he'd felt like an ogre for wanting to take her sweet young body, but desire had rapidly turned into indifference.

Daniel's wayward heart kept telling him that Melinda Ballard was different. He'd never seen anyone who worked harder—and without complaints. He remembered how she had pitched in and fought the fire the other night with him and his men, pumping water until her poor hands were raw and blistered. And he thought of the way she had kissed him back; there had been no coldness in her. She wasn't like Millicent. Maybe if he allowed himself to love her, it wouldn't turn sour and hopeless.

But the familiar guilt flooded him when he compared Melinda to his late wife. It hadn't been Millicent's fault that she hadn't lived up to his expectations; it had been his fault for dragging her out here, for putting too many burdens on her, for wanting too much. He had killed her with his selfishness, and he couldn't forget that, couldn't explain it away. It could happen again. What would he do if he fell in love with Melinda, married her, then found their love crumbling around him as the other had? He couldn't allow that. He couldn't bear it again. Fear and doubt and guilt mingled in him, and somehow they all turned into anger—anger at himself, at Melinda, at the world.

He forced himself to look at her with polite indifference as he answered her. "Yes, Mrs. Ballard?"

"It's only two weeks until Christmas."

"Thank you for keeping me informed of the date," he returned, his roiling emotions seeping out in sarcasm. He disliked himself for speaking to her this way, yet he could not help it. It was all he could do not to explode into a rage, churning as he was with so many combustible emotions.

Melinda crossed her arms and set her mouth. He was as cantankerous as always. You'd think he was an old man, given the joyless, nasty way he responded to everything. Her voice was icy as she went on. "I merely wanted to remind you to get out the Christmas decorations. And we need a tree. I should start decorating as soon as possible."

Daniel's brows drew together. "I have no Christmas decorations," he snapped. "Nor will there be a blasted tree in this house."

Melinda's anger rose up to meet his. She wanted to scream at him, but she struggled to control herself. After all, she must remember that memories of Christmas with his dead son must hurt him. "I always celebrate Christmas," she said through clenched teeth.

"It'd be nice to have Christmas." Corley, one of the younger hands, spoke up. "I remember Ma always had Christmas cookies settin' out, and those red flowers she'd buy in town—" He stopped abruptly, silenced by one fierce glance from his boss.

"Of course it would," Melinda agreed stoutly. "No one," she said significantly, fixing her gaze on Daniel, "gets too old or too *mean* for Christmas."

Daniel's eyes flashed and his fist thudded down on the table. "Damn it, woman, I said no! This is my house, and I'll not have you or anyone else telling me what to do." He stood up, and his chair shot back and turned over with a crash.

Melinda jumped up, too, planting her hands on her hips. "Someone needs to tell you what to do! You're too stubborn and cranky to see sense!"

He wanted to roar. He wanted to grab her and shake her. He wanted to kiss her and go on kissing her forever. "I won't have Christmas decorations hanging around, getting in my way, and I will not have a Christmas tree in this house!"

Melinda glared at him, too choked with rage to get anything out. Daniel stared at her for another moment, then growled and stomped out of the room, nearly crashing the door off its hinges as he slammed it behind him.

Melinda wanted to throw things at him; she wanted to scream. She would have Christmas. She refused to let some bitter, nasty-tempered man ruin the holiday for her and everyone else on the ranch. They all deserved to have Christmas, including the cowhands. If Daniel MacKenzie wouldn't help, well, that was fine. She would do it without him. He couldn't keep her from cooking Christmas cookies and candies or a feast of a meal. Let him refuse to get out the Christmas ornaments. She would make her own. And if he wouldn't have a tree—well, she would figure something out.

Right after dinner Daniel saddled his horse, packed a few supplies and rode off to visit the north line shack for a few days. He said he was going to ride the fence, although he and everyone else knew that the hands regularly rode along the barbed wire fence all winter long, checking for breaks or fallen posts. No one would have dared to mention that fact, however.

Melinda turned to cleaning the dinner dishes with such vigor that by the time she was through she had broken one pottery serving bowl and two glasses, bent a spoon and dented one of the enameled metal coffee cups. Then she marched out onto the porch and surveyed the countryside. What was she going to do for a tree? She had to find something to hang the ornaments on, something that would satisfy the letter of his law, but that would also show him that she meant what she said.

Her eyes happened to hit on the northwest side of the corral, where several tumbleweeds had piled up, and she stopped. A grin spread across her face. Now she knew what she was going to do. Still smiling wickedly, she started off across the yard toward the fence.

DANIEL SPENT two miserable days riding the fence and sitting alone in the line shack, staring at the wall and listening to the December wind whistling around the corners of the little house. Finally he decided to return home. He was still irritated with himself and Melinda, but not nearly as irritated as he was lonely. After two days of thinking about Melinda as he rode through the cold, he figured that if she was going to be constantly on his brain, he might as well go back where he could actually see her and hear her voice—and live in a clean, warm house while he was doing it.

He amazed himself, he thought as he rode into the ranch yard and dismounted. For seven years he hadn't cared that he lacked creature comforts, hadn't even noticed, really, that the food was always cold or burned, or that dust balls gathered beneath the furniture and along the baseboards, or that the laundress in town starched his shirts too much. He hadn't missed the comforts any more than he'd missed the company of ladies or the sight of a woman's lips curling into a smile or the sound of her laughter. Now, in just a few weeks, Melinda Ballard had spoiled him until it seemed that he not only didn't *want* to live without those comforts, he damn well near *couldn't*.

When he had unsaddled his horse and turned him loose with the others in the corral, Daniel walked across the yard and into the house through the kitchen door. He told himself that he hadn't entered through that door in the hopes of seeing Melinda, it was just the easiest way. But he couldn't deny the fizzle of excitement in his stomach as he took the steps two at a time or the disappointment that pierced him when he found the kitchen empty.

The house smelled deliciously of vanilla and hot cookies. All along the table cookies were spread out on racks and brown paper to cool. They were cut into Christmas shapes of stars, trees and bells. Two small bowls of red and green icing stood at one end of the table, with paper cones beside them. Some of the cookies were already iced.

The rich, warm scent teased at Daniel's nostrils, and a nostalgic longing darted through him. He felt strangely as if he wanted to both cry and smile. Melinda was having Christmas no matter what he'd told her. It didn't surprise him—but, oddly, it didn't really displease him, either. The pantry door opened, startling him, and Melinda stepped out. She stopped abruptly when she saw him, a little gasp escaping her.

"You're back."

Daniel looked at her, feeling absurdly ill at ease. He

took off his hat. He didn't know what to say. "Yes." He continued to stand, just gazing at her, until he realized that he must look like an idiot. He supposed he ought to say something about her baking, ought to point out that she had ignored his orders, but he suspected that if he did, he would manage to appear even more foolish. It was best to ignore it.

"How were the fences?"

"The what? Oh. Oh, they were all right. In good condition." It had been only two days, yet he couldn't keep from staring at her as if he had been gone for weeks. He thought of the last time they had been alone together in the kitchen, when he had kissed her.

He stepped back, almost as though he could physically avoid the thought. "Well. I, uh, better see to some, uh…paperwork."

Daniel left the kitchen and strode down the hall. He didn't know where he was going. He had no paperwork to speak of, except the bookkeeping that he was always behind on—and he had no intention of doing that. He could go down to the barn and inspect what the men had done. Or he could talk to Will and find out what had gone on in his absence. But he had just told Melinda that he was going to do some paperwork, and it would look crazy for him to leave the house now.

He headed for the study, casually glancing into the parlor as he walked. He passed it, then stopped and backtracked to the door. He looked inside again. His eyes hadn't been playing tricks on him. There was a large tumbleweed sitting on a table in the center of the parlor. Strings of popcorn and cranberries and brightly colored paper chains were looped around it. Bows in various colors, materials and sizes adorned its dry, flimsy branches. A homemade felt angel was balanced near the top. The woman had made a Christmas tree out of a tumbleweed.

"Well, I'll be damned."

Melinda, who had followed Daniel into the hall, a little leery of his reaction to her tree now that the time of discovery was upon her, let out a sigh of relief. He didn't sound furious.

Daniel heard Melinda's sigh and swung around to face her. "A tumbleweed."

Melinda shrugged. "It's not a tree."

He struggled to keep his mouth from twitching into a smile. "You're one determined lady."

"I've been told that."

"Oh, hell." He moved away, slapping his hat against his thigh. He paused partway down the hall and glanced back at her. He should get mad at her now. He should tell her what he thought of her flouting his authority. But he couldn't find any anger or indignation in him. He felt too funny inside, too inclined both to laugh and cry, as he'd felt in the kitchen, smelling those cookies. He sighed and turned away, heading for the front door. Melinda barely caught his words as he walked away. "I might as well give up and get you a tree."

He stalked out the door. Melinda stood, staring after him, and began to smile.

It was after dark when Daniel rode in again. Supper was through, and Melinda had finished the dishes and was sweeping when the kitchen door opened and Daniel walked in, a short, scrawny juniper tree hoisted on his shoulder.

"What are you still doing here?" he growled. "Don't you ever go home?"

Melinda just smiled. "I was finishing up. I kept you some supper." She motioned toward a plate on the counter, a napkin over its contents.

"You work too late. Whatever happened to Will's girl, the one that used to help you?"

"Oh, that was a welcoming gesture on Mrs. Moore's part. I couldn't presume on her."

He grimaced. "No presumption. I'll pay the girl. She ought to do it willingly enough for money."

Melinda stared at him, not sure she'd heard him right. "You mean you want to hire her? To help me?"

"That's what I said, isn't it?"

"Well, yes, but…" Melinda's voice trailed off. She wasn't about to argue against having someone to help her clean. The big house and cooking for so many men made for exhausting work, and she was usually running behind. She smiled. "All right. Thank you."

Daniel looked uneasy with her thanks. "Where do you want this thing?"

"In the parlor, I guess." He'd already nailed crossed wooden planks to the bottom of the trunk for a stand. Melinda thought of the Christmas tree skirt in one of her trunks. She hadn't been able to use it with the bottom-heavy tumbleweed.

She followed him into the parlor, where he unceremoniously dumped the tumbleweed on the floor and set the low tree on the table. Daniel stepped back and looked at it uncertainly. "Scrawny thing, huh?"

It was indeed. It was little more than a bush, and there were big gaps in the branches. But at least it had green needles on it. At least it was a tree. It was the only kind of evergreen tree she'd ever found out here, except where someone had planted a row of fir trees for a windbreak beside their house.

"It'll look fine," she reassured him. "Where'd you find it?"

"In one of the breaks over in the southwest quarter. They grow on the walls of the gullies sometimes. Stubborn things." He grinned, and his eyes slid to her. "Like some people."

Melinda grinned back. She would have liked to hug and kiss him for bringing her the tree, but there was no indication on his part that it would have been welcome. They both looked at the tree.

"I brought another one, case you needed it," he continued, studying the tree. She knew that he was embarrassed at revealing any kindness. "I left it outside. Thought you might want it in your house."

Her smile turned a little wobbly, and tears shimmered in her eyes. "Yes," she said softly. "Yes. Thank you."

OVER THE NEXT FEW DAYS the house seemed suddenly filled with Christmas. The delicious smells of Melinda's baking and candy making hung in the air. The men couldn't resist popping in now and then throughout the day to grab a cookie from one of the full jars or a piece of candy from a glass dish. Once Melinda heard one of the hands joke that her candies had even sweetened ol' MacKenzie's disposition.

Daniel did seem milder, more ready to smile or even laugh. Though he often snapped at people, as he always had, the perpetual frown had eased from his forehead, and his voice was no longer heard rising in anger all over the place. To everyone's slack-jawed amazement, he shaved off his beard, keeping only the mustache. When Melinda saw him, she almost didn't recognize him. He appeared younger, not so hard and far more handsome. Every now and then he would come into the kitchen in the late afternoon or evening, while Melinda was working, and he would sit at the table, sipping a cup of coffee. Much to her surprise, he even chatted with her in a normal way, without flaring up into argument.

He climbed into the attic and brought down two big boxes of Christmas decorations, telling her in his usual gruff way that she might as well use them, they were just gathering dust. Use them she did. She had hung the strands of popcorn and cranberries and the paper chains on the tree Daniel had brought, but she didn't have enough ornaments at home to do justice to two trees, so the poor thing had had a rather naked look. Inside the boxes she found dozens of beautiful ornaments, fragile glass or delicately carved wood or daintily sewn tiny cloth dolls. There were green and red bows, both large and small, made out of velvet, grosgrain and satin. She pulled out garlands of tinsel to hang on the tree and festoon the mantel. There was a large, handsomely carved and painted nutcracker and a delicate porcelain crèche. She even found a mistletoe ball made of two small, crossed, ribbon-covered hoops to hang in a doorway. Of course, there was no mistletoe to put in it, but Melinda hung it anyway, and in her mind's eye she pictured Daniel catching her beneath it and kissing her.

However, she was careful not to let herself think that way too often. After all, he had made it clear that he had no intention of following up on that one kiss. She wondered if her kiss had repulsed him. Had she seemed too bold? Or was it that she wasn't skilled enough? Or perhaps he had found their kiss lacking in the love that had been there with his wife. The possibilities were inclined to sink Melinda into a most un-Christmaslike state of unhappiness. She tried to make herself concentrate only on the observances of the season and not on Daniel MacKenzie.

Despite the crush of work, she had more free time now that Daniel had hired Opal to help her, so she was able to use most of her evenings to work on the gown she was making over for the Christmas ball. When she finished it, two days before the ball, she tried it on in front of the mirror, turning this way and that to get the full effect. It had turned out beautifully. She had done away with most of the lace overdress, leaving only the satin gown with just a few rows of lace around the hem. Then she had dyed it a pale, dusky pink that did wonderful things for her eyes and skin. She'd taken the skirt in so that it had the new, slimmer silhouette, and she'd ripped out the lace sleeves and inset at the neck to make the neckline fashionably bare. The dress showed off her white shoulders and neck to advantage, but even though it was no more daring than the pictures in the women's fashion books, she had made a small lace shawl to drape over her shoulders. The result of all her work was a simple but stunning dress, and she knew that with her hair artfully swept up and decorated with a few pale satin rosettes, she would look the best she possibly could.

It was disappointing in the extreme to think that Daniel wouldn't even see her in the gown, for everyone had assured her that he never attended the Christmas Ball.

However, the next morning, much to her surprise, as she was standing at the sink washing dishes, Daniel walked into the room and asked abruptly, "You going to that silly Christmas Ball in Barrett?"

Melinda turned, her eyebrows lifting. "Yes."

"Figured as much. Well, long as I'm going, too, you might as well come with me."

Melinda's jaw dropped. She didn't know if she had ever heard a less graceful invitation, but she couldn't think of one she'd ever wanted more to accept. However, she couldn't think only of herself. "Lee is coming with me."

"Bring the boy, too."

Melinda stared. "Well…well, all right, then."

"Be ready at seven o'clock sharp."

THE NIGHT OF THE Christmas Ball, she prepared a quick, early supper. Since everyone on the place was attending the ball, they were all in an equal hurry to eat and get ready. For the first time since she'd started working there, Melinda left the supper dishes to soak and hurried over to her house. There wasn't much time. Knowing that, she had already bathed and washed her hair early this afternoon, brushing her hair dry in front of the fire. Now she took it down, brushed it again and piled it on top of her head in a fuller, more elegant style. On one side she fastened a cluster of satin rosebuds dyed to match her gown. Then she dressed as quickly as possible.

The knock on the door came promptly at seven, and Melinda almost ran to answer it. It was foolish to be so excited, she knew, but she couldn't help herself. She draped the lacy shawl around her bare shoulders, holding it closed at her breast, and opened the door. Daniel stood outside, stiff and nervous-looking and unbelievably handsome in a dark suit, with a blazing white shirt beneath and a narrow black string tie. His boots were polished until they shone, and the black Western hat in his hand looked as if it had never before been taken out of its box. His eyes swept over her, taking in the bare shoulders with their filmy covering and dropping to the white tops of her breasts, barely visible above her dress.

"You look beautiful." He said the first thing that came into his head, his voice slightly shaky.

"Thank you. You look quite good yourself." Melinda felt as if she were bubbling, effervescent with excitement and happiness. "Come in." She stepped back and called, "Lee, it's time to go."

"Coming, Mama."

Melinda reached for her coat on the hook near the door. It would look awful with the dress, spoiling the effect, but it was the only one she had, and she had to wear something or she would freeze on the long drive into town.

Daniel reached out a hand and stopped her. She glanced up at him in surprise. "No, wait. I just thought. There's something in the house I need to get. I'll be back in a moment."

Curiously she watched him trot across the yard. Lee joined her at the window. "Where's Mr. MacKenzie going?"

"I don't know. Now, Lee, I want you to promise you'll be on your best behavior tonight." She turned to him and bent to button up his coat. "No horseplay. Mr. MacKenzie isn't used to being around children, and this will be your first time alone with him, and I—"

"No, it isn't."

"Isn't what?"

"My first time around him. He took me riding with him three days ago. We went clear down to the breaks and back."

"What?"

He looked at her strangely. "I just told you, he took me—"

"No, I heard. It's just that it's… I can hardly believe it."

"Yeah. I was kinda surprised, too. I know he didn't like me at first. But sometimes he comes around when Jimmy's working on my riding, and a couple of weeks ago he even came over and showed me how to do something. He was nice when we went riding. He told me all kinds of neat stuff about the ranch, and when we came back, he told me he enjoyed it. He said he'd let me help when the roundup comes in the spring. Can I, Mama?"

"I suppose so, if it's all right with Mr. MacKenzie," Melinda replied absently. Daniel was changing even more than she had realized.

Daniel returned in a few minutes, a large, wrapped box in his hands. He held it out to Melinda. "Here. It's your Christmas present. I want you to open it early."

Melinda reached out to take the box with suddenly trembling hands. She hadn't even dreamed that Daniel would give her a present. Carefully, she opened it, knowing that she was so foolishly in love with him now that she would save all the wrappings. She lifted the lid. Inside lay something made of thick black material. She lifted it out. It was a heavy cloak, one that fell all the way to the floor. The inside was lined with black satin, and it fastened at the neck with a silver clip. She held it up, staring at it, and tears gathered in her eyes and rolled down her cheeks. A cloak. He had seen her in her coat, and he'd understood why she wore it. He had cared enough to notice and then to want to change it. Melinda stroked a hand down the cloak.

"I meant it to make you happy," Daniel said, his hand coming out to touch her wet cheek.

"I am. Oh, I am," she replied, her voice thick with tears. She turned and let him slide the cloak around her shoulders and fasten the clip. For an instant she stood within the circle of his arms, his gift heavy and warm around her, enveloping her, and she was utterly, blissfully happy. "Thank you. Thank you."

He smiled slowly and held out his arm, elbow crooked, for her to take. "Then let's celebrate."

CHAPTER SEVEN

THE BARRETT HOTEL was festively decorated for the Christmas Ball and packed with merry people, all dressed in their finery. A band consisting of a piano, fiddle and guitar played away at one end of the open room that was normally the location of the hotel's restaurant, but at the opposite end, in the lobby, nothing could be heard of the music because of the hubbub of laughter and talking. Melinda supposed the party was lovely and enjoyable; she didn't notice. She was too busy floating on a cloud of her own. Men paid her compliments, and she smiled in return. But she didn't really hear what they said to her. She could think of nothing but sitting beside Daniel on the long ride into town, their thighs touching, with only the material of their clothes between them, the lap robe across their legs enclosing them in their own warm, private cocoon. Wherever she was and whomever she was talking to or dancing with, her eyes sought out Daniel.

Melinda had so many invitations to dance that she wouldn't have had to sit out even one if she hadn't wanted to, but afterward she couldn't remember any of the dances except the three she had had with Daniel. It had startled her when he asked her to dance. She hadn't seen him with anyone else, and he didn't seem to be the type to dance, but when he swept her out on the floor, she found that he moved well. More importantly, his arm was around her waist as they waltzed, and he was gazing down into her eyes. They were only a breath away from each other, their embrace just shy of causing comment. She could feel the heat of his body; she could see the pulse in his throat. His eyes were hot and probing, and she felt as if she were melting. She was in love with him, and she couldn't keep hope from rising within her.

Melinda wasn't sorry when the evening ended. She looked forward to the ride home. Lee, who had been running around all evening, stuffing himself with treats and playing with the other children, was exhausted. Not long after he climbed up into the buggy seat behind Melinda and Daniel, a heavy blanket across his lap, he was sound asleep.

The night sky was as clear as it could be only in the Panhandle, pure black except for a thin slice of pale moon and the faraway white light of the stars. It was cold and utterly beautiful and, snuggled safely under her lap robe, Melinda gazed at the view in delight. Once or twice Daniel glanced over at her, and a small smile touched his lips. She could see the beauty in this fierce, huge land. Perhaps she didn't hate it as much as she said.

When they reached the ranch, Daniel stopped the horses in front of Melinda's house and jumped down to help her alight. They looked into the backseat, where

Lee lay sound asleep, stretched out on the seat with the blanket wrapped around him. Melinda hated to wake him up to get him out, but he had gotten far too big for her to carry, so she leaned forward to shake him awake. Daniel stopped her. He nodded toward the house. "You get the door."

He scooped Lee, blanket and all, up in his arms and carried him onto the porch. It took a stunned moment for Melinda to realize what he was doing; then she darted to the front door and opened it for him. Quickly she preceded him into Lee's tiny bedroom and turned down the covers of his bed. Daniel laid the boy down on the bed and bent to remove his boots. Then he pulled the covers up and, for a moment, stood gazing down at Lee. Melinda watched, seeing pain and pleasure mingle strangely on his face.

When he turned and left the room, Melinda followed him, closing the door behind her. Her throat was choked with sympathy and regret, but she didn't know how to express them. Daniel was not a man who welcomed sympathy. She came up beside him and laid her hand on his arm. He looked down and smiled.

"Would you like some coffee?" she asked, reaching up to unclasp her cloak. "I could fix us some. Or how about hot chocolate?"

Daniel lifted the cloak from her shoulders, his hand grazing her bare skin. "I don't want anything to drink," he said, his voice low. He tossed the cloak onto a chair and stared down at her as his hands came up to touch her throat. "You were beautiful tonight. Did I tell you that?"

Mutely Melinda nodded her head.

"I rarely tell you, do I?" he admitted, his fingers drifting down over her shoulders. "It's one of my many faults. I'm too rough, too blunt, lacking in the social graces."

"I didn't say that." Melinda's voice came out breathlessly.

"Oh, yes, you have. Many times. Perhaps not tonight." He paused. "You are beautiful. I kept watching you all evening, dancing...talking...laughing. And I wanted you so badly I could hardly remember where I was." His fingertips slid across the smooth white skin of her chest down to the quivering tops of her breasts, exposed by the low neckline. "God, you're lovely."

He bent and brushed his lips against the soft flesh. Melinda drew in a sharp breath, part surprise and part sharp delight. "Daniel..."

His lips trailed kisses across to her other breast, sending shimmering sensations through her. Her knees went weak, and she gripped his arms tightly to stay steady. His mouth worked its way upward, tasting her skin from her breasts to her throat. Melinda let her head fall back, offering up more of herself for his delectation. Daniel's hands went to her waist, his fingers digging in as though to keep her from moving away from him. He murmured her name, his breath ragged and hot on her flesh, exciting her almost as much as the touch of his lips.

Melinda moved restlessly, and her hands went up to Daniel's head, weaving into the thick mass of his hair. Shamelessly she tugged at his head, urging him upward to her mouth. Smiling, he kissed her. His kiss was long and deep, compelling. Melinda felt as if her bones were turning to wax and melting away beneath her. She swayed against him, and Daniel answered by squeezing her body more tightly to his. He still wore his heavy overcoat, and the thick material frustrated her desire to feel his hard, masculine body against hers. She wriggled against him, and her nipples tightened in response to the friction of the cloth across them.

Daniel kissed her again and again, his tongue plundering her mouth. He kissed her face all over, hard, quick kisses, always returning to her mouth. His tongue traced the whorls of her ears, and he nipped gently at the lobes. He pushed the narrow straps of her gown off her shoulders and down her arms, freeing her breasts from their restraint.

Melinda had worn a corset on this special occasion, to make her waist infinitesimal, and it had the effect of pushing up her breasts so that they swelled above the frilly white cotton chemise, only the deep rose nipples still covered. Daniel stared down at her, his breath rasping in his throat. Slowly he reached out and took the chemise between his fingers and gently pulled it down. The material scraped over her sensitized nipples, making them harden and swell even more. Lush and erotic, her breasts thrust up at him, the nipples pointing provocatively. The blood pounded in his head as he reached out a forefinger and lightly touched one nipple. He circled it, watching the bud tighten beneath his touch. He went to the other and worked the same magic on it. Melinda sucked in her breath, and Daniel glanced at her face. Her eyes were closed, and her lower lip was pulled in, her teeth biting down into it, her face a mask of ecstasy.

Daniel shuddered and pulled her to him. His mouth fastened on hers, and he kissed her as though he would never stop. His hands cupped her breasts between their bodies, his fingers teasing and stroking her nipples, until Melinda moaned at the devastating pleasure and moved her hips against him, blindly seeking fulfillment.

He bent, sweeping her up into his arms, and turned to carry her into the bedroom. As he did, his eyes fell on the door to Lee's room. Her child was here; he had forgotten that. He could not take her with the child lying only a room away. It was too crude, as though he did not value and respect her. Daniel stopped.

Melinda opened her eyes and glanced questioningly at him. Her eyes followed his gaze, and she, too, came back to reality with a thud. She was a mother, not a wanton strumpet who didn't care where she coupled.

Slowly, regretfully, Daniel set her on the floor. Melinda's hands flew up to her breasts, quickly tugging up her chemise and dress to cover them. A blush stained her cheeks.

"I'm sorry—I—oh, hell!" Daniel turned away and strode out of the house.

Melinda watched him go, then sank into a pile on the floor, her knees too weak to help her stand. She felt hot and aching and thoroughly frustrated. Yet at the same time she couldn't stop grinning like an idiot. Daniel wanted her. He wanted her almost past reason.

FOR THE NEXT FEW DAYS Melinda was so busy that she had almost no time to think about Daniel. Almost. Nothing, not even the preparations for a huge Christmas feast, could completely take her mind off him. She was too lost in love. She thought about the way he smiled, the things he said, the wild, marvelous sensations his kisses evoked in her. She wanted to be with him, wanted him to make love to her. It was obvious that he wanted her, too. However, it was equally obvious that he had no intention of making her his wife. He hadn't spoken one word of love when they had kissed. He had said nothing to her of commitment or marriage. No doubt he still cherished the memory of his late wife too much to put another woman in her place. He obviously desired her, but he was fighting it, because he didn't want to seduce a woman whom he considered a lady. He knew that her only position with him could be that of mistress.

Melinda would lose whatever position and respect she had in the community if she became his mistress. People would whisper about her, and when she went into town, she would be the target of sidelong glances and leering grins. There were times when she desired Daniel so much that she thought she would be willing to undergo those things. She was afraid that she could put aside her moral beliefs if that was the only way that she could have him. But then she would think about Lee, and she knew that she couldn't do that to him. Whatever she did would taint him as surely as it did her. How could he grow up here with people calling his mother a whore?

She tried hard to suppress her desire, to take her

mind off Daniel, and so she threw herself into her work. She chopped, sliced, seasoned, baked, boiled and, most of all, cleaned. The entire house had to be sparkling for Christmas Day, and the good china, crystal and silverware had to be taken out and cleaned of the dust and tarnish that had accumulated on them. And, of course, with all the cooking and mixing that she was doing, she was forever washing dishes.

She didn't see much of Daniel, fortunately. But sometimes she would glance up during a meal and find him looking at her from the opposite end of the table. His blue eyes would be filled with smoky secrets, and her pulse would leap, and she could do nothing but stare at him, all her senses thrillingly alive. At night, after she went to bed, she found it difficult to sleep, no matter how tired she was. Her mind always turned to Daniel, and soon her body would be thrumming with desire, with no hope of satisfaction. And always there would be the little flicker of hope, the irrepressible desire that Daniel would change, that he would grow to love her as well as want her, that he would ask her to marry him.

After all, Daniel *had* changed already. He talked and laughed and joked more. Two days before Christmas he went into town and returned with crates of oranges and apples, boxes of Christmas candy and sacks of nuts more exotic than the pecans they were used to. By the way the men stared, Melinda could tell that it wasn't a Christmas custom at the ranch. He also brought in a sprig of mistletoe, shipped in by train from farther south, and placed it in the mistletoe ball Melinda had hung in the doorway of the parlor. One day when she had carried a dish of fudge into the parlor and was turning to leave, Daniel surprised her by stepping into the doorway and stealing a kiss from her beneath the mistletoe. Then, just as quickly and quietly, he had stepped back from her and left.

Finally Christmas Eve came. When Lee had complained that there was no chimney for Santa Claus to come down, since Melinda's house was heated by an iron stove, not a fireplace, Daniel had graciously offered to let Lee hang his stocking from the parlor mantelpiece in the ranch house. After supper on Christmas Eve, Lee hung his stocking under his mother's watchful eye. Afterward he put on his coat and ran down to the foreman's house. As a special treat, Lula Moore had invited him to spend the night with her youngsters and join them in popping corn and roasting nuts. After all, she told Melinda, as wild as her children were on Christmas Eve, she wouldn't notice one more, and Lee's absence would free Melinda for the massive work she had to do for the meal tomorrow.

Melinda spent her evening making cakes: one Lord Baltimore cake and two coconut layer cakes. She had already baked the pies this afternoon, and the pie safe in the corner of the kitchen was full of apple, pecan and mincemeat pies, six in all. By ten o'clock she was done with the cakes, too, and after she checked to make sure that everything that could be done ahead of time for tomorrow's meal had been, she left the big house and hurried to her own cabin. High on a shelf in the wardrobe closet of her bedroom was a big bag, which she pulled down and carried across the yard to the ranch house.

Quietly, thinking that Daniel might already have gone to bed, she slipped down the hall to the parlor. To her surprise, she found him sitting there with the lamps lit. Her surprise must have shown on her face, for he chuckled and said, "I've been waiting for you." He nodded toward the limp stocking hanging from the mantel. "I figured you'd be back to fill that."

Melinda smiled, pleased that he had wanted to be with her. She took her presents out of the bag and laid them beneath the tree, feeling both awkward and pleased at having Daniel's eyes follow her movements. She remembered what had happened the last time they had been alone together, and a tingle ran through her. She glanced over at him and saw the same hot memory in his eyes. She looked away, very aware of how quickly she was breathing and how fast and furiously the blood was pumping through her veins.

She went to the stocking and dropped nuts, an orange and an apple to fill the toe. Then she began to stuff in the little goodies she had bought: a whistle, some marbles, a small ball, licorice whips, a few hard candies, a new slingshot. Daniel came over and squatted down beside her, so close to her that their arms were almost touching.

"I thought you might want to add these things," he said, holding out his open hand.

Melinda looked at him in surprise; then her eyes dropped to his hand. He was holding a jackknife that would delight any boy and a pair of child-size spurs.

Melinda stared. He had bought them for Lee. "Why, Daniel!" She looked at him, her face warm with gratitude and love. "You didn't have to…."

He shrugged. "It's not much. I got him a real present for tomorrow. But I thought he might like these, too."

"He'll adore them." Melinda took the knife and spurs and added them to the stocking. She turned to Daniel and smiled warmly at him. "Thank you. It was very kind of you."

He shook his head, a little embarrassed by her thanks, and looked away. "I—I had a child once, a boy. He died when he was very young. I thought—that I could never love anyone again. I thought that I was dead to emotion." He paused. Melinda stayed very quiet, afraid to speak or even to move for fear she might break the fragile moment. "That's why I didn't want children around here. They made me think of Matthew. But I've found that I don't mind so much. At first, whenever I looked at Lee, I felt that old pain, but then the longer I was around him, the more I saw him as a person, as himself, and not just some reminder of Matt. I like Lee. I enjoy being with him."

"I'm glad." Melinda put her hand on his arm.

He looked at her, then bent down and kissed her once, briefly and hard. She felt the familiar surge of longing, and an ache started deep inside her. She swallowed, wondering if she would be able to resist him if he began to kiss and caress her.

But Daniel did not kiss her again. He stood and took her hands in his. Melinda stood, too. She wasn't sure whether she was relieved or disappointed. "I have something I want to give you. Now, not tomorrow, when all the others are here."

Melinda looked puzzled. "But, Daniel, you've already given me my Christmas present. Remember?"

"This is something different." There was a strange look in his eyes, hesitant and hopeful and, strangely, almost frightened. He released her hands and moved away. He took a small box from the mantel and handed it to her.

Melinda looked at it. The box was so clumsily wrapped in red tissue paper that she was sure Daniel must have wrapped it himself. Giving him another puzzled glance, she unwrapped it and lifted the lid of the tiny box. Inside, lying on a bed of cotton batting, was a woman's ring. In the center was a large, square-cut emerald, and all around it in a sparkling circle were small diamonds. "It's beautiful!" she gasped and looked up at him.

What did it mean? Was this the sort of gift with which men paid their mistresses? Her heart tore within her, and she found herself begging inside, *Please, oh, please, don't let him be asking to set me up as his kept woman.* No matter how many times her desire had led her to consider the possibility of accepting that role, she realized now that it would break her heart to have him ask it of her.

He saw the questioning in her eyes, and although he did not realize why she was confused, he explained. "That was my mother's ring, and before that, my grandmother's. If you don't like it, I'll get you another.

It's just that it's a tradition in my family, the betrothal ring of the first son."

"Betrothal?" she breathed, her chest tightening. She hardly dared to believe that it was true. "You're asking me to marry you?"

He nodded. "I never thought I'd ask that again. When Millicent died—well, frankly, our marriage had been so wrong, so disappointing that I—"

"Disappointing!" Melinda's jaw dropped. "But I thought you loved her terribly! That you built this house for her!"

"I did love her, at first. But then, when we lived here together—well, she hated it here. We never seemed to agree. It wasn't right between us. Millicent was desperately unhappy, and I grew to dislike her. It was my fault, all my fault. She died because of me. I didn't want her to leave, you see, and take Matthew from me. I practically forced her to stay. Then she died."

"Oh, Daniel, no!" Melinda went to him, wrapping her arms around him and laying her head against his chest. "You mustn't blame yourself because she died. None of us choose the way we'll die—it just happens. It was out of your hands."

"Perhaps. I don't know. But I decided that I wouldn't marry again. After Matthew died, I didn't want children. And I'm not good with women. I'm blunt and ill-tempered. I don't know the right things to say, and I always wind up hurting their feelings. I love this country—it's the only place I want to live. But women hate the loneliness and barrenness. For a long time it didn't matter. I didn't feel capable of love anymore. It was easy to avoid it."

He sighed. "Then you came here. I couldn't avoid you. I couldn't run from you or push you away. You just stood your ground and gave back as good as you got. You were so damned beautiful, so desirable. You turned me inside out. You lit up everything in my life and made me see how cold and lonely I'd been for years. You made me want to have more than that. Melinda, I love you. I can't bear to live without you. I want to marry you. Will you? Could you bring yourself to—"

He looked down at her with such hope and trepidation that Melinda had to laugh. She threw her arms around his neck. "Yes! Yes, you silly man. Of course I'll marry you. I love you."

He grinned, then forced his face into sober lines. "Are you sure? I know you don't like the Panhandle, but I—"

She chuckled again. "As you might say, 'I don't give a damn where I live.' I just want to be with you. That's all that's important. Besides, I've even gotten to think it's kind of pretty—in its own strange way."

Daniel grinned, and his arms went around her hard as he bent his head and kissed her, his lips moving over hers slowly and lovingly. But then the pressure increased as passion took him, and she parted her lips to grant him possession of her mouth. Their tongues met and twined in a dance of love until his skin grew searing hot and his breath ragged. Finally he pulled away and looked down at her, a faint question in his eyes.

In answer, Melinda smiled up at him and pulled

his head down to hers again. He kissed her thoroughly, then lifted her up into his arms and carried her out of the room. Up the wide staircase he carried her and into the bedroom that was so masculinely his, where she had often worked and dreamed, but had never been with him. He set her down tenderly by the bed, and his hand went to the row of buttons down the front of her dress. Eagerness and passion made his big fingers clumsy, and Melinda, smiling, took his hands away and began to unfasten the buttons herself.

Daniel stepped back, his eyes on her hands and what they gradually revealed, as he, too, unfastened and removed his clothing. His garments fell scattered on the floor, and he stood before her naked and powerful. But Melinda was no longer a girl, and though her cheeks might color a little at the sight of him, she did not take her eyes from him, but looked her fill. The desire on her face when she gazed at him naked was too much for Daniel, and he had to go to her and take her into his arms. He kissed her as his hands swiftly removed the last of her light cotton undergarments.

He jerked down the covers on the bed, and they lay back on it, their hands and mouths eagerly exploring each other's bodies. Melinda sighed shakily, afire with sensations she had never known before. She hadn't known it could be like this, not just sweetness and love, but fire and storm and raging need, too. She reveled in the differences between them, his hardness against her pillowy softness, the hair-roughened skin that abraded her sensitized nipples and tender flesh, the aggressive thrust that found eager acceptance in her.

His mouth was hot on her breast. His hands found the soft, secret places that aroused her into almost mindless passion, and her hands played over him, delighting in discovering him, urging him on until they were both writhing and panting in their urgent need. When he came into her, she welcomed him, wrapping her arms around him and moving with him in the timeless rhythm of passion. Together they vaulted to the heights and slowly, gently, came fluttering down to earth again.

With soft murmurs and kisses, they separated; then Daniel settled her into the crook of his arm, and they lay together, dreamily quiet. Melinda had never felt so content, so happy. She thought about the next day— well, this day, really, for it was past twelve o'clock. Christmas Day.

She thought about the morning that would come— the eager unwrapping of presents, the huge breakfast with its reading of the Christmas story, the surprise when they announced their marriage plans—and she smiled. She knew that she and Daniel would have many more Christmases together. There would be more children, and they would make new customs and traditions, and in time there would even be grandchildren around them to share the joy.

But there would never be a Christmas more special than this one. For this night, they had both given and received the greatest gift of all: love.

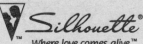

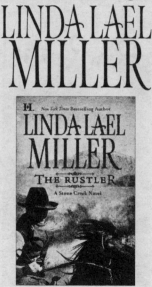

REQUEST YOUR FREE BOOKS!

2 FREE NOVELS
FROM THE ROMANCE/SUSPENSE
COLLECTION PLUS 2 FREE GIFTS!

YES! Please send me 2 FREE novels from the Romance/Suspense Collection and my 2 FREE gifts (gifts are worth about $10). After receiving them, if I don't wish to receive any more books, I can return the shipping statement marked "cancel." If I don't cancel, I will receive 4 brand-new novels every month and be billed just $5.49 per book in the U.S. or $5.99 per book in Canada, plus 25¢ shipping and handling per book plus applicable taxes, if any*. That's a savings of at least 20% off the cover price! I understand that accepting the 2 free books and gifts places me under no obligation to buy anything. I can always return a shipment and cancel at any time. Even if I never buy another book from the Reader Service, the two free books and gifts are mine to keep forever.

185 MDN EF5Y 385 MDN EF6C

Name _____ (PLEASE PRINT) _____

Address _____ Apt. # _____

City _____ State/Prov. _____ Zip/Postal Code _____

Signature (if under 18, a parent or guardian must sign)

Mail to **The Reader Service:**
IN U.S.A.: P.O. Box 1867, Buffalo, NY 14240-1867
IN CANADA: P.O. Box 609, Fort Erie, Ontario L2A 5X3

Not valid to current subscribers to the Romance Collection,
the Suspense Collection or the Romance/Suspense Collection.

Want to try two free books from another line?
Call 1-800-873-8635 or visit www.morefreebooks.com.

* Terms and prices subject to change without notice. N.Y. residents add applicable sales tax. Canadian residents will be charged applicable provincial taxes and GST. Offer not valid in Quebec. This offer is limited to one order per household. All orders subject to approval. Credit or debit balances in a customer's account(s) may be offset by any other outstanding balance owed by or to the customer. Please allow 4 to 6 weeks for delivery. Offer available while quantities last.

Your Privacy: Harlequin is committed to protecting your privacy. Our Privacy Policy is available online at www.eHarlequin.com or upon request from the Reader Service. From time to time we make our lists of customers available to reputable third parties who may have a product or service of interest to you. If you would prefer we not share your name and address, please check here. ☐

BOB08R